the galaxy, and the ground within

the galaxy, and the ground within

becky chambers

HODDER &
STOUGHTON

First published in Great Britain in 2021 by Hodder & Stoughton
An Hachette UK company

1

Copyright © Becky Chambers 2021

A CIP catalogue record for this title is available from the British Library

Hardback ISBN 9781473647664
Trade Paperback ISBN 9781473647671

Typeset in Sabon MT by Palimpsest Book Production Ltd, Falkirk, Stirlingshire

Printed and bound in Great Britain by Clays Ltd, Elcograf S.p.A.

Hodder & Stoughton policy is to use papers that are natural, renewable
and recyclable products and made from wood grown in sustainable forests.
The logging and manufacturing processes are expected to conform to the
environmental regulations of the country of origin.

Hodder & Stoughton Ltd
Carmelite House
50 Victoria Embankment
London EC4Y 0DZ

www.hodder.co.uk

For the strangers who helped.

Prologue

....

OPENING HOURS

Received message
Encryption: 0
From: Goran Orbital Cooperative Info Team (path: 8486-747-00)
To: Ooli Oht Ouloo (path: 5787-598-66)
Subject: Possible service outage today

This is an update from the Goran Orbital Cooperative regarding satellite network coverage between the hours of 06:00 and 18:00 today, 236/307.

We will be performing routine maintenance and adjustments on a portion of our solar energy fleet. While we hope to avoid any disruptions in service, there is a possibility that residents and business owners in Neighbourhoods 6, 7, and 8 (South) may experience a temporary decrease or loss in power during the hours stated above. Our maintenance crew will do everything in their ability to prevent this from being the case, but please prepare accordingly. We recommend activating and testing your back-up power system ahead of time.

If you have any questions, please feel free to contact our info team via this scrib path.

Thank you for supporting your local planetary co-op!

OULOO

In the Linkings, the system was listed as Tren. The science section in those same files was remarkable only for its brevity, as even the most enthusiastic astronomer would find it hard to get excited over this lonely section of the map. Tren's namesake star was middle-aged and run-of-the-mill, and when you discounted the assorted dust and debris you could find in any stellar system, the only thing orbiting it was one bone-dry planet of mediocre size, possessing no moon, no rings, nothing to harvest, nothing worth mining, nothing to gasp at while on vacation. It was merely a rock, with a half-hearted wisp of atmosphere clinging meagrely to its surface. The planet's name was Gora, the Hanto word for *useless*.

The sole point worth noting about poor Tren and Gora was that on a navigation chart, they had the accidental chance of falling at a favourable distance between five other systems that attracted a lot of to-and-fro. The interspatial tunnels branching from these more vibrant ports of call were old, built with technology that lacked the range of modern wormholes. Tunnels couldn't stretch as far back in the day, is what it came down to, and the old routes from the Harmagian colonial era were commonly punctuated with spots where ships could pop out into normal space before heading down the next leg. At last, the boring little rock that spun around the drab little sun was given a use: that of an anchor between the places people actually wanted to visit.

Traffic at a tunnel hub like Gora was complicated, as the

comings and goings through wormholes had to be meticulously tracked. Swooping out of one tunnel and into the next without any sort of regulation was a perfect recipe for accidents, particularly if you were entering a tunnel someone else had yet to exit. As was the case in all such places, Tren was under the watch of the Galactic Commons Transit Authority. Any ship exiting or entering had to first submit a flight plan indicating their time of arrival, their point of origin, and their final destination. The Transit Authority would then grant access to the destination-bound tunnel in question and assign a departure time. Crossing normal space from one tunnel to the next would only take a few hours, but waits in the Tren system were rarely that short. A layover of at least half a day was common, unless traffic demand was unusually light. And so, the solitary planet had acquired much more company over the decades. Gora was flocked with bubbled habitat domes, each containing diversions and services of varied flavours. There were hotels, tech swaps, restaurants, repair shops, grocery vendors, sim vendors, kick vendors, smash vendors, gardens, *tet* houses, and swimming pools, each courting weary spacers in need of some real gravity and a brief change in scenery.

One of these domes, on a flat plain in the southern hemisphere, encased a modest-sized establishment. Its name – as was painted in a wreath of multiple languages on the shuttlepad outside – was the Five-Hop One-Stop.

It was Ouloo's self-appointed mission in life to make you want to land there.

She awoke, as she always did, before dawn. Her eyes opened easily in the ebbing dark, her body long accustomed to transitioning out of sleep at this exact hour in this exact lighting. She stretched against the nest of pillows heaped in her sleeping alcove, pulled her head out from where it rested beneath a hind leg, and shook errant locks of fur from her eyes. She reached out a paw and shut off the alarm that hadn't been needed (she couldn't even remember what it sounded like).

Ouloo swung her long neck out into the room and saw that the sleeping alcove across from hers was empty. 'Tupo?' she called. It wasn't like her child to be awake this early. Every morning in recent memory had begun with a prepubescent war, each more tedious than the last. Ouloo felt a faint glimmer of hope arise, a fantastical fancy in which Tupo had gotten up on xyr own, started xyr chores, perhaps even *cooked*.

Ouloo nearly laughed at herself. There was no chance of that.

She padded across the room, entered her grooming cabinet, shut herself in the spacious compartment, put her feet on each of the four placement markers, and tapped a button with her nose. She sighed as a company of clever machines got to work, combing and curling, washing and rinsing, massaging her paw pads and cleaning her dainty ears. She loved this part of the morning, though she did somewhat miss the days before Gora, when her morning routine included scented soaps and herbal powders. But as the host of a multispecies establishment, she knew all too well that what might smell delicious to her might trigger anything from an allergic reaction to a personal insult in someone else, and she valued the long-term satisfaction of her customers exponentially higher than the fleeting indulgence of a rich springweed lather. Ouloo was a woman who took details seriously, and in her mind, there was no detail too small to note, not where her customers were concerned.

'Tupo?' she called again. Properly groomed, she exited the cabinet and headed down the hallway that connected the sleeping room to everything else. Their home was not large or elaborate, but it was just right for two, and they needed nothing more than that. It wasn't typical for Laru to live in a group that small – if a pair even counted as a *group* – but Ouloo didn't think of herself as typical, in any respect. She took pride in that fact.

The hallway was lined with skylights, and the view through them was busy as always. Tren had barely begun to shine that day, but the sky was alight all the same, glittering with satellites, orbiters, and the ever-constant parade of ships launching and landing and sailing by. Ouloo noted, as she passed a window, that the shuttlepad paint could use a touch-up. She mentally added it to Tupo's list.

The scene she found at the end of the hallway sent her fresh curls into an angry ruffle. 'Tupo!' Ouloo scolded. Her eyelids fell shut, and she sighed. She remembered a day long ago when she'd peered into her belly pouch and seen this pearl-pink nugget finally looking at her. Two tendays after being born, Tupo's eyes had just begun to open, and Ouloo had stared back into them with all the love and wonder in the universe, rendered breathless by this moment of pure connection between herself and her marvellous, perfect baby, cooing softness and safety at this tiny living treasure as she wondered who xe might grow into.

The answer, depressingly, was the consummate disaster snoring in the middle of the floor, limbs sprawled like roadkill. Some goofball vid was playing unwatched on the projector nearby, while its lone audience member slept face-first in a bowl of algae puffs.

Ouloo had no time for this. She marched over to her child, wrapped her neck around either side of xyr torso, and shook firmly. 'Tupo!'

Tupo awoke with a snort and a start. 'I didn't,' xe blurted.

Ouloo stomped over to the projector and switched it off. 'You said you would come to bed by midnight.'

Tupo raised xyr neck laboriously, blinking with confusion, algae-puff dust clinging to the fur of xyr face. 'What time is it?'

'It's *morning*. We have guests arriving soon, and . . . and *look at yourself.*'

Tupo continued to blink. Xe grimaced. 'My mouth really hurts,' xe whined.

'Let me see,' Ouloo said. She walked over, swinging her face close to Tupo's, trying to ignore the fact that Tupo had drooled all over the contents of the snack bowl. 'Open up.' Tupo opened xyr mouth wide, habitually. Ouloo peered in. 'Oh, dear,' she said, sympathy bleeding through her annoyance. 'That one's going to come in by the end of the tenday, I'll bet. We'll put some gel on it, hmm?' Tupo's adult incisors were making their first appearance, and like everything else on the child's body, they were being inelegant about the process. Growing up was never a fun experience for any species, but the Laru were longer-lived than most, and had that much more time to drag the whole unpleasant business out. Ouloo didn't know how she was going to stand at least eight more years of this. Tupo was still so soft, so babylike in temperament, but had finally crossed the threshold from *small and cute* to *big and dumb*. Nothing fit right and everything was in flux. It wasn't just the teeth, but the limbs, the jaw, the adult coat coming in like a badly trimmed hedge, and the smell — stars, but the kid had a funk. 'You need to go wash,' Ouloo said.

'I did last night,' Tupo protested.

'And you need to again,' Ouloo said. 'We have Aeluons coming in, and if *I* can smell you, they definitely will.'

Tupo dug absentmindedly around the snack bowl with a forepaw, searching for puffs that weren't wet. 'Who is coming today?'

Ouloo fetched her scrib from where she'd set it on a side table the night before, the same place she always left it. She gestured at the screen, pulling up that day's list of arrivals. 'We've got three scheduled for docking,' she said. Not the best day ever, but decent. It would give her time to get some repairs done, and Tupo could start on the shuttlepad painting. Ouloo gestured again, pulling the details on screen into projection mode so Tupo could see.

The list read:

Today's scheduled dockings

Saelen (Est. arrival: 11:26)
Melody (Est. arrival: 12:15)
Korrigoch Hrut (Est. arrival: 13:06)

'Which one's the Aeluon ship?' Tupo asked through a full, crunching mouth.

'Which one do you think?'

'I dunno.'

'Oh, come on. Yes, you do.'

Tupo sighed. Normally, xe was all for guessing games like this – and could be a real show-off about it – but mornings were not xyr best time even when xe hadn't spent the night in a snack bowl. '*Saelen.*'

'Why?'

'Because that's obviously an Aeluon name.'

'How can you tell?'

'Because of the way it ends. And the *ae.*'

'Very good.' Ouloo pointed at the third ship name on the list. 'And what language is this one?'

Tupo squinted. 'Is that Ensk?'

'Not even close. Look at the consonants.'

Tupo squinted harder. 'Tellerain!' xe said, as if xe'd known all along. Xyr sleepy eyes perked right up. 'Are they Quelins?'

'Quelin, singular, even if it's a group, and yes, correct.'

Tupo was visibly excited. 'We haven't had any Quelin people in a long time.'

'Well, there aren't many of them who travel in common space. You remember not to be nosy with them about why they're out here, right?'

'Yeah. Their legs are so *weird*, Mom.'

Ouloo frowned. 'What have we talked about?'

Tupo huffed, making the fur below xyr nose shiver. 'Not weird, just *different.*'

'That's right.'

Tupo rolled xyr eyes, then turned xyr attention to the list once more. 'Who's the second one?'

'Could be anyone,' Ouloo said, as was true for a ship with a Klip name. 'Probably a mixed crew.'

'You could looooook,' Tupo wheedled.

Ouloo gestured at the list, bringing up the details filed with the Transport Authority.

Melody
Ship category: Family shuttle
Associated orbital ship (if applicable): Harmony
Length of planetside layover: Two hours
Pilot: Speaker

'What kind of a name is Speaker?' Tupo said. 'That's not a name.'

'It's clearly *xyr* name,' Ouloo said, but now she was curious, too. A modder, most likely. Modders always had funny names like that. She pulled up the pilot licence that had been submitted with the docking request. The file appeared on screen, complete with a photo of the pilot in question.

Ouloo gasped.

Tupo was fully awake now. 'What is *that*?' xe cried, pushing xyr face in close. 'Mom, what is *that*?'

Ouloo stared. That . . . that couldn't be right.

Day 236, GC Standard 307

. . . .

COURSE ADJUSTMENTS

SPEAKER

When Speaker awoke, Tracker was nowhere in sight. This was to be expected. Tracker was always the first to be up and about. As egglings, Tracker had been nearly free of her shell by the time Speaker had started to crack through her own – a fact neither twin remembered, but one their relatives relayed time and again. Speaker had never known a life without Tracker in it, nor a morning when she'd awoken with her sister still in their bed. As such, it was not the sound of a busy sibling which roused Speaker that morning, but instead, the loud chime of a message alert.

'Can you get that?' Speaker called, reluctant to let go of the cushion she was curled around.

The message alert continued, which gave Speaker her answer.

Reluctantly, Speaker crawled to the edge of the hanging bed. She reached out a forearm, using the large keratin hook at the end of her much-smaller hand to anchor herself to the nearest ambulation pole. She then swung her body out to grab the next pole with the opposing hook, and so on, and so forth. As was the case on any Akarak ship, every room in the *Harmony* was filled with lattices of floor-to-ceiling poles, each a constructed course designed to mimic the arboreal byways her ancestors had used. Speaker had never moved about using a real tree, nor, she imagined, did she move as dexterously as her predecessors had. Like many, Speaker had been born with what her people called Irirek syndrome – an environmentally triggered genetic condition that limited the use of her legs.

The two short limbs that hung below her as she swung across the room could grasp and passively support, but nothing beyond that. Her arms were what carried her, and these were strong and tireless, even on a morning when she'd been awoken rudely.

Speaker reached the comms panel embedded in the wall, and settled herself into one of the woven seating hammocks that hung before it. She gestured to the panel, and looked at the incoming call data. A local transmission, not an ansible call. Speaker took a breath and willed herself into a state of calm. Who knew? Maybe it would go well this time.

A Laru appeared on screen – her destination's ground host, Speaker assumed, for the vowel-heavy name she'd previously noted when requesting a docking slot at the Five-Hop could be nothing *but* Laru. Most Akaraks found this species difficult to read, what with their thick fur obscuring so much of their facial musculature, but Speaker could interpret Laru expression and body language both, just as she could with most GC species. She had doggedly practised at this, and knew her skills in this regard to be sharp.

In any case, this particular Laru was nervous, a fact which made Speaker feel both exhausted and utterly unsurprised.

The Laru addressed her in laborious Hanto. '*I am Ouloo, the ground host. Please state your business here.*' The lack of polite greeting or welcome was unmissable, especially in the flowery colonial tongue. One might have chalked that up to Ouloo's obvious difficulty with speaking the language, but experience had taught its recipient better.

Speaker adopted a posture that she knew worked well on Laru: slumped shoulders, head extended farther forward than was natural for her. To a Laru, this would hit the approximate visual markers for a person at ease. 'Hello, Ouloo,' Speaker responded in polished Klip. 'It's a pleasure to meet you. My name is Speaker. You should have our shuttle reservation on file – the *Melody*.'

Ouloo's clay-red fur fluffed in surprise, and Speaker didn't have to guess at why. Akaraks were not known for conversing easily in Klip. 'Oh, I, um . . .' The Laru scrambled on her end, entering commands with her shaggy paws. 'The . . . ?'

'The *Melody*,' Speaker repeated. She doubted Ouloo had not seen the reservation before this point.

The Laru's large eyes darted up and down as she read a file on an unseen screen. 'Yes, I see,' Ouloo said. Her voice remained uneasy, adrift. 'Sorry, I didn't realise you were, um . . .' She paused. 'Could you . . . could you send over your ship's travel registry permit?'

Speaker resisted the urge to snap her beak in annoyance, and kept her head soothingly extended. 'My pilot's licence should be there with our reservation,' she said. 'Is that not sufficient?'

'Yes, um, it is. This is just for extra verification. Standard security policy.'

Speaker wondered if that policy had existed prior to this conversation. 'One moment,' she said. She called up the file and sent it forth.

There was a chirp on Ouloo's end as the file was received. The Laru's eyes went up and down, up and down, a few more times than one would assume was necessary to read such a short file. 'Thanks very much,' Ouloo said. 'All seems in order.' She was trying to sound friendly now, but there was still an edge to her voice. 'Welcome to Gora. We're looking forward to having you at the Five-Hop. I'll be in the office upon your arrival to assess your needs and show you around our facilities.' She paused again. 'I'm sorry, but we haven't had Akarak guests before. I make a point of offering something for every species, but I don't have – I don't know—' She laughed awkwardly. 'I mean – I suppose it's an oversight on my part—'

'Not to worry,' Speaker said. 'Our stop here will be short, and we'll be most comfortable in our shuttle anyway. I just need a few supplies.'

'Right,' the Laru said. 'Well, I hope it's a pleasant stop all the same. Um . . . you saw in the docking reservation guide that we have a strict no-weapons policy, correct?'

Speaker let the mild insult slide, like so many others. 'We don't carry weapons,' she said.

'Oh,' Ouloo said, surprised once more. She brightened, trying to salvage the conversation. 'You'll be less fuss than the Aeluon, then. We got a shuttle in from some border mess, and she *definitely* had to lock a few things up. You'll see her around, I'm sure.'

'I'm sure I will,' Speaker said. 'See you when we dock.'

The screen went black. Speaker exhaled, deeply. She glanced at the clock – an hour until they reached Gora. Time enough for a few creature comforts.

She swung from pole to pole, out of the bedroom and into the washroom, where she drank some water, relieved herself, and put a pack of meadowmelt dentbots to work. Meadowmelt was *her* preferred flavour, not Tracker's, but Tracker had been the one to put in the grocery order at the last market stop. Knowing this made Speaker smile as she spat the last of the cleansing froth out of her mouth. Her sister had a knack for unspoken kindnesses.

Feeling more herself, Speaker made her way down the corridor, peeking in each room as she passed by. The *Harmony* would've been far too cramped for a typical Akarak family of ten or more, but this ship was home to Speaker and Tracker alone. The unlived-in rooms were far from empty, however. Each was stuffed to the brim with tech, medicine, shelf-stable food, bedding, air tanks – whatever leftovers they'd scrounged or gifts they'd accepted. Speaker and Tracker did not carry this cargo for themselves, but for those they encountered in their work. There was no way of knowing who would need what, and so it was best to carry everything.

Tracker was, predictably, in one of the only two rooms on the *Harmony* that the sisters had set aside for something other than practical use. One of the rooms belonged to Speaker, who was in the slow process of kitting it out to be an acoustic paradise for listening to music. Tracker's room – the one Speaker entered now – was a garden, in a way. Tracker had an affinity for growing crystals, and she'd developed the room solely for this purpose. The lower part of the room was stuffed with shelves holding beakers, burners, jars of powders and salts. The walls were decked in coloured lights, affixed here and there at asymmetrical angles. Tracker's inorganic creations filled the remainder of the space, hanging from twine-supported bowls and cups in the open air between ambulation poles. Some of the crystals were fuzzy, others chunky and smooth. Some looked like water ice, or engine char, or melted glass. Their colours were varied as could be, and every movement Speaker made, no matter how minute, resulted in the room shifting into a new arrangement of kaleidoscopic glitter born out of the play between the character of minerals and the wavelengths of light.

Tracker hung by her feet from the ceiling netting, her hands arranging the contents of a likewise hanging bowl. 'This batch is turning out beautifully,' she said in their native Ihreet.

Speaker climbed toward the bowl in question, but halfway up, the maze of poles and jars that Tracker had configured around her own motions no longer worked for someone with legs of different make. Tracker noted Speaker's difficulty, and without a word from either sister, shimmied down to help. Tracker turned horizontal, vertical, back limbs flipping her body in ways Speaker's could not. She linked wrist-hooks with Speaker. She supported, boosted, guided. Speaker leaned, followed, trusted. This was a dance they knew well.

Pressed close against Tracker's torso, Speaker could hear the rattle of her sister's lungs. 'Bad day?' Speaker asked.

'Not the best,' Tracker said. Irirek syndrome had passed her by, but she had challenges of her own. It had been Speaker who had noticed the first signs of brittle lung in Tracker, three full years after the improperly filtered air they'd breathed as egglings had kicked off a slow-burn mutative revolt. Speaker hadn't known what was wrong, only that at night, when she rested her ear near her sister's nostrils or against her heart, sometimes she could hear those sleeping breaths catch and stumble. If she hadn't dragged Tracker to a doctor, Speaker would've become a sibling alone – the worst thing an Akarak could bear.

'Did you take your medicine?' Speaker asked.

'I will,' Tracker said. She gave Speaker one last gentle tug, up to the seating hammock by the bowl she'd been working on.

'Take your damn medicine,' Speaker said calmly as she sat. She leaned forward and peered into the bowl. The mineral spires within were a bottomless blue, mysterious and pacifying, branching outward in beguiling geometry. She picked one up and admired it, turning it this way and that in the coloured light. 'Is this why you didn't pick up the call?'

'No,' Tracker said, reclining on a hammock below. 'I just didn't want to deal with it.'

Speaker flicked her eyes toward her sister. 'Thanks,' she said.

Tracker spread her arms out to the side in congenial argument. 'Tell me it wasn't some bullshit.'

'Oh, it absolutely *was* some bullshit,' Speaker said.

'Mmm-hmm,' Tracker said. 'And nothing makes bullshit worse than someone with an accent like mine.'

'Your accent is fine,' Speaker said. 'It's not like you're the only person in the galaxy with a thick accent.'

'Okay, well, I don't know half as many words as you. Not even half. Like . . . an eighth. A sixteenth.'

'It's still good enough for a docking call.'

Tracker linked her wrist-hooks together behind her head, lounging in a manner that said she was not going to concede this point. 'You're Speaker, not me.'

Speaker put the crystal back in the bowl. 'Do you want to come with me this time?'

'No,' Tracker said. This was of no surprise. She rarely left the ship unless there was good reason to. This was a common trait for their kind, but Tracker had fostered it with aplomb.

She was a master of not going anywhere. Still, something occurred to her after her initial answer. 'How *much* bullshit was that call?'

Speaker understood the underlying question: *is it safe for you to go alone?* 'Not the dangerous kind,' she said. 'She seemed fussy, not violent. Besides, she doesn't allow weapons.'

'Okay. You're sure?' Tracker said.

'I'm sure.' Speaker began to make her way down, carefully. Tracker moved to help, but Speaker waved her off. 'I'm fine.' She swung herself to Tracker's hammock, and her sister made room. They arranged themselves around each other in familiar choreography, taking on a configuration that came as naturally to them as the shapes the crystals formed. Tracker started to cough, and Speaker held her sister's hands as the short fit peaked and passed. 'Hey, while I'm gone?' she said.

Tracker took a few slow, deliberate breaths, making sure everything within her chest was working as intended. 'Yeah?' she said at last.

Speaker looked Tracker dead in the eye. 'Take your medicine.'

ROVEG

The ocean beach was as beautiful as it was every time. The sky above was the pale amethyst of noon. The water below lapped at the shimmering black sand with a tender, rhythmic caress. People of all species milled about, some napping, some swimming, some collecting shells. The beach was lively, but not raucous; peaceful without being dull. A place where a person had ample space to stretch one's own thoughts while still benefiting from the reassuring company of others at a distance.

Roveg sat in the middle of the tableau, his abdominal legs folded properly beneath him while his thoracic legs engaged with the serious business of finishing a lengthy breakfast. A variety of foods were spread across the table in front of him, all carefully selected from the stasie that morning. He'd arranged a somewhat Aandrisk-influenced spread: grain crackers with snapfruit preserves, spicy fermented fungus paste rolled in fresh *saab tesh*, and a few choice slices of hot smoked river eel (this was an Aeluon addition, but it complimented the other offerings well). A bowl of tea tied the arrangement together – a delicate Laru blend, as it happened – along with a small glass of seagrass juice. The latter beverage was the only part of the meal that originated with Roveg's own species, and though he'd had many sorts of breakfasts on many different worlds, he still swore by that hard-shelled Quelin tradition of starting the morning with a cleansing shot of the stuff. Some habits, he could never break.

Roveg spread preserves onto the last of the crackers with a lower set of legs while holding a fungus roll in the set nearest

22

to his mouth. He nibbled as he watched a school of fur fish jump playfully in the water beyond the waves. A breeze rustled in the sandy scrub a short distance behind him, and the sound of chorus beetles rose in accompaniment, their haunting song low and sweet.

'Friend,' Roveg said clearly. He angled his head toward the place where he knew the wall vox lay camouflaged. 'Turn off the beetles.'

Friend chirped in acknowledgement from the speakers, and the chorus beetles ceased.

Roveg liked beetles just fine, but today, he wanted something else, something . . . 'Play Relaxation Mix #6,' he said. 'On random.'

Friend chirped again, and the music began to play.

'That's better,' Roveg said. He continued to eat, humming softly as he chewed. 'How long until descent?'

'Twenty minutes,' Friend replied.

Roveg flexed his abdominal plates in mild surprise. 'Is that all? Well.' He looked down at the last of the morning delicacies. 'Damn.' He thought briefly about bolting the remainder of his meal, but eating food without savouring it was almost as bad as throwing it out. He gathered the remnants with care, drank the seagrass juice with an appreciative shudder, and got to his feet. 'Friend, please continue music playback throughout the main sound system.' He gestured at a panel and the beach disappeared, leaving only projection hardware and smooth walls in its stead. He passed through the doors and into the hallways of his ship.

The *Korrigoch Hrut* had been Roveg's shuttle for standards, and he loved it well. It wasn't his home – that, he had left back on Chalice, a charming dwelling built into a cliff overlooking the city centre. But space travel suited him best when embarked upon in a ship that *felt* like home, and he had decorated the interior of the *Korrigoch Hrut* accordingly. There was not a wall outside of the engine core that didn't have art hanging from it. There were abstract Aandrisk paintings, Aeluon colour-opera masks, exquisite baubles made of Harmagian glass, some gifts, some memories, some passing fancies stumbled upon during a marketplace stroll. He patted a Human-made landscape painting with a leg as he walked into the kitchen. He was particularly fond of that piece.

He packed away his leftovers with meticulous care, placing them on the stasie shelves just so, then headed for the control room, still humming along to the music that followed.

The planet Gora dominated the viewscreen; he'd not abandoned his breakfast a moment too soon. He'd never travelled by way of Gora before, and his first impression was of a very orderly mess. The other transit hubs he'd been through were all situated around living planetary systems, where life happened down on the ground and traffic stuck to the orbiters above. But here, where the planet served no other purpose than to cater to the temporary needs of those in passing, where every dome was individually owned and the only shared territory were the traffic lanes guiding ships to and fro, everything smacked of utilitarian artificiality. There were no seas, no forests, no great cities. This was a place to be used, not lived in.

Roveg's compound eyes were capable of tracking many objects in motion at once, but even he struggled to parse the scene before him. The open space he flew through was thick with ships of all sorts: sleek cruisers with polished white hulls, colourful teardrops made for going fast and looking good doing it, hefty haulers fat with cargo, luxurious vacation skiffs, cheap-ride deepods, and shuttles that appeared held together with nothing more than a welding torch and hope. The vessels moved as though they were following a pheromone trail, each marching along, one after the next, docking here and turning there, waiting patiently in the wormhole queue for their turn to hop through the space between space. Heavy as the traffic was, Roveg took comfort in the tidy streams of ships and the calculated rows of buoys. Roveg liked space travel just fine, and he rather relished any opportunity to take his shuttle out for a few tendays, but he didn't do it particularly often. Space was not his life. He wasn't the sort to enjoy an unplotted jaunt through the off-road sections of the galactic map, and he certainly didn't like landing in places where travel law was approached as more of a suggestion than a rule – especially not given the course he was on now. The task at hand was fraught enough without adding traffic violations to the mix.

As Roveg waited for Friend to guide the *Korrigoch Hrut* into a proper entry angle, he noticed a second dance of machinery occurring in the space below the ship traffic – or, at least, inasmuch as 'below' had any sort of meaning in three-dimensional space. The orbital layer cocooning Gora was as thick with satellites as any world he'd ever seen. He noted comms tech, and solar harvesters as well. The latter's distinctive shape was unmistakable – huge photosynthetic panels blooming among the weeds of the comms dishes. Their panels glittered as they soaked up raw sunlight undiluted by atmosphere, and he took care not to look too long at the concentrated beams making their way down to collection stations on the surface. Solar was the only sort of power that made sense on a windless, waterless world, and he was glad that *this* portion of infrastructure seemed to be communally distributed. He didn't much fancy the idea of each dome being a bubble unto itself, powered by whatever generator the owner could manage. Roveg was nothing if not a champion of playing one's own tune, but there were some areas in which individuality stopped being a virtue and became more of a game of chance.

'We're ready for entry, Roveg,' Friend said. The AI was neither sapient nor sentient, as Roveg detested the use of their soulful kind. Even so, he had made a point to tweak Friend's linguistic files into something companionable – in Klip, of course, never Tellerain. Roveg was sparing about the contexts in which he welcomed his mother tongue.

'Thank you, Friend,' Roveg said, even though the AI had no

capability with which to care about being thanked. 'Let's begin.'

There were some individuals for whom landing a spaceship manually was a point of pride, but Roveg took no chances when it came to physics. He did not see the need to flex one's frills over being able to do something that every species in the GC had taught their machines to do centuries prior.

He walked himself into the safety harness hanging in the centre of the room, holding still as the robotic straps wove themselves between his abdominal legs and around his thorax. 'Friend,' he said, reaching for a nearby compartment as he spoke. He opened the small cubby and retrieved a packet of grav tabs. 'Check with the surface for landing confirmation.'

'One moment,' Friend said. The flight status monitors shifted accordingly as the AI worked.

Roveg tore open the packet and ate the disks of chalky medicine within, his spiracles flaring in fleeting disgust as he did so. This was a necessary precaution, as he knew from queasy landings of yore, but he could think of few worse ways to chase a lovely breakfast than with grav tabs. Whoever manufactured them really could stand to flavour them more palatably.

Friend reported back. 'The ground host has confirmed they are ready for our landing.'

'Excellent,' Roveg said. He folded the empty packet in half twice, then set it back in the cubby, ready to be retrieved for the incinerator at a later time. 'You may begin landing.'

There was the floating lurch of the artigrav turning off, the loud whirring of the engines changing position, the roar as Roveg's ship threaded itself in a precise parabolic curve. All at once, the *Korrigoch Hrut* threw itself at Gora, and natural gravity grabbed it with inescapable authority. Roveg forced himself to relax into the harnesses, as he'd long ago taught himself to do. Bracing only made atmospheric entry worse, even though every instinct in him demanded otherwise. Intellectually, he was aware that he had done this countless times and had nothing to worry about. Still, the visual of *an entire planet rushing toward you* was a hard thing to tell your body to ignore. But Roveg did, in fact, manage to relax, letting engineering lead the way. Both of his stomachs held as the ship split Gora's paltry air. Breakfast, thankfully, stayed down. He no longer regretted taking his medicine.

Dome after dome flashed past as he made his decent, and he craned his torso toward the viewscreen as much as the harnesses would allow. Everything was going too fast for a proper look, but he made out multiple bursts of green and blue: the signatures of plant life and water fixtures, hauled between stars and corralled for the purpose of travellers' comfort. He warmed at the sight of the colours alone, even though their details were lost. He loved his simulated environments dearly – as only made sense for one of his profession – but it had been over two tendays since his last docking, and he was more than ready for the real thing, curated as it might be. In all honesty, Roveg much preferred gardens to untended biomes, and had spent as little time in the latter as possible. Wild places had every right to exist, and the galaxy needed them, to be sure, but he was content to leave them to their own devices behind fences and walls and the thickest of windows.

The ship began to slow, and the world along with it. The *Korrigoch Hrut* coasted to its destination, landing as comfortably as one could. The view outside was pretty much what one would expect in such a place: a circular shuttle tarmac outside of a modest-sized habitat dome. An airlock tunnel connected dome to landing pad, its six universal latching ports branched outward like airways. As Friend nudged the ship into docking position, Roveg glanced idly at the other shuttles he now neighboured. One looked both military and Aeluon – white as a child's shell, smooth as wet ceramic, its brawny hull ready to take a beating. It was in excellent condition and a feast for the eyes; he'd never encountered an Aeluon vessel that appeared otherwise. The other two ships looked like the sort of prefab kits that anybody with a modest budget could pick up at a multispecies dealer, but that was where their similarity ended. One obviously belonged to the ground host, as the exterior was painted unmissably with the phrase 'VISIT THE FIVE-HOP ONE-STOP!' on every side. The other . . . well, it was a cheap ship, to be sure, and the longer he looked at it, the more it became clear there had been repairs involving components from other kits. It was mismatched and homely, but it wasn't falling apart, and the build didn't look dangerous. It simply looked like the efforts of someone who was doing what they could with what they had. For all his love of aesthetics, Roveg could respect that. Sometimes all you could do was make it work.

There was a clank, a whir, a quieting-down. 'Docking is complete,' Friend said. 'You may safely exit the shuttle, when ready.'

'Thank you, Friend,' Roveg said, as the harness let him go. Stars, but he was ready to get out. He wasted no time in heading to the hatch, stepping into the airlock, standing patiently as he was scanned for contaminants, and going on through.

Awaiting him at the airlock entrance was a Laru – a large child, too young to have chosen a gender yet, comprised of angles that didn't look comfortable and feet that didn't match xyr body. Xyr fur looked halfway groomed, and was too long for xyr face. It hung listlessly over xyr large black eyes in a helpless manner that suggested it didn't know why it was still growing but didn't know what else to do.

'Welcome to the Five-Hop One-Stop,' the Laru child recited in the flat tone of the unenthused. Xe stood on three legs, holding a scrib in the paw of xyr fourth. Xe looked at the screen, craning xyr limb-like neck. Xe looked then at Roveg, then back to the screen, then turned the scrib around so that Roveg might read his own shuttle licence.

It took Roveg a moment to realise this was the child's attempt to verify his identity. Apparently this was what passed for docking security here. 'Yes, that's me,' he said, hoping he was correct in his interpretation of whatever was going on.

The Laru bobbed xyr long, shaggy neck in acknowledgement and holstered the scrib in the light satchel strapped across xyr back. Xe swung xyr head to the left and plodded along after, leading Roveg inside without another word.

A pair of doors slid open. The Five-Hop One-Stop lay beyond. The place was . . . quaint. Charming, in a bucolic way. Roveg was not the sort to condescend about such things; arrogance was a quality he strongly disliked, and took care to dig it out of himself whenever he found it. But he'd have been a liar if he'd said this establishment was his first choice. He'd hoped to stop over at the Reskit Afternoon, a well-reviewed restaurant in Gora's southern hemisphere, but their dock had been fully booked, as had the Goran sculpture garden, and the Harmagian baths, and the city field. Much as Roveg would've liked a bit of a treat to ease the journey, the only thing that was truly necessary for him was fuel, and when it became clear that docking space on Gora was in high demand that day, he changed tactics and jumped on the first open reservation slot he could grab.

He looked around, assessing just where that choice had taken him.

Someone had worked hard on this place, someone who substituted love for money whenever the latter ran short. The circular space within the dome was home to a selection of fab-printed, bubble-shaped buildings of varied size, all painted in benign whites and greys – a palette clearly intended for the comfort of Aeluons, who could grow fatigued from more colourful architecture that their species would interpret as yelling at them. The walking paths branching between the buildings looked hand-laid, and were paved in a manner suitable for Harmagian carts. The filtered air was warm – warmer than a densely coated Laru would choose on xyr own, he assumed, but quite comfortable by his standards, managing to strike a considered compromise between his own Quelin preference for a soothing cloud of humidity and the Aandrisk penchant for desert dryness. It wasn't perfect, but it would make most people happy. Roveg had the feeling that was the underlying aim with everything in this place.

A sign hung over the entry pathway, and it was crammed with so many words in so many languages that the well-intended attempt at universal communication had rendered it nearly unreadable. The Tellerain was grammatically jarring (he respected the effort, at least), so he skimmed through the Klip instead.

WELCOME TO THE FIVE-HOP ONE-STOP!
THE LITTLE DOME WITH A LOT OF OPTIONS!

YOUR GROUND HOST: OOLI OHT OULOO
YOUR ASSISTANT GROUND HOST: OOLI OHT TUPO

Beside this was a close-up picture of the ground hosts in question, both enthusiastically mugging for the camera. Tupo had to be the child Roveg followed now, for the little one in the portrait looked exactly like xyr, only half the size, twice as fluffy, and in a good mood.

The overwhelming signage continued.

OUR RULES:
NO WEAPONS!
NO MAGNETS!
NO BAD TIMES!!!

THIS WAY:
OFFICE AND SUNDRY SHOP
- CERTIFIED TRAVEL PERMITS
- CERTIFIED IMUBOT SOFTWARE UPGRADES
- OFFICIAL GC TRANSIT AUTHORITY MAP CHIPS
- WATER FILTRATION STATION
- SOUVENIRS!
- GIFTS!
- SNACKS!

HOST RESIDENCE AND
LIFE SUPPORT/COMMS FACILITIES
NOT OPEN TO GUESTS

THAT WAY:
FUEL AND FIX-ITS
- BARRELLED ALGAE
- ALGAE STARTERS
- PHOTOVOLTAIC REPAIR
- MECH TECH BITS AND BOBS
- NO COMP TECH SUPPLIES ON SITE,
BUT WE CAN COURIER THEM IN!

THE ONE AND ONLY GORAN
NATURAL HISTORY MUSEUM
DON'T MISS IT!!!

STRAIGHT AHEAD:
REST AND RELAX DURING YOUR LAYOVER AT
THE FIVE-HOP'S WORLD-FAMOUS MULTISPECIES
BATHHOUSE AND FLOWER GARDEN!
- FIXTURES AND FAUCETS FOR EVERY SAPIENT!
- TRY OUR HOMEMADE SCALE SCRUB, BATH FIZZ,
STEAM TABS, AND SOAP!
- TRADITIONAL LARU DESSERT OFFERED FREE IN THE
GARDEN EVERY DAY FROM 14:00 - 17:00
- WE PROUDLY GROW AND USE NOTHING BUT
HYPO-ALLERGENIC PLANTS ENGINEERED BY UTLOOT
AGRICULTURAL LABS
- NO BUGS! NO RAIN! BETTER THAN OUTDOORS!
- HARMAGIAN-STYLE SWIMMING LANE COMING SOON!

Just as Roveg was beginning to feel overwhelmed by the glut of exclamation points, their presumed wielder appeared in front of him.

Laru were, to his eyes, a hilarious-looking species. He'd never say it to one of their faces, and he knew well that biological normality was extremely relative. He was sure he looked odd to plenty of people outside of his own phenotype. But stars above, Laru were so *floppy*. Their limbs were like animated noodles, their stubby torsos thick and bumbling, their long tail-like necks somewhere between a nightmare and a grand cosmic joke. This Laru – Ouloo, he assumed – had styled her fur in an explosion of intense curls that reminded him of nothing so much as the stacked rows of icing he'd once seen at a Human bakery. She definitely looked to be the sort who would love a good exclamation point (or twelve).

Roveg was proved correct, though the Laru's volume was directed not at him, but his young guide. 'Tupo!' the older Laru scolded. The child visibly cringed. 'I thought I told you to restock the steam bath before Captain Tem got here.' She pointed an angry paw at the middle path. Roveg saw enticing angled hedges down that way, and among them, an Aeluon walking contemplatively – the owner of the fine shuttle, one would assume.

The child exhaled from the depths of xyr lungs, as though this were just one more injustice from a universe that existed only to conspire against xyr. 'You also said to be there for the 13:06.' Xe gestured at Roveg, who now found himself in the role of evidence in a trial he hadn't anticipated.

'If you'd started earlier, you could have done both,' the older Laru said. 'Go on.'

The younger voiced no further argument, and marched past, radiating annoyance.

'And *trim your fur*,' Ouloo called after xyr. She arched her neck in exasperation, and swung her face toward Roveg. 'I am so sorry about that. Puberty, you know?' Ouloo leaned in confidentially. 'Poor thing's quite uncomfortable, what with xyr teeth coming in. But that doesn't excuse . . .' She craned her neck so that her head was facing fully over her haunches, watching Tupo plod off. 'Well, all the rest of it.' She tutted as her head came back around. 'But just because xe's forgotten xyr manners doesn't mean I have.' She beamed, bowing her neck low. 'Welcome to the Five-Hop One-Stop. I'm Ouloo, and you must be Roveg.' She hushed her voice discreetly. 'No honorific?'

'No,' he said, a quiet twinge accompanying the answer. The old sting had faded, but was always there.

Ouloo bowed her head again. 'We're very happy to have you, Roveg,' she said, and this, he appreciated. Quelin customarily were never addressed without an honorific; exiles, however, were allowed none. The fact that Ouloo both knew to enquire about it and to smoothly move on from the question showed courtesy and cultural savvy. Roveg forgave her a few of the exclamation points. Not all of them, but a few.

'Thank you,' he said. 'I understand from your Linking page that you carry high-skim algae fuel.'

'We sure do,' she said smartly. 'You're here for a . . . four-hour layover, correct? Would you like to take care of fuelling up now, or later?'

'Later, if that's all right. I've been on my ship for tendays, and could use a walk around.'

'Oh, I understand,' the Laru said in a knowing tone. 'I haven't been on a long haul in standards, but my paws twitch whenever I remember it. Where is it you're headed?'

'Vemereng,' Roveg said.

Ouloo apparently knew it. 'Oof, that's a long way,' she said. 'Remind me where home is for you?'

'Chalice.'

'Goodness, yes. Must be an important trip to take you that far. Business or pleasure?'

'I have an appointment there,' he said.

Ouloo waited expectantly, but he provided nothing further. 'Well,' she said, the barest hint of disappointment creeping into her otherwise chipper tone. 'If it's a walk you want, our garden will be just the ticket. Are you hungry? We haven't got a restaurant, I'm afraid, but we've got a wonderful selection of nibbles.'

Roveg wasn't hungry, but nothing piqued his interest like regional food. 'I never say no to nibbles,' he said.

Ouloo laughed – which wasn't like a laugh at all to Roveg, but he knew what the huffing sound meant – and gestured with a paw for him to follow. 'Come on, we'll sort you out,' she said. 'Do you like jenjen cake? I got some fresh from my neighbour this morning.' She padded along, making small talk in good cheer. But as Roveg followed, he couldn't help but notice her throwing the occasional glance toward the fuel shed across the way. Something in there was on the Laru's mind. Whatever it was, it wasn't his concern. He was here for fuel, a stretch, and apparently, cake. Under the circumstances, he had no appetite for anything more complicated than that.

PEI

One of the first things Aeluon children learned after they mastered the complicated matters of walking and eating and using their colours with intention was that the world around them did not use the same language people did. People, of course, communicated via the swirling chromatophore patches covering both cheeks. Their plant-and-animal neighbours, however, did not. The purplish fur of *lumae* did not mean they were angry. Nectarwings, with their orange spots, were not sad. Shiver fish were not friends, no matter how kind their blue scales might look. Pei had a hazy memory of struggling with this concept, of feeling like the natural world was untrustworthy, that it was lying to her in some way. Colour was colour, and colour *meant things*, and if it was obvious to *her* that laughter was green and annoyance was yellow, surely other creatures must know this, too.

From the vantage point of her middle years, she could not pinpoint the moment in which that errant conception had faded, but once she crossed that threshold, she understood that every aspect of life had layers. There was the colour on the surface, and the meaning underneath. Yellow, when not seen swimming through a person's face, was often nothing more than yellow, full stop. You had to pause in the face of reflex, ask yourself if the narrative you attached to the knee-jerk was accurate. Once she'd grasped this, she could never again see life as a static thing, something with one immutable definition. The universe was not an object. It was a beam of light, and the colours that

35

it split into changed depending on whose eyes were doing the looking. Nothing could be taken at face value. Everything had hidden facets, hidden depths that could be interpreted a thousand ways – or misinterpreted in the same manner. Reflexes kept a person safe, but they could also make you stupid.

Pei knew this fact in the same way that she knew how to breathe, and yet all the same, the Akarak made her wary.

She'd never seen one of their kind in a place like this – in a spaceport, sure, but always on the fringes, digging through scrap, scuttling through alleys, conversing only among themselves. Never in the thick of a marketplace. Never alone. Never walking around a fuel shed, browsing algae starters and fuel pumps, as the individual she was watching from a distance was doing now. Akaraks were not a common sight in GC space, but Pei had assuredly had dealings with them – not in words, but with weapons. She'd caught a pair of them snooping around her shuttle once, and had scared them off with nothing more than a pistol drawn. Another time, a crew of them had been in the process of stealing the cargo she and her own crew had been sent to collect. That incident hadn't been so easily resolved. Pei had never spoken with an Akarak, but she had a pulse-rifle scar on her upper arm thanks to one, and had ended the lives of two more with her own hand.

That was the sort of fact whose layered meanings she had no desire to unfold further.

Pei turned her attention back to the spiral of blooming hedges she stood within. Their long, horn-like flowers were pretty (despite being yellow), and their scent was pleasingly sweet. A small swarm of pollinator bots moved among them in a soothing sway, meandering from blossom to blossom, rolling their soft, dusty brushes with a mechanical hum. Pei was glad to be outside, glad to have her feet on the ground. Her ship – her main ship, not the shuttle she'd travelled in – had a garden, like most did, but it just wasn't the same as one woven into a planet. She knelt down, grabbed a pinch of the mulch blanketing the hedges' roots, and rubbed it between her fingers with reverence. She loved her ship, loved her crew, loved a life spent above instead of below, but stars, there were times when she missed *dirt*.

The back of her neck prickled with the empty touch of being seen.

She glanced up, and over.

The Akarak was looking at her.

They were too far apart for Pei to see the Akarak's face – not that she would've been able to read the expression anyway, knowing as little about them as she did. Like all of xyr kind, the Akarak was housed within a bulky, bipedal-bodied mech suit, sealed away in a windowed cockpit that occupied the space where an ordinary-sized head might be. The suit itself was a bit taller than Pei, but its operator was child-sized – no, smaller than that, even. Pei could've placed xyr in a satchel without difficulty. She could make out a few physical details: spindly limbs, short torso, the hint of a beak hiding in shadow. But even without a good view of the Akarak's face, Pei could tell they were staring at one another. The moment in which they could each pretend they weren't had gone.

There was movement within the suit: a lever pulled, buttons pressed. The suit obeyed, straightening up and raising both of its four-fingered metal hands. At the Akarak's command, it turned the palms outward, and tipped the fingertips gently to each side.

Pei's inner eyelids flicked with surprise. The stance the Akarak's suit had adopted was that of an Aeluon greeting, the kind you gave a person when you were too far apart to press palms. It was an unremarkable, everyday way of expressing a friendly hello, performed by the last sort of figure she would've expected it from. The combination was nothing if not surreal.

Pei stood still for a moment, then cautiously returned the gesture.

The Akarak's suit gave a polite tilt of acknowledgement, then returned to the business of buying algae.

Before Pei could process that exchange, a loud rattling sound approached. Pei had no natural sense of hearing, but the auditory-processing implant embedded in her forehead allowed her to cognitively register sound and understand its associated meaning (the sensation was something like reading, but without a screen present). Vital as this need was in a galaxy where everyone else insisted on carrying out vibratory conversations delivered via air, the implant could not communicate the sound's *direction* in the same neural way that it relayed the sound itself. This simply wasn't something a non-hearing brain could comprehend. To accommodate for this, the implant gave her skin a gentle buzz on the right side of her forehead, letting her know where the noise was coming from.

She turned to see the younger Laru ambling in her general direction, walking on xyr hind legs and pushing a three-tiered cart with xyr forepaws. The garden had a clearing at the centre, a spacious, short-cut lawn with tables and benches designed for a variety of species' posteriors. It was here that the Laru was headed with xyr cargo.

Pei approached, and the smell of warm sugar caught her attention. 'What've you got there?' she asked, mentally operating the talkbox implanted on the outside of her throat (a talkbox could be implanted anywhere, really, but other sapients preferred it when your 'voice' – computerised though it was – came from the same direction as your head).

The child – Tepo, was xyr name? Tuppo? something like that – parked the cart and turned to face Pei. Except . . . xe didn't *quite* face her. The Laru were a species that Pei *was* familiar with, but it didn't take an expert to grasp that the shaggy kid was shy. Xe looked somewhere in the vague vicinity of Pei's face, just short of looking her in the eye. 'Please enjoy these traditional Laru desserts, compliments of your hosts at the Five-Hop,' xe said in joyless recitation. Xe gestured at the cart with all the enthusiasm of someone cleaning out a clogged drain.

Pei managed to squash the laugh that was about to leave her

talkbox, and hoped the amused green she could feel tickling her cheeks would go unnoticed. 'You know, I don't think I've ever had *any* kind of Laru dessert,' she said. 'Can you walk me through them?'

The kid squirmed, clearly having hoped xyr introduction of the cart would've served as both hello and goodbye, but xe dutifully turned xyr attention to the treats. 'We've got, um, crushcake, mellow-mallow pudding, sweet-and-salties, baby paws, and . . . mint crisps.'

'Hmm,' Pei said. 'Very interesting.' She was trying to make xyr more comfortable, but the remark was genuine. The festively decorated bowls and cups before her did look tempting. 'Which one is your favourite?'

'Umm . . . I like mellow-mallow pudding.' Xe pointed a stubby toepad toward a bowl filled with something black and gelatinous, topped with swirls of . . . some kind of plant shavings? Or maybe spun sugar?

'All right,' Pei said. 'Will you have one with me?'

The child shifted on all four feet, pawing lightly at the grass. 'Oh, um . . . it's for guests only.' There was regret laced through those words, and it sounded as thick as the pudding appeared.

Pei threw a theatrical glance over her shoulder toward the office. 'I can keep a secret,' she said with a cheeky flick of her eyelids.

The kid finally brightened. 'Yeah?'

'Yeah.'

That was all it took for the Laru to transform. With a sudden burst of animation, xe grabbed two bowls of pudding, handing Pei one and keeping the other for xyrself. Pei noticed that xe had hung onto the bowl with a more generous helping. She had no problem with that.

They both sat down in the grass, Pei cross-legged, the youngster on xyr haunches. 'Sorry, what's your name again?' Pei said.

'Tupo,' xe said. Xe cupped the bowl in xyr forepaws and began lapping up the pudding with xyr fat purple tongue, having no need for the alien spoons xyr mother had provided.

Pei, on the other hand, *did* need a spoon, and with it, she took a confident bite of the pudding. 'Huh,' she said through her talkbox as she swirled the stuff around her mouth.

'D'you like it?' Tupo mumbled, xyr own mouth partially full.

'Yeah, I think I do,' Pei said. The pudding had a strange consistency, more fluffy than creamy, and the taste did not fall into an easy category. Sweet and earthy, with a bitter tang that both surprised and encouraged. 'I don't think it's *my* favourite, but it's really good.'

Tupo looked pleased. Xe swallowed, and said, 'That's so weird.'

'What's weird?'

'That you can talk while you eat.'

'It's weird to me that you *can't* talk while you eat,' Pei said, smiling blue. 'Eating's the only thing we use our mouths for.'

'Not drinking?'

'Well, drinking, too.'

'And breathing?'

'Okay, yeah, we can breathe through them. But I mostly do that through my nose, like you.'

Tupo looked at her for a moment. 'Can I look close at your nose?'

Pei blinked. 'Um . . . yeah, sure, I guess.'

The Laru stretched xyr neck all the way out, getting far closer to Pei's face than was anywhere in the realm of comfort or good manners. Xe studied her face with keen interest. 'It's so *small*,' Tupo said.

'And yours is really big, to me,' Pei said, as she experienced the best view she'd ever had of a Laru's broad, fleshy nostrils.

Curiosity apparently sated, Tupo retracted xyr neck and went back to xyr pudding. 'What kind of captain are you?'

'Cargo,' Pei said.

'I thought you were maybe a soldier.' Tupo sounded disappointed at her answer. Xe took another long lick of pudding. Xyr bowl was already about halfway empty. 'My mom said she locked up a bunch of your guns.'

'If two is a bunch, then yes,' Pei said.

'But you're *not* a soldier.'

'No. I get soldiers the supplies they need. That's what most of my work entails.'

'Do you go where they're fighting?'

'Yes,' said Pei, matter of fact.

'Is it scary?'

'Yes.'

'Have you ever been shot?'

Pei cocked her head at Tupo's bluntness. Xe seemed harmless, but this wasn't a turn she'd expected. 'Yes,' she said, her tone unchanged.

'Did it hurt?'

'What do you think?'

'Probably.'

Pei laughed. '*Probably*.' She looked at Tupo with affable admonishment. 'Yes, it hurts.'

'How bad does it hurt?'

While Pei did not *need* to be quiet while eating, she took a long moment to weigh that question. 'Are you sure your mom would want me to be talking to you about this?'

Tupo licked some pudding from the corners of xyr mouth. 'I dunno.'

'Mmm-hmm. Maybe we should find something else to talk about.'

Tupo looked a smidge sulky about that prospect, but shifted gears. 'If you're a captain, where's your crew?'

'On shore leave. We just finished a . . . a big job—' she was *definitely* not discussing the details of that, even though she could see them plain as day every time she shut her outer eyelids '—so now we get a break. Everybody's off in different directions for a while, then we'll get back together and head on to the next.'

'Where are you going?'

'To visit a friend.'

'Where's your friend live?'

'On a ship. He's a spacer.'

'Aren't you a spacer?'

'Yes.'

'So . . .' Tupo looked unimpressed. 'For your vacation, you're going to a *different* ship.'

'I mean, vacation's about the company, right?'

Tupo was not convinced. 'What kind of ship?'

Stars, but the kid didn't stop once you got some sugar in xyr. 'Mixed. My friend is Human.'

Tupo let out a fizzing chuckle. 'Humans look so funny.'

'What?' Pei said. 'Why?'

'I dunno, they're just funny. They have furry heads and nothing else.'

'They have fur all over,' Pei said. 'It just grows really, really thin in most places.'

'Yeah,' Tupo said. 'Like *babies*.'

Pei laughed at that, her face flushing green. 'I don't know,' she said in friendly disagreement. She took a thoughtful bite of her pudding, letting it spread across her tongue, savouring the sugar as it melted slowly. A few private notes of fond blue bloomed here and there. 'I think some of them look nice.'

A different shade of blue appeared down the path leading back to the Five-Hop's main buildings, and Pei noted it with interest. Ouloo was giving the grand tour to a Quelin, whose ship had presumably been the one that landed before the pudding arrived. His bold cobalt exoskeleton glinted in the sunlight, but there were no other colours visible on his shell, none of the embedded jewellery his kind commonly wore. Pei could see the dull scarring where the gems had been forcibly pried loose, the harsh lines carved through formerly intricate etchings detailing his class and lineage. An exile, barred from home. The only individuals you really saw outside of their territory. She pressed her tongue against the back of her teeth with quiet pity. The Quelin Protectorate were a real bunch of bastards.

'You get all sorts here, huh?' she said to Tupo as she watched Ouloo excitedly showing the Quelin around. He seemed particularly interested in one of the flowering hedges, and bowed the vertical half of his body low to inspect it closer.

'We've had Quelin before,' Tupo said, looking forlornly at xyr empty bowl. 'Not a lot, but sometimes. Never had an Akarak, though. My mom won't let me go talk to her alone.' This fact made Tupo look even glummer than the lack of dessert did.

Her, Pei noted. She had no idea how Akaraks defined gender, so she had to follow the child's lead. 'Did your mom say why you can't?' she asked carefully. She really wanted to know what the Akarak's deal was.

'No,' Tupo said. 'Just that I can't.' Xe reached over to the cart and took another bowl of pudding. 'Is it true they're all pirates?'

Pei paused, because of course they weren't, but that was the exact same knee-jerk thought *she'd* had when she'd caught her first glimpse of the mech suit. 'No,' she said. An Akarak was just an Akarak. Yellow could just be yellow. Reflexes could make you stupid.

This answer yet again disappointed Tupo, but xe looked unsurprised. 'She didn't have *any* guns, so she's probably *not* a pirate.'

'Your mom's pretty serious about locking up weapons, huh?' Pei said.

'Yeah,' Tupo said, swallowing xyr mouthful of dessert with the same vigour as all previous ones. 'She doesn't like guns at all.'

'My friend's the same way.'

'Your Human friend?'

'Yeah,' Pei said. 'He'll probably make me leave mine on my shuttle.' Which was fair, even if she didn't like it. His house, after all.

'Why do Humans—' Tupo stopped talking with a jolt. Xyr eyes grew huge.

'Bite your tongue?' Pei asked. The talkbox had delivered the question teasingly, but as soon as the words left it, Pei realised the kid wasn't looking at her. Xe was looking up.

'What's *that*?' Tupo shouted.

Pei followed Tupo's gaze, and turned toward the horizon. Her cheeks flooded with colour, her blood with adrenaline.

'Captain Tem, what—'

'Stay here,' she said, getting quickly to her feet. 'I'm gonna—'

'What is it?!'

'I don't know,' she said. Her first instinct was to reach for her gun, but of course, she didn't have it. She took a step forward, in between Tupo and the sight that was making xyr freak out, trying to understand what she was seeing.

Far above the dome, way up at the edge of the sky, something in the atmosphere was burning.

SPEAKER

Looking upward in a mech suit was difficult. The cockpit window allowed Speaker some degree of peripheral vision, but swinging her view properly *up* required manoeuvring the suit so that it would tip her seated body backward. She wouldn't have thought to do this if she hadn't glanced up from the engine compatibility specs she'd been reading and seen the aliens in the garden pointing and shouting.

Speaker hurried the suit out of the shed and tipped the torso so she could see. Gaseous white streaks now criss-crossed the sky. *Clouds*, was her first thought, followed quickly by the realisation that Gora didn't have atmosphere enough to *get* clouds. This fact was confirmed as one of the streaks' edges shifted from billowing white to the unmistakable colour of flame. Another like it appeared elsewhere, then another, and another, an ever-growing chorus of far-away fires in free fall.

Heavy as the suit was, it could run pretty quickly.

'What's going on?' she called as she ran to the others. The words exited the vox on the outside of her suit, but were lost in the din of everyone else yelling things of the same nature.

'What's happening?' the Quelin cried.

The Aeluon came running over with the Laru child close by her side. 'Mom!' the youngster said, rushing toward Ouloo.

'Does the planet have emergency comms?' the Aeluon demanded.

Tupo wove xyrself under and through Ouloo's legs. 'Mom, *what is it?*'

'Some kind of alert system?' the Aeluon said.

'I – I—' Ouloo stared at the sky in shock, her mouth open and eyes wide.

'There's so many,' the Quelin said. 'Could it— oh, *shit*.'

A large explosion joined the fray – silent at this distance, but stomach-twisting all the same. Tumbling debris scattered from it, mere flecks in the sky, deceptively small. Something big was breaking into pieces, and it wasn't the only thing up there doing so.

Everyone reacted in their own manner: the Aeluon turned red as gore, the Laru's fur fluffed, the Quelin threw each of his upper legs out to the side. Speaker sat motionless in her cockpit, every muscle tense, one thought piercing through the dozen tangled questions racing through her own head and in the voices of everyone around her.

Tracker was up there.

The Aeluon took charge. She moved decisively to Ouloo, looked her in the eye, and said, 'Where's your sib tower?'

Ouloo gulped air and pointed a paw down one of the paths.

The Aeluon ran.

Speaker followed her.

The ansible tower wasn't far, and Speaker caught up quickly, arriving just a few steps behind. The Aeluon opened the manual access panel, pulled her scrib free of its belt holster, and looked around, searching for something not present. Her cheeks speckled purple with frustration.

Speaker understood; the Aeluon didn't have the tower's wireless access code, and therefore needed to plug her scrib directly into it. Speaker dug the suit's hands through the storage compartments attached to its midsection and retrieved a standard intermix cable. 'Will this work?' she said, extending the cable forward.

The Aeluon looked up with obvious surprise, as though she were only now registering Speaker's presence. 'Uh, I think so,' she said, grabbing the cable with her long silver fingers. She held both it and the scrib up, inspecting port and jack. 'Yeah, yeah, that'll work.' She made the connections, giving Speaker a brief glance as she did so. 'Thanks.'

Ouloo hurried up behind them, having seemingly pulled herself together. 'Try the emergency beacon network,' she said. 'The channel is 333-A.' Her child was nearly attached to her side, and the Quelin was close behind.

A broad streak of flame tore across the morning sky, and Speaker felt as though her heart would burst from her chest. She had to get out of there. She had to get to Tracker. Whatever was happening, she and her sister needed to get away from it, *now*.

The Aeluon gestured at the scrib's screen. It responded to her command, displaying a dizzying stream of polychromatic flashes. This had meaning to the Aeluon, assuredly, but Speaker winced at the sight, unable to look directly at it. The Aeluon gestured again, and said aloud, 'Disable colour translation. Enable Klip audio playback.'

The scrib obeyed; a voice emerged. '—*advising everyone to stay calm as we assess the situation.*'

'I can't stay calm if you don't tell me what the situation is,' the Quelin huffed.

'Quiet,' the Aeluon said.

The Quelin's frills bristled at that.

The emergency broadcast continued. '—*refrain from calling emergency channels unless you are in actual need of assistance. We are aware of the situation and will have more information once we have properly assessed the*—' A burst of static cut the voice off. '—*is ongoing – don't – halt all launch – for the time*—'

'I just had this tower serviced,' Ouloo said frantically. 'I don't understand; it should be working.'

'It's not the tower,' Tupo said. Speaker turned the suit toward the child. Tupo was craning xyr neck out from under xyr mother's legs to face the sky. Xe still clung to Ouloo, but xyr voice possessed the calm of a person who'd come to a terrible conclusion. 'Look.'

The adults all looked.

The sky was nearly choked with smoke by now, offset by flashes of flame. The debris had grown thicker, and chaotic though it was, the longer Speaker looked, the more she began to see shapes. Angles. Jagged edges. The occasional glint of shattered photovoltaic blue.

'Satellites,' Speaker said. 'It's the satellites.'

Roveg stepped forward beside her, his many pointed feet tapping the ground. His voice came out a whisper. 'It's *all* the satellites.'

Day 236, GC Standard 307
....
SHELTER

Received message
Encryption: 0
From: GC Transit Authority – Gora System (path: 487-45411-479-4)
To: Ooli Oht Ouloo (path: 5787-598-66)
Subject: URGENT UPDATE

This is an urgent message from the Emergency Response Team aboard the GC Transit Authority Regional Management Orbiter (Gora System). As both standard ansible and Linking channels are currently unavailable, we will be communicating via the emergency beacon network for the time being. We ask that you leave your scribs locked to this channel until proper communications are restored.

This is an emergency. Please shelter within your ships, homes, or any other reinforced structure until you receive an all-clear message from the GCTA. Habitat domes may not provide adequate protection against large debris that survives reentry.
Please prepare to continue sheltering for at least one GC standard day.

At this time, the Goran satellite network is experiencing severe cascade collisions and orbital destabilisation. As this unexpected event is still developing, we cannot provide full details as to the nature of this system failure. However, we are working closely with Goran Orbital Cooperative representatives in orbit to assess the situation, and our joint agencies are working as fast as possible to provide you with more detailed information.

As the Goran Orbital Cooperative is likewise unable to access standard comms channels on the surface, the GCTA will be handling public updates for as long as necessary.

We do not yet have an estimate as to when an all-clear will be possible. We are asking all travellers to anticipate a delay of approximately one GC standard day. We understand this will cause major disruptions to travel plans, but launches and landings pose extreme risk in current conditions. Any attempts to travel to or from the Goran surface at this time will result in an immediate suspension of your pilot's licence and possible confiscation of your vessel by the GCTA (provided your vessel remains intact).

Thank you for your patience. We are all in this together.

ROVEG

Roveg returned to his shuttle as fast as his legs would carry him. The hatch shut behind him, and he felt profound gratitude as he heard it thud into place. He stood motionless in the airlock, unsure of what should come next. He'd never been in a situation like this. He was aware that all civilised life ran on machines and constructs. Such things were the bedrock of his work, and he knew this truth well. But possessing the intellectual knowledge that *infrastructure can break* was a far cry from *watching* it break in real time. He didn't know what to do with that.

Even so, the orbital calamity still in progress wasn't the thing making him quietly panic – or at least, not the primary thing. No, the thought making his frills twitch and his spiracles widen was:

Am I going to be late?

'Friend,' he said loudly. The AI was everywhere and there was no need to yell, but shouting seemed the only reasonable thing to do under the circumstances. 'I need to make some calculations.' There was no point in telling the AI this. It wasn't a command, or a question. A non-sentient model would take nothing away from the statement other than the fact that one of its computational programs would soon be running, which, in turn, would mean absolutely nothing to a utility without an agenda of its own. Roveg wasn't talking for Friend's sake. He was stating his intent, voicing the first step in an actionable plan. He hurried down the hall toward the control room, passing windows as he went. Through them, he could see the sky burning. A chunk of metal was briefly visible before being swallowed in the heat of its own freefall.

'Friend, please shade the windows, maximum opacity,' Roveg said. Friend obliged, and the plex windows shifted into a pleasing bedtime purple. The ambient lighting adjusted as well, increasing its warmth. Roveg flexed his thoracic legs in approval as he moved down the hall. It was enough to *know* something awful was going on. He didn't need to look at it.

Status panels leapt to life as he entered the control room, readying themselves for his instructions. 'Friend, please access our current travel route.' At his command, a star chart filled the display, drawing his course in a neat brushstroke of pixels. The small yellow light that represented the *Korrigoch Hrut* was three-quarters of the way to its destination. 'Please calculate our arrival date if we were to leave Gora one – no, two – standard days from now.' The emergency alert had stated only *one* day, but better to be over-prepared than under.

The yellow light zipped along its course, and a series of numerical dots displayed themselves alongside (unlike language, math was something Roveg always preferred to do in Tellerain; his brain disliked translating numbers). Their results were calculated, and Friend delivered the conclusion: 'At our current rate of fuel consumption, the altered departure date would result in an arrival time delayed by five days.'

Anxiety ran laps through Roveg's body. He'd meticulously planned this trip to allow for a three-day buffer zone before his appointment, in case of any mishaps (plus time to rest and breathe and summon some courage). Three days had seemed generous, at the time. But now Friend was telling him he was at risk of being *five* days later than planned. Five days would mean he'd miss his appointment entirely. 'How does a two-day delay result in a five-day difference in arrival time?' he asked, trying (and failing) to keep his voice from shaking.

'A delay at Gora is likely to cause a further delay at Bushto, which will result in you losing your reservation in the queue,' Friend said.

'But I made that reservation tendays ago,' Roveg said. 'I made it before I left home.'

'I do not understand,' Friend said.

Roveg took a breath, pulling air through his abdomen with deliberate slowness. In moments like these, he could understand the appeal of a thinking, conscious AI (but, of course, therein lay the danger; convenience was morality's most cunning foe). 'Please explain your calculation regarding the delay at Bushto,' he said.

'Leaving Gora on 238/307 will result in an arrival at Bushto on 242/307. Our current reservation for the Bushto tunnel hub queue is for 240/307. The local branch of the Harmagian Travel Office has a cancellation policy of one standard day. A 242/307 arrival will result in a cancellation of our reservation, thus—'

'We'll lose our spot and will need to get back in the queue. Yes, I see.' Roveg sighed. Damn the Harmagians and their point-less bureaucracy. 'If we increase our speed, could we arrive at Bushto by 240/307?'

Friend calculated. 'Yes,' the AI said. 'An increase of travel velocity to seventy-five SUs per day would result in a 240/307 arrival.'

Cutting it close, but doable. 'And how would that affect our fuel consumption?'

Friend calculated further. 'Fuel consumption would increase by two hundred and fifty-eight kulks.'

At last, Roveg felt himself relax. He happened to be parked right outside a fuel depot with only two other customers present. Money wasn't a problem, and even if it had been, an extra barrel or two of algae was a trifling price to pay for arriving on time. He'd buy all the fuel Ouloo had, if that's what it took. He'd sell his art, his gear, everything that wasn't an engine or an oxygen filter. He'd sell his *ship* after the fact, so long as he got there on time.

'Reset our course with the current calculations for arrival date and travel velocity factored in,' Roveg said. His voice held steady this time. He left the control room as Friend worked, and went to the kitchen to brew a full pot of mek. He didn't usually drink the soporific stuff in such quantities, but on a day like today, it was justified.

SPEAKER

The shuttle was too small.

This hadn't been the case in the past. Speaker had used the shuttle for its intended purpose many times – quick hops between ground and orbit, or ship to station, or ship to ship, typically ferrying supplies one way or the other, sometimes with her sister in the seat beside her. She had never found it cramped then, and the shuttle was equipped with the basics needed for unexpected circumstances such as the one she found herself in now. There was water, a pair of sleeping hammocks, plenty of dehydrated food, a decent-enough toilet, breathable air – everything you needed for a quick bail-out if need be. But right then, Speaker needed something else, something the shuttle *couldn't* provide, and that lack was driving her out of her head.

She needed to *move*.

Speaker swung from pole to pole, her wrist-hooks hitting the metal loud and angry. She went from one side of the too-small shuttle to the other, back and forth, back and forth, always with one eye on the comms screen. A progress wheel had been spinning there for ten excruciating minutes, and any second now, it would—

The screen went white, indicating an update was on the way. Speaker shimmied down, scrambling to the console. 'Come on,' she said. 'Come on, come on, come—'

The hull of the shuttle was thick, but a terrifying noise bled through it all the same: a crunch of impact, a hail of dirt. Speaker did not see what had happened, nor did she need to.

She wasted no time in sliding down the nearest pole and bolting into the space on the floor beneath the console. She bent her head and covered the back of her neck with her arms. Something had crashed outside, and though there were no decompression alarms, no further sounds of danger, she braced all the same. She'd done this in safety drills, but never before with real cause. Her pulse pounded and her hands shook, but she locked her fingers together and shut her beak tight, waiting for whatever came next.

Nothing came next. The shuttle and the world beyond were as quiet as they'd been minutes before. This should have been a relief, but Speaker didn't trust it. How could anyone find comfort in silence that could end without warning?

Timidly, she crawled out of the nook in which she'd sheltered, and climbed up to the nearest window to see what had caused the sound. She did not have to look hard. A crumpled mass of metal had slammed down a short distance away – far enough that she did not feel the need to inspect the outer hull, but close enough to see the unsettled dust still hanging in the thin air around it.

Speaker's stomach churned as she thought of the incalculable variables that had led to the careening junk landing *over there* and not *right here*. She tried to still her shaking hands, tried to hush the racing horror of *oh stars, what if?* She closed her eyes and took a breath, then made her way back to the comms console, attempting to focus on just one heart-rending worry at a time.

Error, the comms screen read. *Comms signal cannot be established with requested recipient. Atmospheric disturbance suspected.* 'No fucking kidding,' Speaker said under her breath.

Nothing about the lack of signal was a surprise. It hadn't been a surprise the three times before, either. The shuttle didn't have an ansible; it had a short-range comms dish, and that required a clear, uninterrupted channel between transmitter and receiver. Given that the latter was impeded by the exponentially multiplying debris of the former, there was no way she was going to get a call out.

She tried again anyway, selecting yet another signal-searching algorithm before resuming her elevated pacing.

'You're okay,' she whispered to her still-shaky self, the words becoming a rhythm as she grabbed each pole. 'You're okay, you're okay, you're okay.'

Tracker would know how to secure a signal, Speaker thought. Well, maybe. Maybe Tracker would have come to the same conclusion the comms screen had, that sometimes things were just too broken for even the cleverest of workarounds. But puzzling these sorts of things out was Tracker's skill. It was why she had the name she did. She loved patterns and order; so did Speaker, but in an entirely different capacity. Where Speaker loved the weave of grammar, Tracker found solace in the march of numbers. Where Speaker treasured nuance, semantics, word roots, double meanings, Tracker feasted on riddles of calculus and the satisfaction of solution. The ends to their respective means were the same: finding the most elegant way of expressing a desire. They were two components of the same tool, in that respect. All Akarak twins were halved souls, but Speaker and Tracker's bond was what was called a *triet*. 'Straight cut' was the literal definition, but the word in Ihreet was weighty, reverent, a way of describing a pair made whole by the other's complement.

And now Speaker couldn't reach her.

The screen went white, and like a fool, Speaker hurried up to it once more. *Error*, the screen read. *Comms signal cannot be established with requested recipient. Atmospheric disturbance suspected.*

'Stars!' she spat. 'Dammit!' She hit the screen with her palm and yelled in wordless frustration. This behaviour wasn't like her. Tracker was the one who got angry, the one who popped off, in contrast to Speaker retreating inward. Tracker made noise; Speaker calmed her down. This was their balance, the flow of their emotional tide. But therein lay Speaker's problem: the other part of herself was in the sky. It wasn't that Speaker never left Tracker's side. She did so often on stops like these, given her sister's reluctance to leave the *Harmony*. But that was always a matter of hours. An afternoon, maybe. The stretch between waking and sleeping. She'd never been through a night without Tracker, not ever.

She thought of the times she'd awoken to a particular sound – or rather, an absence of sound. The sound of Tracker not breathing. From time to time, her struggling lungs simply forgot what they were meant to be doing, and though Tracker's imubots were supposed to sound the alarm on her scrib if her blood oxygen dropped too low while she slept, rarely did they react as quickly as her sister beside her. There had been dozens of nights interrupted by Speaker shaking Tracker awake, helping her to sit up, pull in air, take her medicine. Tracker was often quick to fall back asleep, accustomed to it as she was. Speaker, on the other hand, never did. Commonly, she lay awake and listened until the morning hours came and Tracker got up to start her day. Only then did Speaker feel safe in returning to sleep.

Would Tracker wake up at all, Speaker thought, *without her there?*

Speaker swung herself to the sleeping hammocks and sat down in one. She closed her eyes. She unclenched her beak. This frenzy would not help. This was panic, and while panic was a normal sort of response to have when the world was falling apart, the place her mind had leapt to was unhelpful and unlikely. Tracker wasn't an infant, and she wasn't stupid, and the mere *presence* of Speaker was not what determined whether Tracker's lungs behaved or not. Tracker was resourceful, resilient. Speaker told herself she did not need to worry like this.

She worried all the same.

Speaker rubbed her palms together. No, this would not do. She would not spend a day or however long like this – and she doubted *approximately one GC standard day* was an accurate estimate as to how long this would take. *Approximately one GC standard day* was exactly the sort of cut-and-paste response given when the authority in question wanted people to ready themselves for a long wait, in the same way that *please be twenty minutes early* could mean anything from instant service to an hour. *One GC standard day* was an empty phrase, a figure that offered fast-absorbed comfort in the foundational concepts of *one* and *day,* then defused any real meaning with the administrative application of the word *approximately.* Speaker had stood in enough queues and filled out enough formwork to know better than to trust phrases like that.

So, then. If the comms were a lost cause and the shuttle was already making her insane, what else could she do? What was a better use of *approximately one GC standard day?*

She got back on the poles, and went to find her scrib.

PEI

The *eelim* moulded itself around Pei as she sat down, its putty-like polymer flexing and curving around her body. Doorways had melted open in a similar fashion as she'd gone from room to room, on her way to getting off her feet. The shuttle, like all Aeluon living spaces, was an object whose interior shapes and fixtures changed to suit her needs. The item of furniture she settled into now was a large, practical piece, which could serve as a communal bench or a shared bunk by three people (or more, if you didn't mind getting close). But for this trip, Pei had travelled alone, and that meant she could enjoy the luxury of spreading out without bumping elbows with her crew. She normally didn't mind being crowded – comfort was so often a secondary consideration in her places of work – but with no other option than the alternative here, she had to admit it was awfully nice to have the ship to herself.

It was odd to be enjoying such things while the sky was on fire.

Pei was not a stranger to an atmosphere aflame, as underlined by her initial reflex to run, move, shoot, react, protect. But Gora was not a war zone. Her guns were in a locker and her real ship was elsewhere, and the Rosk border appeared in the Goran sky as nothing more than one star among millions. The current problem at hand – the *sky on fire* problem – was taking place in low orbit, and there was nothing a person *down here* could do to help the people dealing with the mess *up there*. Nothing but sit in your shuttle and wait, as instructed.

Waiting was another activity Pei was accustomed to, but it almost always went hand-in-hand with *preparing*. The list of things she had to keep in mind when *waiting* for something was endless and forever increasing. She had to consider ambushes, crossfire, thievery, arguments, equipment inspections, entry trajectories, exit plans, fuel levels, bulkhead integrity, proper formwork, customs inspectors with no sense of humour, middlemen with no ethical framework, translations and digital stamps and whether or not the shields would hold this time. She had crew she could delegate to handle such things – and a damn good crew, too – but as captain, the buck stopped with her, and there was no issue that didn't require her input, be it *your pilot lost an eye* or *we're out of mek, again*.

So in the approximate hour since the emergency message had come through and everyone had retreated to their respective shuttles like good little creche-kids, the primary thing Pei felt about a situation in which there was nothing for her to do but follow someone else's instructions and wait for them to do their job was . . . relief.

She felt guilty about that. This whole to-do was an ordeal for the people responsible, no question, and the ripple effects were no doubt fucking over the schedules of an entire planet full of people with places to be. She was losing a day of shore leave because of this, and that definitely soured her mood, but she was sure things were far worse for others with strict schedules and urgent business. No one had died, as far as she knew. No one in her immediate locale was hurt. Still, though, harm was harm, and she found herself wrestling between two truths until she realised neither was a zero-sum:

This wasn't the worst that could happen.

It was a bad thing all the same.

But all of this consideration was a moot point. She had no control, and no responsibility to do anything but sit and wait. That sort of permission was something she was almost never granted.

Right or not, relief conquered guilt.

She let her shoulders go and her head dip. From where she sat, the idea of anything being wrong seemed preposterous. It was quiet. She was safe. The garden she'd been walking in earlier was visible through her window, and the angle of the hills beyond the dome was such that she couldn't see the sky at all. She drew her eye back to the garden, which really was lovely, in a humble way. It reminded Pei in spirit of the garden at the creche where she'd grown up, the one her father Le had tended every day. She fondly remembered the triangular beds planted specially with things for kids to poke and nibble at. Nothing bad could ever happen in that place, and she'd felt the same, for a moment, in Ouloo's garden. She knew such sentiments weren't true, that bad things could and did happen anywhere, but it was a nice illusion to buy into, temporarily. She allowed herself to continue indulging in that fantasy, even though she knew the view above told a different story.

As her mind quieted, thoughts began to drift freely, and Pei began to idly pick at their threads, feeling her cheeks shift colour this way and that as she did so. It was important for her, in her line of work, to scrutinise the things going on within herself, and she did this sort of maintenance in any spare moment she had. The immediate state of affairs was one she'd unravelled easily, and had no need to examine further. But there was a bigger snarl beyond, one she'd been wrestling with for tendays. She'd made small progress with it, and the more she picked, the more she found its messy components trying to entwine with one another, like roots planted too close together. She wished she had Le's garden shears, that she might chop it apart and be done with it.

She exhaled, running a palm over the crown of her head. She was so tired of the tangles, so tired of immediately running into them anytime her mind wandered as it liked. *This* was not the time for it, she told herself. There truly *was* a problem outside, disconnected from it though she was. She'd been told to take shelter and stay calm. The former was easy; the latter was a treat. She saw no need to muddy the time she'd been given with things that would not leave her be.

Pei pushed with steady firmness back against the *eelim*, prompting it to recline all the way down. She eased into the supportive nest, folding her hands across her chest, allowing herself the comfort of being cradled. Through the skylight overhead, the remains of a weather tracker tumbled into distant view, flaming like tinder as they hit the thin air. She shut her eyes before the pieces ceased burning. Within minutes, she was asleep.

Received message

Encryption: 0

From: GC Transit Authority – Gora System (path: 487-45411-479-4)

To: Ooli Oht Ouloo (path: 5787-598-66)

Subject: URGENT UPDATE

This is an urgent message from the Emergency Response Team aboard the GC Transit Authority Regional Management Orbiter (Gora System). As both standard ansible and Linking channels are currently unavailable, we will be communicating via the emergency beacon network for the time being. We ask that you leave your scribs locked to this channel until proper communications are restored.

This is not a full all-clear. Individuals on the planet's surface may now move freely within habitat domes, but surface travel between domes is not recommended. All spaceworthy vessels are required to stay grounded until further notice. No launches or landings are permitted at this time.

We are continuing to work with the Goran Satellite Cooperative to fully assess the situation. What we know as of now is as follows:

Earlier today, a hardware failure disrupted a routine satellite course adjustment procedure. This created a cascade collision, which at this time has damaged or otherwise negatively affected an estimated seventy-eight percent of the Goran satellite fleet. This percentage is expected to grow over time, as there is still damaged hardware in descent. As you have likely already noticed, this has disrupted communications channels planetwide.

The circumstances surrounding this hardware failure have yet to be thoroughly investigated, but initial data suggests this incident was both accidental and mechanical in nature. We are aware of rumours regarding an untracked asteroid or orbital weapons fire. These rumours are completely false.

As always, your safety is our top priority, both on- and off-world. It remains our goal to have launch and landing capabilities restored within approximately one GC standard day, and are working to find solutions as quickly as possible.

Thank you for your patience. We are all in this together.

ROVEG

All-clear or no, Roveg was in no hurry to leave his shuttle, not when things could drop out of the sky at any moment. He'd brewed more mek and put on some music, and was quite comfortable among his own walls and decor. The urge he'd had upon landing to get out and see something new had faded. Comfortable and familiar were what his nerves needed now, and though he trusted that everything was indeed under control, he saw no need to rush back outside.

The wall vox switched on. 'Sorry to disturb you,' Friend said. 'There is a visitor at the hatch who wishes to speak with you.'

'Who is it?' Roveg asked. He assumed it was Ouloo, checking in.

Friend paused as it asked a question at the other end of the ship. 'Her name is Speaker,' the AI said.

Roveg lowered his cup of mek. He hadn't spoken to the Akarak, but he had overheard Ouloo using her name. Curious. He thought for a moment. 'Allow her to come aboard,' he said. He'd never talked to an Akarak before, and felt it was best to experience such moments face to face. He drained his cup, got to his feet, and headed for the airlock.

The noise of the Akarak's mech suit walking through the hatch was louder than the machinations of the hatch itself. Stars, but the suit was unwieldy – and ugly, too. He wondered, as he looked at her, how she moved when she wasn't inside of the thing. In truth, he had difficulty picturing an Akarak *without* a suit, for he'd never seen one that way. The whole business was disconcerting, what with not being able to smell her. Roveg took in more of the world through smell than through sight, and the Akarak being tucked away behind metal and plex made her feel ghostly, artificial, more like a bot than a person.

The Akarak, however, quickly made him rewrite that impression. Within her cockpit, she bowed her torso forward. Her body could not have been more different than his, but the gesture was understood all the same. Roveg bowed as well, as was his custom. It was a pleasant surprise, to be doing this with someone like her.

'Thank you for inviting me in,' Speaker said. 'I hope I'm not intruding. I would've been happy to talk outside.'

Again, Roveg experienced a note of surprise. He'd heard that Akaraks were maddeningly difficult to converse with. You could count on a language barrier the size of a small moon, he'd been told. But Speaker's Klip was flawless, delivered with the affable, neutral vowels you'd hear humming around the respectable cities of Central space. She sounded like someone from a diplomat's office, or a recording studio. The thing that marked her as someone who didn't use Klip as her primary language wasn't a particular accent, but rather the absence of any sort of accent whatsoever.

Roveg was intrigued.

'It's no intrusion at all,' he said. 'You're Speaker, yes?'

'Yes. And you're—'

'Roveg,' he said with another little bow. A thought occurred to him, and he straightened up quickly. 'Are you all right? That thing that came down didn't hit your ship, did it?' He hadn't planned on having a shuttle guest, and he didn't particularly *want* one, but if need be, he had the space.

'No, I'm fine,' Speaker said. 'You?'

'No, not a scratch. Safe and snug, I'm happy to say. So what is it that I might do for you?'

Within her cockpit, Speaker picked up a device – an Akarak-sized scrib, Roveg belatedly realised. He'd never seen one so small, but then, the device didn't look mass-manufactured. This was a hand-hacked object, as evidenced by the thick glue around the edges, the mismatched screws at the seams. Speaker gestured at the screen, and as she did so, Roveg experienced a peculiar dissonance. He knew that the individual within the cockpit and the mech suit itself were not one entity, but it was strange all the same to see an Aandrisk-sized bipedal figure – a body type he was well accustomed to encountering – standing lifeless, hands at its sides, while the tiny person within its metal head busied herself with other things.

'Well, that's actually what I came to find out,' Speaker said. She looked up, but on her way to meet his gaze, her eye was caught by the projection mat covering the ceiling above. The active rendering displayed the sort of sky you'd see on a typical spring day in the equatorial regions of Sohep Frie – seafoam green with lazy wisps of cloud. Speaker pulled a lever, tilting the suit's torso back so she could view it from a better angle. 'That's . . . beautiful,' she said.

'Thank you,' Roveg said. He glanced up with her, admiring the everyday sight with pride. 'I'm rather pleased with it.' She cocked her head at him, and he explained: 'I'm a sim designer. I made this.'

'Oh, nice,' she said, still looking at the ceiling. 'Do all Quelin ships have projections like these? I've never been in one of your vessels before.'

'No, no. This is just one of my own fancies. What's the fun in only making things for other people to enjoy?'

The Akarak watched the digital clouds drift and sway. 'Must eat up a lot of power,' she said.

'It does,' Roveg said. 'But it's entirely worth it if you're going to be off-world for a while. Helps keep my head clear. I can only do spacer life in small doses.'

'I see,' Speaker said, still watching the clouds. Her tone was hiding something, but Roveg couldn't determine what.

'Sorry,' Roveg said, 'but you . . . I didn't quite understand what you were getting at before my clouds interrupted us. You said you were wondering . . . what I can do?'

'Yes,' Speaker said. She righted the mech suit and held her scrib at the ready. Roveg tried not to stare at her hands. Hands were an odd-enough alien feature to begin with, but he was accustomed to slender Aeluon digits and bold Aandrisk claws, not the backward hooks that sprouted from each of her wrists like gnarled thorns. Something about them made Roveg's antennae bristle nervously, but he shoved the errant feeling aside. Speaker looked at him, her wet vertebrate eyes sharp and focused. 'I'm making the rounds and finding out what skills everybody here at the Five-Hop has.'

'Why?' he asked. He didn't understand the point of this endeavour.

The feeling was clearly mutual, because Speaker looked back at him with a gaze that seemed to say *why wouldn't you?* 'It's an emergency. We need to know who can contribute what.'

Roveg looked out the window in the bulkhead beside him. Everything outside appeared exactly as it had hours before. 'Has something more happened?' he asked with a stab of concern. Had he missed something important while sitting on his belly and drinking mek?

Speaker stared at him. 'Something *more* than the planet's satellite network falling apart?'

'Well, I – I mean, of course, that's *serious*, and an emergency for those who have to sort it out, but all's well for us on the ground, isn't it? Barring more sudden landings?'

'For now,' Speaker said. 'But we have no idea how long this is going to drag on, and comms are severely limited. If something happens, it'd be wise for us to know how we might handle it.'

This seemed unnecessarily cautious to Roveg, and a tad silly to boot. 'The Transit Authority said it'd be a day,' he said.

Speaker looked at him, saying nothing, tangibly unconvinced.

'Well,' Roveg said. He felt as though he'd lost an argument, but hadn't the faintest notion of what the argument *was*. 'I'm good with tech.'

Speaker made an entry on her scrib. 'Mech tech or comp tech?'

'Both,' he said, 'but in rather superficial ways. I can patch a fuel line or fix a buggy input panel, but I can't, say, build an engine or recode an AI.'

'That's not superficial, that's great,' Speaker said, gesturing her input with efficient speed. 'You're saying you can fix everyday stuff, but nothing too specialised.'

'Exactly. Or, well . . . it depends on what sort of item we're discussing.'

'Got it. What else? Don't just think of things related to your profession. Think of every practical thing you know how to do, even if it seems trivial.'

Roveg was unprepared to deliver such a résumé on the fly, and had never really taken inventory of himself in this way before. 'I can . . . hmm. I can pilot a ship. I know how your average life support system works. I can write well.'

'In what languages?'

'Klip and Tellerain, same as I speak. I understand a bit of Hanto and Reskitkish, slowly, but I don't speak either.' He gave a short, good-natured laugh. 'Trust me, you don't want me to try.'

'Can you read Aeluon colours?'

'About as well as anybody who hasn't studied. I can gauge a general sense of what they're feeling, not what they're saying.'

Speaker logged every word. 'What about first aid?'

Roveg did not foresee a scenario in which this would be necessary, but he played along. 'For my own species, yes, in a very, very basic sense. I could bandage someone's shell for long enough to get xyr to a doctor. For any other sapient, no.'

'What about *your* needs? What should the rest of us know about?'

'In regards to . . . ?'

'Allergies, health issues, that kind of thing.'

Roveg felt nervous at the question, just as he had with the query about first aid. What did the Akarak think was going to happen here? They were stuck in a hab dome filled with cakes and blooming hedges, not crash-landed on an asteroid or venting oxygen into space. But Speaker was making her enquiries with earnest, and he did not want to insult her, no matter how alarmist he found this line of questioning. 'No allergies. Well . . . that is, none beyond the norm for my species. I wouldn't react favourably to physical contact with a Harmagian or to a meal made with suddet root, but I don't see any danger of either of those situations taking place, given our present company. And I'm in perfect health, or so my bots tell me. No underlying issues, mental or physical.'

'Good,' Speaker said. 'That's great.'

'Oh, and I can read annotated galaxy charts,' he said. 'That's not a health matter, but it is a thing I can do.'

Speaker added a note about that. 'You and Captain Tem both, in that regard.'

'That's the Aeluon?'

'Yes. I already spoke to her, and with both of our hosts.'

'Saved the best interview for last, eh?' he said congenially.

Speaker paused, and did not mirror his light banter. 'To be honest, I . . . wasn't sure if you'd speak to me at all.' She paused again, as though she were still processing. 'I definitely didn't think you'd invite me in.'

'Ah,' Roveg said. He needed no explanation as to why she thought this. 'Rest assured, while I may share my species' aversion to suddet root, I do *not* recoil from socialising with other sapients. On the contrary, I highly value any opportunity to do so.' He lowered his torso with gracious slowness. 'In fact, I'd be very glad to chat more with you, Speaker, on subjects less dire. It seems we have the time!'

The Akarak seemed to relax a bit. 'I appreciate that,' she said. Her tone was sincere. 'Actually, that brings me to the other thing I'm here to tell you: Ouloo is inviting everyone to the garden for "food and chat", as she put it.'

'Ooh,' Roveg said. 'Well, that's kind of her.'

'I think she's trying to keep us all happy while we're stuck here. She's pretty upset about the whole thing.'

'It's hardly her fault.'

'Yes, but it's her home,' Speaker said. 'I understand that.'

Roveg's reluctance to leave his shuttle had fully ebbed. The promise of snacks didn't hurt, but mostly, he'd developed a new-found curiosity about the company he'd fallen into – particularly the tiny person he spoke with now. 'Well, if you're done with your . . . rounds,' he said, 'shall we go together?'

Now it was the Akarak's turn to be surprised. He couldn't smell it, of course, but basic bipedal body language was such an easy thing to glean. If you learned one, you learned them all. 'Oh. Um, sure,' Speaker said. 'I . . . I don't see why not.'

Day 236, GC Standard 307

. . . .

PLEASE REMAIN CALM

EVERYONE

Stars, the Laru was trying.

It was the same garden that Pei had been in hours before, but Ouloo had repurposed the grassy circle at its centre. The tables were laden with what looked like every cup and bowl from the host's own kitchen, each filled with snacks both sugary and savoury. Pei peeked into one of the cups and discovered twisting salt licks. The other containers were filled with similar snack-pack fare: algae puffs, snapfruit tarts, jelly straws – all everyday nibbles you could find at your average mixed market-place. The offerings were *almost* fancy in the respect that they weren't the cheapest algae puffs you could buy, and had maybe flirted with actual herbs or fruit or some other ingredient grown in real dirt before being sealed up. It looked as though Ouloo had grabbed armloads of her stock – or legloads, in the Laru's case – and done her best to make it look as nice as she could, arranging tidbits in hurried arrangements within mismatched tableware.

'Hello, Captain Tem!' Ouloo called. The ground host was busy at the edges of the circle, attempting to assemble a makeshift canopy out of blankets brought from home and poles that looked leftover from a construction project. 'Please, help yourself!'

Pei puzzled at the canopy. What was the point of such a thing in a habitat dome, where there was no weather? No rain, no snow, nothing that could fall out of the—

Oh, she realised. Ouloo was trying to block her guests' view of the sky.

'Can I help?' Pei asked. The Laru seemed to be struggling with the assembly.

'No, no, I've—' Both blanket and poles tumbled to the ground with tragicomic slowness. 'Oh, shit.'

'Mom,' Tupo scolded laughingly from somewhere unseen. '*Language.*'

Pei crouched down and cocked her head in the direction of her implant's buzzing. The kid was curled up under a table, stuffing xyr face with algae puffs straight from the bag. Pei had no way of knowing, but she had a suspicion that the bag in question had been intended for guests. 'Hey, Tupo,' Pei said. 'You doing okay?'

'Yeah,' Tupo said quietly. Xyr tone suggested otherwise. Xe shoved a pawful of puffs messily into xyr mouth. 'You should try the algae puffs,' xe said, holding up the front of the bag so Pei could see the picture printed on it. 'They're good.'

Pei was not a stranger to algae puffs, and she wasn't hungry, but between Ouloo's frantic efforts and Tupo's apparent misunderstanding that Pei needed *all* food explained to her, she could hardly refuse. She picked up a plate and began to peruse the makeshift buffet, but before she could determine her choices, her implant began buzzing again in Ouloo's direction. The Laru was muttering in her cooing language, and though Pei didn't understand the words, the frustration within was clear as day.

Without a word, Pei set down her plate and walked over to Ouloo. 'Here,' she said, holding one of the precarious poles. She eyed the materials Ouloo was using: blanket, pole, twine. 'I don't mean to butt in, but I think I could . . .'

Ouloo relinquished control with a huff. 'If you have better ideas than me, then by all means.'

Pei thought for a moment, then got straight to work, arranging poles and tying sturdy knots. A structure began to coalesce.

'Oh, you *definitely* have better ideas than me.' Ouloo laughed. 'Well done.' She stretched out her long neck toward Pei's

handiwork. 'I hope you don't mind me watching. Your feet –
sorry, *hands* are very fun to see in action.'

Pei flushed chuckling green. She didn't mind at all. 'Just tying
knots,' she said, as she did said-same. 'Nothing special.'

'Yes, but you do it so *quickly*,' Ouloo said. She held up a
stubby paw, wiggling her broad toepads. 'I can't do that.'

'And I can't look straight back over my shoulder,' Pei said.
'I've always thought that must be neat.'

Ouloo continued to watch Pei work, somewhat hypnotised.
'Where'd you learn to do that?'

'Military school,' Pei said. 'Throwing up a quick shelter is
one of the things you have to be able to do in your sleep.'

Tupo's neck extended out from under the table. 'You said
you're not a soldier.'

'I'm not,' Pei said. She wrapped the twine over, under, and
through. 'But I thought about it. On Sohep Frie, we have these
schools – I have no idea what to call them in Klip. They're an
alternative to the standard school you go to once you reach
adolescence. If you're considering a career in the military, you
can go there instead, see if it's a good fit.'

'I take it it wasn't, for you,' Ouloo said.

'No.' Pei tied one last knot. 'I admire the cause,' she said.
'But I like being my own boss.' She stepped back to look at her
work. The canopy held fast.

Along the path, on the flip side of the hedges, the other guests
approached.

'You must be Captain Tem,' Roveg said, bowing his thorax in
greeting. 'It's a pleasure to meet you properly.'

'Likewise,' the Aeluon said. He found himself soothed by her
presence, stranger though she was. Speaker's list of questions
had sparked a nagging worry that perhaps this situation *wasn't*
as controlled as he'd like, but here was this fit, confident captain,
who seemed ready for anything. Her scent conveyed that she
was at ease, and this meshed with the blueish silver of her

cheeks, an easy-to-spot sign of Aeluon calm. If she wasn't worried, then he saw little reason to be so himself. 'Ouloo, this looks delightful,' he said, picking up a plate. 'Thank you so much for your hospitality.'

'Oh, goodness, it's the least we can do,' Ouloo said. 'I'm just so sorry this has happened. Whatever we can do to make this less stressful for you, please, please let us know.' With this, she looked at Speaker, her gaze meaningful. 'We're here for you.'

Something passed between Speaker and Ouloo, and while Roveg wasn't entirely sure what it was, he hazarded a guess that an apology had been made. Speaker responded graciously, as she seemed to do with everything. 'Thank you,' she said. 'I appreciate that.' Apology accepted, it seemed.

A puff of warm air hit several of Roveg's toe joints, making him jump with surprise. As he looked down, he realised it wasn't just air, but *breath*. The little Laru was under the table, trying to get a good look at his legs. 'Well, hello!' Roveg said, laughing.

'Tupo, what have I said about hiding when there are guests around?' Ouloo sighed. 'Can you come out from there, please?'

Tupo did not.

'I'm sorry,' she said to Roveg, hushing her voice in a manner the child could undoubtedly still hear. 'We don't get many Quelin. I think xe's being a bit shy.'

'Am *not*,' Tupo complained. Xe remained under the table.

'That's quite all right,' Roveg said, looking at Ouloo, but intending his words for smaller ears. 'I was fully an adult when I met my first other-specied friends, and they made me want to hide under the table, too.' He lowered himself down to look at the child. Tupo stared back, smelling of excitement and concern. 'I hope you'll come out soon,' Roveg said. 'I could use some support if these bipeds start to bully me.'

The joke flew over the child and landed somewhere in the hedges beyond. 'Why would they—'

'He's teasing, Tupo,' said Ouloo with exasperation. 'Stars.' She shook out her fur and turned her attention to the adults.

'Well, there's no reason for all of *you* to be shy, too. Please, make yourselves at home!'

Speaker had spent her entire adult life learning how to navigate interactions with other species. Her people operated by insularity, and even when they did make their homes in mixed settlements, they kept largely to themselves (for reasons no Akarak needed reminding of). Speaker had honed her natural talents of linguistic quickness and what Tracker called 'social sponging' in order to enter the multicultural melee, to gain entry to places her peers typically could not. Her skills in this regard were malleable by necessity, as you never knew what sort of sapient you'd need to talk to. She prided herself for her flexibility in that regard. With the exception of a small collection of trusted market stops and reliable contacts, she rarely found herself in the same place twice, and part of what made her and her sister good at their work was her ability to adapt to whatever the scenario called for.

But as she stood at the edge of the garden, faced with food and flowers and small talk, a realisation dawned on her. Varied as the places she visited were, they all shared one element: practicality. She frequented fuel depots, tech swaps, hydroponic suppliers, medical clinics, libraries, bustling markets, water stations, government bureaus, shuttledocks, and other such functional locations. She knew how to trade and enquire and haggle and win over, and had done all of these with alien species of every shape and size.

Not one of them had ever invited her to hang out with them.

Easy as this scenario should have been, Speaker found herself facing a tremendous challenge. She had to maintain the air of confidence she knew was so crucial to appeasing other species, while navigating a situation she'd never been in and was unexpectedly nervous about, while *also* keeping the part of herself that was desperate to talk to Tracker shut away for the duration of the gathering.

She took a breath, and marched her mech suit forward.

Fortunately, she did not have to be the one to launch a conversation. Roveg was keenly chatting to Captain Tem as he heaped his plate with snacks, the frills around his thorax flexing with excitement. 'I have to say, Captain,' he said in his stormy accent, 'that is a beautiful shuttle you have. Caught my eye immediately as I flew in.'

'Ah, thanks,' Captain Tem said, nibbling at something from her own (more modestly filled) plate. Speaker did not grasp cheek colours as well as she wanted to yet, but the Aeluon looked pleased, and said nothing further on the matter. Captain Tem didn't boast or brag, but neither did she demur. She acknowledged that her shuttle was a nice one, and left it there. Speaker noted that.

Roveg leaned toward Captain Tem just a touch. 'I would assume from the, ah, *robustness* of your ship that you're joining us from more dangerous territories,' he said. His voice took on the sort of well-intentioned yet clueless empathy of someone who knew nothing of real violence beyond the fact that it was *bad* and you had to be careful bringing it up. Not that Speaker had any real understanding of the matter herself. Though she commonly worked with people who had an intimate relationship with mortality and the means by which it could be used, she and Tracker had both long ago resolved that their home would have no weapons and their hands would never get bloody. The darker sides of the galaxy were something she knew by proxy, not directly. Still, what she *did* know was enough to ensure that she'd never raise the topic herself, not as Roveg was doing now. His interest was blatant, despite being smothered beneath an imposed layer of tact.

But whatever personal insights Captain Tem had, she kept them to herself. 'That's right,' she said, as nonchalant as she'd been at mention of her shuttle. A short reply, Speaker observed, followed by a deft pivot. 'Just finished a cargo drop and now I'm on leave. Going to visit a friend for a few tendays.'

'Her friend's a Human,' the child said from under the table, joining in at last.

'Ah, I love Humans,' Roveg said jovially. 'All the ones I've met are just the most fascinating people. And such a history they have! I hear Mars is quite a charming little place.'

Captain Tem continued to swerve. 'My friend's Exodan, so I wouldn't know.'

'Oh, *really?*' Ouloo said. It was her turn to become inquisitive. Speaker wondered if she and Roveg together might be a bit much. 'That's so . . . gosh, I don't know. So rugged, isn't it?'

The Aeluon did not laugh aloud, but Speaker got the feeling she was laughing all the same. 'I'll be sure to tell him so,' she said dryly. Her inner eyelids flicked across sideways, and she shifted her gaze, pulling Speaker into the conversation. 'And what about you?' she said. 'Where are you headed?'

Speaker swallowed her nervousness, and moved the suit into the circle.

Pei had no idea how to interpret an Akarak's facial expressions, and she found that gap in knowledge uncomfortable. Roveg's face didn't move at all, but she'd long ago learned to accept the impossibility of reading Quelin. Speaker, on the other hand . . . well, who knew much of anything about Akaraks to begin with? She knew they were a nomadic, scattered species, their home-world stripped by the Harmagians of anything and everything usable in the years before the Hashkath Accords put an end to that sort of thing. She knew their species lived in GC space proper, not the fringes, but she was pretty sure they did not have a seat in Parliament (which, now that she was thinking about it, seemed off). She knew the only ones she'd ever come face to face with had been trying to steal her shit, and that those were the only stories anybody ever told about their kind. Beyond that, she knew nothing. She'd never had reason to think about that realm of ignorance before, but now that it was standing right in front of her, she found herself bothered.

Who was this person?

Pei turned herself toward Speaker, adopting an open stance. The only way to answer that question was to ask.

'I'm en route to Kaathet,' Speaker said.

'And what's taking you there?' Pei asked.

'We've got a rendezvous with another ship. My sister and I, we help other Akarak ships acquire supplies.'

Pei's eyelids twitched with reflexive suspicion. She couldn't tell if *acquiring supplies* was a euphemism or not. 'What kind of supplies?'

'Hydroponic gear, mostly. And some assorted odds and ends.' She looked Pei in the eye. 'We purchased everything they needed at Port Coriol, and now we're on our way to drop it off.'

Everything about Speaker's tone and cadence was disarmingly pleasant, but Pei knew a *don't fucking insult me* stare when she saw one. She didn't know how well Speaker could read her, but she made her cheeks swim easy blue all the same. 'So you're a cargo runner, too,' she said congenially.

Speaker gave the slightest of pauses. 'I suppose you could call it that,' she said. 'But I don't think of myself that way. And I don't think our jobs are much the same at all.'

Roveg couldn't suss out the sliver of tension that had entered the gathering, but he didn't like it. Moreover, the way this round robin was going, the next question was going to focus on where *he* was headed, and that, he didn't want. He swooped in, reaching for lighter fare. 'You know, on the subject of Humans, there's something I've long wanted to ask someone about.' He paused in thought. 'Cheese. Is that a real thing?'

Pei erupted in laughter. 'Ugh,' she said. 'Stars. Yeah, cheese is real, unfortunately.'

Roveg was both delighted and horrified by her answer. 'Not really?' he said.

This was finally enough to coax Tupo out from under the table. 'What's cheese?'

Speaker cocked her head. 'I second the question.'

'Oh, please don't make me explain this,' Pei groaned.

The Akarak leaned back in her cockpit. 'Well, now you have to,' she said.

'Mom, what's cheese?' Tupo whispered loudly.

'I don't know,' Ouloo said back. 'If you listen, you'll find out.'

Pei set down her plate and exhaled apologetically. 'Cheese,' she said in a clinical manner, 'is a foodstuff made out of milk.'

Ouloo blinked. 'You mean like . . .' She gestured at her own underbelly, where her mammary glands presumably lay beneath thick fur.

'Yep,' Pei said. 'Exactly that.'

'So, a children's food,' Speaker said, her tone suggesting that this struck her as no stranger than the concept of milk itself.

Roveg laughed. 'Go on,' he said to Pei goadingly. He continued to snack, enjoying the show.

Pei winced. 'No,' she said to Speaker. 'It's not for kids. I mean, kids eat it, too, but . . . so do adults.'

Everyone present – with the exception of Pei – let out a reflexive sound. There were low growls from Ouloo and Tupo, a short trill from Speaker. Roveg, for his part, let out a triple-clicked hiss. A brief cacophony of varied species all communicating the exact same thing: complete and utter disgust.

'*No*,' Ouloo said.

Tupo cooed in fascinated horror.

'Wait, so, how . . .' Speaker made a hesitant face. 'I'm going to regret this question. How is it . . . prepared?'

Pei grimaced. 'They take the milk, they add some ingredients – don't ask me, I have no idea what – and then pour the mess into a . . . a thing. I don't know. A container. And then . . .' She shut her eyes. 'They leave it out until bacteria colonise it to the point of solidifying.'

The cacophony returned.

'I knew I'd regret it,' Speaker said.

Roveg laughed and laughed. 'I'm so glad I asked about this,' he said.

'Mom, can we order some?' Tupo said.

'Absolutely *not*,' Ouloo said.

'They don't *all* eat this, do they?' Speaker asked.

'I don't know,' Pei said. 'I know they don't make it in the Fleet, and a lot of people there *can't* eat it without getting sick.'

'Understandably.'

'No, it's not that. Humans need a . . . oh, what is it . . . it's something with their stomachs. An enzyme, I think. For digesting milk. Only some Humans produce it naturally. But here's the thing: they're all so fucking bonkers for cheese that they'll ingest a dose of the enzymes beforehand so that they *can* eat it.'

'That seems a bit extreme,' Roveg said.

'Have you eaten it?' Tupo asked.

'Not if my life depended on it,' Pei said.

'How is it that their milk makes them sick?' Speaker said. 'That's got to pose a problem if they can't feed their young.'

'Oh, no, I – stars, I forgot the worst part.' Pei rubbed her neck with her palm. 'They don't make cheese with their own milk. They take it from other animals.'

At that, chaos broke out.

'I didn't know *that* part,' Roveg said, his forelegs shivering. 'That's . . . oh, that's vile.' And it truly was, but this fact did nothing to derail his glee.

Tupo had become scientific fervour incarnate. 'How do they take it from them?'

'Tupo, *please*,' xyr mother said wearily.

The Akarak looked dumbfounded. 'But . . . but *why*?'

'I have no idea,' Pei said. 'No idea.'

'I knew they *ate* other mammals, but . . . *ugh*,' Roveg said.

'They eat *mammals*?' Tupo said, xyr voice heading toward a shriek.

Speaker cocked her head. 'Is that worse?' she asked. 'Killing and eating them, rather than harvesting something from them while still alive?'

'Do you not think so?' Roveg asked.

'We only eat plants,' she said, 'so all of this is outside my realm of expertise.'

'What sorts of plants do you eat?' Ouloo said, pouncing upon the opportunity for a change in topic.

'Oh,' Speaker said, blinking. She looked surprised to have someone interested in the subject. 'Well . . . hmm.' There was a long pause. 'I don't know the names for any of our foods in Klip.' This bothered her, clearly. 'I guess I've never talked about them with . . .' She gestured at the group. 'People like yourselves.'

'Broad strokes?' Roveg said. 'Fruits, leaves, nuts . . . ?'

'All of the above,' Speaker said. 'Fruits especially, and flowers. We need a lot of sugar.'

'See, *that's* nice,' Ouloo said. 'That sounds like very nice food. Perhaps you could give me a list of your favourites before you go? I'm sure I can look up the translated names.'

'Why?' Speaker said.

'Well, so I could carry some here! That way if you come back – or if you send any of your friends our way – I can make something more to your liking.' The Laru blinked her large eyes hopefully.

Roveg popped a snapfruit tart into his mouth as he watched Speaker's reaction to this. Something had caught the tiny sapient completely off guard.

It took Speaker a moment to understand what Ouloo was saying. She looked around at the others, each holding a plate or snacking from the table – or in Tupo's case, straight from the bag. She saw herself as they did, hanging about the edge and not taking any of the offered food. But . . . surely. Surely they knew . . . ?

The others looked at her expectantly.

No. Of course they didn't. The core detail that had determined everything – *everything* – for her species in the past two centuries, and they didn't even fucking know about it.

A tangle of frustration began to surface, one that grew more and more knotted with every standard – every tenday, it sometimes felt. To the others, she was sure this question was nothing, and in the grand scheme of things, that was true, just as a speck of dust was nothing. But a million specks of dust, gathered over time, became something big and ugly and impossible to ignore, something that could jam your ship's filters and ruin your day. Stars, she was tired of needing to be the Linking file for her entire species wherever she went. She'd learned about *them*; why hadn't anyone she met ever done the same for her?

She located her tension. It resided in her shoulders, her hands, the joints of her jaw. Mindfully, deliberately, she let it go.

'I'm so sorry,' she said to Ouloo with a smile in her voice. 'I didn't mean to insult you. This all looks delicious.' In actual fact, she had no idea what any of the foodstuff around her was, but in a different reality, she *would've* loved to try some. 'The thing is . . .' She decided to give them the benefit of the doubt, even though she knew what the answer would be. 'How much do you know about our suits?'

A silence fell over the group, and there was a weight to it that suggested more than just ignorance. *Ah*. So they did know *something*, or at least some of them did. Captain Tem and Roveg had an inkling, she guessed, from the way the Aeluon's colours were mixing and the fact that a morsel in the Quelin's grasping toes had paused on the way to his mouth.

Captain Tem was the one to answer, and she did so with a question. 'Do you mean how they work, or why you use them?'

'Both. Either.'

'I know they were mining equipment, once,' Captain Tem said. Her tone was careful but direct. 'The Harmagians made your species use them, before the Accords.'

'That's right,' Speaker said. A few minutes of conversation was nothing to form an opinion on, but she did respect the Aeluon's frankness, even if she disliked her profession. 'Do you know why we *still* use them, off our ships?'

'I . . . no. I don't. I assumed it was because you wanted to . . . to compensate for . . .' Captain Tem stopped, reframed. 'You're a lot smaller than the rest of us.'

'We are,' Speaker said, 'but it's not a matter of being able to see eye to eye.' She wasn't about to fault an individual for simply not knowing something – she'd certainly been on the end of that equation many times. But stars, was that what they all thought? That her people just wanted to be *bigger*? 'In part, it's because we can't move around public spaces the way the rest of you do.' She raised her left wrist-hook. 'We don't walk around our homes. We climb. We swing.' She pointed from where she stood to one of the tables. 'Without my suit, I'd have to crawl on my belly to get from here to there. I could. But that's not ideal.'

'So you use it as a mobility device,' Pei said. 'Like a Harmagian cart.'

Speaker loathed that comparison, but she let it go in the same way as the knots in her shoulders. 'In part. But I couldn't crawl around here even if I wanted to.'

'Because?'

'Because I can't breathe your air. I can't leave my suit if I'm off my ship.'

There was no joy in being the object under the microscope in a social gathering. Roveg had been cast in that role a thousand times – the only Quelin at the party, answering the same questions again and again and again, summoning the patience to let people gawk at his shell, finding himself thrust into the undesired role of political analyst for every ludicrous decision his former government made in Parliament. He didn't want to leave this young woman – was she young? He suddenly realised he had no idea – in that unenviable position, and was already trying to engineer a conversational way of getting her out of it . . . but dammit, he was curious, too. Fine. A few questions, then he'd devise a rescue. 'You're allergic to something commonplace, you mean?'

'No,' Speaker said. 'We don't breathe oxygen. It's toxic to us, in the quantities you need. We mostly need methane, which, of course, is toxic to you.'

This statement took Roveg completely aback. 'But I thought . . . forgive me, it's been a long time since I took a biology class, and it was never my best subject, but I thought all sapient species breathe oxygen. I thought that was one of the Five Pillars.'

'What are the Five Pillars?' Speaker asked.

Tupo burst into energetic song. '*Water for drinking, oxygen for breathing—*'

'Tupo—' Ouloo said pleadingly.

The child continued singing the bouncing tune, despite xyr mother rubbing her face with her paw. '*Sunlight to make life go! Protein for building, carbon for bonding, that's how all sapients grow!*'

'It's the basic ingredients all sapient species need,' Pei explained.

'I thought everybody knows that,' Tupo said. 'Don't you know the song?'

Speaker was quiet. 'I don't,' she said at last. 'Because it doesn't apply to me.'

Now it was everyone else's turn to hush.

Roveg bent his thoracic legs decisively. The time for a rescue had come. 'Well, if you can't enjoy the food, perhaps we can share in some other entertainment,' he said. He looked around the group. 'Does everyone here enjoy vids? I have a portable projector on my ship, and I'd be happy to bring it out.'

'Oh!' Ouloo brightened, looking relieved. 'Yes! What a good idea.'

Speaker seemed surprised by the conversational detour, but took it in stride. 'I . . . yes,' she said. 'Why not.'

Roveg turned to the Aeluon. 'Captain Tem, are you in?'

'Sure,' she said easily. She flashed a wry, laughing green. 'It's not like I've got any other place to be.'

Part 4

ATTEMPTED REPAIRS
DAY 237,
GC STANDARD 307

PEI

Sleep was not something Pei generally had much of a problem with. She'd always been the sort who could sleep anywhere, at any time, whether it resulted in short snippets or total oblivion. As she'd gotten older, her body had become less eager to lean against crates or to let her head tip back as she snoozed upright in a chair, but so long as she had a bed – or at least, a horizontal platform – she could count on remaining asleep once her consciousness switched off. This was not always the case for her crewmates, some of whom had a tough time keeping their minds quiet for the duration of a night after a difficult day, but whatever unpleasant memories Pei carried with her, sleeplessness was not the way in which they manifested. Once she was asleep, she was asleep.

Lately, though, her rhythm had changed. Naps were still easy as ever, but when it came to coasting through the night, she found herself waking in the middle just as she awoke now, wide-eyed and bright-brained. She sighed with frustration, staring at the smooth bulkhead above. It wasn't the same view as that of the ceiling in her quarters aboard the *Mav Bre*, but an unfamiliar bed wasn't the problem. She'd slept in the shuttle many a time, usually with multiple crew members for company. No, she'd been having this specific problem for tendays, and minor annoyance though it was, it was still . . . well, annoying.

She knew why she was awake. This was her body's way of communicating that there was a problem left unsolved, and some stupid part of her thought it best to wake at random intervals until the matter was closed. This had happened to her before when there were open questions about flight paths, landing strategies, contracts that became complicated. It didn't matter that there was no new information to process; her mind simply wanted to review the facts, over and over. It was a maddening habit, and especially so since the subject these days wasn't her job, but Ashby – the person with whom she'd created a space in which she *didn't* have to think about her problems.

She was in no mood to go over the whole thing again, and steadfastly refused to at this hour, but even so, she exhaled, and tossed the blankets aside. The bed moved with her, moulding itself into a chair-like shape as she sat up, then rounding into neutral standby as she left it behind. She gestured at the light panel, and a twilight glow accompanied her as she walked down the hallway to the kitchen. The kettle was half-full of water; she gestured at this as well, and the heating element began its work. She pressed her palm against the pantry wall and it melted gently in response, yawning itself into an opening through which she could peruse the contents stored within. She retrieved a box of instant mek powder, then opened another compartment in search of a mug and a mixing stick. Tools and single dry ingredient retrieved, she tapped the powder into the mug – she knew the exact amount needed, by muscle memory – and waited for the water to boil.

Pei pulled each arm in a light stretch, and as she did so, felt a lingering twinge in her right forearm. The fading shadow of some long-removed shrapnel that had embedded itself there during her last job. A few tendays prior, she'd been at the Rosk border, trying to land the same shuttle she stood in now at the drop site. Now *that* had been a sky on fire. Strike ships had protected her as she'd flown in, raining blinding bursts on the Rosk cruisers that were emptying their ammo bays in an effort to keep anyone from landing. It had not been the first time she'd been in such a situation, but it had gone sideways fast. In the end, the cost of her landing on a planet for ten minutes and unloading a few crates had been a laundry list of broken shit and two destroyed strikers. Repairs to her own ship had been a pain in the ass, but all things considered, it was fine. Her employers had sung her praises, her crew had gotten paid, and nobody who was her responsibility had died. It was, in the end, just another job.

The indicator light on the kettle flashed to let her know its own job was done. She began to fill her mug, and in doing so, distractedly spilled the water. The liquid splashed scalding on the counter, leaping from there to her bare torso before she could get out of the way. It was the most minuscule of misfortunes, but she reacted to it as though it were true insult, her cheeks bruising a shade of purple so dark it felt nearly black. This, too, was a new disruption to her rhythm, and not one she liked. Her temper was always waiting just a scale's width away these days, simmering below the surface and ready to pop at the drop of a scrib or the loss of a signal or, as seen here, the spill of a drink. Anger was not typically an emotion that took up more space in her than joy or fear or any of the others. She always gave it as much room as it needed, and let it out freely. There was nothing healthy about bottling, and anger was useful when wielded wisely. But why it was so quick to appear *these* days, she didn't know. She felt like an adolescent, raw and volatile with no apparent cause. She had tried, many times, to unpack the feeling. Emotions left unchecked could so easily metastasise, and she worked hard to never be that personally negligent. But she couldn't figure this one out, any more than she could sleep a full night, any more than she could keep her mind from immediately leaping to the same weary topic when granted the briefest pause.

She filled her mug. She did not spill this time.

She blended powder and water with the stir stick, summoning an approximation of the drink she really wanted. The tree bark required for a proper cup of mek didn't have the longest shelf life, so for practicality's sake, she always purchased instant. But stars, she missed the real thing. She remembered the brewer her father Po had, with its intricate tubes and pipes, a beautiful, elaborate machine that served no purpose beyond concocting a soothing beverage. Most mek drinkers did not make the stuff fully from scratch, preferring the freeze-dried powder that was a good step up from instant but wouldn't take hours of your day to prepare. Father Po, however, insisted that mek had to be done right or not at all. She had a memory of peeking around the kitchen wall with a creche sibling or two in tow, watching as Father Po performed the ornate ritual of shaving the bark he'd harvested from the garden that morning, grinding and regrinding the potent stuff by hand, adding spices and dried flowers and whatever else he fancied for that particular batch. It was an enormous amount of work for the ten or so cups it would produce, but Father Po insisted it was worth the effort. Not that Pei had ever been able to test that theory. Kids were too young for mek's mild narcosis, and Pei had forgotten to ask Father Po to make her a batch before she went off to school. She still visited the creche, when rare occasion allowed for it, but she could never bring herself to make him go to all that trouble just for her.

She'd never tried traditional mek – made by her father's hand or anyone else's – but lately, whenever she made a cup of the instant stuff, she found herself longing for that intricate delicacy, the one she'd never tasted. She longed, too, for the creche's vegetable garden, even though she had no patience for gardening and no interest in cooking. She longed for the days when a bug or a joke or the movement of her own face was enough to keep her attention rapt all afternoon. She did not long for childhood, as such. On the contrary, Pei was extremely happy to have left that clumsy messiness behind forever. What she longed for, rather, was the simple space to think and explore nothing more complicated than *can I kick my shoe over the tree?* and *how do hands work?* and *if I flash my face at this flower for long enough, can I make it change colour?* Sillinesses such as these had been vital once, a key component in learning the basic rules of the universe within and around her. She no longer needed to discover those rules, but it would be nice, she thought, to have the time to become that intimate with them again.

Pei raised her mug with both hands and opened her mouth to drink. A light panel on the wall flashed before she could do so, signalling a message received. It only did this for channels she'd tagged as important, so she did not think twice about setting her untouched drink down and heading for the control room.

She did, however, wish she was still asleep.

Received message
Encryption: 0
From: GC Transit Authority – Gora System (path: 487-45411-479-4)
To: Gapei Tem Seri (path: 3541-332-61)
Subject: URGENT UPDATE

This is an urgent message from the Emergency Response Team aboard the GC Transit Authority Regional Management Orbiter (Gora System). As both standard ansible and Linking channels are currently unavailable, we will be communicating via the emergency beacon network for the time being. We ask that you leave your scribs locked to this channel until proper communications are restored.

Our team has completed a full orbital survey of Gora's satellite network and the debris cloud. Wreckage drones have been dispatched, and are hard at work removing the debris as quickly as possible.

Due to the unprecedented nature of this situation, debris clean-up sufficient enough to resume normal ground-to-orbit traffic will take longer than originally estimated. **Based on current data, we hope to restore safe spaceflight conditions within approximately two GC standard days.** These estimates are based on the most recent survey data. Given the evolving nature of this situation, the actual time of resolution is subject to change.

We understand and sympathise with the impact these delays are having on both business and personal affairs. We appreciate your continued understanding as we work to resolve this situation as quickly as safety parameters allow.

We are aware of isolated attempts to launch spacecraft despite the current traffic shutdown. **Do not attempt launch of any vessel, crewed or uncrewed, at this time.** The current risk to both sapient life and ship integrity is extreme. Though we share your frustration at the situation, please follow the current traffic regulations for your own safety and the safety of those travelling with you.

The GCTA and the Goran Orbital Cooperative are working together to bring Gora's solar power network back online. The Goran Orbital Cooperative will compensate you for all fuel resources used for back-up power supplies until the solar network is restored.

We understand that some debris from the collision has deorbited and landed planetside. We plan to work directly with affected individuals to assess the damage and necessary repairs once comms channels are restored.

The safest place to be during this situation is within your ship or your habitat dome. Do not attempt exosuit walks in unshielded environments until the all-clear is given.

Any satellite debris that has landed on Gora's surface remains the property of the GC Transit Authority or the Goran Orbital Cooperative. GC salvage rights do not apply in this scenario.

We are working to restore ground-to-orbit comms as soon as possible. We do not have an estimate for this repair work yet.

Thank you for your patience. We are all in this together.

SPEAKER

Speaker focused on the horizon, and tried to keep her breathing slow.

She wanted to pace. She wanted to break something. She wanted to say *fuck it* and hit the launch sequence and navigate the debris herself. But the first option hadn't helped, the second was wasteful, and the third was the sort of thinking that got people killed. So she sat, she breathed, and she tried to calm down.

Out the shuttle window, there was nothing but desert. Not the good kind of desert, like she'd seen on supply stops at Hashkath, full of wildflowers and the strange scurrying lives of animals in their natural niche. This was pure emptiness, a lifeless monument to all the different configurations rock could assume. The sheer amount of *nothing* frightened her. Gora was as undeveloped a place as she'd ever seen, and the bulkhead between her and the outdoors did less to reassure her than usual. The sight of other habitat domes out there – their signs illegible thanks to distance – was a comfort, of sorts. But the domes were so far apart from one another that it did not take much imagining to picture Gora without any sort of buildings at all.

The thought of an untouched planet unnerved her, and the fact that it did made her angry.

She looked down to the hammock beneath her. She wasn't sure when she'd dug her fingers into the edge of the fabric, but it took conscious effort to make herself let go. As she glanced back up, she noticed motion outside.

Roveg's shuttle was parked beside hers, and she could see him in his own control room, looking . . . well, she wasn't quite sure *how* he looked, beyond looking like himself. Quelin were such a conundrum. How were you supposed to understand a face that never changed? She continued to watch him, intrusive though she knew this to be. Roveg gestured at panels, spoke words unheard. The longer she watched, the more it became clear that something wasn't right. An individual in distress was an easy thing to identify, movable face or no. Speaker ran her fingertips over the dents they'd created in the hammock fabric. She thought for a moment, then got out of her seat and climbed into the bubbled window.

'Hey!' she yelled. She doubted he could hear her, given they were each behind a pane designed to keep the vacuum of space away. But it felt odd to wave her arms *without* yelling something, so yell she did. 'Roveg! Hey!'

She waved furiously, feeling awkward, but at last, Roveg noticed her. Everything about his body language noted surprise – the shift of light in his glossy eyes, the way his antennae and frills perked up. He scuttled over on his dozens of legs to face her. She could see his mouth moving, but the words were lost.

'I can't—' *I can't hear you*, she started to say, before realising that phrase was particularly pointless when it held true for the listener as well. If she knew his ship's comms path, she could've called him, but she'd neglected to ask for that when she'd checked in on everyone the day before. What a stupid, basic thing to forget. She raised a hand with deliberateness and pointed in the direction of the airlock. He mirrored the gesture with the legs attached to his thorax. Understanding was reached. She saw him exit his control room as she did the same.

Speaker clambered into her suit, let the cockpit hiss shut, and stepped out of the back hatch of her ship and into the airlock. The hatch clanked closed behind her, and there was another hiss as unseen machinery pumped out the filtered air that had drifted in from Speaker's ship and replaced it with the differently filtered air Ouloo provided for her habitat dome. This was a normal procedure, for Speaker – seals within seals within seals. A constant reminder of the danger posed by an environment without barriers.

Roveg was waiting for her in the Five-Hop's entry tunnel, flexing his upper legs. 'Are you all right?' he asked.

'I was wondering the same about you,' she said. 'I saw you through the window, and it seemed you were upset. Unless I misread?'

Expressionless though he was, Roveg seemed taken aback by this, as though he hadn't thought about the fact that windows worked both ways. 'Oh,' he said. There was a long pause, a touch beyond the boundary of comfort. 'I assume you saw the alert?'

'Yes,' Speaker said.

Roveg paused once more. 'I've had to recalculate my course again, given the increased delay,' he said. 'A bit of a complicated thing, as I'm sure you're familiar with, but the new adjustments I've made will still allow me to arrive in time for my appointment. Arriving the night before isn't ideal, but here we are.' Roveg's tone grew lighter the longer he went on. It reminded Speaker of the way she'd forced her hands to let go of the hammock minutes before.

'That sounds stressful,' Speaker said. 'Is there anything I can do?'

'Not unless you've got a wreckage drone tucked away in that shuttle of yours,' he said. His tone was joking now, forcibly so.

'I'm afraid not,' she said. Strange as the sapient before her was, his anxiety was as palpable as the fact that he didn't want it to show. Speaker understood everything about that state of being, and had no desire to pry (peeking in windows had been bad enough). His business was his business. She respected that. But proximity to someone else's pain wasn't something she could ignore, and if she was unable to provide tangible help, then the next best thing she had to offer was an echo. 'I'll be late for a rendezvous, too,' she said. 'It's not the end of the world, but as you said, it complicates things.'

'You mentioned your sister last night,' Roveg said. 'Have you been able to contact her?'

Now it was Speaker's turn to feel exposed. Windows went both ways, of course, but he'd cut right to the heart of it. 'No,' she said. 'I haven't.'

'Watcher, was it?'

'Tracker.'

'Ah, yes. My mistake. Are you worried about her?'

Speaker took a deep breath. 'I am,' she said. The understatement of the standard. She tried to keep her words measured, but rooted in her heart as they were, they attempted to race away. 'She wasn't well when I left. She's – she's probably fine, she just has, um – she's always had—' Speaker steadied herself, slowed down. 'She has a lung condition, and she was having a difficult day when I left our ship. I'm sure she's—' She paused to take another breath, and as she heard the air slip smoothly through her open throat, she thought of how Tracker's breath had sounded the day before: tight and stuttering, far from effortless. Speaker shoved the thought away. She was embarrassed by letting her fear get the better of her, and frustrated to be in the position of talking about *herself* when her intent in coming out here had been to help *someone else*. With effort, she found her poise, found her words. 'I just want to make sure she's all right.'

Roveg's eyes shifted in their keratin sockets, scattering reflected sunlight. They reminded Speaker of the crystals Tracker grew. 'You know, I can't promise anything,' Roveg said, 'but I . . . hmm. Do you know what kind of comms receiver your ship has? Your ship in orbit, I mean, not your shuttle.'

'Oh, uh, it's a . . .' She closed her eyes and tried to remember. This was her sister's domain, not hers. 'I'm not completely sure.'

'Does it look like a dish, or does it stick out? Like a small tower?'

'A tower, I think.'

'Ah, good. Again, no promises, but I have an idea.' The decorative frills around Roveg's upper torso waved gently. Speaker had no basis for thinking this, but something about the gesture felt friendly. 'Come,' he said. 'Let's find Ouloo.'

PEI

Pei's implant buzzed to the right as the door to the Five-Hop's office slid open. She looked in the buzz's direction and saw a robotic percussion instrument, playing a short tune to announce her arrival. Her brief recognition of the sound was drowned out a split second later by the sort of input her brain was far more receptive to: a veritable avalanche of colour. Pei was no stranger to environments that seemed to be shouting – she wouldn't get far in a multispecies market otherwise – but given the tactfully neutral paint of the building's exterior, she hadn't expected the inside to be so *loud*.

The Five-Hop One-Stop's permit office and traveller's shop was jammed to the gills with items for sale, each emblazoned with a label or logo designed to make people of other species sit up and take notice. Pei noticed, all right, but not in the way their designers had hoped. She gave an involuntary wince as every hue hit her eyes at once. She felt as though she were staring directly into the sun, and that the sun really wanted her to buy something.

'Oh dear, I know, I'm so sorry,' Ouloo said. Pei hadn't yet registered the ground host sitting behind a desk at the far end of the room. 'There's a basket of monocs just to your left there.'

Pei looked over and saw the basket in question, hanging from the wall and fixed with a computer-generated colour-sign that read *Please take them if you need them! Return them before you go!* Inside, as stated, there were several pairs of monochromatic spectacles, which, when worn over Aeluon eyes, rendered the world a tranquil grey. Despite her discomfort, Pei did not pick up a pair. Monocs were dorky as hell, the sort of thing you only wore if you were very young or very old or very fussy or never left your homeworld. The fledgling headache that had made its appearance would pass in a minute or two, she knew, and in this case, pride won out. 'Thanks, but I'm okay,' she said.

'All right, well, they're there if you change your mind.' Ouloo sighed apologetically. 'I can control how the buildings look, but not the labels on things.'

'I completely understand,' Pei said. 'And honestly, the grey paint is more than I'd expect in a place that gets traffic from all over.'

Ouloo beamed at this. 'I got that paint special-ordered from an Aeluon manufacturer,' she said. 'Everyone knows your rods are extra sensitive and can pick up colours the rest of us can't see, so I wanted to make sure I wasn't getting something that was . . . you know, sloppy. I know that what's grey to me and what's *purely* grey to you are different things.'

Pei smiled appreciative blue, because everyone *didn't* know that, and Ouloo had clearly done her homework. That point was underlined as Pei perused the screaming shelves. There were baskets of all manner of fresh fruit, bags of spicy dried insects, jerky made from a broad swath of animals and plants alike, and a plex-doored stasie filled with single-serving tubs of roe and Hanto-labelled mysteries Pei could only guess at. A little something for everybody.

No species was a monolith, but if Pei had been asked to describe the Laru in broad strokes, she'd simply point to what Ouloo had constructed at the Five-Hop. The Laru had been even less technologically capable than Humans – believe it or not – when the GC had made contact about a century back. Their furry species hadn't gotten any farther than space tele-scopes and short suborbital flights before Aandrisk ambassadors sent along a friendly hello. Pei had read that it was always difficult to predict how a sapient species would react to contact, but in the Laru's case, the overwhelming reaction to learning they were far from alone in the galaxy was one of joyous enthusiasm. The Laru wasted no time in throwing themselves wholeheartedly into a life among aliens, opening their planetary system to metal mining and gas harvesting and whatever else the GC wanted, leaving their homeworld in droves to absorb all the lessons they could from interstellar exchange. Pei had met many Laru in her time, and they were each their own people, but the one thing they had in common was that she'd never met any who'd been born on their homeworld. She wasn't even sure what their homeworld was called, come to think of it. All the Laru she'd encountered were transplants from elsewhere. She'd met one from Port Coriol, one from Hagarem, one from Kaathet who could speak Reskitkish so perfectly she would've thought they were an Aandrisk if she'd closed her eyes and plugged her nose. Ouloo appeared to have come straight out of the same mould as her predecessors – a champion for multispecies life, someone who dove headlong into the melting pot and was loving every minute of it.

'Did you make those?' Pei asked, nodding at Ouloo's desk. A heap of office supplies had been shoved aside to make way for an enormous stack of iced buns, which Ouloo was in the process of transferring one by one into a drone delivery box.

'Yes,' Ouloo said, sounding quite unhappy for someone wielding that much sugar. 'I made them for my neighbours who own the *tet* house across the way. I can't call anyone, but Tupo has a telescope, and I used that to look around and see what was going on out there, and it looks like some of the debris hit their dome. There's pieces of it all over.'

Pei straightened up. 'Are they okay? Can you tell?'

'Well, their shuttle was there, so nobody left, and I could see some people moving around, so I guess they must have some kind of shielding, or maybe it didn't hit hard enough to break the seal, or – I don't know. I don't know, and it's making me crazy. But I'm going to send them these, along with a note to send the drone back with a note of their own if they need help, because that's the only thing I can do.' The filaments of fur around Ouloo's ears stretched vertically in agitation. She picked up one of the buns and took an enormous bite, for what looked like therapeutic purposes. 'I just can't believe this is happening,' she said as she chewed. 'We've never had anything like this here. Not ever. I'm shocked the Transit Authority let something like this happen.'

'Things just happen,' Pei said kindly. 'All the rest of us can do is react. And do our best.'

'Well, I suppose, but . . . stars, what a disaster.' Ouloo took another bite; icing stuck to the fur around her mouth. She looked at Pei, and swallowed. 'Captain Tem, if there is anything I can do for *you* to make this easier, please, please let me know. Any hour of the day. No matter what it is.'

'I will,' Pei said, trying to infuse the words with as much a sense of *it's not your fault, please stop worrying* as she could. She understood that this was likely one of the worst things that had ever happened to Ouloo and that her fretting was proportionate to that, but for Pei, a few unexpected days of shuttle camping and catching up on vids and books was far from a hardship. It was annoying, not distressing. It truly was okay. They weren't the ones stuck under a dome that had shit falling on it. Not yet, anyway.

Pei stopped in front of a rack of snack packs. One in particular caught her eye: an Ensk label bellowing in red font (to her, the words appeared afraid). She understood only a smattering of Ensk – which was pathetic, given how long she'd been with Ashby – but this label she knew, thanks to an unthinkable pair of days she'd had earlier that standard. (Had that rendezvous happened *this standard*? Stars, but it felt like a lifetime already.)

She picked up the bag. *The Original Fire Shrimp!* the label read. *Devastatingly Hot!*

Pei picked up a second pack and headed for Ouloo's desk.

'Ah, Human snacks, of course,' Ouloo said. She took a pack in her forepaw and studied it with suspicion. 'There's no cheese in these, right?'

Pei laughed. 'No, I don't think so. And they're not for me, they're for a friend.'

'The one you're visiting?'

'Well – no, they're not for *him*. But they are for someone on his crew, so I . . . yes, I guess I'm visiting her as well.' Intellectually, Pei was well aware that Ashby did not live alone, but she'd been so focused on spending time with him that she hadn't given much thought to how it would be to spend time with the rest of his crew as well. This was new territory in their relationship, for certain. 'Sorry, where's the . . .' She looked around for the patch scanner, and found it semi-hidden beside a stack of scrib repair kits. She pushed up her wristwrap, swiped her implanted chip over the scanner, and paid for the shrimp bits.

'Anything for yourself?' Ouloo asked. 'I'm not trying to be pushy, I promise, I just want to make sure you've got everything you need.'

'Actually, yes, I could use something,' Pei said. 'Though I don't quite know what I'm looking for.'

Ouloo was instantly attentive. She set her bun down and extended her neck with keen alertness. 'Oh, I'm sure we can accommodate whatever it is.'

Pei paused. How to explain a feeling she wasn't sure of herself? 'I'm not . . . feeling quite right.'

Ouloo's eyes widened. 'Oh dear, are you sick?' She started to get to her feet. 'Come on, I've got a bot scanner over—'

'No, I'm not *sick*,' Pei said. 'I just feel . . . off. Kind of sore. I was wondering if you have any painkillers? Maybe muscle rub?'

'I have lots of things in those categories, but let's narrow it down. Sore, like you hurt yourself?'

'No.' The twinge in her arm from the night before wasn't

bothering her now, and this was a different kind of discomfort entirely. 'It's not any one spot, and it's mild. It's my back and my belly and . . . I don't know. Feels almost like I slept wrong.'

'You *might* have, unless you're in the habit of sleeping in your shuttle.'

'Yeah, that's not an issue with my kind of bed,' Pei said.

'Oh, right!' Ouloo said. 'You have those marvellous squishy things. I slept in one once, when I was young. Really ought to splash out and get one for myself one of these years. Maybe when Tupo stops eating so much. But . . . hmm, yes, I see your point.' Her neck wiggled slightly as she thought. 'Could just be stress, you know. I haven't been sleeping well either.'

Pei wasn't about to tell Ouloo that the current disaster hadn't gotten under her skin. But she *did* have a lot on her mind, and stubborn thoughts had a sneaky way of moving themselves into your body. She was accustomed to stress settling in her shoulders, not lower down, but bodies were anything but static.

'You know, I can sell you some muscle rub if you like, but I think I have something even better.' Ouloo's eyes twinkled. 'Have you seen the bathhouse yet?'

'Oh,' Pei said. She dimly remembered seeing something about it on the signage out front. 'No, I haven't.'

Ouloo got out from behind her desk and began walking toward the door, her decision already made. 'Not to brag, but it's a real treat. I am sure it'll put you right.'

Pei had intended to come away from the office with a tube of this and a jar of that to take back to her shuttle, but Ouloo's suggestion was tempting. Pei couldn't remember the last time she'd bathed for something other than the sake of hygiene and habit. Honestly, disappointed as she was to lose a few precious days with Ashby, if bathhouses and cakes were what being grounded on Gora meant, being stuck there certainly didn't suck. It *did* sound like a treat.

She thought of Ouloo's neighbours, and kept that thought to herself.

ROVEG

Sky full of space trash aside, it was a beautiful day. Gora's thin atmosphere made for a strikingly crisp canvas, and the habitat dome's dulling of this effect was minimal. Without water vapour to scatter its rays, the sunlight pierced down as cleanly as honed metal, leaving you with no illusion that it was anything but a star. And as for stars, they were out, too, despite the sun being high. The satellite debris hid most of them from view, but the boldest shone through anyway, peppering the morning with an elegant tease of night.

Were the sky *not* full of space trash, Roveg would've assumed Tupo was simply enjoying the view. The child was on one of the lawns alongside the walking path, lying in a position impossible for any species but xyr own. Tupo was belly-down in the grass, limbs flopped every which way around xyr. This included xyr neck, which was folded back over xyr spine so that xyr head was fully rested against xyr lower back, face staring upward. It was a horrid configuration, but Roveg supposed that from Tupo's perspective, it was incredibly comfortable.

'Quite a mess up there, eh?' Roveg said as he and Speaker approached.

Tupo looked up, surprised to have been disturbed. 'Yeah,' xe said. 'There's no more explosions, though.'

'That's probably a good thing,' Roveg said.

'I guess.' Tupo sighed.

Not the take Roveg had expected, but he let it slide. 'We're looking for your mother,' he said.

113

'Why?'

'We'd like to make some minor adjustments to your ansible tower, with her permission.' He nodded reassuringly at Speaker. 'We're trying to get a call out.'

'Oh, yeah, that's fine,' Tupo said. Xe got to xyr feet all at once, like some kind of cloth puppet whose performer had returned. 'Come on.'

'Uh,' Roveg said. 'We should ask your mother, shouldn't we?'

Speaker looked at him quizzically from within her suit. 'Why?'

'Yeah, it's fine,' Tupo said again. The child was already trotting down the path. 'Come on.'

Roveg did not immediately follow Tupo, as Speaker did. The adjustments he was planning were as minor as advertised, but the tower in question was Ouloo's, not Tupo's, and . . . and, dammit, they were already around the corner ahead of him. He hurried after, still unsure about this.

The path that led behind the office was as tidy as the others, but less decorative. There were no signs here, no lawns, no flowers. A small dwelling came into view, and unlike the drab grey buildings that comprised the rest of the Five-Hop, this one was painted in patterns of vibrant yellow and seashore blue. 'Is this your home, Tupo?' Roveg asked.

'Yep,' Tupo said.

'Must be nice to have all that space just for two,' Speaker said.

Tupo looked at her sceptically. 'I guess,' xe said. Xyr tone did not suggest agreement.

The sib tower stood right by the Laru house – a standard model, nothing flashy. Roveg opened his mouth as Tupo approached the tower, beginning to ask if xe was *sure* they shouldn't check with Ouloo first, but the child had already pried off the access panel. 'Do you need any tools?' Tupo asked.

Roveg raised the tool bag he carried by way of answer. 'I believe I'm set,' he said. He approached the tower and got to work.

Speaker sat the suit down beside him at a courteous distance that still allowed her to get a good look. 'What exactly are you attempting here?'

Roveg reached into the tower and pulled out a bundle of wires. 'I think,' he said, 'with a few adjustments, we might be able to boost the signal enough to get at least a text message through. We might even get voice, if we're lucky, but let's see how we get along.'

'I don't understand why the sibs aren't working at all,' she said. 'If they can get signal from one system to another with all the dust and planets in between, why can't I reach my ship that's right up there?'

Roveg began to answer, but Tupo beat him to it. 'Sibs need sublayer buoys to work, and you, um, still need a satellite network to connect to them if you're calling from the ground. You can't have buoys inside a planet. That wouldn't even work.'

Roveg stared at this completely accurate technical summary from a youngster who appeared to have some kind of custard on xyr chin, but Speaker seemed nonplussed. If anything, she seemed to warm to it. 'I didn't know you were a tech,' she said approvingly.

Tupo laughed. 'I'm not a *tech*,' Tupo said. 'I just . . . know some stuff.'

'You sound like you could be a good tech,' Speaker said.

'I dunno,' the kid said, shuffling xyr feet.

Roveg was concentrating on not knocking circuitry out of place, but out of the corner of his eye, he could see Speaker readjusting herself in her cockpit, taking an interest in the child. 'So how old *will* you be, when you decide on a profession?' she asked. 'Round about?'

'I dunno,' the kid said again. 'When I'm grown up.'

'And when would that be, for you?'

'Um . . . I guess . . . well, I can get my shuttle licence when I'm twenty-six.' Tupo delivered this information with authority, as if this were a number they were keenly aware of and eager to reach.

'Twenty-six,' the Akarak mused. There was a subtle awe in her tone.

'And how old were you, Speaker?' Roveg asked. 'When you got *your* shuttle licence?'

Her eyes crinkled. 'Very subtle of you,' she said.

He waved a pair of pliers at her in acknowledgement. 'Thank you.'

'I was three and a half,' she said.

Tupo's head rushed right up to Speaker's cockpit window, propelled in a spring-like manner by xyr neck. '*Three* and a *half*?!' the kid exclaimed.

Roveg did not stick his face straight into Speaker's, but he shared the sentiment. He lowered his pliers. 'Forgive my ignorance,' he said, throwing subtlety to the wind, 'but how old *are* you?'

'I'm eight,' Speaker said.

Tupo was agape. 'You're eight standards old.'

'Yes.'

The child looked at Roveg with sheer bewilderment, then back to Speaker. 'You're a kid?'

Speaker shifted her beak, amused. 'No. I reached adulthood before the end of my first standard. By my species' rubric, I'm approaching middle age. We live to be about twenty, twenty-five, or so.'

'That's *it*?'

Roveg intervened. He shared the child's surprise, but gawking at another's relatively imminent mortality felt uncouth. 'Lifespans vary as much as our bodies,' he said. He looked away from his work to address Tupo directly. 'And *your* species lives much longer than the rest of us, so your childhood is equally lengthy – as I'm sure you're aware. Remind me how long it takes a Laru to leave xyr mother's pouch and start walking?'

'Um . . . like four years.'

'Stars,' Speaker said with a laugh.

'Mmm-hmm,' Roveg said, returning to his work. 'And how old are you now?'

'I'm *seventeen*,' Tupo said, still agog. Xe pointed a shaggy paw at Speaker. 'I'm more than *twice as old* as you.' Xe frowned mightily. 'Wait, if *you* can have a shuttle licence, why can't I?'

Speaker laughed again. 'That's a good question, actually. Shuttle licences are based on whatever age your species independently determines marks the cognitive maturity needed to fly a ship. Roveg, when did you get yours?'

Roveg tied off a bit of cable and reached for his glue gun. 'Twelve,' he said.

'See?' Speaker said to Tupo.

Roveg looked to Speaker, more questions on his mind. He understood, conceptually, everything that he'd just explained to Tupo about the relativity of aging, but the ramifications of a twenty-standard lifespan were beginning to dawn on him. 'I spent twenty standards in school before I was a barely competent adult,' he said. 'And here you are, fully educated and well cultured at *eight*. How?'

'Well, that's the thing,' Speaker said. 'We don't have the opportunity to be as *broadly* educated as the rest of you. In a person's first year, we carefully scrutinise what skills xe's got the most aptitude for, and then that's what xe learns. So, if a kid demonstrates a knack for wiring panels together, xe'll be an engineer. If xe shows an interest in plants, xe'll be trained for food gardening, and so on. The time in which we exist is enough to learn one subject really, really well. We're specialists, not generalists. That's what our names reflect. We don't have abstract names like you do. Your identity is what you do for your community. So, for example, my mother is Kreiek – *water maker*. She manages her ship's life support systems. Every big ship has a Kreiek; I simply know which one is mine.'

'So what is your name, then?' Roveg asked.

'You know my name.'

'I mean in your own language.'

'I don't have a name in Ihreet,' Speaker said. 'My name is Speaker, just as it is in Klip.'

'Because you *speak* Klip,' Roveg said. 'That's *your* speciality.'

'It's not the only language I speak, but it's the one that benefits my community most, yes.'

Several pieces began to click into place. 'Is that why so many of your species *don't* speak Klip? Because there isn't time to learn? It took me . . . oh, let's see . . . would've been about nine years of Klip lessons before I was fluent.'

'That's part of it. The other piece is that Klip is a challenging language for most of us. Hanto comes more easily, but that's because modern Ihreet is largely based on it. It's essentially a Hanto skeleton with a hodgepodge of whatever remnants of our pre-colonial languages we managed to retain.'

Roveg could hear her skimming past a painful history there – not her own, not something she'd lived, but something burned black into her shell (or her bones, he supposed – the Quelin idiom didn't work well for vertebrates). He followed her lead, and did not press that subject further. 'But *you* can pronounce Klip,' he said. 'You do so beautifully.'

'Thank you,' she said. Speaker appeared to be done with that line of conversation, and instead turned her attention to his work. 'I have no idea what you're doing, but it looks like you're doing it well.'

He laughed. 'We'll see. This isn't the kind of thing I do every day.' It had, in fact, been a long time since he'd delved into the guts of a machine like this. He was a designer, not a mechanic, and he usually deployed fixbots when things went awry. But basic mech tech skills had been part of that schooling he'd mentioned, an essential foundation for anyone who wished to play intimately with software. He remembered the common plaza at his university, where he and his peers would race robots and do mild hacker pranks and dazzle onlookers with elaborate pixel animations. It was an old memory, a nothing memory, but one made painful by the simple context of what life had once been. He knotted it up tightly and sealed it away.

'I love sims,' Tupo interjected with a blunt absence of segue. Roveg's profession had been established at the garden gathering the night before, and it sounded as though Tupo had been feverishly waiting since then to discuss the matter further. 'The last one I played was *Scorch Squad 19* and it was really, really good.'

'I haven't tried that one,' Roveg said, and he wouldn't, because you didn't need to see anything beyond the previews to know that series was the purest of trash. 'If that's your sort of taste, my sims might not be for you. I make vacation sims.'

'What's a vacation sim?' Speaker asked.

'You know, the sort where there's no story, it's just a lovely blank-slate environment for you to enjoy for as long as you please.'

'Oh,' she said.

'Not your cup of tea, either?'

'No, it's just . . . I've never played a sim before.'

Roveg and Tupo turned in tandem to stare at her. 'You've *never* played a sim?' Tupo said. It was the exact same tone xe'd confirmed her age with.

'No,' Speaker said simply. 'I haven't.'

Roveg continued to stare, then laughed. 'I'm sorry,' he said. 'When something's your whole life, and you meet somebody outside of that bubble . . . do you know the feeling I mean?'

'Yes,' Speaker said. 'I do.'

'How have you *never* played a sim?' Tupo said.

Speaker gave a nonchalant gesture. 'They don't make them for Akaraks,' she said.

'Why not?'

The answer came to Roveg immediately, and he didn't like it at all. 'Sims have to be tailored to the nervous system of the player,' he said. 'An Aandrisk and a Harmagian can enter the same sim, and it'll behave identically from both of their perspectives, but they're accessing different versions of the software. A designer like me will build the base world or story, then port it to different species-specific templates. Brain maps, we call them.'

Tupo frowned. 'Why?'

'Well, if one player has arms and one player has tentacles, the—' he reached for a kid-friendly word '—the rules that make the sim work behave differently for each of them. Otherwise it won't feel like the players are actually *touching* something.' He looked back at Speaker. 'And nobody's ever bothered mapping Akaraks, it would seem. I'd never thought of it before, but you're . . . you're not an option in the design tools I use.' His words came out quiet, bothered.

'I guess nobody expects us to buy them,' Speaker said.

'Yes, well, you *can't* buy them if they don't exist, can you?' He huffed air through his spiracles, and rattled his mouthparts in disapproval. Carefully, he replaced the machine's innards, and closed the panel back up. 'All right. There. Let's give that a try.' He moved to the control terminal and started to gesture commands, but immediately ran into a problem. 'I . . . can't read this,' he said, facing an unfamiliar alphabet. Laru, presumably, but he'd never seen their language written before. 'Where are the translation settings?'

'Oh, uh . . .' Tupo came over and swung xyr neck under Roveg's thoracic legs so as to get a better look at the screen. 'Um . . . that one that looks like a square. Here, lemme.' Xe entered in some quick commands, and the screen transformed into Klip.

'Ah,' Roveg said with relief. 'Thank you.'

'Is it working?' Speaker said.

'Can't say yet. We'll need to reboot in order for the changes I made to be recognised. It'll take several minutes, at least.'

Speaker shifted in her suit. It was evident she did not want to sit by even one minute more, but she accepted the situation and leaned back into her seat. 'So we wait?'

Roveg bent his legs affirmatively. 'We wait.'

PEI

The bathhouse, it turned out, was pretty nice.

It wasn't huge, like the spas and saunas you'd find in a big city, and it wasn't plush, like some of the places she'd treated her crew to after a long haul. From the outside, the Five-Hop's bathhouse looked like it had room for maybe six people; inside, it was quiet, inviting, and sparkling clean. The walls were tiled with affordable faux silicate (it looked decently close to the real thing), and across these, decorative trails of pillowy moss had been coaxed to grow in spiralling lines. The floor was so polished that Pei could almost make out her reflection in it, and upon seeing this, she wasted no time in removing her boots. She placed them in one of the large cubbies by the entryway intended for this purpose, and her clothing followed in short order.

On the other side of the hallway, two rows of automated dispensers were built into the wall, each labelled with a pixel frame. All manner of soaps and scrubs and oils were on offer, and Pei smiled as she imagined Ouloo tying herself in knots trying to narrow down the scale scrub scent that would appeal best to Aandrisks, or a tonic spray that most Harmagians would find suitable. The animated pictures on each dispenser did look tempting, but Pei decided to check out the facilities first.

Just as the crammed sign out front had advertised, the bath-house offered a broad variety of culturally specific bathing fixtures, all of which were installed in a single, large room with waist-high dividing walls between. There were curtain rods circling each setup as well, and the intent of this was clear. If visitors wanted to chat with others, they could, but privacy was equally available. *Do you*, Ouloo's handiwork said.

Pei walked around the room, enjoying the sensation of cool tile on bare soles. She stopped in front of a very familiar apparatus: an Aeluon douser. This was the traditional way of getting clean – a sustained blast of steamy mist to kill germs and loosen dirt, followed by a single splash of cold water emptied from a tank overhead. Pei had used one of these nearly every day of her life, but she wasn't in the bathhouse because she needed to clean up. She was in the bathhouse to kill time and chill out, and if *that* was the goal, there was one species who had those things down better than most.

She turned her back on the douser and instead set her eye on the Aandrisk-style steam bath – a windowed, ovular container, made of stone and big enough for a single occupant to walk into. A gate was installed around this, for the sake of Harmagian safety. A Harmagian wouldn't dare enter such a contraption anyway, but any steam that escaped when the door was opened would be unkind to their slimy skin. Pei herself was not built for the temperatures Aandrisks craved, but she knew from experience that a steam bath was a real treat if you used the button marked with the Reskitkish term for *child's setting* (for years, she'd thought the button read *low heat* – a small but recoverable blow to her pride).

She returned to the dispensers in the hallway and found one containing scented steam tabs. She swiped her wrist over the patch scanner and a round capsule popped out, containing two powdery pucks flecked with dried herbs. She decided to be fully Aandrisk about it and bought a tiny pot of scale scrub as well – saltmoss-scented, a taste she'd acquired in her travels. Aandrisks had a much thicker, rougher exterior than her own, but scales were scales, and she'd found that just a tiny bit of scrub used lightly gave her a nice shine.

She returned to the steam bath, stepped in, closed the door behind her, popped the tabs into the receptacle on the wall, and

entered her settings into the control panel. Her implant registered the instantaneous hiss of water being pumped through
hot metal, and continued to let her know that the sound was
present. She sat with that feeling for a few seconds, then did
something she almost never did when away from the *Mav Bre*:
she reached up to her forehead, and shut off her implant.

Pei had received implant and talkbox both when she was
small, and it had been so long since she'd known life without
them that turning the processor off was always jarring at first.
She felt like when she'd reached for her locked-up gun two days
prior – startled by the absence of something that wasn't actually
part of her but always came along for the ride.

After a few seconds, the weirdness wore off, and Pei allowed
herself to be cradled by silence. Not silence in the way that
other species spoke of silence. When hearing species said *silence*,
they meant *I can hear nothing but the wind and the leaves*, or
No one is speaking, but the sounds of the city are still present.
That wasn't true silence. *Real* silence. Her species' natural state.
The only time Pei realised how tiring it was for her brain to
constantly process a type of input it wasn't built for was when
she made the decision to shut it out.

The silence wasn't enough to fix the mental discomfort she'd
awoken with, but it did make her care about it less, and right
then, that would do.

A smooth lounging stone stood in the middle of the steam
bath, its shape intended for the face-down posture of someone
with strong haunches and a long tail. Pei had neither, but she
lay on her belly anyway, wrapping her arms and legs around
the stone, letting her shins and forearms settle into the grooves
carved for that purpose. Scented steam began to billow from
the tiny nozzles embedded throughout the walls and ceiling.
She watched it swirl, felt it pull her airways wide. As her body
let go, her mind took its cue to wander, and in doing so, pulled
itself toward the inevitable topic of Ashby.

The man himself wasn't the problem. He was what made

problems bearable, what softened her angles and quieted her thoughts. They saw each other rarely – usually only a few days snatched here and there within the bulk of a standard year – but when she was with him, everything made sense. There was no work, no danger, no complications. There was only him, and her, and a bed beneath them. With him, there was a depth of conversation she couldn't find with anyone else, an effortless surety that everything said between them was true and that nothing – no matter how messy or unflattering – would be judged. Not that all they did together was talk. Thinking of the way he moved when she touched him made the deepest part of her kick. She never stopped being intoxicated by the choreography they'd invented together, a dance made for two bodies that hadn't evolved for each other. Everything fell into place when she locked herself away with him.

But then, inevitably, there was the other side of that door. There, she became someone else, and he loyally pretended not to know her even though she could see the sadness in his eyes as he did so. There, they fell into a different rhythm, one of secrets and denial. That reality was increasingly difficult for both of them to stomach, but she *did* stomach it, and *had* stomached it, because Ashby was Human. Ashby was Human, and Pei wasn't ready to blow her life up.

She had no idea when exactly the Aeluon taboo against interspecies relationships had taken root in mainstream society, only that it was older than the GC and as much of a given as rain on a winter's day. She knew there were accepting communities in the more socially liberal places of the galaxy – neutral worlds and modder hubs and the like. She'd once seen three Aandrisks and an Aeluon joyfully fucking in an open-air park on Port Coriol in the middle of the afternoon, uncaring about the fact that they were on broad display to anybody walking through the street below. She'd been jealous as she passed their revels by – not for their public display, which she did not share the Aandrisk ambivalence for, but for the fact that the Aeluon getting railed by an alien simply didn't care who knew. She, on the other hand, went through endless acrobatics to keep Ashby safely quarantined from the rest of her life. They had elaborate protocols for how to meet at hotels and guesthouses without anybody knowing they were staying in the same room, and how to communicate when apart so that her crewmates wouldn't notice messages between them. She'd gone to the absurd length of writing to him on *paper* and sending it via mail drone, and while he apparently saw a certain romance in that, she saw only how ridiculous things had become.

Ashby was a piece of her life she would grieve if he were gone. Every time she pretended he didn't exist, every time she dodged her crewmates' good-natured questions about why it'd been so long since they'd seen her take a lover, it felt as though she were throwing mud in his face. Such deception was disrespectful to who he was and all he'd given her. He followed every rule of hers to the letter, even though no one else in his life would've minded in the slightest. He hid and lied and kept her quiet, for her sake. She hated it, fervently.

. . . and yet.

It was one thing for some modder or artist or crunchy bohemian on Coriol to cast tradition to the wind. It was entirely another for someone like Pei, who was not politically radical and had never been and for whom reputation was the framework everything else in her life clung to. She didn't have a clear map for what would happen if her relationship with Ashby became public knowledge, but she could guess. She wouldn't lose her ship over it – that was hers, bought and paid for. But her job as she knew it would be over, once word got around. Military contracts would evaporate, and the big businesses most worth hauling for would probably vanish as well. She could go elsewhere, pursue more work in multispecies space, maybe focus on Aandrisk or Harmagian clients instead. But those weren't the networks her best contacts were in, and rebuilding a list of people who *would* work with her would be all the harder while looking for a new crew. Some of hers would leave, no question. Most, probably. She'd confided in her pilot and her algaeist about Ashby and they hadn't abandoned her for it, but then, she was friends with them to a degree that she wasn't with the rest. She didn't know how the others would react. She wouldn't bet on a positive outcome.

Pei was nothing if not resourceful. If push came to shove, she *could* start from scratch. What it came down to was . . . she didn't want to. But she didn't want to keep playing in the shadows, either. She wanted to keep her job. She wanted to fuck in a park (metaphorically). She could not see a reality in which those two desires might coexist.

And around and around it went.

She hadn't told Ashby that this was tearing at her as it was. On the contrary, she'd written to him and told him she didn't care who knew anymore, that if someone found out, *oh well.* She'd meant it, at the time. The last drop had been dangerous, one of the worst Pei'd ever taken part in. It had rattled her, but not half as much as when she'd seen the news from Hedra Ka and known *exactly* which civilian ship the Toremi had fired upon. Ashby was the farthest thing in the universe from a soldier. He had no business finding himself in a situation like that. But as she'd sat there alone in her quarters, clutching her scrib so hard she bruised the screen, she wondered how many times those tables had been turned. How many times it had been *him* reading the news, sifting between the lines and trying to determine if she was okay?

In that moment, she'd had enough of pretending.

In the moments that followed, the tangle returned.

She thought about what she'd written to him then, scribbled onto a piece of dead tree and shot across the void. *I won't say anything to my crew one way or another, but they might piece it together. If they do, I'll deal with it. I don't care anymore.* To some extent, that was true. It was a risky thing, for her to spend shore leave on the *Wayfarer.* She knew some of her crew had found her destination odd, given that they'd been there themselves and seen nothing but a homely tunnelling ship that had lent them a hand. Part of Pei *wanted* her crew to figure it out, put the pieces together, hit the detonator for her. She normally hated things being outside of her control, but in a twisted way, that felt like the best possible outcome. She'd spent standards trying to determine the right course of action, the right words to say. Having somebody else erase all of those decisions sounded like a relief, of sorts.

She didn't want it to happen.

But she likewise did.

She began to pant softly, her body's unconscious way of trying to cool down. The nameless ache in her belly began to ease. She turned her head and pressed her cheek hard against the stone, plunging into the dizzying warmth, trying to sear away the unsolvable.

SPEAKER

Speaker assumed that Roveg could read her about as well as she could read him, but even so, she did her best to mask her sadness as the sib tower let them know that it could not, in fact, establish a transmission path.

'Damn,' Roveg said. He returned to the access panel, picking up his tools. Speaker was fascinated by both components of this action: the bifurcated ends of his legs, which could do nothing more than grasp objects between them like pairs of tweezers, and the tools designed for such appendages, which were so slim they seemed fragile. But Roveg wielded these with far more dexterity than Speaker would've thought his toes could manage, and he dove back into the access panel to tinker further. 'All right, let's give it another go.'

'Are either of you hungry?' Tupo asked. Xe paused. 'Right, you can't have snacks.'

Speaker clicked her beak kindly. 'I *can* have snacks, just not out here. But no, thank you, I'm not hungry.'

'Me neither,' Roveg said.

'Okay,' Tupo said. Xe paused again. 'Well, *I'm* hungry.'

Roveg laughed. 'You go on, Tupo, we might be a while out here.'

Tupo made an awkward exit without another word, padding up the path to the house.

'Xe's a funny one,' Roveg said once Tupo was inside.

'I don't really understand kids,' Speaker said. 'Ours are in that state so briefly that it doesn't make much of an impression.

A few tens of tendays of chaos, and then they're on their way.'

'You don't have any of your own, I take it.'

'No.'

'And your sister?'

'No.'

Roveg continued his work, using four pairs of feet at once, and nearly as many tools. Speaker had initially thought all those legs must be a bother to keep track of, but she was starting to see the benefit. He sat back and dug through his tool bag. 'Speaker and Tracker,' he mused. 'You speak. What does she track?'

'Other Akaraks,' Speaker said. 'Or, more specifically, their ships.'

'To what end?'

'So we can help them.'

'Yes, you made mention of that work last night. Acquiring supplies, I believe you said.' He paused. 'Forgive me, I still don't understand.'

Speaker considered how best to answer. She had no qualms about sharing the shape of her life with others, but had so little opportunity to do so that she wasn't sure which pieces to include and which to skip. This had gone beyond small talk, now, and Roveg's interest seemed as sincere as her fascination with his feet. Given that she could contribute nothing to his work – which he was doing as a favour to *her*, after all – she saw no reason not to explain in full. 'Once a standard, all – or, well, *most* – Akaraks gather for an event we call *rakree*. Literally, it means *exchange*. Or *sharing*, I guess. That's a better fit. Anybody who wants to gather with other ships does so. We all go to the same coordinates and we link our ships together with these . . . oh, I don't know the word. They're essentially portable airlocks. A big, airtight tube that links two ships together.'

'And you use these to link . . . all of them?'

'Right. Imagine . . . imagine if there was one tenday a standard in which every house in a city opened its doors, and everybody was free to go in and out of wherever they wanted.'

Roveg's frills rippled. 'That sounds a bit hellish to me, to be honest. But I'm getting the impression you feel the opposite.'

'It's wonderful,' Speaker said honestly. 'It's my favourite thing.'

'And what's the purpose?' Roveg asked. 'Trading, politics, partying, sex?'

'Akaraks don't have sex.'

Roveg's tools froze in place. 'What?'

'We *reproduce* sexually, but we don't have social sex. I'm fully aware of how that works in other species, but we . . . physically don't have the capability for what you're referring to, or the need. We can't. We don't.'

The Quelin absorbed this information. 'I'm not sure whether that's tragic or whether you've been spared a lot of bother. Anyway, sorry, continue.'

'You got two of the activities right: trading, primarily, and partying, second. We don't do politics, or at least not in the way you mean. We don't have a government. Each ship makes its own decisions. But I'm getting sidetracked: you wanted to know about my job, not my culture.'

'Well, now I'm interested in both.'

Speaker crinkled her eyes at him. 'The point of *rakree* is to be open with others. You tell people what you need, and you give others whatever you can provide. Maybe you've got a big crop of food, and there's surplus to share. Maybe you need a compressor coil, and there's someone three ships over who's got a spare. Maybe your ship needs a doctor, or a pilot, and you find someone with those skills who's been looking for a new home. Or maybe it's as simple as needing to sleep in a different place for a few nights, or talk with people you don't live with all day every day. A change of pace. That's the thing about *rakree*. Needs can be big or small, but they all matter.'

'So it's not a barter, then. It's a truly open exchange.'

'It *can* be a barter, but yes, you've got it. There's no expectation of receiving something in return for what you give, and no guilt about taking what you need.'

Roveg's hard-surfaced eyes rotated in their sockets with an almost mechanical quickness. 'Is *that* why you came to my ship and quizzed me on my skills? Because that's what you do among yourselves?'

'I suppose,' she said. 'Did you find it unusual?'

'Yes, I admit I did. Not in a bad way. It's just not what I would've done.'

Speaker clicked her beak contemplatively. 'It would've felt odd not to, especially in an emergency,' she said.

'Even though we're different species?'

Speaker considered that. She *had* been apprehensive about approaching a group of sapient strangers one by one, but as she reflected on it now, she understood that her fear of their hostility had been lesser than that of facing danger alone. 'I was operating on the hope that such things wouldn't matter when the sky is falling apart.'

'Such things shouldn't matter at all, regardless of what the sky is doing.' Roveg swapped one tool for another, and continued his work. 'So, do I correctly surmise that under normal circumstances, you and your sister offer something to your people that fits a *particular* need?'

'We do,' she said. 'We offer me.'

'You?' He leaned his shelled torso back, and thought. 'You speak Klip. You understand other customs. You're . . . you're their Speaker.'

Speaker warmed with the quiet joy of being understood. 'Exactly.'

'You can get access to things others can't. Go into shops where they might get turned away, or . . .'

'Help them finish the formwork to get an official pilot's licence. Get a bunch of seedlings from the nursery that didn't understand what they wanted. Track down a medical specialist for something particular. Set up a standing order with a fuel depot. Buy groceries for someone who's too nervous to go to a big market stop.'

'Are these imaginary examples, or . . . ?'

'My last five jobs.'

'Fascinating,' he said. 'That's fascinating.' He returned to the panel, twisting a wire here, loosening a clip there. 'Right, let's try that.' He went once more to the interface panel and rebooted the system. 'You still haven't answered my question, though.'

'Sorry, which?'

'What does Tracker do?'

Again, Speaker gathered all the components this answer required, and tried to filter them down to the most necessary. 'So: a ship is a family, and a ship is autonomous. We're not an instinctively hierarchal species, like many of you are. We do best in groups, but each group is an entity unto itself. We don't have any sort of larger government, or ship registry, or anything like that. We don't log flight plans, we don't submit travel routes. We just go where we need to, as we want to. That freedom is very important to us, but it also means—'

'You're hard to find.'

'Right. But that's also by design.' She paused. 'If I explain this, you have to understand it's not intended as an insult.'

'Now I'm dying to know what it is.' His face was stone, but his voice was kind. 'Don't worry. I won't take it personally.'

She continued, carefully. 'Most Akarak ships go to great lengths to not show up on anybody else's wake scan. Both in a navigational sense and a technological sense. We mask our ships' signals. We make flight plans that look nonsensical to outsiders. By and large, we avoid contact with other species as much as possible, but the side effect of that is it's hard for us to find *each other* as well. And *that's* what Tracker does. When we take on a task for someone else, we know roundabout where they're headed, and we know their data wake signature, but we don't often make a hard and fast rendezvous plan. Plans change.

Circumstances are unpredictable. And a ship that *really* wants to stay off the map might not even feel comfortable sharing their flight plan with us, beyond what system they'll be in. That's where Tracker comes in. Her speciality is tracking untrackable ships.'

'How?'

'You would have to ask her. I don't understand it at all.' Tracker had tried to explain, of course, many times, but Speaker had had as much luck understanding Tracker's monitors filled with nav charts as Tracker had made purchase with syntax.

'Well, hopefully, if we get this thing working, I'll be able to say hello, at least.' Roveg glanced at the monitor, watching the reboot progress. 'That must be extraordinary difficult, treasure-hunting your peers across the galaxy.'

'Depends on who it is and how seriously they take their privacy. Some ships don't care at all. Aversion to other species isn't a universal rule – we're not all the same, obviously. But most of us prefer to travel incognito. And that's because . . .' She paused. 'Again, please don't take offence at this.'

'You don't trust the rest of us,' Roveg said simply. 'I under-stand that completely, and I don't take offence.' He gestured at himself. 'My species' reputation hardly makes me one to judge on that front.'

'It's . . . not quite the same.'

'Isn't it? Sure, we're talking xenophobia on very different scales, but fear of outsiders is fear of outsiders all the same.'

Speaker disliked that categorisation, but in keeping with her own request, did not take it personally. 'I'm not sure I'd call it xenophobia in our case. It's just . . . experience.'

'Hmm.' Roveg considered that. 'Yes, perhaps I'm not viewing it in the proper context. My peers would argue your situation and ours boil down to the same principle, but then, they're wrong about most things.'

Now it was Speaker's turn to be curious about delicate matters. She hesitated, not sure how he'd take this question, but the ease of the conversation made her feel bold. 'May I ask why the Quelin Protectorate . . . why it is like it is?'

All the holes along Roveg's abdomen pulsed air at once. 'We could sit here for days discussing that. Do you know anything about our history? What happened after contact?'

'I know there was war, but not the specifics.'

'Right.' He idly rubbed one of his eyes with a toe as he thought. 'When we first made contact with other sapients, there was an inevitable explosion of cultural evolution, as there always is. Technology, philosophy, art, all of it in flux. You know how it goes. And as is sadly common during periods of rapid change, things that had been simmering for my species for a long time came to a boil. There was war. You can read about it, if you must, but all you need to know is that it was horrific. Cloned soldiers became one of the weapons of choice, suffice it to say, and it was a hideous mess. People died, treaties were drawn, and so on and so forth, and when it came time to cast blame, the fact that we could point to people who weren't even from our planet was deliciously convenient. It was *their* influence that had caused the fractures among us, you see, not centuries of our own inanity. It was *their* tech that fuelled our genetic wars, *their* ideas that had corrupted the sanctity of true Quelin civilisation.'

'And what's *true Quelin civilisation?*'

Roveg laughed ruefully. 'Now *that* would take tendays. There are tomes upon tomes written on the subject, and they're all equally stupid. Anyway, it became very fashionable very quickly to perform cultural purity for others, and that fashion became dogma, and dogma became law, and tada! Here we are.'

Speaker thought. 'Yet you're part of the GC. You trade. You're in Parliament. Your borders aren't closed.'

'Oh, of course not,' Roveg said. His frills bristled. 'Perish the thought that we stop *trade*. It's a relationship of greedy conven- ience, and everyone knows it. The fact that both the GC and the Protectorate are willing to quietly shelve their principles just so they can keep ore and ambi flowing is nothing short of disgusting.' He had no muscles to tense, but his body had gone rigid anyway. Speaker wondered how it felt, being unaware of your own softness. Roveg shook from head to end, as if dusting himself off. 'I cannot tell you what a constant relief it is, even decades after I left, to be in places where I can say something like that freely.'

Speaker had a word for how she felt right then: *eerekere*. A moment of vulnerable understanding between strangers. It did not translate into Klip, but it was a feeling she knew well from gatherings among her people. There was no need being expressed here, no barter or haggling or problems that required the assistance of a Speaker, but *eerekere* was what she felt all the same. She'd never felt it with an alien before. She embraced the new experience. Were Roveg an Akarak, were he linking wrist-hooks with her and opening himself in the radical way required if you truly wanted someone's help, she would hold nothing back, couch nothing in pretence. And so, she said exactly what she wanted to say next: 'May I ask what it was that led to your exile?'

Roveg was silent for a long time. Speaker feared she'd swung too far, but eventually, his motionless eyes glittered. 'I told the wrong stories,' he said.

'You said you make vacation sims.'

'Nowadays, yes. But in my younger years, I designed narrative sims, and . . . well. My political subtext wasn't as clever as I thought.'

That seemed a callous reason to drive someone out of an entire region of the galaxy, but such extremity matched what she'd been told of the Quelin, and why she and Tracker never flew through their space. 'Why did you stop telling stories?'

'I enjoy giving people templates in which they can make their own stories. Telling my own requires a mindset I just can't return to.' Roveg was quiet for several seconds. 'Just because I was right doesn't mean it doesn't hurt.' He stared off, past the garden, past the dome, all the way to the horizon. 'But you're correct. Our species – no, forgive me, our *cultures* – aren't the same at all. Quelin fear outsiders because we use them as scape-goats for the things we fear about ourselves. We bar cultural exchange because change frightens us. Whereas your people . . .' He looked at her. 'You fear outsiders because they gave you no choice in the change they forced upon you.'

'There's more to it than that,' Speaker said. 'But that's a piece, yes.'

The progress monitor chimed completion. Roveg leaned forward; Speaker did the same with her suit.

Error
Connection lost
Cause: unknown

'Agh,' Roveg moaned. 'Stars, I don't know what's wrong, that should've—'

'It's all right,' Speaker said. She was disappointed, of course, but the beak-snapping anxiety she'd felt in the shuttle had ebbed. The feeling remained as a background hum, still imagining the same horrors, still desperately wanting solutions. But she'd tamed it, for the moment. She, and the stranger who had attempted to help. 'It's enough that you tried,' she said. 'Really.'

His frills drooped with defeat, but he turned his inscrutable face to hers once more. 'I *am* sorry it didn't work. But thank you for the *rekree*, Speaker. Am I saying that correctly?'

'*Rakree*,' she said.

'*Rakree*,' he repeated.

'That's right. And yes. Thank you, as well.'

Day 237, GC Standard 307

. . . .

YOUR CONTINUED PATIENCE

ROVEG

The building was the same shape as the other pre-fab bubbles that comprised the Five-Hop, but that was where the similarity ended. The outside had been painted – in amateur fashion and drab monochrome – with images of erupting volcanoes, careening meteorites, glittering gems, and . . . and . . . some shapes. The shapes had meaning, Roveg was sure, but whatever their artist's intent had been, it was lost in the execution. He stood pondering one lopsided blob that was probably a cliff. Maybe a rock. Could also be a water tank, if you turned your head to the side. There was no way to be sure.

A sign hung above the entrance to the building, its style quite unlike that of its prodigious cousins. This sign was engraved, not printed, and embellished with thick lacquer and faux-metal highlights. A custom order, commissioned by someone who wanted it to look elegant but without the means for heavy expense.

The sign read:

THE GORAN NATURAL HISTORY MUSEUM
ESTABLISHED GC STANDARD 304
HEAD CURATOR: OOLI OHT TUPO

A beaded curtain hung beneath the sign. Roveg passed through it, taking a moment to disentangle a few of the strings from where they'd caught in the ridges of his shell. He took in his surroundings, and his heart melted. 'Oh, stars,' he chuckled to himself.

The Goran Natural History Museum consisted of a single room crammed with tables, and atop the tables lay . . . well, rocks, mostly. There were big rocks and small rocks, rocks in boxes, rocks in stacks, rocks atop sagging pedestals, shards and pebbles and vials of dirt. The ostensible exhibits were marked with placards made from the same printer as the rest of the Five-Hop's signage, and proclaimed titles like 'Planetary Formation', 'Early Eras', and 'Anthropological Relics'. This last sign was posted above the only table in the Goran Natural History Museum which did *not* contain rocks, but rather, everyday bits and bobs that appeared to have fallen out of the pockets of dozens of travellers. Every cheap gadget and forgotten trinket was displayed and labelled as though it were precious treasure. Roveg thought that perhaps, to the curator, that's exactly what they were.

Outside, someone came running – four paws, hitting the path hard. The sound grew closer and closer until at last Tupo burst through the curtain with a loud clatter, nearly getting xyr feet tangled in the beaded strings as xe skidded to a halt.

'Welcome to my museum,' Tupo gasped. There was glee in xyr voice, a sound that had been completely absent when Tupo had greeted Roveg at the airlock, or offered him cakes in the garden, or recited anything that had been xyr mother's idea. But said glee was somewhat smothered, as the child was out of breath. (Lungs were limited in that respect, Roveg had learned; he was grateful for the much more sensible layout of his multiple abdominal airways.) 'If you have – if you have any quest— whew, hang on.' Tupo rested xyr head against the back of xyr lower neck and tried to catch xyr breath. 'I was in the kitchen when I saw you come in.'

'Sorry, should I have found you before entering?' Roveg asked. He hadn't seen any signage out front about checking in or buying a ticket or anything like that. If there was one thing he was sure of about the Five-Hop, it was that there was a sign for *everything*.

'Yeah, no, it's always – it's always open.' Tupo's breaths were beginning to steady. 'It's just . . . not a lot of people come in here, so I got excited.' Xe pulled xyr head back to a respectable angle and looked at Roveg with huge, eager eyes. 'Can I give you the tour?'

Roveg's initial intent upon entering the building had been to simply take a peek at the place, and his impression once he'd come through the door had not given him any desire to stay long. But the situation had changed. Now, he had but one goal, and that was to give his full, undivided attention to the head curator. He'd have been a monster to do otherwise.

'Tupo,' he said, 'I would love to see your tour.'

The child nearly began to glow. 'Cool,' Tupo said. 'Have you been to a natural history museum before?'

'I have indeed.'

'It's really hard running a natural history museum on Gora.'

'Because visitors are so unpredictable?'

'No, because there's no life here.'

'Ah,' Roveg said. 'Yes, I can see how that might affect the study of natural history.'

The little Laru looked at xyr displays and huffed. 'Everybody has such high expectations,' xe said, delivering this opinion with the gravity of someone far more mature. 'They think natural history museums have to have fossils or plants or bugs and stuff, and I'm here to tell you that *no, they don't.*' Xe gestured proudly at xyr displays. 'Rocks are natural, and they have a history, and they're awesome.'

'I quite agree. But . . . I do have a question.'

'Okay.'

'And you'll have to forgive me, as I'm not a scientist.' Roveg said this with all the courtesy he would utilise in a professional setting. 'If your study is primarily rocks, is your field not . . . geology?'

Tupo waggled xyr neck in acknowledgement. 'That's what Mom said at first, but listen. I've done a *lot* of sims of natural history museums, and they all have the same story.' Tupo rose up and walked on xyr back legs, so as to be able to gesture with both forepaws. 'You start with planetary formation. How the planet got here.' Xe pointed to the first table, which held a stick-and-ball model of the Tren system – an easy thing to make when you only had two orbital bodies – plus an ancient scrib that was playing a pop-up pixel projection of planetary disk formation on loop. Tupo nodded at the scrib apologetically. 'I couldn't find a vid of Tren, so that's a vid of Hagarem. But planets all happen the same way.'

'Yes, I see,' Roveg said. 'And there's no shame in using a different vid. This one gets the message across. I'd say that was a good educational instinct.'

Tupo beamed and continued on. 'Okay, so then, there's rocks.'

Stars, yes, there *were* rocks, all tagged and dated diligently. *Slate, 158/306, found by Tupo. Gneiss, 6/305, found by Tupo. Calcite, 184/307, present from the Aashikset feather family.* 'Who's the Aashikset family?' Roveg asked.

'They own the *tet* house north of here,' Tupo said. 'We're neighbours, I guess. Mom gives them a discount on fuel and they give her a discount on . . . um . . . I don't know. I'm not allowed to go there yet.'

'I would imagine not.'

'Because there's sex there.'

'Yes, I'm aware of what a *tet* house is, thank you.'

'It's usually Hirikk who comes to buy fuel, and he always brings me cool rocks they find if they go outside their dome. He's nice. Anyway, you can learn a lot from rocks.' Tupo paused again as xe stared at xyr massive collection, seemingly overwhelmed by choice. 'Do you know what an igneous rock is?'

'Yes.'

'What about a sedimentary rock?'

'Yes, I know those, too.'

'Okay.' Tupo paused again, at a loss. 'Well, you can just read the labels, then.'

'I will,' Roveg said. By this, he meant he would skim them, but he kept that to himself.

'Oh, and also—' Tupo ran over to a table off to the side that held an old-fashioned portable data server and an access monitor, both of which looked like well-loved hand-me-downs. 'You can access the GC reference files here, if you want to look up something you don't know about.'

'Ah, you run a storage node!' Roveg said approvingly. 'Excellent. I have a number of friends who volunteer for the reference files, and they're always on the prowl to find people willing to maintain nodes. Keeps the whole network more robust, as I'm sure you know.'

'Yeah. I mean, I know I could just go on my scrib and access it through the Linkings, but I think this is cooler.'

'It *is* cooler. And since you can't get on the Linkings right now away, at least you've got this, hmm?' He looked back to the other tables. 'So. Explain to me how rocks fit into this omni-story you see at every museum.'

'Oh, right, okay, so . . . you have a planet. It's full of rocks, and the rocks tell you stuff about how things used to be on the planet. There basically wasn't anything on Gora, ever. Well, there were volcanoes once, but not anymore. They're dead. And there wasn't any water, so we don't have as many kinds of rocks as other places. But we do have some pretty ones from where the volcanoes used to be. Look, this is my favourite.' Tupo picked up an unpolished gemstone for Roveg to see – murky blue and flecked with black.

'That's a nice piece,' Roveg said. 'Have you ever thought about polishing it?'

'None of my rocks are polished,' Tupo said firmly. 'It removes the rock from its proper context and then people don't know what it really looks like.' Xe paused. 'Plus I don't have the stuff you need to polish them.'

'That's fair.'

'So, at other museums, after rocks, you get exhibits about

life. And the thing is, there *is* life on Gora. It just didn't *start* here.' Tupo gestured at the table of *anthropological relics*. Roveg noted a broken Harmagian piercing, an empty bottle of Whitedune, an immaculate Aandrisk feather presumably given to the child. 'It *is* natural history,' Tupo asserted. 'Life came to Gora, just not in the way . . . not in the way most people mean.'

Roveg started to grasp what Tupo was trying to say. 'You're arguing that calling your collection *natural history* rather than *geology* is valid because life *did*, in fact, establish itself here, and is therefore a key part of the planet's history.'

'Yeah. Exactly.'

'Tupo, I have to say, I've never heard that perspective before, but I truly enjoy it. You should write a thesis one day.'

Tupo made a face. 'I hate writing.'

'Well, then stick to curation, because this is a very fine museum.'

The child shuffled xyr paws. 'It's okay,' xe mumbled happily.

Roveg's gaze shifted away from the feather as a surprisingly familiar item leapt out of the crowd. 'Ah!' Roveg said, reaching forward. He picked up the three-dimensional ceramic object from the table. 'You have a poem stone! Wonderful!'

Tupo blinked at him. 'It's a what?'

Roveg looked at the label the child had affixed below the stone: *Unknown sculpture, 248/306, found by Tupo*. 'Where did you get this?' Roveg asked.

'Oh,' Tupo said. Xe looked around the floor. 'There were some other Quelin here a while ago, and they forgot it in the garden.'

Roveg tried to catch Tupo's eye. 'Did you take it for your collection before or after they left?'

The child became interested in a pebble near xyr forepaw. 'Umm . . . well . . .'

'I'm not your mother, Tupo,' Roveg said. 'You *could* always try to mail-drone it back. But theft is a long, proud tradition for many museums, so that decision's up to you.' He turned the poem stone over between his toes. It was of charming make – the sort of thing you'd buy at a tourist trap, but endearing all the same. He hoped its former owner hadn't been too sad over its loss. 'So you don't know what this is?'

Tupo quickly stuck out xyr tongue, the Laru body language for *no*.

'Do you know how Quelin writing works?'

Another blip of the tongue.

Roveg set the poem stone down and looked around for something he could use. A vial of dirt – that would do. He walked to the *Early Eras* table and pointed. 'Would it be all right if I emptied out one of these?' he asked. 'I'll clean it up, of course.'

'Uh . . . sure?'

'Thank you,' Roveg said. He emptied the vial onto the table. 'Could you assist me, please? I need this as flat as possible, and I believe your paws are much better for that task.'

Tupo did as asked, looking puzzled but intrigued. A few seconds later, xe'd provided Roveg with a flat patch of dirt.

Roveg flexed his frills. Yes, it would do. He extended a right foreleg, and with its pointed tip, he drew a neat vertical line in the dirt, dividing the makeshift canvas cleanly in two. Then, with deliberateness, he took both a left and right foreleg and began to tap tidy indentations, starting near the dividing line and then spreading horizontally in opposite directions. He completed one pair of lines, then another pair above it, then another. After a moment, he leaned his torso back up and looked at Tupo. 'What do you see?' he asked, gesturing at the patterns.

'Dots,' Tupo said.

Roveg expanded his abdomen happily. 'To you, yes,' he said. 'To me, these are sentences. This is how we Quelin write.' He pointed closer. 'Look carefully. What do you see?'

The child squinted, rubbing xyr lips together fervently as xe extended xyr head over the dirt. 'They're the same on both sides. Or . . . wait.' Xe frowned harder. 'They're kind of different.'

'Ah, you're clever, Tupo. Yes, that's exactly right.' Roveg gestured at the sentences. 'Everything I've written on the *left* side has the same literal meaning as everything I've written on the right. They are the same words. But each side represents a different means of speaking. Right now, I'm speaking to you with the vocal organ in my throat.' He tapped his exoskeleton right where it lay over his oesophagus. 'This is the only thing I use when speaking Klip. But when I speak Tellerain—'

'That's your language,' Tupo interjected.

'That's right. When I speak Tellerain, I use both my throat and my . . . hmm. You don't have a word for them in Klip. The . . . hard structures I have in the back of my mouth. They make sounds like *this*.' He rattled his mouthparts together in quick staccato, releasing a chord of loud clicks that amounted to nothing but pure gibberish.

Tupo was delighted. 'Do that again.'

Roveg obliged; the child laughed. Roveg continued with the impromptu lesson. 'Tellerain is, in a way, two languages in one. Take the word for . . .' He looked around the museum. 'Rock. What's the word for "rock" in Mululo?'

'I don't speak Mululo.'

'No?' Roveg was surprised by this. It seemed extreme for Ouloo to not teach her child xyr own official language.

'I know, like . . . a few words. But I speak Piloom with Mom.'

'Oh, my mistake. I didn't realise your mother's from Ulapot.' A small Laru agricultural colony, located in Aandrisk territory. He'd heard *of* their regional language, but never heard it spoken.

Tupo was surprised. 'Nobody ever knows Ulapot.'

'Of course I know Ulapot. They export the best redreed in the Commons. So, what's "rock" in Piloom?'

'*Oelo*,' Tupo said.

'Interesting. In Tellerain, there's only one word for "rock", but you make it in two ways. Spoken through my throat, the

word is *trihas*. Spoken with my . . . other things, the word is—'
He released a crisp set of clicks. 'Put the two sounds together,
and you get . . .' He demonstrated the layered word.

Tupo attempted to mimic the clicks with xyr tongue, and
failed spectacularly. 'I can't do that.'

'You don't have the mouthparts for it. No one does, and so
no one can speak proper Tellerain aside from us, just as no one
can fully speak Hanto or colour language. There aren't many
other sapients who make the attempt, but those that do only
speak Simplified Tellerain, which uses the mouth sounds only.'

'But that's not . . . that's not the whole word,' Tupo said.

'The meaning comes across. If you were to say *trihas*, I'd
know you meant *rock*. But the . . .' How to explain this to a
child? 'The *flavour* is missing. You know how some words just
feel better than others?'

'I guess.'

'Well, I can change the way a word feels a *lot* by just changing
the clicks. Listen again as I say *trihas*.' Roveg spoke the word
in full, throat and mouthparts together. 'That's a boring way
to put it. That's how you'd read it off of a dictionary feed.
Now, if I was telling you that the rock in question is quite
beautiful, I'd say it like this: *trihas*.' The clicking this time was
made further back in the mouth, a little sharper, a little deeper.
'But if I was annoyed at this rock, if I had just stepped on it
and hurt my toes, I'd say *trihas*.' The accompanying clicks were
exactly the same as before, only harsher, messier. Roveg exag-
gerated the sound like an operatic villain, so that Tupo could
clearly hear the difference. He gestured again at the writing in
the dirt. 'So, you see – the left side of our writing tells me the
throat sounds, the right side tells me the mouth sounds. At first
glance, you're right, they look like mirror images of each other,
because each side represents the same words. But those differences you see, like how *this* letter is higher than its counterpart
– those are directions. They communicate the feeling I'm trying
to get across.'

'So what's it say?' Tupo asked impatiently.

Roveg traced a pair of legs in the air above the words, pointing to each as he translated. 'My name is Roveg. I am with Tupo, a . . .' He paused, seeking the right words in Klip. 'An esteemed museum curator. Xe has a poem stone in xyr collection.' He looked warmly at the child. 'That's the literal meaning. But if you add in the feeling as I've written it, it will tell you that I think Tupo is brilliant and that I admire xyr collection very much.'

Tupo was so pleased that xyr fur began to fluff.

'So,' Roveg said, moving along, 'your poem stone.' He picked the object back up. 'You see?' He held it so that Tupo could look straight down the forward edge of the triangle. 'Right-side words, left-side words. This is an ancient style of writing. Before scribs and screens and whatnot, we wrote using sheets of clay. The writer would pour wet clay into a flat mould and inscribe their piece before the clay dried. It's a skill that takes a lot of practise, but it's still the loveliest way to write, because – here, look.' He directed Tupo to lean xyr face in closer. 'Do you see how the *depth* of each letter changes?'

'I guess,' Tupo said. 'Oh. Yeah.'

'This changes the word as well. These are specific directions on how the poem should be performed when read aloud.'

'So *what does it say?*' Tupo demanded.

Roveg turned the stone toward himself and began to translate. 'All right, it won't rhyme in Klip, and the meter will be awful, but it begins: *Think of home when you are far from here—*'

'No, no,' Tupo said, wiggling xyr neck. 'I want to hear what it really sounds like.'

'You won't understand it.'

'You can tell me after.' Xyr paws danced. 'I wanna hear you click again.'

Roveg laughed. 'All right,' he said. He lifted the stone to the light, and began to read.

Think of home when you are far from here
Let it be your comfort
Think of us when you are alone
Remember always our bright days
Remember song, remember joy
Remember the purple sky
Remember dark faces, old and beloved
Remember children, their—

The verse stuck in Roveg's mouth and would not leave. He'd known what the poem was on sight – the lover's farewell from the second act of *The Summer Sorrows*, one of Vemereng's most paraded classics – but it had been ages since he'd read it. There was a reason he avoided Tellerain, and classic literature, and sentimental pap like *this* especially. He'd been so caught up in humouring Tupo that he hadn't considered the dangerous territory he'd foolishly wandered into. Now that he was mired there, he could not see how to break free.

'Is that it?' Tupo asked. Xe craned xyr head right behind the stone.

'Yes, that's it,' Roveg lied. He returned the stone to Tupo, placing it in xyr cupped paws.

'That sounded really cool,' Tupo said. 'Though . . . kinda scary, also.' Xe paused. 'Mom says I shouldn't say stuff like that.'

Roveg didn't reply, though he did not take offence. His mind was elsewhere now, and this place was no longer distraction enough. 'Tupo, thank you very much for the tour. I look forward to exploring your exhibits more thoroughly later, but for the moment, I think I should return to my shuttle. I'm feeling a bit tired and could use a snack.'

'I can get you a snack, if you want,' said the ground host's child.

'No, thank you. I – I think a short rest in my shuttle will do me well.' He headed for the exit, then paused. *Remember children, their shells still white.* He turned back to Tupo. 'It really is an exceptional museum you've built,' he said. 'Gora's lucky to have you.'

He exited without another word, leaving the child to xyr scavenged treasures.

PEI

Pei walked out of the bathhouse a few hours after entering, enjoying the coolness of the filtered air. The smell of saltmoss lingered on her skin, and her freshly scrubbed scales felt smooth as soft metal. She raised her arm, admiring the intense glitter the sunlight created. She couldn't remember seeing herself this bright since her early days of adulthood, that time in her life when her body had been at its absolute best in a way her younger self hadn't remotely deserved. Ouloo certainly knew where to get the good stuff.

She glanced up at the sight of people walking toward the garden – Speaker, with her arms full of some kind of tech, and Tupo, trailing happily afterward on two legs as they pushed a cart overflowing with what appeared to be the contents of xyr entire house: cushions, light fixtures, ribbons, basically anything bright and colourful that hadn't been nailed down.

'What's all this?' Pei said, walking their way.

Tupo arched xyr neck toward her. 'Speaker's gonna make a concert!'

'A concert,' Pei echoed. 'That sounds cool.'

'Yeah,' Tupo said. The kid was excited – paws bouncing, fur fluffed. 'Speaker's brought all her stuff, and her and me are gonna share our favourite music. Mom's making snacks. Do you wanna share some music, too?'

'I think I'll just . . . be in the audience,' Pei said. This event was not going to be something she could contribute much to, but she wasn't about to squash the kid's enthusiasm. Besides, any sort of distraction was welcome at this point.

She meandered over to Speaker, who was setting her cargo down on the garden lawn. Pei looked at the equipment in question. She'd seen sound tech before – at bars, at parties, in other sapients' homes – but had no idea how to set it up, and had never paid it much attention. All the same, she asked: 'Can I help?'

Speaker looked at her, then around at her gear; she moved her head, but the mech suit stayed still. 'Uh, yes, if you like. Are you able to lift the speakers?' She made a funny expression. 'The common-noun speakers, not . . . me.'

Tupo laughed much harder at this than was warranted, chuffing through xyr nostrils in that strange Laru way.

Pei looked at the equipment. Speakers were basically talkboxes made large; that much, she knew. She picked up a fat, keg-shaped thing she was *pretty sure* was a common-noun speaker, and when proper-noun Speaker did not object, Pei knew that she'd got it right. 'Yeah, it's not too heavy,' Pei said. 'Where do you want them?'

Speaker adjusted the mech suit in order to look around the lawn. She pointed one of the suit's hands and said, 'Just evenly distribute them around the edges. Make a circle.'

Pei lugged the thing over as directed, and as she set it down, a small etching in the outer plating caught her eye. 'Are you *sure* this isn't you?'

'What?' Speaker said.

Pei pointed at the etching: a single-line drawing of an Akarak's face, carved into the metal with something thin and sharp. 'That's definitely you.'

Speaker walked the suit over, bent it down to look, and let out a laugh. 'Tracker must've done it,' she said with fond exasperation. 'That's very much her sort of stupid joke.' With this, Speaker fell quiet.

Tupo dropped the wires xe'd been trying to suss out and trotted over to Speaker. 'She'll be okay,' xe said. Xe patted Speaker's suit with a forepaw.

Speaker met Tupo's eye. 'Thank you,' she said.

Pei did not chase that subject further. This Akarak was still an enigma, a walking, breathing blank space in Pei's inner reference manual for the galaxy at large. But unaccustomed to her kind as she was, she knew better than to press on what was clearly a sore spot, especially with a stranger. It wasn't her business, plain and simple.

Still, though: Speaker's silence had dampened the previously congenial mood, and Pei understood that she was not the only one in need of distraction. 'Hey Tupo,' she said. 'What'd you think about that vid we watched last night?'

Speaker gave her a quick glance; it was hard to say, but there seemed to be an air of gratitude in it.

'Um, it was pretty good,' Tupo said. Xe rubbed xyr chin against the lower end of xyr neck. 'Some parts were kinda boring, though. I like vids that are more exciting.'

Pei leaned against one of the lighting posts. 'Yeah? Like what?'

Tupo did not need to think about this. 'Have you seen *Creds and Revenge?*' xe asked, eyes growing wide.

A laugh barked through Pei's talkbox. 'Have *you* seen *Creds and Revenge?*' she said. 'That's a . . . pretty intense vid.'

'Yeah! It's so good!' The kid was theoretically standing on all fours, but xyr feet were dancing around so much that there was never a moment in which there were more than three paws touching the ground at once. Xe whipped xyr head in Speaker's direction. 'Speaker, have you seen it?'

Speaker's attention was focused on her cockpit controls. 'I have not,' she said. 'That sounds like a bit much for me.'

Tupo *tsked*. 'You're missing out.' Xe turned xyr attention back to Pei. 'You know the part where that bad guy gets hit with a plasma cannon way up close, and he turns into a skeleton and then he explodes?'

'Yeah,' Pei said, not sure where this was going.

'Could that really happen?'

Ah. *That's* where it was going. 'Absolutely not,' Pei said.

Tupo's neck drooped. 'Not even maybe?'

'Not even maybe,' Pei said. She didn't mind Tupo asking, per se, but she did not share the kid's enthusiasm for this pattern of questioning. She couldn't tell xyr that she knew precisely why a person's skeleton would *not even maybe* be visible if you hit them with a plasma cannon, because then xe'd ask what a plasma cannon at short range would do instead, and that was not a detail a kid needed to be privy to. She didn't know how to tell Tupo that vid war and real war were not the same thing at all, that it wasn't a stylish series of heroics punctuated by kick-ass music and witty retorts. War was ugly, exhausting, and above all else, tedious – an odd thing to say about a situation in which there *were* more explosions and adrenaline than you knew what to do with. But for all the strategising, for all the narrow escapes and near misses, when you boiled it down, war was nothing more than an argument in which no one had landed on a better solution than killing each other. The suffering, at some point, became commonplace. Pei did not mind working on the edges of that. She did not mind the things she saw or the things she did. Her stomach was strong and her conscience was clean. But what did sometimes unsettle her was the disconnect between *here* and *there*. *Here* was a kid with big eyes and busy paws, for whom war was a fun story you watched before bedtime – a sugar rush, a metaphor. *There*, there were no kids. There were only exhausted adults who were desperate in a way Tupo would hopefully never be, people who wanted nothing more than for the miserable business to be done so they could go home. Except it never *was* done, and many would never see home again.

'Where is it you've travelled from, if you don't mind my asking?' Speaker said. Her suit's hands were busy with gadgets whose names Pei did not know.

'The Rosk border,' Pei said. That was as much of an answer as she was allowed to give, and she knew there were only a few reactions to this that would follow. She'd heard them all. As soon as the Rosk were invoked, people would say 'wow' or 'whoa' or 'holy shit', or anything else along those lines. Some were impressed. Some were sympathetic, in a clueless sort of way. Most people, unless they were military themselves, merely stumbled through the moment in which war stopped being a story – fun or otherwise – and instead found themselves talking to a piece of it.

But Speaker surprised her, for she did none of those things. 'Ah,' was all she said. *Ah*, as though Pei had told her she was a fruit farmer or that she'd come from the Capital or that she'd bought a new pair of shoes last tenday. *Ah*, as though Pei had confirmed something Speaker found obvious. What that might be, Pei had no idea, and Speaker offered no insights to help her along. She continued her work, saying nothing else.

Pei didn't particularly enjoy the gawking responses she was used to, but she was so accustomed to them by now that their absence puzzled her. All right, so the Akarak didn't care. Or maybe she didn't know what else to say. Most likely, she was just an alien that Pei couldn't read. So what?

The exchange stuck in Pei's teeth all the same, a single grain of sand she didn't really give a fuck about but also couldn't ignore.

'Ah, shit,' Tupo said. The phrase left xyr mouth exactly as it had left Ouloo's the night before, and it took everything in Pei's power to keep her talkbox from laughing. The kid held up a pawful of tangled wires. 'I dunno what I did.'

Pei walked over and sat down by Tupo. 'You made a mess, is what you did,' she said congenially. 'C'mon, let's sort this out.' She picked up a knot and began to work through it. As she did so, she glanced over at Speaker. The Akarak wasn't looking at her, but she shifted her beak ever so slightly, as if she, too, had something stuck in it.

ROVEG

A cup of tea sat upon the table before him. The projection walls were dark. The tea was untouched. He had made the drink with the intent of comfort, but though it was sitting right in front of him, he'd forgotten to pick it up.

There had been a time once when the galaxy had been simple. There were Quelin, and there were aliens. Quelin were people. Aliens were . . . aliens. They were *almost* like people, but not quite, and never would be. Never *could* be. You could talk to an alien, and trade with an alien, but aliens were not like you. You should be polite to them. You should respect the laws you shared.

You should not be their friends.

The thing that held a society together, Roveg had been taught, was shared narrative. A common history, a bedrock of ethics. This was the shell that held the world together, and protected all that was soft and fragile. Turning away from your own story was to open yourself to chaos. This was not academic opinion, his teachers had told him. This was observable fact. This is why good Quelin made pilgrimages to the Silent Warfields, so they could gaze upon the crumbling ruins of the civil war. The land there was still scarred from caustic artillery fire, still littered with debris. This was not to be disturbed, nor were the exoskeletons to be removed. Some of their faces remained, those of the old soldiers, their insides long eaten away by rot and time. One of these in particular was scarred into Roveg's memory – a single eye casing, partially crushed, bleached with sun, all that was visible of a body embedded in a fallen rock face. He had stared at it, living gaze meeting dead, and his teacher had stood with him, nodding with approving sympathy as Roveg rattled his mouth in the percussion of grief.

The Silent Warfields were what straying from Quelin teachings brought: destruction and decay. The Quelin could not pretend they were alone in the universe, and it was wise to cooperate with your galactic neighbours (especially when said galactic neighbours were bigger and stronger and had more toys than you). But you could not try to *think* like them. People who had tried that were lost. Wretched. They were forever torn inside, and they would never know peace.

Roveg had believed that once, wholeheartedly. As a child, he'd been determined to live a good life, a virtuous life. He heard the way adults clicked with pride when he memorised the Twelve Central Tenets or made paintings of the founding of the Grand Library. He fed on that approval as though it were the only nutrient he required. He remembered the day of his First Brand in the Watchful Hall. He'd been afraid, of course. He'd watched the older children go through it, heard their shouts and the hissing of the iron, smelled the acrid stink of scorched keratin that lingered for tendays after. One could not watch that and not be afraid. But something had happened when the Curate held the sizzling metal to Roveg's shell. There'd been pain, yes, and the panicked scent of his own body burning, but he'd looked at the joyful assembly, and he'd understood that he was just one in an immeasurable chain of people who had stood exactly where he was standing and born the same brand, that he was part of something noble and incredible and beautiful, that he could not only *look* at history but *further* it. The crowd around him roared their support as he screamed, and truly, in that moment, he had felt no hurt. For a moment, he transcended it. He was whole. He was loved.

He had tried, in his adult years, to re-contextualise that moment, to understand whatever it *really* must have been.

157

Adrenaline was the obvious main ingredient, combined with other potent neurotransmitters and the irresistibility of eusocial belonging. A heady cocktail, that. He'd had many other transcendent moments since, things that made that ghastly ritual pale in comparison. He'd seen the artwork of dozens of different planets, pieces beautiful enough to make him feel like there was no one in existence but him and the artist, each breathing air into the other. He'd seen a rare, synchronous sunset born out of three different stars. He'd seen the glittering ice of Theth's rings through the window of a plex-bottomed cruiser. He'd made friends that were family, and held infants with fur or claws or tails. He could swear in a dozen languages and sing along to songs he didn't understand. He had eaten the finest foods the galaxy had to offer. He'd had sex that bordered on the spiritual. His life was a marvel, and he would trade it for nothing.

But he'd yet to find an experience that was anything like his First Brand.

This should not have mattered. The life Roveg had built for himself was a celebration of difference, of variety, an endless exultation of questioning and learning and questioning again. He knew there would never be a point in his life in which he knew everything there was to know, and while part of him despaired at the puzzle that would never be solved, the rest of him embraced this truth fully, for what satisfaction could there be in having nothing else to ask? There was only one absolute in the universe, Roveg was (relatively) sure of, and that was the fact that there *were* no absolutes. Life was fluid, gradient, ever shifting. People – a group comprised of *every* sapient species, organic or otherwise – *were* chaos, but chaos was good. Chaos was the only sensible conclusion. There was no law that was just in every situation, no blanket rule that could apply to everyone, no explanation that accounted for every component. This did not mean that laws and rules were not helpful, or that explanations should not be sought, but rather that there should be no fear in changing them as needed, for nothing in the universe ever held still.

Roveg took great solace in this. This was the core belief of all he did and said and made. He'd given up everything for it, and he would do so again. There was nothing that could make him do otherwise, even though he knew how much pain that choice had brought to others. How much pain he'd caused himself. It was worth it, in the end. It was worth seeing the universe as it was.

But there was a great irony in that. If the root of all things was chaos and change, and if there were no true answers, if no one was capable of figuring everything out, Roveg could take *comfort* in that knowledge. Comfort, however, was not the same as peace. So in that respect, the Curates had been right: away from the Tenets, peace was something he would never know.

The wall vox switched on. 'Ouloo is at the hatch,' Friend said. 'She says she'd like to invite you to the garden.'

'Thank you, Friend. Please tell her I'll be outside in a moment.' Roveg got to his feet, and went to join the aliens. He left his tea where it was. It had gone cold anyway.

PEI

As far as parties made for only five people went, this one had turned out pretty good.

The lawn made for a decent dance floor, and the hedges surrounding it were strewn with the ribbons and craft supplies Tupo had gathered from home (Pei had assured everyone, repeatedly, that she was fine – really, fine – with the colourful decor). Ouloo had prepared desserts enough for twice their number, and was laying them out on a table off to the side as the others danced. Pei, for her part, lay on her side in the grass, propped up on one arm as she enjoyed the spectacle.

Speaker, it turned out, had an enormous repository of music at her disposal, and seemed to know her shit in that regard. She emceed from within her cockpit, selecting songs from her scrib and jamming along in her seat. She slammed her head hard when the drums kicked up, and closed her eyes blissfully as the vocals overtook them.

'Who is this?' Roveg asked, his body in motion. He moved his legs in bizarre symmetry, each pair performing the same move but no two pairs moving in tandem. The result was hypnotic – difficult to watch yet impossible to look away from.

'The Bathtub Strategy,' Speaker replied.

'I've heard the name, but – stars, they're good. You'll have to send me their Linking details.'

Speaker's eyes suggested a smile. 'If you like this, then I know *exactly* what we're playing next.' She gestured at her scrib with vigour, skimming through titles.

Tupo danced in the space between them, limbs and neck in a frenzy. What xe lacked in technique xe made up for with enthusiasm, and there was no question that the kid was having a blast. Xe caught Pei's eye, by chance, and this was enough to make xyr run across the lawn, straight toward her.

'Come on, Captain!' Tupo said. 'Come dance!'

Pei smiled blue, but made no move to get up. 'I'm happy watching you,' she said. 'I don't know how to dance to this.'

'You just . . . *move*,' Tupo said. Xe flailed xyr legs and neck chaotically; Pei guessed this was meant to look *extremely cool*. 'However you feel like.'

'Well, that's the thing,' Pei said, keeping the tone from the talkbox light. She didn't want to bring the kid down. 'Music doesn't make me feel anything.'

'Oh,' Tupo said. Xe thought. 'Do you not like this song? We can change it.'

'No, it's not this song, it's . . . music. I don't understand music. Not like you do.'

Speaker caught this, and turned the volume down. 'Does your implant not register music?'

'Oh, it does,' Pei said. 'I'm aware of the sounds. But it doesn't *mean* anything to me. It doesn't make me feel anything. My brain understands language; it doesn't understand music.'

Roveg looked at her now. 'What?'

'It's just . . . sound. Like if I'm walking through a market-place, I can hear talking, movement, and machinery. If I go to . . . I don't know, to a park, I might hear insects, or a fountain, or whatever. I know *what* those sounds are. I can identify them. So, right now . . .' She paused, angling her forehead toward one of the speakers, colours swimming as she concentrated. 'I know there are drums. Flutes. Singing. I can tell that it's complicated. I could make you a list of everything I'm processing, as I process it. But that's as far as it goes for me. You're feeling something, right? This makes you feel something?'

'Stars, yes,' Speaker said. She closed her eyes. 'It gets way down in my bones. It makes me feel . . . triumphant. Powerful. I want to swing back and forth as fast as I can. And it makes me ache, too, in a way I can't possibly explain. Like . . . like the way you feel when you're saying goodbye to someone, and you're so excited for where you're going, but you don't want to leave, either.'

'See,' Pei said. 'That's where you lose me.'

'But rhythm,' Roveg said. 'This, I know you understand. I've seen Aeluons dance at festivals. That stomping thing you do.'

'Okay, but that's – that's different.'

'How so?'

'Well . . .' She thought hard. She knew exactly how to explain this in colour; less so in words. 'I can follow a beat, and I can make one happen. But that's not about *sound*, to us. That's about sight and touch. When we dance, we can feel the vibrations through the bottoms of our feet, and the larger the group is, the more intense the feeling. And you can see the . . . the call and response, I suppose. I move one way, you move another way, we move together.'

'That *must* make you feel something.'

'Absolutely. It feels . . .' She flashed understanding blue at Speaker. 'Triumphant. Powerful. I've worn myself out doing it, and I wake up sore, and I never regret it.'

Speaker seemed to warm to this. 'That's pretty close to what music is.'

'Can you show me?' Tupo said. 'Can you dance?'

Pei hesitated. 'It'd be really weird doing it by myself. There's this whole back and forth to it. We don't dance *alone*.'

'So show me!' Tupo said. 'Look, I can be *two* Aeluons.' Xe laughed as xe stomped both sets of legs.

'I can be twenty-two,' Roveg said, deadpan. Everybody laughed at that.

Pei looked at the pleading kid for a moment, her cheeks speckling amused green. 'Okay, sure,' she said. 'Why not.' She began to unstrap her boots.

'Would you like the music off?' Speaker asked.

'If you wouldn't mind,' Pei said.

Speaker tapped her scrib, and the noise stopped.

'What are you doing?' Tupo asked.

'I'm taking off my shoes,' Pei said. 'Dancing's best done barefoot.'

Tupo watched her actions intensely. 'Shoes are so weird,' xe said. 'I can't imagine wearing shoes all day.'

'Same,' Roveg said.

'Same,' Speaker said.

Pei looked around at the group. 'They're just clothes for your feet.'

'I also can't imagine wearing clothes,' Roveg said.

'Same.' Tupo giggled.

'Fair,' Pei said. She pulled her foot free and set it in the bare grass. She couldn't help but wiggle her toes in it. Stars, it felt good. She did the same with her other foot. 'Ouloo, you joining us?'

Ouloo was in the middle of fussing over some icing that had gone askew. 'You go on, I'm content watching.'

Pei stood up, gripping the grass between her toes indulgently. The others faced her, falling into an informal line. 'All right, let me think.' She knew herself to be a good dancer – very good, to be honest, but she'd never boast about that – and she had dozens of options at her disposal. There were festival dances, funeral dances, dances that were playful, serious, sexy, sweet. But selecting something for a group of beginners who all had different types of limbs was a trick she'd never attempted before. She mentally dug around for something easy that wouldn't scare them off. 'Okay, this is a cute dance you learn as a kid. It's called . . .' She paused. There was no translating this. She thought for a moment, then gave up and pointed at her cheeks as she flashed the name of the dance. 'That. It's called *that*.'

'*Green Blue White Spots*,' Roveg said. 'Marvellous. Teach us *Green Blue White Spots*.'

Pei laughed. 'Okay, to start, I'm going to slide my left foot forward.' She demonstrated. Tupo hopped up on xyr back legs and started to mimic. 'No – no, don't do what I'm doing. I'm the leader. Your job is to *respond* to me, not copy me. I slide my left foot, and now *you* – you slide your right foot back. Like this.' She turned her back to them, performed the correct response, then turned back around.

Tupo slid xyr back paw away, wobbling a bit. Roveg took a step back with all the abdominal legs on one side. Speaker thought, pulled a few controls, and made her *suit* slide a foot back.

'Awesome,' Pei said. 'Now, I do *this*.' She lifted her foot and slammed it full-sole onto the ground. 'And you—' She turned around again and performed the response: two equally hard stomps. 'Do that.'

And so they went, doing *this* and *that*, learning the pattern, learning the rhythm, repeating sequences faster and longer each time. Her students laughed, Ouloo clapped her forepaws to the beat, and Pei blossomed in sparkling green. The vibrations made by alien feet felt so strange as they travelled through the dirt to the soles of her feet, but it was an oddness that delighted her. She'd danced *Green Blue White Spots* at parties more times than she could count, but always with her own kind, never with other species.

Wait, she thought as she continued to lead. *That's not true.* She'd taught Ashby to dance, once, during one of their trysts on Port Coriol. They'd shared a snapfruit tart in bed. She'd laughed the brightest shades at stories about his techs, and he'd listened with such softness as she told him about where she'd been. He'd touched her colours as they moved. She'd played with the curls on his head. And after all of that and so much more, she'd taught him to dance. Not this dance, though. She'd taught him – well, she'd taught him *Deep Blue Light Grey Soft Blue Black*, a dance for lovers. Neither of them had needed to take off their shoes then. They'd gotten rid of those hours before, along with their clothes.

'Am I doing it right?' Tupo said. Xyr neck was bent way down so xe could watch xyr own feet as they stomped.

Pei snapped back from the memory and cheered the kid on. 'Ha, yeah! You've got it! And now from here, we do *this*.'

She fell back into the rhythm, and her thoughts drifted once more to memory – not to Ashby, but to her creche. To when *she'd* learned to dance. Not that it had happened in one day. Dance lessons were a constant part of her childhood, both in school and at home. The whole family had taken part at the creche, but Father Gilen had been the best dancer, by far, and she fondly recalled a time when he'd picked her up, put her feet on top of his feet, held her steady by her shoulders, and danced so that she could feel the rhythm done properly. She couldn't see his face, but she could see her father Le watching her across the circle, swirling blue with love and pride. *You're going to be a great dancer, Pei*, he'd said. *You'll turn everybody's head at Shimmerquick. I bet you'll—*

Pei missed a step as Father Le's words landed in her head, heavy as the slam of a foot. She froze in place. The others were still dancing, demonstrably, but to her, they seemed to freeze as well. Her implant buzzed with their chatter, but she didn't parse the sounds. Words and noise became one and the same.

No, she thought. *That can't be it.*

Her heart thudded in her chest, and it had nothing to do with the dancing.

'Are you all right?' It was Speaker, her suit standing still, her tiny head cocked to the side.

Roveg and Tupo looked at Speaker, then to Pei. They stopped as well. 'Did we do it wrong?' Tupo asked.

Pei shook her head. 'I'm so sorry,' she said. 'I, um . . .' Her cheeks swam hot and fast, and her thoughts raced along with them. 'I'm sorry, I'm not – I'm not feeling well.'

Ouloo stepped forward, fur fluffing with concern. 'Do you need help?'

'No, I'm fine. I just, um . . . I'm so sorry, I need to . . . go

The Galaxy, and the Ground Within

get something.' She did not leave room for questions. She did not care if they thought her strange. She picked up her boots, turned around, and walked barefoot back toward her shuttle, trying not to run.

SPEAKER

'Do you think she's all right?' Ouloo asked, taking a seat as she watched Captain Tem walk back toward the shuttlepad.

'She strikes me as someone who can take care of herself,' Speaker said. She flicked through band names on her scrib as if perusing a cupboard full of spices. There was Orange Fizz, Five on Five, Augment – *Ah,* she thought. *There we go.* 'Tupo, I want to keep seeing those cool moves of yours,' she called as she conjured the song.

Grinding beats and the soaring wail of strings poured forth, sparking an instant fire in Speaker's belly. Roveg let out a loud series of escalating clicks – the lungless version of a cheer. 'Yes!' he cried, flexing his abdominal plates in time with the music. 'Oh, Speaker, *excellent*. You have excellent taste.'

She swelled with pride at this. 'You know Augment?'

'Oh, of course. I saw them play live at a sim launch two standards ago.'

'*Ugh*,' Speaker said enviously. 'I'd love to have seen that.'

Roveg began to sink into the music, moving each pair of legs along his torso in a different yet complementary pattern. 'Well, if you're ever in the neighbourhood of Chalice, let me know. We could summon a few bands, invite some interesting people, have a proper little soiree.' The legs along his abdomen joined the party, marching in place in a mathematical fashion.

Speaker didn't know what to say to that. She wondered if it was the fancy kind of thing Roveg said to everybody. It would be in character for a person with a home big enough for *parties with live bands* to throw empty invitations around, for the sake of politeness and posturing. But extravagant though Roveg might be, she also couldn't help but feel that he *was* genuine, and that his offer was as well. Perhaps it wasn't posturing. Perhaps he was simply a man who knew he had much, and enjoyed sharing it with others. 'I might just do that,' she said. Her reply wasn't empty, either. If he meant it, so did she.

'Turn it up!' Tupo cried raucously. Xe stomped xyr feet in a furious pitter-pat, as though trying to put out a fire.

'Yes!' Roveg agreed.

'Not too loud,' Ouloo pleaded Speaker. The request was good-natured, but delivered with the weight of someone who spent all day wrangling an already loud child.

Speaker gave Ouloo an understanding look, and nudged the music up *just* a bit more. She laughed as both paws and shelled legs responded accordingly, intensifying their movements. The Quelin and the Laru's dancing styles were discordant as could be, and yet, somehow, the sight of them together made a strange sort of sense.

Ouloo did not get up to dance, but she bobbed both head and neck from where she sat, watching her child's goofy moves with unmistakable adoration. 'Stars, I love that kid,' she sighed.

'You two are an interesting pair,' Speaker said, 'if you don't mind my saying.'

'How so?' Ouloo asked.

'Well, you are just a *pair*, right?'

'Yep,' Ouloo said happily. 'It's just us.'

'May I ask why?' Speaker hadn't spent much time with Ouloo's species, but she had seen their homes in spaceports: large, communal buildings that belonged to no one and served all Laru in the neighbourhood (an arrangement Speaker could easily understand). And yet, here were Ouloo and Tupo, tucked away in a literal bubble that belonged only to them. It reminded Speaker in some ways of Tracker and herself, but she was sure the context could not be more different.

Ouloo thought for a moment. 'You don't speak any of *our* languages, right?' she asked.

'No, unfortunately,' Speaker said. 'All I know about them is they've got a lot of vowels.'

Ouloo laughed heartily. 'That they do,' she said. 'They don't have much in common, but there's one thing true for all of them: we don't have a word for *family*. We have lots of words for groups – sizes of groups, people who hang out together often . . .' She trailed off.

'What?'

'I don't know how to translate this type of . . . of word. I'm not sure it *has* a translation in Klip.'

Speaker was immediately interested; these were her favourite kinds of words. 'What's the gist?'

'*Moh*. It's a specific kind of noun, and it means . . . um . . .' Ouloo frowned. '*Gathering mood*, I guess? *Mood* isn't quite right. *Gathering sense*. Or . . . mmm!' She bobbed her neck definitively as a connection was made. 'Gathering *flavour*. That works.'

'Gathering flavour,' Speaker said, savouring the new concept. 'Give me an example.'

'Well, like . . . an energetic crowd, we have a *moh* for that. Like a crowd at a big party. Or a small group of good friends. A group of young people who do foolish things. A group that likes to have sex with each other. A group of people all keeping to themselves within a shared space. These are all types of *moh*. Is this making sense?'

'Yes. I love it.'

'Do you have anything like it in Ihreet?'

'No, we don't.'

'I didn't think so,' Ouloo said. 'I haven't met anybody else who has *moh*. But see, there is no *moh* for *family,* because we don't . . . have that concept. I know the rest of you draw those lines in many different ways, but we don't. The only concept Laru have of family, among ourselves, is *other Laru*. Our *species* is a family. On *that* level, we understand, but anything smaller than that is not something we traditionally *do*.'

'I see,' Speaker said. She turned that idea over and around. 'That's . . . that feels somewhat overwhelming to me. Not in a bad way.'

'How so?'

'To me, family is the group within your ship, but there are . . . tiers of a sort within that. Siblings are paramount. Twins, specifically – the person you hatched alongside. That's . . .' *That's the other half of yourself,* she intended to say, but the words evaporated as the worry she'd worked so hard to distract herself from took the opportunity to return to the forefront.

Ouloo reached out a paw and placed it on Speaker's suit. A detached gesture of reassurance, given that she wasn't actually touching Speaker, but the intent was appreciated all the same. 'Roveg told me about the sib tower,' Ouloo said kindly. 'I put an alert on my scrib that'll let me know the *second* signal's restored. You'll be the first to know. I know that's not much, but—'

'No, it helps,' Speaker said. It really did. Ouloo seemed the type to wake someone in the middle of the night over something like that, which was exactly what Speaker wanted.

Ouloo bobbed her neck in acknowledgement. 'So. Siblings first, for you. And then . . .'

'Then your mother. You always, always honour and respect your mother, even if you don't like her.'

'Hmm!' Ouloo said. 'I like that. You should tell Tupo.'

Speaker laughed. 'Beyond that, everyone you share a ship with is family on an equal level. What you're describing about your people – about *your* notion of family – feels like the same thing I feel toward the shipmates I grew up with, but on a scale of millions. Billions. However many of you there are.'

'I have no idea how many of us there are. We've spread so much, there's no way of knowing. But yes, that's the idea. Laru are family.' She swung her head around to watch her child. 'And that's why I don't live with them.'

'I don't understand,' Speaker said.

Ouloo tipped her face upward, staring at nothing in particular as she spoke. 'The closest concept we have to family is this saying: *Laru are bone, and Laru are blood, and bone and blood are one.* It really doesn't have the same punch in Klip, but I think you get it. The way it comes across in Piloom, it paints this image of Laru as distinct from all others. That idea made sense when we were one sapient species alone on one single planet. It means that we must take care of each other, and learn from each other, and love everyone we encounter the same as anyone else we meet – even if we don't, as you said, *like* them much. But . . . oh, stars, how to explain this . . . there's something in the nuance that makes it feel . . . insular.'

'I don't think of your species as insular,' Speaker said. Every Laru she'd ever encountered had been embedded in the thick of multispecies life. She saw them as enthusiastic immigrants, wherever they went.

'I know what you're saying, but . . . ah, I have it.' She stamped a paw with confirmation. 'Laru are bone and blood and so on, but you'd never use that phrase toward other species. You just . . . wouldn't say that. It'd sound wrong. And we don't use the term *species* toward ourselves. There are Laru, and Laru are just . . . Laru. *Species* are . . . all the rest of you. *You,* versus *us.*'

'So . . . Laru are family, other species are friends?' Speaker said.

'Yes! Exactly. And I think that's wrong. It's completely wrong! If we are out here to benefit from all the rest of you, to learn everything we can and become part of your lives and follow your example, then you *must* be blood and bone, too. You must *also* be family. I wanted Tupo to understand that – to *truly* understand that. I thought the best way to do that would be to remove other Laru from the equation entirely, give xyr a childhood full of nothing *but* other species. What could be a better education than that?'

'I suppose,' Speaker said slowly. She wasn't on board with this idea, but wasn't about to insult Ouloo over a mere difference in principle. 'But then, the trade-off is xe'll never know Laru ways of doing things.'

Ouloo scoffed at this, batting it away as though it were a troublesome bug she'd seen before. 'Of course xe will. Or xe can, if xe wants to. Xe'll grow up one day, and wherever xe wants to go, xe'll go. If xe wants to embed xyrself in a Laru neighbourhood, xe absolutely can. But until then, xe's going to learn all there is to learn about *you*. I mean, look!' She gestured proudly toward Tupo, dancing xyrself breathless in the blue-shelled company of a laughing Quelin. 'What would xe learn sitting in a stuffy interspecies-relations class that xe isn't learning ten times better here?'

Speaker considered this. 'I have to say, Ouloo,' she said. 'I didn't expect you to be such a radical.'

Ouloo beamed. 'Ha!' she said. 'Oh, I like that. I'm keeping that.' She sat glowing for a moment, then got to her feet and hurried over to the others, doing a waving dance as she went. Roveg let out a clicking cheer, Tupo laughed, and the three of them danced all the harder, an uncountable number of limbs trampling the formerly pristine lawn.

Speaker smiled, turned up the music, and joined them.

PEI

Pei rushed into her shuttle the moment the hatch opened, beelining to the med room. She switched on the patch scanner, sat down on the *eelim*, rolled her sleeve, pushed up her wristwrap, and . . .

. . . hesitated.

There's no way, she thought. The only colour in her cheeks was anxious red.

With a breath and a quick swipe, she pressed the scanner against her wristpatch. The scanner flashed successful contact, then cycled lights back and forth as it processed the information transmitted by the imubots patrolling her bloodstream.

The scanner's screen flashed colours in question:

What kind of assessment do you require?
- *Basic check-up*
- *Illness diagnosis*
- *Injury assessment*
- *Reproductive check-up*
- *Other/custom (warning: only use this option if you are a medical professional or have medical field training)*

Pei swallowed, then selected *Reproductive check-up*.

The lights cycled. The scanner hummed against her palm. She could feel her heart, beating harder and harder and—

The screen flashed completion.

Pei read the results.

She reset the device.

She ran the scan again.

She read the results.

She ran a diagnostic on the device.

The device was fine.

She reset the device.

She ran the scan again.

She read the results.

Spoken languages had words for moments like this, and Pei knew a great many of them. There was *bosh* in Klip, *hska* in Reskitkish, *fok* in Ensk. But Aeluons did not have profanities in their native language, for the concept simply didn't translate. For her, frustration existed beside her nostrils, debates blossomed near her jawline, insults roared from two spots straight down from her eyes. Spoken words were something separate from the speaker, something loosed into the air. When your words were embedded in your flesh, when they existed as an intrinsic piece of you, how could any of them be considered profane?

So instead of barking something cathartic and crass, Pei's cheeks erupted in red and yellow – a reflexive display, at first, but she indulgently held the chromatophores in place, venting with a dash of purple.

Her skin didn't look good because of the fucking scale scrub. She was shimmering.

She lay down and let the *eelim* decide what shape she needed to be held by. Nervously, she pushed up her shirt and lay her palm against her skin. She ran her fingers over the familiar scales and scars, and nothing felt different at all. But somewhere within her, the scanner had said there was – for the first time ever – a fully formed egg, and that egg was making her body pump out hormones that were screwing with her abdominal muscles and the shine of her skin. How had it not even occurred to her? The symptoms of shimmer had been drilled into her as a kid, and there'd been a time in her late adolescence when every random cramp or odd angle of light had made her go *oh stars, is it happening?* But she'd been too young for it then, and was on the cusp of too old now, and she'd long figured, over the decades of nothing happening, that she was one of the many who wouldn't.

Why the fuck was it happening now? Here? On top of everything else? Was this *really* the best time her body could come up with?

Her head swam. She felt like the shuttle was upside down, or that the gravity had been switched off. *It's a lot to take in,* her father Gilen told her and her siblings in an old, old memory. *Your shimmer doesn't care about your job or your travels or whatever plans you had. It's a wonderful thing, but shifting gears like that is stressful, and that's why it's so important for us to make all the mothers who come here feel like this is their home for a little bit.*

Pei remembered them, the women who'd come to the creche. Some had been nervous. Some had been shy, or quiet, or in a hurry. But most, she remembered, were really happy. They seemed it, anyway. It was hard not to be happy when you were on six tendays of culturally mandated vacation that every job in existence bent itself backward to accommodate. Six tendays of sex and pampering until it was time for you to lay your egg and get back to your life. Six tendays of knowing that you were doing something vital for the species, something you were so privileged to do, something your friends would throw a party for once you were back home. Pei had thrown a lot of parties like that for crewmates over the years.

She pressed her palm down, even though she knew she wouldn't be able to feel it. The shell wouldn't harden until the egg was fertilised. It was just a soft ball of protein and instructions at this stage, which was a bizarre thing to picture within herself. She thought instead of her creche's incubation pool, full of greenish-white speckled-shelled marvels about the size of an adult's fist. The light in there was kept low, but sometimes one of her fathers would lift one out of the water with heartbreaking gentleness and hold it up to the window so you could see the extraordinary being inside shift and pulse. She and her siblings had been encouraged to look at that, to hang out in the pool room whenever they pleased (so long as they didn't touch). Her fathers wanted no secrecy in the matter, especially not for the girls and *shon* who would produce eggs of their own one day.

Four tendays. Pei had four tendays to get this egg fathered. After that point, the window would close, the egg would break down and be reabsorbed, and . . . that would be that. Opportunity lost. For most would-be mothers, there was only the one chance. This was Pei's, apparently. She closed her eyes and pushed out what felt like every breath she'd ever taken.

Why *now*?

Pei thought about her mother, Seri. She'd never met her, but she carried her genes and her name, and knew her story well. Unlike her creche siblings, Pei had no biological relation to any of her fathers at the Tem creche; she'd been *raised* by them, not *made* by them. Seri, the story went, had been a soldier on deployment when she'd started to shimmer. Typically, soldiers entering shimmer were shipped out of combat immediately, but Seri was the commander, and the situation was one of those where she just *couldn't*. So, she'd engaged in what translated as *wild fathering*. One of Seri's comrades, a *shon* named Tova, had been the obvious pick for the task, given their close friendship, but Tova had been female at the time. Undeterred, Tova took herself to the medic, popped a hormonal cocktail, went through the shift as fast as medically possible, and had a few respectful, practical rounds of sex with his friend. The egg that had been pre-emptively named *light blue glass blue misty green* – in the Aeluon naming language, Gapei – was then laid in a portable emergency incubator and ferried back to uncontested space, where it was placed in the happy collective hands of the Tem creche fathers.

Pei had been told the story many times, both from her fathers (who constantly reminded her that having a *shon* parent gave her good luck), and from Tova herself, who had personally come to the creche one summer day to deliver the news that Seri had been killed in combat. Pei hadn't been old enough then to understand what that news actually *meant*, but not having a living mother was of no concern to her. Some children at the creche got visits from their mothers – both regular and sporadic – but just as many did not. This didn't matter either way to an Aeluon child. A mother was a nice thing to have, but then, so was a best friend, or a close sibling, or a father you were particularly attached to. Nobody had the same mix of people in their lives. There were no requirements when it came to what constituted a family.

And yet . . . Pei, as a child, had sometimes thought about the fact that none of the fathers at the creche had made her.

It was the smallest of bothers, even then, and anyway, it shouldn't have mattered. All three of her fathers were hers in equal measure, and that would've been true even if she'd shared a set of chromosomes with one of them. Any child raised by a father was *his* child, and all the children understood this. But sometimes, as a girl, Pei had taken note of the similarities that were expressly not spoken of – the way her brother Kam laughed like Father Le, the fact that Dux and Tre had the exact same eyes, the way her siblings Hib and Malen looked practically identical despite being four years apart. Pei looked like no one at the creche, and though this did not make her feel any less loved, it did, on occasion, make her feel slightly unanchored. She wanted to feel that through-line, unremarked upon as it was. Once she'd learned about shimmer and how it all worked, she'd made the firm decision that whenever her time came she'd go to a creche and have her egg fathered properly. It was better, sometimes, to have an unremarkable story.

But now, here she was, stuck on a nothing planet in the middle of nowhere, with no idea how far away the nearest creche was, facing down the strong possibility that she was going to have to— a realisation hit her, and she covered her face with her hand. Fucking hell, she was travelling alone. Her ship wasn't nearby. If this had happened two tendays ago, she would've asked her pilot Oxlen to help her take care of it, and he would've said yes, and they'd have a good laugh at each other afterward, because that's what friends did. But Oxlen wasn't here, or any of the rest of her crew. If there weren't any creches nearby, she'd have to find . . . someone.

Just . . . *someone.*

The idea made uncomfortable yellow seep slowly across her cheeks, but if that's how it was, that's how it was. Gora was a crowded planet, and she'd seen plenty of Aeluon ships in orbit. Maybe Ouloo would know someone. Pei relaxed a touch at this idea. All right, it didn't have to be a *complete* stranger, just a stranger that the relative stranger she was docked with now could vouch for as being *decent.*

She wrapped her forearms across her face.

She didn't want to talk to Ouloo about this. Oxlen wasn't there, but if he had been, she wouldn't have wanted to talk to him either. She didn't want her friends or her fathers or the mother she'd never met.

In that moment, the only person she wanted to talk to was Ashby.

. . . .

THESE DISRUPTIONS
WERE UNANTICIPATED

Node identifier: 4443-115-69, Roveg
Feed source: Galactic Commons Reference Files – Local Access/
Offline Version (Public/Klip)
Node path: 239-23-235-7
Node access password: Tup0IsGr3at

Archival search: Akarak history and culture
Top results:
  Akari (planet)
  The Harmagian Colonial Era
  Harmagian colonisation of Akari
  The Hashkath Accords
  Galactic Commons Membership Hearings (Akarak, GC standard
    261) Ihreet
  Akarak anatomy
  Modern Akarak diaspora and recorded subcultures

Selected file: Galactic Commons Parliamentary Session, public record
3223-3488-5, recorded 55/261 (highlighted text – Akarak represent-
ative)
  Encryption: 0
  Translation path: 0
  Transcription: [vid:text]

Effective immediately, the Akarak Gathering is formally closing
our negotiation channels with the GC Parliament, and with-
drawing our pending application for GC membership. If this
news comes as a surprise, allow us to remind you of our history
with your government.

Following the signing of the Hashkath Accords, the Sapient
Sovereignty Act went into effect, in which all homeworlds
colonized by Harmagian invaders were returned to their original inhabitants. Akari, of course, had no relevant natural
resources nor sustainable ecosystems left at this point, making

it impossible for us to survive there. We requested a supply line from the GC, in which the resources necessary to rebuild and continue life on Akari would be delivered to us as needed. This request was refused on the basis that the Colonial Wars had put severe strain on existing resource stockpiles, and there was no surplus to be spared. Your needs were greater than ours, in effect. Instead, we were granted refugee status in what you had designated as your space. Eventually, our repeated demands for citizenship were heard, and we were promised a new system to settle in.

We have waited nearly two centuries for this.

Our environmental needs were too challenging, you told us at first. We have searched and searched, but have not yet found a suitable world.

Then build us a world, we said. Terraform a planet for us, as you have done for yourselves.

We have a new law, you said. The Biodiversity Preservation Agreement. It is now illegal to terraform planets that have so much as a microbe on them, as we don't want to disrupt future evolutionary pathways.

Surely, we said, our extant species is more important than a hypothetical biosphere that may or may not arise a billion years from now.

It is the law, you said.

There must be a solution, we said. Our children are hungry. The Harmagian ships we scavenged are old and breaking. You give us rations and tech, but we need a world. We need a home. We need to be able to provide for ourselves. Give us habitat domes. Orbiters. Something.

Those kinds of concessions require you to have an organisational structure that we can interface with, and we don't understand yours, you said. You have no formal government.

Fine, we said. We'll make a government for you. We'll make an organisation you will recognise.

We're still confused, you said. We were negotiating with your representatives, and then we had to file motions and wait for processes and debate with each other, because that is the only way to do things, in Parliament. We've come back with options, but we don't know who to talk to now.

That's because you took five standards to do so, and the representatives you were working with grew old and died. Someone new had to take their place.

We can't negotiate like this, you said. Every time we talk to you, we have to start over. How are we supposed to negotiate without consistency?

Indeed. Let us discuss consistency.

The only consistency we have had from you is the word *no*. The only matter in which the GC has proven itself constant is in explaining to us why the things we ask for are impossible. And yet, elsewhere, you have proved yourselves extremely capable of creating possibilities. We have all seen the news about the Human species being granted full GC membership. The Human species, which destroyed its own world and which no one in the GC knew existed seventy-five standards ago. You will grant them full rights. You will give them a star to park their ships around. You will allow them to build colonies. When we expressed our outrage about this, we were told that the circumstances were so very different with them. Humans breathe the same air you do. Their ways were easier for you to understand. They don't die in the middle of political talks.

How convenient for you, to at last work with a species whose bodies are compatible with your bureaucracy.

Our time in this galaxy is, as you have constantly reminded us, limited. We will no longer waste it on waiting for you to do what is right.

SPEAKER

The sound of an incoming message took Speaker from dead asleep to wide awake in the span of a digital chime. She grabbed her scrib from where it had lain beside her as she slept. She read the text, and hope immediately shifted into confusion.

> *A mail drone has arrived.*
> *Do you accept this delivery?*

Speaker squinted at the screen. That had to be a mistake, a misfire of some random satellite dying above. She dismissed the alert, set the scrib down, rolled over, and shut her eyes.

A few seconds passed before the scrib chimed again.

> *A mail drone has arrived.*
> *Do you accept this delivery?*

Speaker clicked her beak with annoyance. There was no way this could be a legitimate signal. Even if that were possible with the comms network in pieces, she hadn't ordered anything. Who would be sending her cargo *here*?

'Display sender details,' she said to the scrib. She anticipated nonsense in reply.

4443-115-69, the screen read. *Sender: Roveg.*

Speaker remained confused, but intrigue crept in.

'Accept delivery,' she said, and got out of her hammock.

The boxy drone that came through the airlock was unlike any she'd seen before. It was small, for a start – smaller than Speaker herself, and a far cry from the huge delivery crates she and Tracker usually had to clamber up. The drones she was accustomed to always flew themselves in and landed on the floor, but this one, in contrast, *walked*. The drone had what looked like a flight module on the back, but the loco-motion it currently utilised was that of ten mechanical legs bent out from the sides of the box, marching along in steady obedience. The style of movement was undeniably Quelin, an impression Speaker likely would've had even if the sender of this cute little thing had been unknown. And it *was* cute, in an eerie way. As soon as it was clear of the hatch, it folded its legs up and threw its lid open, as if to say, *Hello! I've arrived!*

Speaker crawled over to the drone, peered inside, and was filled with wonder. The box contained food, none of which she recognised but all of which looked beautiful. There were yellow things and blue things and white things and leafy things – all fruits and vegetables, seemingly – cut into crescents and spirals, some raw, some cooked, some dusted with sugar or spice or salt. Each culinary mystery was packaged in a neat bundle of translucent wrapping and tied with thin, shiny ribbon. She had no idea what any of it was, no idea how to eat it, and no idea why this was being given to her. This reaction had apparently been anticipated, because resting atop the enticing contents was a small box that *wasn't* food. It had no lid, no visible seams, only a small button and a hand-printed message that read *Press this*.

She pressed it.

The box popped open, and as Speaker jumped back, a burst of confetti-like pixels shot out, danced around, then dove back inside. The device extended an arm upward, and from this, a written message in a rectangular frame projected into the air above it.

Good morning, Speaker! I was hoping you might join me aboard my shuttle for breakfast. As I know you're unable to leave your suit, I thought perhaps you could pack these into your cockpit and join me in that fashion. I tried to make everything small enough to fit into your compartment (and hope I estimated correctly). I also took the liberty of researching what your species can safely eat, so I'm fairly confident all of these will be suitable for you (though, as I'm sure you know your needs best, the ingredients are printed on the ribbons on each package, just in case).

If this idea doesn't suit, or you simply don't feel like coming by, please enjoy these tidbits in your own time and your own space. I will not take offence.

Your temporary neighbour,

Roveg

Speaker sat in stunned silence. She picked up one of the bundles and held it in both hands. Beneath the wrapping, there were long, artful curlicues of something purple and earthy, flecked with green seeds and cut with a steady hand. Or steady toes, rather. Whatever Quelin appendages were called.

She placed the bundle back in the box with care, and went to ready her suit.

PEI

Ouloo was not difficult to find. Pei spotted her with a paint tube in her forepaw, touching up the fuel shed where it had been worn by the clumsy comings and goings of algae barrels.

'Can I help?' Pei said as she approached.

Ouloo craned her neck around. 'Captain Tem! Are you feeling better?'

Pei freckled yellow and red, a touch embarrassed over her exit the night before. Making a fuss was not her style. 'Yes, I'm fine, thanks. Some good sleep put me right. It was just time lag, I think.'

This was entirely untrue, because Pei had barely slept at all, and wasn't time lagged in the slightest, but the excuse seemed to work for Ouloo. 'Oh, you wouldn't be the first. I had a Human here two tendays ago who was so out of sync he slept right through his turn in the tunnel queue.' She raised herself on her back legs so she could paint a high-up spot. The effort made her pant ever so slightly.

'Can I help?' Pei asked again.

'Oh, no, no, no,' Ouloo said. 'I've got it, and I wouldn't dream of putting guests to work.'

'What if I *like* painting?' Pei asked. 'What if painting's the thing I want to do most right now? You said if there was *anything* I wanted, I should tell you.'

Ouloo threw her a sceptical look. 'That's cheating.'

Pei laughed and picked up another spray tube from the nearby cart of paint supplies. 'I can only take so many baths, Ouloo. And I could do with something other than sitting around.'

'Well . . .' The Laru huffed. 'Fine, if you *really* want to.'

Pei didn't feel one way or the other about painting, but it *was* something to do, and honestly, she welcomed the opportunity to help. She felt sorry for Ouloo, trying so hard to be a good host in the midst of all this. 'Any news beyond the emergency updates?' she asked. She searched the wall for the nearest scuff.

'No, nothing,' Ouloo sighed. 'I wish they'd let us leave the dome. I've been wondering how my neighbours are doing. I mean, I'm sure we're all in the same boat, but it's uncomfortable not being able to check in.'

'Your friends didn't send a note back?'

'No. Which is good, honestly, because their lights have been on, and them not sending anything means they're busy but not in a bad way. Or the *worst* way, I suppose. I wish I could say that's made me stop worrying.'

Pei began to spray paint as needed – a simple task, but quietly pleasant. 'Do you know all your neighbours well?' she asked.

'Oh, we have a wonderfully supportive community. It's interesting – everybody's in their own bubble, and everything is designed for self-reliance. The only things we share between ourselves are, well, comms and power.' She gave a small laugh at these, the things they no longer had. 'It's all very to-each-their-own here, but we help each other out. Someone might look after someone else's comms while they're away, or loan each other some spare tech if needed. Tupo goes over to the gambling house across the way every couple of tendays to practise xyr Hanto.'

'Good for xyr,' Pei said. Hanto was a smart thing for the kid to have in xyr pocket, no matter where xe wanted to go. (Not that Laru *had* pockets, but still.)

Ouloo gave her a flat look. 'Xe's dreadful at it,' she laughed, 'but then, so am I, and at least xe's trying. Xe could be trying *harder*, but . . .' She trailed off, and in doing so, said all that was needed about her losing battle against preadolescence.

'Anyway. The point is, it's a great bunch of people on Gora. Or in this corner of it, at least. It's made me twitchy the past few days, not knowing how everyone else is doing. Nice to know I *can* take care of almost everything on my own—' she gave a nod in the direction of the solar generator and the life support system '—but that isn't how I like it. Did you see people flashing their lights last night?'

'Oh,' Pei said, her inner eyelids blinking. 'I saw some lights on the horizon, but I thought it was just . . . power trying to come back on. Or something.'

Ouloo stuck out the tip of her tongue in the negative. 'That was on purpose. I don't know who started it. I saw someone's lights flash, and then I saw someone else do the same in reply, so I turned *my* lights off and on four times, and then we just . . . did that for a while.'

'Was it some kind of code? Four for okay, three for help, that kind of thing?'

'No, not at all. Though that kind of thing would be smart to have, in hindsight. No, we weren't saying anything. Or at least I wasn't. We were just letting each other know we were there, I think. That's what I got out of it, anyway.' She bobbed her neck approvingly. 'Made me feel a little better.'

Sympathetic though she was to Ouloo feeling isolated, the conversation had arrived at a point of opportunity for Pei to ask what she most wanted to. She saw no reason not to pounce on it. 'Are there any Aeluons living nearby?' she asked easily.

'Oh, yes.' Ouloo turned and pointed. Pei followed the line of her paw out past the dome and through the desert. 'Tobet works at the Halfway Hotel. And there's Sila over at the art walk – you can't see the dome from here, but it's a hop and skip away. Let's see . . . I know of several Aeluons on the TA orbiter. One's called Sen, she's usually the one who renews my business licence. And, of course, there are lots of places here that mainly cater to you folks. There's a city field on the other side of the planet. We do get a lot of you passing through.'

Pei mulled that over. She was hardly the only Aeluon stuck on Gora, but walking into a city field and chatting up random people with her predicament was the last solution she wanted. 'Any of them in particular you know well?' she asked. She worked to keep the tone of her talkbox light.

'Tobet and I are quite friendly. She sent over that jenjen cake I had out when you all first got here—'

Pei tuned out everything that came after the female pronoun, because no matter how good her jenjen cake was, Tobet would be of no help to her. 'I see,' she said once Ouloo had finished. She paused, trying not to tip her hand too much. 'What about men? Or *shon*?'

Ouloo thought about this. 'Well, there's Kopi at the tea garden. I don't know—' She paused, stumbling on something. '*Shon* don't use neutrals, right? I don't know what Kopi is right now, so I don't know what to call – not *xyr*, but—'

Pei came to the rescue. '*Shon* only use neutrals when in the middle of a shift. Whichever gender Kopi was the last time you saw Kopi is the polite thing to use.'

'Ah, thank you. I'll remember that. In any case, I don't know Kopi well at all, beyond running into him on the orbiter and at parties and whatnot, but he's quite nice. A little buttoned up, but—' She paused and rocked her neck. 'Why do you ask?'

Pei shrugged and continued to paint. 'Just curious. I—'

Whatever feint she was about to attempt died the second she felt a warm, fuzzy paw gently push up the edge of her jacket sleeve so as to reveal the bare skin underneath.

Ouloo held Pei's arm, staring at the scales. 'Oh, stars,' she said in a hush. She stared a moment longer, then looked up at Pei with shining eyes. '*Congratulations.*'

ROVEG

He was so happy Speaker had joined him. He hadn't been sure how she'd feel about his invitation – not because he could think of anything in it that would be poorly received, but because Speaker was still a stranger to him. Did meals and socialising mix well, for her? Was she the sort to go to the home of someone she barely knew for breakfast?

Apparently, she was.

As she walked through the airlock, she seemed markedly different than she had two days before, when she'd come in, scrib in hand, confidently asking him what it was he could do in a pinch. Today, there was no scrib, only the bundles of food he'd prepared for her, carefully tucked around both sides of her cockpit seat in an endearing way. She looked . . . not nervous, no. *Shy.* That was it. Speaker looked a touch shy, and even with his limited knowledge of her, that was not a trait he'd expected.

'I'm delighted you're here,' he said, bowing his torso. 'I was thinking we could eat in the projection room, if that's all right by you?'

'Oh,' Speaker said. 'Um, yes, that sounds fine.'

She followed him down the hallway, the clank of her mech suit providing a funny harmony to the familiar patter of his own legs. He had been ready for small talk, as she'd been pleasant company in the days before, but she was quiet now. Glancing back, he could see her studiously taking in the hallway, the architecture, the artwork on the walls. What did she make of it, he wondered. He thought of her weary shuttle parked next to his, and of what he'd known of her species before he met her, and of what he'd learned of them since. At this, he became self-conscious. Embarrassed, almost. He wondered if this was insulting to her in some way, if it came across like he was some wealthy bastard with more than he deserved. He knew he *was* a wealthy bastard, and he certainly didn't deserve it any more than anybody else. These were facts, but he hoped she didn't dislike him over it. He shuffled his abdominal plates, and told himself that however she felt was simply how she felt. He could do nothing about that, but what he *could* control was the embarrassment, which was antithetical to the point. He'd been taught that if one person had more than another, feeling guilty about it was the least productive reaction. The only proper way to approach such inequities was to figure out how best to wield them, so as to bring others up to where you stood. (This lesson was one of the better-known components of the Central Tenets; not everything in there was nonsense, and not all of it were things he'd felt the need to root out. Most, but not all.)

'Well, here we are,' he said, leading her into the projection room. The background he'd chosen for the occasion was a giant terraced fountain, with languid waves of water cascading slowly down its mossy sides. He'd wanted something that would serve as accompaniment, not distraction. His table in the middle was already set, laden with plates containing larger portions of the treats he'd packed for her. The meal was far more lacking in protein than he was accustomed to, and he was sure a bellyful of nothing but plants was going to call for a follow-up snack once she'd gone, but enjoying a meal with someone was as much about sharing an experience as it was about sharing space. 'I'm very much looking forward to trying these things. They're all ingredients I had aboard, of course, but I did some reading, and I prepared them in a way I hope will suit. I wasn't wrong about them being safe for you, correct?'

'They seem to be,' Speaker said. 'I'm not familiar with most of them, so I ran it all through a scanner before I came over. No offence, I hope.'

'Oh, not at all. A wise precaution. I once made the mistake of *not* doing that before tucking in at this little Harmagian eatery once, and I couldn't feel the inside of my mouth for a tenday.' He looked her up and down. 'I'd invite you to sit, but . . . I suppose you're already sitting.'

Speaker laughed from her cockpit chair. 'I can sit the suit down so I'm not towering over you.'

He chuckled in agreement, and lowered his abdomen to the floor, folding his legs in neatly. Speaker pulled her controls, setting the suit down with an industrial thud.

'*Vehlech hra hych bet*,' he said magnanimously, then translated: 'May it be to your liking.'

She cocked her head with interest. 'Tellerain is such a beautiful language.'

'Do you think so?' he said. He reached for a plate of quick-pickled marshpears. 'Sounds and beauty are such relative things. I know Aandrisks don't like the sound of us much, but then, I think Reskitkish sounds like someone trying to choke to death as quickly as possible, so to each their own.'

'I love the layers in Tellerain,' Speaker said. 'It's like a song.'

He made an appreciative sound, then a much louder one as he bit into the marshpear. 'Oh! Mmm! Oh, I think this turned out quite well, what do you say? And please know, I won't be bothered *at all* if you don't like any of it. I'm sure we have very different palates.'

Speaker looked at what he was eating, then searched the bundles around her seat to find the matching stuff. She pulled out a marshpear with an intrigued look, studied it for a moment, then took an investigative nibble with her beak. 'Stars, that's tart,' she said.

'Too tart?'

'No, no. I think I'll eventually like it; I just had no idea what to expect.'

'*I think I'll eventually like it*,' he repeated with approval. 'Spoken like a true adventurous eater.'

She took a more confident bite. 'I wouldn't call myself that,' she said. 'I don't eat much alien food.' She swallowed. 'Hardly ever, honestly. I hadn't really thought about it, until you sent me this.'

'It would make sense, if you can't go out to eat,' he said. He began to tuck in with gusto, grasping delicious things with each of his thoracic feet. 'If you're getting groceries for a long haul, you want to make sure it's something you know you like.' He poured himself a cup of mek with the one leg that wasn't holding a piece of food. 'Who is the better cook, you or Tracker?'

'*Me*,' Speaker said with conviction. 'She always overcooks anything leafy. And she likes things burned.'

He laughed. 'I sense a long-standing argument.'

'*Very* long,' she said.

He continued down that road with delicate steps. 'Are you feeling better in that regard than you were yesterday?'

Speaker finished the marshpear she had in hand, then began eating another one. 'No,' she said frankly. 'I'm not.'

'I rather suspected as much. That's why I thought you might appreciate a distraction.'

She did nothing but eat for a moment. 'That's kind of you,' she said. She studied him, crunching the fruit she held with both hands. 'Would I be right in guessing you also needed distracting?'

'Hmm,' he said. 'Yes, you would.'

The frankness continued. 'You're not looking forward to going home, are you?'

Roveg looked up at her. 'Ouloo mentioned where I was headed, I take it?'

Speaker chuckled. 'She did.'

'Well, it's *not* home. Home is on Chalice, for me. But I am headed to Quelin space, yes.' He took a strip of sugared snap-fruit. 'It's been a long time.'

'How long?'

'Fifteen standards.'

She considered this. That was nearly a lifetime for her, he realised. It rather felt like one to him, too. 'What's taking you back there now?' she asked.

Roveg almost told her. Part of him wanted to purge the anxiety he'd shoved inside for days on end, but he was so afraid of the possibility of things going wrong that he dared not speak his fear aloud. That would make it too real. So instead, he relayed only the logistics, the piece that was nothing more than a means. 'I'm barred from *living* in Quelin space, but it's been long enough since I was thrown out that I'm now eligible for a . . . hmm, I don't know what to call it in Klip. A visitor's permit, essentially. Extremely temporary, and my permissable activities will be equally limited. I'll have a law-enforcement escort with me wherever I go, to make sure I don't do or say anything disruptive. I'm sure whoever xe is will be *delightful* company.'

The way Speaker looked at him suggested she was well aware that this was a half-answer. But to her credit and his relief, she did not go digging for missing details. 'So that's your appointment,' she said. 'To get your permit.'

'Yes. There's a tedious interview process and other assorted nonsense. It's very strict.' He paused. 'Tardiness would not factor favourably, for me.'

'Ah,' she said with understanding. She clicked her beak together, looking at the table. 'Hence the distraction.'

'Indeed.'

Speaker turned the suit so she could get a better look at the projection walls. 'Is this one of yours?' she asked, watching the digitally rendered water tumble down.

Roveg curled his legs proudly. 'It is indeed,' he said. 'And I'm not too modest to say that it's a favourite. Though, of course, this is just the visual playback, not the whole experience.'

'I've always thought sims sounded a bit overwhelming. I don't know how I feel about plugging something into my brain.'

'Nothing's *plugged in*, it's all wireless,' Roveg said. 'The patch you wear doesn't hurt, and it's not invasive. But you're right, the actual sensory experience can take some getting used to. Work like mine is a nice entry point. You can get accustomed to the concept of feeling and seeing something that isn't there without being asked to *do* anything.'

Speaker took that in. She nodded at the wall. 'This isn't a real place, right? You didn't model this after somewhere that exists?'

'No, this one's made up. Sometimes I do real-world environments, but it depends on the mood I'm in.'

'Can you show me one?'

'Certainly,' he said. He was always pleased when someone took an interest in his work. 'Friend, can you display Reskit, unpopulated version?'

Friend obliged. The fountain vanished, and the Aandrisk capital was summoned in its place. Roveg and Speaker now sat in Reskit's famous Old Marketplace, surrounded by ancient doorless buildings adorned with flags and banners of every colour waving merrily in the bone-dry breeze.

'Wow,' Speaker said. 'Wow, it looks just like it.'

'You've been?'

'Yeah, Reskit's a fairly regular stop for us. The market there is . . . well, friendly.' She did not elaborate on what *friendly* meant, but Roveg could guess. 'It looks funny, without the people.'

'You can add people in if you wish, but being able to admire the scenery without all the hustle and bustle is nice, too.'

'I suppose it is,' she said. She observed quietly, deep in thought. 'Do you have any of Vemereng?'

The question hit Roveg beneath the shell, but he did not let this show. 'No,' he said. 'I've never made a sim based anywhere on my planet. Not since, I mean.'

Speaker's pensiveness became heavier. 'Can you tell me what that's like?'

'You mean Vemereng? Well, it rather depends on which continent we're talking about, just like anywhere. I was born in the eastern islands, which are cool but temperate—'

The Akarak cut him off. 'No, no,' she said. 'I want to know what it's like to *have a planet*. You've visited many, and so have I. Tell me what you feel when you say that one is *yours*.'

Roveg stared out at the projection, the spiracles along his back rising and falling with each breath. 'My planet,' he said, but not to her. He spoke the words to himself, experimentally, studying them from an angle he had never thought to consider. He looked at the Old Marketplace, and it was a marvel, truly, but not his, not at all his. 'You know how it feels when you hop between worlds? How you begin surrounded, in a place like *this*—' he gestured at the screen with his legs '—and it's everywhere, it's every*thing*. It appears flat and endless. But then you push away with as much engine thrust as you can muster, and it all zooms out at once, and quickly begins to *curve*. And once you're above, you see it's just a sphere like all the others, a giant ball that becomes a marble that becomes a speck. And then you approach *another* marble, which becomes *another* ball, and when you land on that, it becomes that flat endlessness once more. There's no centre to it. There's no up or down, there's only close and far. You know this feeling?'

'I do,' Speaker said.

'Well . . . to have your own planet means that despite knowing the universe is edgeless, that everything is relative to everything else, you feel there's one place that's the true centre of it. I don't mean the true centre in an astronomical way, or a topographical way. I mean the *true centre*. It's the anchor, the . . . the weight that holds the weaving together. It's not the true centre for everyone, but it is for *you*. And that knowledge reframes all that zooming in and out. You're not drifting. You're *attached*, somewhere. It may be far, but you can always feel it. And it reminds you, when you go back, that it's yours. We travellers, we move through so many artificial environments – so many combinations of air pressure, humidity, temperature, gravity – that we forget how achingly good it feels to step into the natural environment your body spent millions of years evolving for. Everything in you settles instantly, as if you are water and the world is the cup. When you look to the horizon, even though you've been above it, even though you know better, you can fully *believe* in the flatness, the endlessness. You wrap yourself in that illusion, and you will never feel safer.'

The Akarak looked him in the eye. 'Even if you can't go back?'

Another cut below the shell, but perversely, he welcomed it. Nothing about the question felt like a challenge, merely a desire to get to the crux of things. It made him feel quite vulnerable, but paradoxically at ease. 'Even if you can't go back,' he said. He angled his body toward her. If she could be blunt, so could he. 'Does it hurt you, not having a place to call your own?'

Speaker shifted her weight within the suit's cockpit, breathing air she could not share with him. 'Yes,' she said slowly. 'But also . . .' She sighed. 'I don't know if I can explain this.'

'I'd be happy to hear you try.'

She clicked her beak together three times. 'It is difficult to feel sorrow for something I've never known. What you describe sounds magical. But swimming also sounds magical, and I've never done that, either. Or—' She reached for something else. 'Aandrisks can see in infrared. They can walk the world in the dark. That sounds like a magical thing, too. But it's an experience I'll never have. It's impossible for me to have it. Likewise, it's impossible for me to have a world of my own. So, I both grieve and am incapable of grieving, because I don't know what it is that I've lost. And none of my kind can tell me. Nobody's left who remembers.'

'You are like the Humans, perhaps,' Roveg said. 'They likewise know only their ships.'

'Maybe,' Speaker said. 'I've never spoken properly with one, so I don't know. But something in me says we're not the same.

Their world isn't dead, not completely. It's being repaired, little by little. They can visit, if they want to. There are some who live there still. And their planet wasn't taken from outside. They killed it from within. They chewed their own hearts out. No, I don't think we're the same at all.' She moved restlessly in her chair, casting aside an unspoken rage. 'I'm sorry.'

'Please, don't be. You have every reason to be angry. We can talk about something else, if you—'

'No.' She took a steadying breath. He saw her hands unclench. 'Tell me about your favourite place on your planet.'

Roveg did not need to think before answering. 'Wushengat. It means *Flower Lake*, rather unoriginally.'

'What's it like?'

An ache spread through Roveg as he conjured the place in his mind. The memory was as sweet as summer syrup and twisted as an executioner's blade. 'It's perfectly quiet,' he said. 'I never saw a time when the waters weren't calm.'

'What colour are they?'

'They're – I'm not sure you and I perceive colour in the same way.'

'I don't care.'

'The gentlest, lightest purple. The sand on the shore is soft as clouds, and the trees around it explode with flowers in the springtime.' The ache thickened and bloomed. 'It is the sort of place where you can sit all day and be utterly sure that so long as you are there, everything will be all right.'

Speaker hung on every word. 'I don't think anywhere has ever made me feel that way.'

'Well, it isn't *true,* of course. But it feels that way at Wushengat.'

'I think you should make a sim of it,' she said. 'You should make other people feel that, too.'

Roveg fell silent once more. 'Tell you what,' he said at last. He poured himself another cup of mek. 'If I make this appointment, and if I get my permit, perhaps I will.'

PEI

Pei froze as Ouloo smiled at her. Her cheeks roiled purple at the intrusion, at being touched even in such a casual manner without being asked. But angry as she was, part of her was likewise relieved. She shut her eyes and resigned herself to the fact that covering her arm back up would not change what had been seen. Fine. It was one less topic to avoid.

As she looked into Ouloo's face, she knew they were nothing alike. They had different bodies, different blood. Their respective ideas of what a 'mother' was could not be more disparate. For Ouloo, the concept seemed a core part of her identity, and why would it not be? It wasn't an embryo that she'd given birth to, but an entire being that had swum within her, no shell keeping them separate. That same being had clung to her for years, living mostly in a pocket on her belly, a constant communion of one body against another. That level of attachment was unsettling to Pei, just as she found the whole concept of live birth horrifying. But the differences between herself and Ouloo were not limited to that of physicality. In traditional Aeluon culture, a *mother* was not a *parent*. Parents were men and *shon*. Parents went to school for it. Parents were the people who actually *raised* children, not those who had done the easy business of *creating* them. The gendered expectations of parenting were dissolving, but even though women could be found working in creches now, there was still an enormous difference between the person who produced an egg and the person who took care of the little being that crawled out of it.

Parenting was a profession, and it was not Pei's. She could not imagine living like Ouloo, performing two distinct jobs at once, splitting herself for decades until Tupo reached adulthood. The whole idea was overwhelming.

But in the absence of everyone else she wished she could talk to right then, Pei found herself oddly comforted by the company of Ouloo – someone who had, in extreme essence, been in a situation like this before.

'How are you feeling?' Ouloo asked. 'Are you hungry? Do you need some proper exercise? I can keep everyone out of the garden for a while if you need to run around.'

Pei was mildly surprised that Ouloo knew any of the ancillary symptoms of shimmer, but with everything else she'd learned about her, such attention to detail made sense. 'No, I'm fine,' Pei said. She paused. 'Please don't, um—'

'I won't mention this to anyone,' Ouloo said. 'I know I'm chatty, but this is personal. I understand.' Her neck bobbed thoughtfully. 'Oh! But – oh, I can help! Here, come on.' She dropped the paint tube and hurried down the path toward the office. Pei followed.

Tupo was in the office when they entered, standing on xyr back legs and placing snack packs onto the shelves, one bag at a time, not even remotely in a rush.

'Tupo, I need you out,' Ouloo said as she trotted in.

Tupo swung xyr neck around, confused. 'You said to restock the—'

'I know what I said, but you need to go outside.'

Tupo looked at Pei, dumbfounded, then swung back to xyr mother. 'Is . . . everything okay?'

'Everything is *fine*,' Ouloo said, 'but we need grown-ups only. Shoo.'

Relative as both parenting and childhood were, the look on Tupo's face of *what the hell is wrong with my mom* was universal. Tupo dropped xyr snack packs back into the crate and muttered vehemently as xe trotted off. 'If I'm playing outside, I'm supposed to do my chores. If I'm doing my chores, I'm supposed to go outside. It's *ridiculous*.' This general vein of complaint continued until the kid was out and the door slid shut.

Ouloo ignored her child's negative feedback, and instead began to dig through a storage cabinet behind her desk. 'There was . . . hmm, where is it . . . there was this Aeluon man who . . . no, not here . . .' She shut one drawer and opened another. 'I want to say he stopped with us two or three standards ago, on his way home from vacation. He . . . no, that's not it . . . wait . . . aha!' Her paw came up from the drawer, triumphantly holding an info chip. She walked over to Pei on her back two legs and handed it to her. 'He was a creche father from Ethiris and gave me this just in case any interested parties came through. It's details about the creche he works at. Or at least, he worked there then.' Ouloo bobbed with satisfaction. 'This is why you never throw anything out.'

Pei took the chip. 'Where's Ethiris?' she asked.

'Oh, very close. Tunnel number four connects there directly,' Ouloo said. 'It's just one hop and a tenday away.'

Pei flashed approving blue, for that was a good answer. Her window of opportunity would still be wide at that point, and she could stop pursuing the undesirable avenue of one of Ouloo's neighbours. She could do this at a proper creche, with proper fathers, the way she'd always wanted to.

But while one hop and a tenday was good news for the biological countdown she'd been thrust under, there was a problem. She did some math. One hop and a tenday, plus five or six tendays at this creche, then a tenday back to Gora, and one and a half more back to the *Mav Bre*. That would encompass the entirety of her leave, and then some.

She wouldn't be able to meet Ashby.

Pei scolded herself for thinking that way. She was *shimmering*, for fuck's sake. Everything in life paused for that. Holidays were cancelled, jobs were frozen, soldiers got sent to safer space.

That was just how things worked. Ashby knew that. They'd discussed it, many times. She knew he would understand. There would be other chances, other shore leaves. It was fine to be disappointed, but this was how it had to be.

She told herself these obvious things. She took a breath, waiting for their indisputable reason to chase the tightness in her chest away.

They did not.

Ouloo's face rose up, startling Pei out of her reverie. 'I'm sure this whole thing must be a surprise,' Ouloo said. 'But don't worry. From everything I've heard, it sounds like a wonderful experience.'

Pei forced herself to smile blue. 'That's what they say. And, thank you,' she said, sticking the chip in her pocket. 'This is . . . thank you. Really.'

The Laru beamed. 'I'm just so happy I could help.' She moved her face closer, confidentially. 'And I'm glad it doesn't have to be Kopi. He's rather boring.'

Pei laughed at this, her cheeks freckling a bit of genuine green. 'Well, then I'm glad, too.' She glanced around at the snacks and sundries. 'Uh, one more question.'

'Of course.'

'Do you sell anything to drink?'

'Oh, goodness, yes. We've got water, plenty of mek powder, plenty of fizz—'

'No, no,' Pei said. She looked Ouloo square in the eye. 'Something to *drink*.'

. . . .

COMPOUNDED SYSTEM FAILURE

Received message
Encryption: 0
From: GC Transit Authority – Gora System (path: 487-45411-479-4)
To: Ooli Oht Ouloo (path: 5787-598-66)
Subject: URGENT UPDATE

This is an urgent message from the Emergency Response Team aboard the GC Transit Authority Regional Management Orbiter (Gora System). As both standard ansible and Linking channels are currently unavailable, we will be communicating via the emergency beacon network for the time being. We ask that you leave your scribs locked to this channel until proper communications are restored.

We are now able to provide a firm estimate of 240/307 for the restoration of safe travel conditions. We know this comes a day later than our previously stated estimate, and we apologise for the inconvenience. As this situation is ever-changing, we have been unable to provide travellers with information that meets our typical standards for accuracy.

We are pleased to report that we will be deploying a small, temporary fleet of communications satellites throughout today, 238/307. Restoration times will vary depending on your location, and we cannot provide an estimate for your specific area. As this stop-gap network is limited in capacity, it will not be able to support the same user load as Gora's standard network. To ensure that everyone has the ability to use comms as required, we ask that all calls and messages be limited to emergency needs, or matters relating directly to your travel plans.

We will be contacting you with your updated tunnel queue details as soon as comms are available.

Thank you for your patience. We are all in this together.

Hello, future mother! From all of us at the Rin creche, we wish you heartfelt congratulations on your shimmer, and we hope you'll consider us to be your child's fathers.

Location

Ethiris is a beautiful planet, and we're proud to call it home. Sapient settlements here are located on the north coast of the equatorial continent, which makes for mild winters, gorgeous summers, and easy transitions in between.

Our town is Kestrith, a multispecies community anchored around fibre farming and textile manufacture. We have easy access to beautiful beaches, and sunny hillside hikes are just a short shuttle trip away. Though Ethiris falls within Aandrisk territory, there is a large Aeluon population here, and your child will feel right at home. Colour panels can be found on every public sign, and our sapient neighbours are very familiar with our customs. Shimmerquick is arguably the most publicly celebrated holiday here, even more so than Kish Kesh Kep. If you're hoping for your child to grow up with a strong connection to Aeluon tradition and the benefits of a cultural melting pot, Kestrith offers the best of both.

Our Kids' Home

Above all else, we want our kids to feel safe and comfortable here. Our creche includes:

- Cosy sleeping quarters (including temperature-controlled pods for little ones who haven't grown out of hibernating yet)
- Indoor and outdoor play areas
- Warm saltwater swimming pool (with a slide, of course!)
- A sim room for older kids

- A wildflower garden where kids can observe native wildlife up close (our settlement has no large predators or venomous creatures of any kind)
- A HUGE kitchen and aquaponic greenhouse (our kids help grow and cook everything)
- An at-home study hall for our hard-working students and curious thinkers
- Two quiet rooms for kids who need some time alone
- The best steam bath in the system (or at least, we think so)

Your Special Retreat

Having fathered twenty-six kids (and counting!), we know that shimmering can be as stressful as it is special. Having to drop everything is not easy, and as excited as you may be, it's also okay if you're feeling overwhelmed. All of the fathers here at the Rin creche understand, and we want to do everything we can to make this time as pleasant and peaceful as possible for you. We value our mothers' contentment every bit as much as we do our children's well-being.

You probably also have questions about coupling with us – learning about it in school isn't the same as going through it for the first time! We're happy to discuss everything in as much detail as you need to feel comfortable about being intimate with us. We'll go over all your sexual preferences beforehand, and if you're joining us from off-planet, you can write to, or call us as often as you like on your journey here, any time of day.

For you, we offer the following:

- Your choice of private sleeping quarters or shared quarters with any of the fathers
- Top-of-the-line medical exam facilities
- Your own private soaking tub (aside from being relaxing, a hot soak helps with the mild discomfort that can arise as your egg's shell begins to harden)

- All the massages, naps, and dessert you want
- An open invitation to spend as much time interacting with our kids as you're interested in. Some mothers like to be able to picture what her child's life will be like; others want some distance from that. We're used to both, and will accommodate either.
- A high-quality incubation pool, where your egg will be monitored day and night until hatching

Meet the Fathers

Femlen
- Special training: medicine, physical activities, egg care, first aid, tutoring (math, science)
- Favourite activities: swimming, playing mystery sims
- Favourite thing about parenting: watching them do something I taught them better than me

Tus
- Special training: cooking, gardening, visual art, egg care, first aid, tutoring (colour control, art)
- Favourite activities: arranging flowers, making dessert, eating dessert
- Favourite thing about parenting: watching a kid speak in full colour for the first time

Drae
- Special training: mental health counselling, performing arts, dance, storytelling, egg care, first aid, tutoring (talkbox use, Klip)
- Favourite activities: going to the colour opera, reading books in the local city field, playing action sims
- Favourite thing about parenting: that age when they suddenly have opinions about everything

Mudi
- Special training: housekeeping, home repair, egg care, first aid, tutoring (home skills, tech repair, Reskitkish)
- Favourite activities: having adventures in town, taking things apart, playing tikkit
- Favourite thing about parenting: making a bad day better

ROVEG

There was a place in the garden behind the main lawn that was perfect for people who needed a moment alone. Roveg had noted it before – a semi-circular nook surrounded by a thick wall of hedges, facing outward toward the dome and providing an uninterrupted view of the dusty hills beyond. Normally, his shuttle felt like a sanctuary, but right then, it was dead weight that could not fly. He had spent an hour after the last update – or was it more? – bouncing from one room to the next, seeking solace in his usual comforts of food, art, music. But the harder he tried to calm down, the less he was satisfied, and the deeper the frenzy in his mind crept. So, with no better ideas, he'd headed for the garden nook, hopeful that some time alone in different surroundings would quiet him.

He followed the path through the tidy hedges. As he rounded the corner, he discovered that Captain Tem had beat him to the punch.

The Aeluon was sitting in the grass atop her folded jacket, her legs crossed beneath her vertical torso in bizarre bipedal fashion. On the ground before her was a bottle, and in one hand, a cup. Her posture was as steady as ever, but there was the air of something new about her. A tension, yes, but also some change in her appearance that Roveg did not have the mental bandwidth to place. She looked different, somehow. Her scent was different, too. But how much of that difference was *her* and how much was the pungent liquid she was drinking, he could not determine.

'Oh! Hello, Captain,' he said. 'I didn't expect anyone to be here.'

'No worries,' she said. The words coming out of her talkbox were ever so slightly delayed. Roveg knew, from the varied Aeluons in his social life, that operating a talkbox while imbibing became more and more of a challenge with every sip.

'I was just looking for a place to gather my thoughts,' he said.

'Yeah,' Captain Tem said. 'Me too.' She thought for a moment, then raised the bottle. 'If you'd like to be alone *with* someone, I do not need to drink all of this myself.'

This hadn't been what Roveg had in mind, and part of him wanted nothing more than to make a polite exit. But given how badly his efforts to calm himself down had failed, perhaps company would do the trick. Company, and a strong swallow of kick. 'Why not,' he said. 'So long as I don't have to talk about said thoughts.' He sat beside her, tucking his legs beneath his abdomen.

'I don't want to talk about mine, either, so . . . we have an accord.' She drained the cup, refilled it, and offered it to him.

He considered the curved drinking vessel, with its wide brim and strange handle. 'I think the bottle might work better for me,' he said. 'That's not quite the right shape for my mouth.'

She retracted one arm and extended the other, handing over the bottle. As she did so, sunlight fell across her scales. They were no longer merely silver, but faintly iridescent, like the skin of a soap bubble. 'Ah, Captain,' Roveg said warmly. So *that* was what was different about her. 'Congratu—'

'Don't.' The word snapped from Captain Tem's talkbox, unhampered by delay. She shut her eyes and took a breath, and with this, her artificial voice softened. 'Please don't congratulate me.'

Her reaction surprised him, but he took it in stride. 'Is that what we're not talking about?'

'Yes.'

'Noted.' He examined the bottle now held between his toes. The glass was frosted, so there was no good way to see what awaited him within, and the label was one he'd never seen before. He did, at least, recognise the alphabet. The dizzy patterns of concentric rings were unmistakably Laru. 'What is this?' he asked.

Captain Tem drank from her cup, and the slightest of winces appeared around her soft eyes as the beverage hit her tongue. 'I have no idea,' she said.

Roveg wrapped his mouth around the pour spout and gingerly took a sip. The Laru kick shot down his oesophagus like a ship on fire, tasting of ash and bitter herbs. 'Ho!' he said with a hoarse laugh. 'Oh, stars, that'd strip paint. Oof.' He turned the bottle this way and that, as though it were a scientific specimen. 'Ouloo's private stash, I take it?'

'Yep.'

'I have to admit, I would've thought her more of a sugarsnap fan. Or something with a big skewer of fruit stuck in it.'

'We all have days,' Captain Tem said. Her cheeks became dabbled with yellow and orange; Roveg recognised this as embarrassment. 'This isn't the way I typically deal with mine.'

'I didn't have the impression that it was,' he said. He angled his head toward her in a sympathetic way. 'But, as you said: we all have days.'

She took another sip from her cup. She did not wince this time. 'What kind of impression *do* you have of me?'

Roveg's forelegs flexed in thought. 'Honestly?'

'Honestly.'

Roveg took a second swig of the caustic stuff, letting it shake his thoughts loose. 'You strike me as someone practical. Someone smart. Someone who – normally – knows how to manage her fear within the context of what I assume is a very stressful job. You hold yourself together extraordinarily well, given the circumstances.'

'Which circumstances are those?'

'The circumstances in which you're a cargo runner, and your shuttle has military permit insignia stamped on the hull,' he said. 'I imagine that you've lost friends, been injured.' He paused. 'It's likely you've killed people.'

She glanced at him. 'Does that bother you?' she asked.

'No,' he said. 'Though that doesn't mean I approve, either.'

'Fair,' she said. She ran her thumb over the rim of the cup. 'The kid keeps asking me about it.'

'Tupo?'

'Yeah.'

'That's hardly surprising. Xe is a *kid,* after all. Xe doesn't understand what xe's asking about. Or, xe's *trying* to understand, and that's why xe won't drop it.'

Captain Tem thought about this. 'Do you raise your own kids? Like Ouloo does?'

'My species, you mean? Not *exactly* like Ouloo does, but our children stay with their parents until adolescence, yes.'

'I can't imagine,' Captain Tem said. 'Do you have any?'

Roveg took a long pull from the bottle, letting the kick take up any space that words might inhabit. He did not reply.

Out of the corner of his eye, he could see Captain Tem watching him, her cheeks orange with sympathy. 'Is that what we're not talking about?'

Roveg looked at the bottle's label once more. The flavour of the stuff bordered on a treaty violation, but against his will, it was growing on him. 'I have another question for you about Humans, if I may.'

Captain Tem's inner eyelids flicked sideways, and the orange in her cheeks subdued. She seemed to understand. 'All right.'

Roveg looked at her with staged seriousness. 'Waterball. Do you understand the rules?'

The Aeluon laughed, her face flooding green. 'I actually do.'

'Good, because I saw a game once, and all it appeared to be was a zero-G tank full of sapients tearing around in rocket boots, trying to drag a big glob of water around with sticks.'

'I mean . . . that's basically it, plus a lot of complicated bullshit tacked on.'

'Not a fan, I take it?'

'I'd say I have a . . . distant respect for it.' She sighed, then flexed her hand toward Roveg, indicating she wanted the bottle back. He refilled her cup. 'Okay. You have two teams of six, but only three play at a time.'

'And they can't touch the water with their hands, correct?'

'Well . . . okay, you're getting ahead of yourself. They *can*, but only under special circumstances.'

'This is already a mess.'

'I know. Stay with me. The object of the game is to get the waterball into the goal, which is called the bucket. It's not actually a bucket – it's this thing that measures the volume of the water to see how much was lost as they crossed the box. Now, the starting players are chosen as follows . . .'

PEI

Pei still didn't know what Ouloo's kick was called or what it was made of or how long they'd been drinking it, but it had to be good, given how much of it they'd knocked back. Roveg was drunk – merrily so – and Pei was well on her way there. She wasn't sure how they'd started with waterball and ended up at colour opera, but whatever the trajectory, Pei was enjoying the ride. This Quelin was a lot of fun. She'd almost forgotten why she'd started drinking her feelings in the garden in the first place.

Almost.

Pei's implant buzzed to the left, and she registered the clanking sound of the Akarak's suit, in motion and headed their way. Speaker appeared moments later, coming around the corner and looking . . . surprised, maybe? Who knew?

'Oh,' Speaker said. 'Sorry, I was looking for Roveg. I didn't mean to disturb.'

'Nothing to disturb,' Pei said lightly.

'Ah, Speaker, please join us!' Roveg said. 'You'll have to forgive me, I've gotten a little . . . frivolous.'

Whatever the Akarak's original intent had been, she seemed to discard it. 'I think I'll leave you to it,' Speaker said, 'since I can't partake.'

'Oh, come now,' Roveg said, 'we're not *that* sloppy, are we? I may not be able to pour you a drink, but I assure you, I can still provide the most *scintillating* conversation.'

'I'm sure.' Speaker laughed. 'But I really don't want to interrupt. I'll find you later.'

Pei's cheeks stippled with yellow. She'd had enough of Speaker dancing around her, of couched replies and things clearly left unsaid. 'Have I done something?' Pei asked.

The Akarak tensed. 'Sorry, what?'

'Have I done something to rub you the wrong way?' Pei asked. She wasn't mad. She didn't care what Speaker thought of her one way or the other, and she wasn't looking to pick a fight. She was simply asking a question. 'It's fine if you don't like me, I just can't figure out *why*.'

Speaker cocked her head. 'I don't know you well enough to dislike you,' she said.

'Okay,' Pei said. That was an answer she could respect, but it didn't satisfy the question. 'So what did I do?'

'You didn't do anything.'

'So you just don't like my species, then? Or what?'

'Captain,' Roveg said.

'I'm not upset about it,' Pei said. 'I just want to know.'

Speaker placed her hands in her lap and folded them together. 'You really want me to answer this?' Speaker said.

'Yes,' Pei said. She really did.

Sounds did not resonate with Pei the way they did with other species, but all the same, there could be no mistake that every syllable hitting her implant was delivered with the quiet accuracy of someone choosing her words with care. 'I don't know you,' Speaker said. 'And I like Aeluons the same as any species.' She paused, gathering herself. 'What I don't like is your job. And if that has bled into my interactions with you, then I apolo—'

'What about my job?' Pei asked. The yellow darkened.

'The . . . spheres in which you operate. I . . .' Speaker clicked her beak and inhaled. 'I believe you and I have differing opinions on the Rosk war. That's all.'

Roveg laughed at this. 'You should've been a diplomat,' he said. 'Or a parliamentarian.'

Speaker did not laugh. 'I'm good where I am,' she said with glacial calm.

Pei's eyes narrowed. She hadn't cared what Speaker thought of her before, but now she did. 'I'm sorry, but you're . . . you're kidding, right? Do you have any idea what's happening out there?'

'Not as well as you, I'm sure,' Speaker said.

'They're bombing civilians,' Pei said. 'Whole settlements, from orbit. What possible opinion could be had about that?'

Speaker opened her palms upward in a crass approximation of what an Aeluon would do if they were trying to back down. 'Captain, I—'

'No, really, I want to know.' Pei was *not* going to back down, and was not about to let Speaker do the same. Speaker hadn't seen what Pei had seen. She hadn't seen the limbs, the char, the craters where towns once stood. *Differing opinions*. Pei had carried the gory corpse of her crewmate – *her friend* – out of an alleyway on what should've been a safe world because of *differing opinions*. She'd spent two days cleaning out her mine-riddled ship – *her home* – because of *differing opinions*. No, she wouldn't stand for this. Her cheeks seethed purple, and it had nothing to do with the kick or the hormones. This whole turn had started because Pei had wondered if she'd somehow insulted Speaker, but now the opposite was true. Even on her best days, she would not let this slide.

'I don't agree with what the Rosk are doing to the Aeluon civilians,' Speaker said. Her words remained obnoxiously placid. 'It's horrific. I'm not arguing that. But I do think, simultaneously, that it's worth asking *why* they're doing it.'

The limbs. The char. The craters. 'It doesn't matter.'

'It does. Nobody bombs civilians from orbit without cause. My understanding of the situation is that the Rosk believe planetary colonisation is abhorrent, and they'll do anything to stop it from happening in their territory.'

The purple deepened to the cusp of black. 'We're not in their fucking territory. They can do – or *not* do – anything they want on *their* side of the map.'

'Yes,' Speaker said. 'But who drew the map?'

Roveg sighed softly from where he sat between them. 'Oh, stars,' he said to himself, and took a hefty drink.

SPEAKER

If the Aeluon wanted to make Speaker angry, she was doing a fantastic job of it. Speaker was trying to keep her head cool, she really was. She didn't want to fight, and she wasn't at *all* comfortable doing so with a species outside of her own, but for fuck's sake, Captain Tem had *asked*. What was the point of asking for an honest answer if you didn't want to hear it?

Captain Tem slammed her cup down in the grass, the kick inside sloshing over the edge. 'The colonies my government are protecting are at the border,' she said. 'Not *across* the border. *At* it. If the Rosk don't want to settle off of their own planet, fine. They do not get to dictate what happens in the systems next door. And even if they *did*, murdering people would not be the answer.'

'I'm not saying it is,' Speaker said. *Calm, calm,* she told herself. *Be the reasonable voice.* 'But you – *your government* – is murdering *them* in response, and I'm sorry, but I can't accept a lesser evil for the sake of it being *lesser*.'

Captain Tem glared. 'Your people kill people, too. You can't tell me that's not for the sake of your own interests.'

'And I wouldn't. I don't agree with *them*, either. But I do understand *why*. I sympathise with the reasoning even if I disagree with the action taken. And in that, I can simultaneously feel sympathy for the Aeluon settlers *and* for the Rosk who don't want them there. Who I *don't* feel sympathy for are . . . well, the people killing over it. On either side.'

'Could we perhaps—' Roveg started.

'What else are we supposed to do?' Captain Tem said over him. 'They won't negotiate. They won't compromise. They won't listen to anything else.'

'Did you ever consider leaving?' Speaker asked. 'Do you need yet another planet so desperately?'

'It's their *home*,' Captain Tem said.

'No,' Speaker said. 'Sohep Frie is your home.'

'Sohep Frie nearly wiped us out. You know this, right? You seem to know a lot.'

Speaker bristled, but let it go. 'You had a population crash of some sort in your pre-spaceflight era. But I don't know the details, no.'

'The details boil down to a lot of fucking volcanoes, all of which popped off at once and killed almost everybody. It's the greatest luck in the universe that we're not extinct. That's why we built our first ships and went in search of other planets, so we wouldn't be tied to the fate of just *one*.'

'Stars, that *is* lucky,' Speaker said flatly. 'That would be a terrible way to end up.'

The sound of Captain Tem's talkbox came out distorted around the edges, a sign that its operator was punching thoughts through it. 'We're not like the Harmagians were,' she said. 'We were *never* like the Harmagians. The Rosk border – nobody was *on* those planets, when people settled them. There was *nothing* sapient there. We've never taken a world from someone, not once.' She stared as though Speaker had lost her mind. 'You know we *stopped* the Harmagians, right? Back in the day? You know the whole reason you're free of them is because of *us*, right?'

That was it. The last load-bearing support in Speaker snapped, and there was no chance of hoisting it back up. 'How dare you,' she said.

'Speaker—' Roveg interjected.

'No,' Speaker said. Her voice shook, and she could not find a way to make it stop. 'No. How fucking dare you. You think

I'm talking about history. You think I'm talking about something that's *over*. You think that because you have your accords and your treaties and your fucking licences, you can keep doing the same shit as always with a clear conscience. Oh, yes, it's all so *civilised*.' She heard the words leaving her mouth, and she was afraid – afraid of what this angry alien might do, afraid of getting into trouble, afraid of all the unpleasant situations she'd spent her whole life teaching herself to avoid. But stars, it felt *good* to just say what she wanted to say, and she had no intention of putting the lid back on this box, not now. 'Just because there's no one living on a planet does not mean it's yours for the taking. Do you not see how dangerous that mindset is? Do you not think that treating the galaxy as if it is something to be endlessly used will always, always end in tragedy? You think you've broken the cycle. You haven't. You're in a *less violent period* of the *exact same cycle,* and you don't see it. And the line of what you find to be *justifiable cause* is going to keep slipping and slipping until you end up right back where you started. You haven't fixed anything. You put a stamp and a permit and a shiny coat of paint on an idea that has been fundamentally damaged from day one. You engaged in bloody theft and you called it *progress*, and no matter how much *better* you think you've made things, no matter how good your intentions are, that will *always* be the root of the GC. You cannot divorce any of what you do from that. Ever.'

'So, what?' Captain Tem said. 'We're all supposed to pack up and go back to our homeworlds? Now isn't *that* a fucked idea. No more mixing, no more learning from each other. Each species to themselves.'

'That's not what I'm saying.'

'Then what *are* you saying?'

'I'm saying stop expanding, stop going places where you're not invited, and stop treating the galaxy like a free-for-all. You've gone far enough. You're no longer in a bottleneck. There's no reason for you to keep doing this. It can only end badly.'

The Aeluon flicked her eyelids sideways. 'You're talking about things you do not understand.'

'If I am, then so are you. And the fact that you don't see that about yourself is why I've decided I *don't* like you, Captain Tem.' Speaker took a breath, squared her shoulders, and unclenched her fists. She looked at Roveg, who she hoped was still a friend. 'I'm sorry we spoiled your afternoon,' she said to him. She pushed controls and turned her suit around, intending to leave.

Instead, she found herself facing Ouloo and Tupo, each holding a tray of cakes.

ROVEG

Roveg had never been happier to see a pair of Laru offering dessert.

He was too drunk for this. Whatever it was Ouloo had given Pei, it had melted his brain, and he had neither head nor heart for a conversation of this sort. He did not want the galaxy to be a mess, but he didn't want to talk about it, either. He had problems enough without arguing over ones that he could not solve. The only solution he wanted was one for his *own* mess, and if he couldn't have that, he wanted to forget about it for a while. And since *that* was apparently out of the question as well, then if nothing else, he wanted some of that cake.

He didn't know how long Ouloo and Tupo had been on the periphery of the conversation, but he leapt at the opportunity to end it. 'And what about you, Ouloo?' he said loudly, jokingly. 'What's your take on the socio-political woes of the Galactic Commons?'

Ouloo stood on the pathway, holding a tray of her elaborate puddings as though she didn't know what else to do. 'I want everybody to get along, and I want to make them dessert,' she said quietly.

Roveg began to laugh. 'An admirable—'

Ouloo turned her head toward him. 'No,' she said, a thread of iron creeping into her voice. 'I'm not being funny.' She set the tray down on the grass and stood on all fours, not looking at anyone, not looking sure of herself. 'I don't know much about politics, or . . . or borders, or whatever it is you're fighting about. And I *should* know about those things, probably, because I'm sure it's irresponsible of me to *not* know how everything works, but . . . but everything is just so *much*. I don't know your histories, not properly. I don't understand all the – the tiny pieces that keep things moving. But I don't *need* to know those things to be able to tell that something isn't working. That something is wrong.' She looked up to face Speaker. 'What happened to your people – what is *still* happening to them – is wrong. Deeply wrong, and I'm sorry I never thought about it before.' She looked at Pei. 'What is happening to your people at the border is wrong. There's something very wrong there, and nobody should have to live like that. And Roveg – what's happened to *you* is wrong. So how do we fix it? How do we fix all of that?' She turned her eyes to the ground again. 'I have no idea. None. If a politician came here and said, "Here is my plan for fixing these things, and here is why my plan is best," I'd probably just believe xyr on the spot. I'd say, yes, that all makes sense, I'm very glad you're fixing it, what a relief. But then another politician could come in the next day, and xe might say, "Mmm, no, that plan's bad, here are a lot of complicated reasons as to why," and then I'd say, hmm, yes, that makes sense, too. And do you know what? I truly don't care which of them is right so long as it fixes everything. I don't have an . . . an ideology. I don't know the right terms to discuss these things. I don't know the science behind any of it. I'm sure I sound silly right now. But I just want everyone to get along, and to be well taken care of. That's it. I want everybody to be happy, and I do not care how we get there.' She exhaled, her broad nostrils flaring. 'That's how I feel about it.'

Everyone was quiet for a moment – even Tupo, who was hanging off to the side with xyr neck down low.

'I appreciate what you're saying,' Pei said tightly. Her eyes flicked to Speaker, then away just as fast. 'But you can't fix everything with cake.' She turned and walked down the path back toward her shuttle.

Roveg exhaled, the spiracles on his abdomen breathing wide. 'Well, maybe not *everything*,' he said. He moved to Ouloo's tray, and picked up the most generously sized portion with an appreciative bob of his torso.

Ouloo looked apologetically at Speaker. 'I'm so sorry I can't give you any,' she said.

'It's really all right,' Speaker said. Her polished voice had gone brittle, but was mending. Roveg didn't know whether to admire composure that recovered that quickly, or to encourage her to yell a bit more. It sounded as though she had needed to.

'Mmm,' Roveg said, hurrying to swallow a mouthful of delicious fluffy frosting. 'You can bring some cake to her ship.'

'Oh,' Ouloo said. Her sagging neck perked up a bit. 'Oh, I hadn't thought of that.'

'Yes, we had a delightful breakfast together this morning,' he said, trying desperately to change the topic and invoke a better mood. Was this the right way to steer the conversation? He had no idea. At this point, he was just talking. 'I made the food, she put it in her suit, and she hopped on over. Lovely time.'

Speaker did not perk up as Ouloo had. 'I really am sorry for the commotion,' she said, not addressing anyone in particular.

'I do not believe any of that was your fault,' Roveg said. He took another bite, every bit as delicious as the first. Stars, why did sugar and drinking go so well together?

'I wouldn't take it too personally,' Ouloo said to Speaker. 'I mean, she is—' Her eyes went wide. 'Oh, um . . . you know, she's *stressed*, we're all stressed—'

Roveg leaned toward Speaker. 'The good captain is shimmering,' he said.

Ouloo's fur fluffed. 'I said I wouldn't say!'

'You didn't,' he said. 'I did.'

'Oh,' Speaker said. Her tone suggested that she hadn't known and likewise did not care. 'I see.' She paused. 'Somehow I don't think that conversation would've been any different if she wasn't.'

Ouloo swung her neck around her legs, looking this way and that. 'Did either of you see where Tupo went?'

They both looked over. Roveg hadn't seen the younger Laru leave, and Speaker did not seem to have, either. Tupo's tray of cakes still lay on the ground, but the child xyrself had vanished.

'How very stealthy,' Roveg said.

'Xe can't stand people fighting,' Ouloo said with a sigh. 'Doesn't mind fighting with *me* all day long, but just *hates* anybody else doing it. Xe's such a sensitive little thing.' She huffed. 'Looks like xe took a couple cakes for xyrself. Stars, I told xyr one was *enough*. And I don't know how xe thinks I'm supposed to carry all of this back to the house on my own.'

'Can I help?' Speaker said.

'Oh,' Ouloo said, surprised. 'Um – you know what, if you don't mind—'

'I don't,' Speaker said.

'Well, I can't be the only one sitting around eating cake,' Roveg said.

Speaker eyed both his cake and the quarter-full bottle lying beside him. 'I think that'd be the best task for you right now,' she said without judgement.

Roveg started to argue, but felt the fledgling sentence crack, crumble, and dissolve. He had no idea what it was he was he'd wanted to say. He reached out and took a second piece of cake for later. 'You're probably right,' he said.

SPEAKER

There was something strange about Ouloo's home, and Speaker couldn't place it. She thought at first it was the decor, which was low and curving and unlike anything she'd ever seen. But in that, the home should've been no different than a mixed marketplace or any other environment in which Speaker could expect to encounter dozens of things she'd never seen before. No, there was something else making the back of her neck prickle. She just didn't know *what*.

'Sorry about the clutter,' Ouloo said with resignation. She stepped carefully around the scattered belongings in the hallway, shifting her tray of cakes this way and that as she rebalanced. 'I *told* Tupo to pick up this afternoon. Not that I was planning to have any of you over, but it's just the *principle* of the thing.'

'It's okay,' Speaker said. She operated her controls deftly, taking care to not make her suit step on anything. 'I've seen worse.'

'Yes, well,' Ouloo grumbled as she made her way to the kitchen. 'I don't want you to think I don't keep a clean house.'

Speaker's hand froze on her controls. That was it. That was what was weird.

She'd never been in a terrestrial home before.

Had she been in spacers' ships? Yes, of course. That was all she'd ever lived in. Shuttles like Roveg's? Not like *his*, no, but small craft serving as temporary homes on long hauls, yes. Buildings? Absolutely. Often. Anytime she was planetside.

But never a *house*.

'Kitchen's this way,' Ouloo called. 'Can you move around okay in here? Is there room for your suit? I know our ceilings are a little low for bipedals.'

'Yes,' Speaker said. 'I'm fine.' She shook her head and continued to follow her host.

It was funny how a kitchen could be so different from what she was used to and yet completely recognisable as *a kitchen*. Speaker didn't know what most of the gadgets were, and she'd never seen a stove in a shape like that, but it was still undoubtedly *a stove*, or at least, a hot thing for cooking food on. There was a worktable of sorts as well. The remnants of that day's baking were still scattered about it, coated in flour and smudged with frosting. Speaker felt slightly sad over the effort Ouloo had made, only to walk into a fight between the people she was trying to please.

Not that Speaker regretted anything she'd said to Captain Tem. Not even remotely. She had no cause to. All she'd said was the truth.

Ouloo put her tray of cakes in the stasie (Speaker recognised *that* appliance, at least). 'Here, I'll take those,' Ouloo said, retrieving the tray from the suit's hands. 'Thank you so much.'

'It's no trouble,' Speaker said.

'Oh, oh – but before I do.' Ouloo set the tray in the stasie with the door open, then darted around looking for something. 'I'll box some up for you to take back to your ship.' She paused. 'Will they be all right for you to eat?'

'I don't know. What's in them?'

'Well, let's see – sun beans, sugar, baking syrup, teth flour—'

'Ah,' Speaker said regretfully. 'I know teth flour, and I'm afraid I can't eat that.'

'Oh, no!' Ouloo said. The Laru became a portrait of disappointment. 'I've done such a bad job looking after you.'

'It's all right,' Speaker said. 'You've never met one of me before.'

'True, but that's a *reason*, not an excuse.' Ouloo tapped a paw on the floor, thinking. 'Does your species have dessert?' she asked. 'You know, as a concept?'

'Yes,' Speaker said. 'We do.'

Ouloo's neck corkscrewed lightly behind her head. 'Any you know how to make?'

'Oh,' Speaker said, surprised by the question. 'Um, yes, actually. Not many, but . . .' She rifled through a mental list of recipes she could reliably succeed at. 'I guess you'd translate it as *rest-day custard*. I know how to make that.' She cocked her head. 'Are you asking me for a recipe?'

'Yes. And if you're keen, I'd love for you to teach me how to make it,' Ouloo said. 'Just in case any more of you come by.' She looked Speaker in the eye and smiled. 'Or if you come back.'

'If I'm travelling this way, I absolutely will,' she said. She meant it. 'So. Custard. I doubt you'll have all the ingredients.'

Ouloo's paws bounced with excitement in a way not entirely unlike her child's. 'Does that mean you're going to show me?'

'Yes.' Speaker laughed. 'Though, I'm going to need to go back to my shuttle. I don't think I have everything I need there, either, but—'

'Oh, we'll improvise,' Ouloo said. 'We'll muddle through, and if it's a mess, it's a mess.'

And so Speaker found herself back on the path outside, heading to the shuttlepad to fetch whatever ingredients she had. *What a strange day it was*, she thought. She'd had a fancy meal with a Quelin, told an Aeluon to fuck off, and was now on her way to teach a Laru how to make her mother's custard recipe. There were other, better, more pressing reasons for why she wanted to talk to Tracker, but once the important things were sorted, Speaker couldn't wait to tell her about all of this. She thought maybe she'd write her a letter later, so as not to forget the details. She wouldn't send it, of course – it wasn't an emergency, and she wasn't about to be one of the people making the comms jam worse over something frivolous. She began to draft a message in her head as she stepped into the airlock and waited for the air to cycle through. *Sister, you won't believe the day I've had,* she thought. *I know you hate coming planetside, but I wish you'd been here for this—*

The hatch opened, and with it, the letter vanished, along with the recipe, the fight, the breakfast, any memory of anything that wasn't in front of her right then.

On the floor, limbs sprawled, neck twisted in on itself, nostrils shut against air they could not breathe, was Tupo. Unmoving. Unbreathing. Unresponsive.

Scattered before xyr, resting where they'd fallen, lay two pieces of cake.

Dys 238–239, GC Standard 307

. . . .

IN THE EVENT OF
AN EMERGENCY

EVERYONE

An alert light flashed; someone was in the airlock and wanted to come through the hatch. Whoever it was, Pei was not in the mood. She stood in her shuttle's kitchen, leaning against the pantry and drinking a large cup of water. She was in that stage of intoxication where she was beginning to entertain the possibility that maybe – just maybe – she'd overdone it.

The light continued to flash. She would get it, of course. It was probably Ouloo, making a fuss. No, that wasn't a kind way to think of it – Ouloo was *checking in*, most likely. Pei knew it wasn't nice to keep her host waiting, but she also really didn't feel like talking anymore. She wanted to sit in proper quiet and be with her feelings and—

Her implant buzzed, and a loud, rhythmic thudding accompanied it.

Someone wasn't just at the hatch. Someone was *kicking* the hatch.

Frowning purple, Pei walked over to a monitor panel and gestured, pulling up the view from the hatch's security cam. Her inner eyelids flicked hard. It wasn't Ouloo. It was Speaker.

As soon as Pei processed what Speaker was carrying, she dropped her cup and ran.

The fucking hatch finally melted open. Captain Tem stared at Tupo, lying limply in the mech suit's arms. 'What the hell—'

Speaker cut her off. 'You said you have medical equipment,' she said.

Captain Tem snapped into action just as Speaker had. 'This way,' the Aeluon said, hurrying down the surreal hallways of her soft-shelled ship. Speaker followed with equal speed. She ignored the empty weapon racks and hanging sets of armoured clothing, saving her disgust for another time. She tried to keep Tupo's long limbs from falling out of the suit's grasp, but stars, it wasn't easy.

She arrived at what amounted to a small med bay – a decent-sized room with a bed, a bot scanner, and various supplies for patching people up. Captain Tem activated panels and monitors with one hand, and opened a hole in the wall with the other. 'Where did you find xyr?' she asked.

Speaker moved the suit in and lay Tupo on the bed as gently as she could. The bed moulded itself around the child, hugging xyr limbs supportively. 'On my ship,' Speaker said.

'And what ha—' *What happened,* Captain Tem presumably began to say, but as she caught sight of Speaker's suit, she fell silent. 'How long has xe been without oxygen?'

'I don't know,' Speaker said. 'I just found xyr a minute ago.'

Captain Tem retrieved a small item from the hidden cupboard she'd opened: a packet of SoberUps. She tore the wrapping open, popped the tabs in her mouth, and crunched furiously. Her cheeks swirled a discordant mix of colours as she swallowed, as though her body was sorting itself out. 'Did you flag the emergency channel?'

'Not yet, I wanted to get xyr out of my ship first.'

'Makes sense. Does xe have a pulse?'

'I have no idea. Do *you* know how to check for a Laru's pulse? Do they even have one?'

'Fuck. I don't know.' Captain Tem ran a hand over her smooth head. 'Okay. Okay, you – you know how to use a bot scanner?'

'Yes.'

'You know the advanced options?'

'Basically. I know the first aid functions.'

'Okay, good, you – wait, shit, no, I'll have to do it. You won't be able to read my scanner. Here—' She opened another previously unseen cupboard and retrieved what appeared to be a breathing mask connected to a handheld canister of super compressed air. 'See if you can get this on xyr, I'll do bots.'

Speaker took the mask and moved to the head of the bed as Captain Tem picked up one of Tupo's forelegs, searching for xyr wristpatch. Speaker gently lifted the child's head with one hand and tried to slip the mask on with the other. She still couldn't tell if Tupo was breathing.

'Dammit, there's so much fucking fur,' Captain Tem snapped. She searched through the thick curls with her delicate fingers. 'Ah, there!' She pressed a fingertip down on one spot, then brought the bot scanner over. 'Okay, kid, let's check you out.'

'There's a problem,' Speaker said. 'Look.' She'd got the mask on, but the device was ill-fitting for a Laru head. Tupo's mouth was too wide, but when Speaker tried to position the mask solely over xyr nose instead, the contours prevented a proper seal. Without that, it seemed, the canister wouldn't activate.

Captain Tem looked up from the scanner and grimaced. 'Maybe we can—'

'Tape,' Speaker said. 'Do you have tape? Or something like it?' Captain Tem reached for a cupboard, but Speaker stopped her. 'No, not medical tape. It's got to be airtight. What would you use to patch a leaky pipe?'

'Not tape,' Captain Tem said. Her cheeks had settled into placid silver. 'I've got sealant guns, but—'

'Would that be safe for xyr?'

The Aeluon's eyelids flicked. 'I mean, it'll rip xyr fur off.'

Unpleasant as that sounded, Speaker considered that an extremely fair trade under the circumstances. 'Where?'

Captain Tem pointed down the hallway and turned her attention back to the scanner. 'Storage room. Straight ahead, then take a right, then the wall opposite from life support. You know how to open our doors?'

'You just . . .' Speaker raised one of the suit's hands and mimed pressing its palm against something.

Captain Tem glanced over as the scanner got to work. 'Yeah, right.'

Speaker worked the suit's controls with one hand, following Captain Tem's directions as she grabbed her scrib. She gestured at it, readying it for verbal request. 'Flag local emergency channel,' she said. 'And make a voice call to the ground host.'

Roveg would never forget the sound Ouloo made when she ran into Captain Tem's shuttle and saw Tupo.

He couldn't call it a scream. A scream was sharp and shrill. This sound was curved, liquid, moaning. It was a frightened sound, a mourning sound. If blood could speak as it was spilling, that was the sound it would make.

'Xe's alive,' Captain Tem said. 'I don't know how, but—'

Ouloo started speaking, but her words weren't directed to any of them. She spoke to Tupo in Piloom, her cooing words at once pleading and angry. Roveg did not need translation to understand her meaning.

'Did you flag emergency services?' he asked.

Speaker, who was in the middle of – what was she doing? gluing something to the little Laru's face, it seemed – threw him a pointed look. 'My signal won't go through,' she said. 'Too many people are trying to use comms.'

'Idiots,' he said. 'What else – what's the point of an emergency channel if you can't—' The sentence trailed off before he could remember where he'd been leading it. Stars, why had he drank so much?

Captain Tem noticed his trouble. She stuck her hand into a wall, grabbed something, and tossed it his way without a word. He fumbled the catch with his first leg, but recovered with the second. A packet of SoberUps. Thank goodness. He consumed the distasteful stuff without delay.

The Aeluon crouched beside Ouloo, putting her hands on

the Laru's forelegs. 'Ouloo, I need you to listen to me. I'm not
a doctor, and neither is Speaker, but we're going to help as
best we can. I need you to answer some questions. Can you
do that?'

Ouloo trembled, but waggled her neck in vigorous assent.
'Anything.'

'Okay. I don't know much about your physiology. My scans
say that Tupo is alive, but not breathing, and everything inter-
nally seems to be kind of . . . shut down. Speaker's trying to
get some air into xyr, but xyr nose is . . . it seems to be closed
up. I don't—'

At this, Ouloo made the sound again, quieter this time. It
was still enough to make Roveg's frills twitch uncomfortably.
'It's *olotohen*,' she said, and wailed once more.

'I don't know what that is,' Captain Tem said.

Roveg bent his torso lower. 'Breathe, Ouloo. You can do this.'

Ouloo took a breath. 'It's a . . . oh, stars, I don't know how
to explain it. It's a – a protective sort of . . . sleep? Not sleep.
Shit, I don't know the word.'

'Torpor?' Speaker offered. 'Coma?'

'Yes, something like that. It's a – a reflex our kids have when
they're – when they're in danger.' Her voice broke. 'I would've
thought xe was too old for that, but I guess – I guess some
things about xyr are still little.'

Captain Tem squeezed her hands around Ouloo's legs. 'Tell
me about this thing. Is it . . . common? How does it work?'

'It's not common. I've never seen xyr do this before. It never
happened to me. It's – it's only a – a last-ditch sort of thing.'

'And what will happen? How long does it last?'

'I – I'm not really sure. I know you're supposed to go straight
to a doctor if it happens, but other than that, I don't know.'

The SoberUps were working fast, and the clearer his head
became, the more Roveg found himself desperate to be of use.
'Ouloo, do you know the remote access code for the reference
file node in Tupo's museum? I know the password, but—' What

was needed was a proper medical crew, but in lieu of that, they could at least know what they were dealing with.

'Oh, um – yes, yes. It's, um, 239-23-235-7.'

Roveg turned to the Aeluon. 'Captain Tem, may I use your comms panel? I don't have my scrib with me.'

'You won't be able to read it,' she said.

'You can use my scrib,' Ouloo said. 'It's set to Piloom, but you can—'

'Everybody, quiet,' Speaker said. She set down the tool in her suit's hands and bent the vox below her cockpit close to Tupo's face. A breathing mask – that was what she'd attached to xyr. Speaker muttered something to herself as she made the suit pick up the air canister. The words were in her own language, and these, too, etched themselves into Roveg's memory. The high-pitched sounds were unsettling to him, but he could feel an uncanny sort of kindness behind them. A plea, maybe. Perhaps a prayer.

No one in the room spoke as the air from the canister began to hiss, forcing itself forward into the mask. Tupo's eyes remained shut. Xyr limbs remained motionless. But after a few seconds, the little Laru's nostrils shot open, and xyr mouth gulped with a primal gasp. Xyr chest rose, and fell, and rose, and fell. The motion was painfully slow, and disturbing without any other hint of consciousness, but Tupo was breathing. Tupo was breathing, and in that moment, everybody present remembered how to do the same.

Feed source: Galactic Commons Reference Files – Local Access/
Offline Version (Public/Klip)
Node path: 239-23-235-7
Node access password: Tup0IsGr3at

Selected file: Olotohen (medical reference)
Encryption: 0
Translation path: 0

Olotohen is a cryptobiotic state unique to prepubescent and pread-olescent Laru children. This defensive reflex is triggered by extreme environmental danger (high or low temperatures, prolonged under-water submersion, oxygen deficiency, etc.), severe illness, or extreme mental/physical stress. When in *olotohen*, the patient's internal func-tions almost entirely shut down. Breathing and heartbeat are impossible to perceive via physical examination, and may temporarily cease until the patient is placed in an ideal environment. Brain activity will appear minimal in standard imubot scans, and may flag a false positive for brain death.

A patient can safely remain in *olotohen* for up to eight GC standard hours without suffering any adverse affects beyond fatigue and increased thirst/appetite (these conditions typically dissipate within two to four days, depending on the patient). Beyond this point, the risk of brain and/or other organ damage increases exponentially. After thirteen hours, death is almost certain.

Patients who have entered *olotohen* must be given medical atten-tion as quickly as possible. As this is an unconscious state, a patient may remain in *olotohen* even after the danger has passed. While xe may wake up on xyr own without intervention, this outcome cannot and should not be taken for granted. Always err on the side of caution with *olotohen* patients.

Patients who are in *olotohen* can be brought back to full conscious-ness and homeostasis by any medical professional who has completed a GC Medical Institute-certified training course in multispecies emergency medicine. This is a neurological procedure involving non-invasive imubot treatment, and takes about ten minutes to complete. This procedure should under no circumstances be attempted by those without certified medical training, as operator errors are likely to result in nerve or brain damage.

The GC Medical Institute recommends the following care for *olotohen* patients while awaiting professional medical help:

- Remove the patient from the dangerous/threatening environment.
- If the patient is wet, dry xyr fur. If water is present in xyr mouth, open xyr mouth and empty it as much as possible by gently tipping xyr neck in a vertical fashion with xyr head pointing toward the ground.
- If the patient was in an extremely cold or freezing environment, bundle xyr tightly with blankets, warm clothing, or any other insulating material.
- If the patient was in an extremely hot environment, cool the room to fifty GC standard degrees. Do not use blankets, clothing, etc.
- Provide clean, filtered air, if possible.
- Avoid an environment with harsh or bright lights, if possible.
- Avoid an environment with loud or sudden noises, if possible.
- Set up an ongoing imubot monitoring scan and watch closely for any of the following signs:
  - sudden drop or cessation of heart rate, after heart rate has resumed
  - sudden drop or cessation of brain activity, if brain activity has previously been detected
  - hyperventilation or cessation of breath after normal breathing has resumed

If any of these signs occur in a situation in which a medical professional is not immediately available, place the patient in a medical stasis chamber, if possible. This should only be done as a last resort, as medical stasis can create serious complications in *olotohen* patients.

SPEAKER

As things stood, there were two good possibilities: Tupo could wake up before the eight-hour mark, or their signal could get through to emergency services. If neither of these came to pass, then they'd have no choice but to put Tupo in medical stasis, and then . . . then they'd have to see. There was no way to make the good possibilities happen, no way to know if they'd happen in five minutes or five hours or never. So the only option before them was to wait, without any idea of which reality they were waiting for.

Speaker stood with the others in the common area, where they'd stepped out to discuss what came next. It was doubtful Tupo could hear them, but nobody wanted to scare the child on the off-chance that some of their words were drifting through xyr unconscious state.

'Well, we've got the scan going, at least,' Captain Tem said. 'I'll keep an eye to make sure none of those warning signs pop up.'

'And I'll keep trying with the comms signal,' Roveg sighed. 'There's not much I can do about jammed traffic, but I can set the scrib up to automatically send a flag every five minutes.'

Speaker glanced at Ouloo. The Laru's eyes weren't focused on anything. She was rubbing her forepaws together, over and over and over. Speaker turned the suit to face her. 'Ouloo, I know this sounds impossible, but you should rest. We might be here a while.'

'I'm not going *anywhere*,' Ouloo said.

'You can use my bed,' Captain Tem said. 'She's right; your body's going through it right now, too. You should take it easy so you can jump in if . . . well, if it's needed.'

Ouloo continued to rub her paws. 'I do like Aeluon beds,' she said quietly.

Captain Tem smiled blue. 'Mine's really good, too.'

Ouloo looked around the group. 'You'll come get me, right? If any – if anything—'

'Of course,' Speaker said.

The Laru bobbed her neck, and let Captain Tem lead her away.

Roveg sighed and flexed his legs. 'Not quite the evening we were expecting, hmm?' He rubbed his face with his top-most toes. 'Stars, I need some water. I should never drink with Aeluons.'

'I saw a kitchen on the way in,' Speaker said. 'Or at least, I think it was a kitchen. There was food in it.'

Roveg leaned in conspiratorially. 'Every Aeluon room I've ever seen looks exactly the same,' he said in an unimpressed tone. 'So your guess is as good as mine.'

The room Speaker had seen did turn out to be a kitchen, but they couldn't find a damn thing. Both she and Roveg put their respective appendages on the walls here and there, trying to figure out where the cupboard openings were.

Captain Tem appeared in the doorway after a few futile moments. 'What . . . is going on?' she said.

'Captain, where the hell do you keep your drinkware?' Roveg said.

The Aeluon made an amused expression. She walked up to a spot on the wall that looked like every other, pressed her palm on it, and opened the panel. She removed a small bowl and held it toward him. 'Will this work better for you than my cups?'

Roveg chuffed irritably at the wall he'd failed to open. 'Yes, thank you. Water, if you wouldn't mind.'

'Is Ouloo lying down?' Speaker asked.

'Yeah,' Captain Tem said. She filled the bowl from a dispenser of some kind. 'I doubt she'll sleep, but . . .'

'I don't see how anybody could,' Speaker said. She shook her head as if drying herself off. 'I can't imagine how she's feeling.'

Roveg took the bowl of water from Captain Tem, but he didn't speak, and he didn't drink. He stood silent, staring at nothing. 'I can,' he said.

Speaker and Captain Tem both looked at him, and the room grew heavy.

The Quelin took a long drink of water and shifted his eyes. 'I have four sons,' he said quietly. 'I carried their eggs on my shell for a standard, and they all hatched on the same day. Their mother and I were friends, nothing more. It's a common arrange-ment – two friends who both want to have children and haven't found a romantic partner to do so with. I enjoyed her company. I cared about her, but I did not *love* her. But my boys . . .' His mouthparts clicked with a fragile sound. 'I never knew what love was until I saw them for the first time. I remember them stumbling around, unable to speak. I tried to clean them off – they were all wet, and covered in eggshell, but they didn't understand to hold still. They couldn't speak. They didn't under-stand what they were, what anything was. But they understood *me*, somehow. Each one of them, in turn. They stumbled, and they tripped, and by chance, they saw me. And once they saw me, they stumbled right at me, deliberately. They shivered against me, as if they – as if they knew I was the one thing that would keep them safe.' He took another sip from the bowl. 'So, yes. I have some idea of how she must be feeling.'

The weight in the room increased. 'That must be so painful,' Speaker said, 'to have been sent away from them.'

'Don't feel sorry for me,' Roveg said. 'Please don't. I knew the stories I was telling might get me into trouble, and I did it anyway. I was stupid and cocky and thought I wouldn't get caught, but I understood the risk. It wasn't enough, though. The risk of robbing my boys of their father wasn't enough to keep me quiet. And I know. I know that makes me a selfish person.'

'You're not,' Speaker said.

'Of course I am. I put my work above them.' Anger entered Roveg's voice; Speaker could hear its sharpness facing inward. 'And the worst part is, I still don't think that was the wrong thing to do. I hate having left them. It kills me every day. But I also couldn't have kept pretending to believe in something I didn't. I cared more in the end about telling the truth than I did about being a father. I wish I regretted that more than I do.' He turned his gaze to the ground. 'And I'm sure you all think I'm a real bastard now.'

Captain Tem's face shifted colour pensively. 'The friend I'm going to see is named Ashby,' Captain Tem said. 'He's a tunneller, and he's Exodan, and he's my . . .' The talkbox went quiet. 'We've been coupling for about four standards now.'

Roveg turned his head to her, his eyes glittering. 'My, my, Captain. I never would've guessed.'

The Aeluon gave him a sharp look. 'Does it bother you?'

'Not in the slightest,' he said. 'I just wouldn't have bet on you being so subversive.'

'I'm not,' she said with a flat laugh. 'Or at least, I never thought I was. I wasn't trying to make a statement, like you were. He was just . . . just this person I liked.'

'A person you still like, I gather.'

'Yeah.'

He studied her face. 'You like him a lot.'

'Yeah,' she said, then frowned. 'You know, it's really annoying that you can read my face but I can't read yours.'

'It's not my fault you can't detect my pheromones.'

'Yeah, well, anyway.' She went to the cupboard to fetch a cup for herself. 'It's gone on for so long that I'm having trouble stomaching it. Not him, I mean. I mean the secrecy. I don't mind us spending time apart. We have different jobs, different lives. We're usually both on a long haul. That's just how we are. But pretending that he doesn't exist . . . do you know how it feels to be with your friends and talk about your life and cut an entire piece of it out?'

'Yes,' Roveg said. 'I do.'

'But you did the risky thing anyway. So maybe you *are* selfish. I don't know. But even if you are, I think you're brave. You're braver than me, for sure. Because I'm hurting him. I know I'm hurting him. But I haven't stopped hurting him, because I'm too afraid. And sometimes fear is good. Fear keeps you alive. But it can also keep you from what you really want. And that's my problem – I don't *know* what I want. I want to keep both halves of myself, and I want them to stay exactly as they are. But—'

'But you can't do that forever,' Roveg said. 'You can't split yourself like that without feeling each side begin to fray. I know.' His spiracles pulsed. 'And even if you do choose one over the other, the one you abandoned is never really gone.'

'How do you mean?'

Roveg drained the bowl. 'One of my sons wrote to me earlier this standard. Boreth. I have no idea how he found me. I was honestly afraid when I got his message, because whatever pathways he took cannot be legal. I admit, part of me was proud of that. I think perhaps he's turned into a troublemaker like me.' He set the bowl down on the counter. 'We have a ceremony – the First Brand. It's a coming-of-age ritual, performed when you've stopped growing and your shell is the same size it will be for the rest of your life.' Speaker could hear the sorrow in his voice at this, the grief over years he had not seen. 'It's happening for my boys in two tendays, and he asked me if I would apply for the entry permit so I could come. I thought they'd hate me for leaving. Maybe the rest of them do, I don't know. But Boreth wants me there, so . . .'

'So that's why you're going back,' Speaker said softly.

'Yes.'

'Are you going to make it?' she asked.

Roveg pulled himself together. 'I don't know,' he said, stating simple fact. 'At this point . . . I don't know.'

'There has to be something you can do to get your permit,' Captain Tem said. 'Some kind of strings you can pull.'

'Not for someone like me,' he said. 'In GC space? Sure. I could call a friend, line a pocket, whatever it took. But in Quelin territory, I'm nothing. Worse than nothing. I'm a dangerous *something*, and all they need is the slightest of excuses – one box unchecked, one toe out of place – to not grant me any favours.'

'That's not right,' Captain Tem said.

'And neither is having to keep your Human partner secret,' Roveg said. 'But here we are.'

The aliens fell quiet, and after a second, Speaker realised they'd both turned their eyes to her. 'Don't look at me,' Speaker said. 'I don't have any secrets. I just want to go home.'

Roveg laughed, but he spoke with sincerity. 'And that's what I like about *you*, Speaker. You don't have any problem telling anybody exactly who you are.'

Speaker cocked her head at him. 'Yes, I do. Of course I do. I can't always speak my mind, not if I want to get the things I need or go places I need to go. Everything I do, every word I say, is calculated to make people comfortable. To make them respect me. None of it is a lie, but it *is* an act, and it's one that gets very, very tiring.'

The Quelin took that in. 'Then I count myself privileged,' he said, 'to have seen you outside of that.'

Captain Tem got up from the table, the hints of yellow and purple in her cheeks unmissable. She hadn't forgotten the garden any more than Speaker had, it seemed. 'I'm going to watch the kid,' she said.

'Captain,' Speaker said. She had no intention of walking back anything she'd said earlier, but she did want to help, for Tupo's sake. This wasn't a job for one person alone. 'I know I can't read your monitors like you can, but if you teach me what basic colours or patterns to watch out for, we can take turns. I learn fast.'

Captain Tem stood in the melted-open doorway, its liquid frame rippling around her. 'Sure,' she said, her voice utterly neutral. 'Come on.'

ROVEG

Aeluon design didn't make sense when you put other species inside of it. It was plenty functional for any sort of body. You could move around in an Aeluon space. You could use their furniture. You could be completely comfortable. But the *look* of an Aeluon living space – be it ship or building or otherwise – really only served to complement one species and one species alone. They treated surroundings as accessory, a backdrop to both fashion and the aesthetic of their own biology. Aeluons always matched the rooms they lived in, and when you substituted another sapient in their stead, the effect just wasn't the same.

Nowhere was this rule more evident than with Ouloo, who looked like she belonged in Pei's bed about as much as Roveg himself would. Her red furry frame sprawled against the pristine white polymer like an old rug – a nicely kept, freshly washed rug, but a rug all the same. Roveg had never seen a Laru belly-up before, and he did his best not to stare in curiosity at the oil-black skin that peeked through thinner layers of fur, or at the subtle seam of the pouch where Tupo had once lived. He thought of the keratin pockets that lined the edges of his own abdomen, where he'd once guarded four bubble-like eggs, two to each side. He'd barely been able to feel them, but he'd been keenly aware of their existence. Every step, every decision to sit or stand or lie down had been made with their safety in mind.

How things have changed, he thought grimly.

Ouloo was not asleep; he had not expected her to be. He

could not dream of sleeping under such circumstances. Even so, he did not wish to startle her, and walked into the room with light steps, carrying a tray he'd brought from his own shuttle. 'I've brought you some food,' he said.

The Laru's eyes were wide open, fixed on the ceiling. She did not look at him. 'I'm not hungry,' she said, her voice barely a whisper.

'I didn't think you would be,' he said. He looked around for a table, or whatever Pei had that would pass for a table. He settled on a lump-like thing that appeared to be made of the same stuff as the bed, only firmer. 'But hungry or no, I thought *you* could use some looking after as well.' He set the tray down on the stylish lump and it moulded itself accordingly, creating a supportive platform. Stars, but it really did feel like it was showing off.

Ouloo gave him the barest of glances, but as she did so, caught a glimpse of the tray. This was enough to make her neck rise up. Roveg had assembled a spread of Laru-friendly nibbles: grilled quickbread, a hurriedly made batch of whitefish salad, tiny wraps of grain paper stuffed with nut butter and edible flowers, and the last of his smoked eel and crackers.

'Did you . . . make this?' she said.

'Well, I'm of no help to them,' he said, meaning the two sapients in the med bay. 'My skills are a bit useless in a situation like this. So . . . this is what I can contribute.'

Ouloo sat up, resting on her back legs. 'I can't remember the last time somebody cooked for me,' she said. Whether she was stunned by the gesture or just the entire terrible night, it was impossible to say.

'Then it's high time someone did,' Roveg said. He lifted the carafe from the tray. 'Mint fizz? I thought about making you mek, but I assumed you'd want to stay sharp.'

'Stars, no, I don't want mek,' Ouloo said. She paused. 'I wouldn't mind some fizz, though.' She examined the tray. 'What are these?' She pointed a toepad forward.

'Flower wraps,' he said as he filled a cup for her.

She picked one up and took a bite. 'Oh, that's scrumptious,' she said. For a moment, her eyes brightened, but they dulled just as quickly. 'I shouldn't be enjoying myself.'

'Oh, don't think for a minute I ever expected you to *enjoy* yourself.' He handed her the cup. 'This is encouragement, not a cure. You're probably going to walk away from this with mixed feelings about flower wraps. Which is a shame, because they *are* scrumptious, and I'm delighted you think so.'

Ouloo popped the rest of the flower wrap into her mouth and moved to take a sip of fizz. She paused. 'Is this one of mine?' she asked, holding up the cup.

'Ah, yes,' Roveg said. 'My drinkware is almost certainly the wrong shape for you, so I took the enormous liberty of retrieving that from your house. I hope you'll forgive me.'

The Laru scoffed. 'After this, you three can *have* my house, if you want.' She said the words with a paper-dry laugh, but her neck sagged as she spoke. Roveg didn't need to be told why. Nobody knew what *after this* was going to look like.

He folded his abdominal legs and sat on the floor before her. 'Am I correct that you overheard what I told the others in the kitchen?'

'Yes,' she said. 'I wasn't being nosy, it's just – you know – it's not that big of a ship.'

'Not to worry. I assumed as much.' Speaking so freely about the subject was new to him, and he found it brought misery and relief in equal measure. 'One of my boys is named Segred, and he was a wild one from the moment he hatched. This one day, I was at a production meeting for a new sim – oh-so very important, like every meeting of that sort is. Life and death, you know. I *had* to be there. I got a call in the middle of it that Segred had been taken to the infirmary. He and his idiot friends had gone to – it doesn't matter where. This lagoon on the outskirts of our city. They'd thought it would be a marvellous idea to climb the tallest rock face there and take turns dropping off of it into the water. Only, there were *other* rocks below the surface which they didn't take into account, and Segred crashed against one as he came down. Cracked his shell all the way through – *here* and *here*.' He gestured at two spots on his thorax.

'Oh my,' Ouloo said, clutching her cup. 'That's got to be bad for you folks.'

'Very bad, especially given the lagoon water that poured into the wounds.' He exhaled through his spiracles at the awful memory. 'I spent two tendays sitting with him in the infirmary as he dealt with a raging bacterial infection that was very difficult to treat. It was ugly. I'll spare you the details. But watching my child fight to stay alive was the worst experience I've ever had.'

'Worse than getting kicked out?'

'Oh, stars, yes. They can name me a cultural threat a hundred times over if it means I never have to go through something like that again.'

'And . . . was he . . . ?'

'He was fine. Physically scarred yet infinitely wiser.'

Ouloo bobbed her neck. 'I hope . . . I hope that . . .' She couldn't bring herself to say the words.

Roveg tilted his head to catch her eye. 'I'm not telling you that everything will be all right,' he said. 'I'm telling you I understand how horrible it feels to be able to do nothing.'

She took another flower wrap. 'How did you get through it?'

'Not easily. But his mother and I started doing this . . . sort of game, I suppose. We would talk about the things we were looking forward to doing with Segred once he had healed. The things we wanted to see him do. It was frightening, at first. I felt as though we were jinxing it. But the longer we did it, the more it felt like we were willing a future for Segred into existence. Like the more we said it, the more certain it was. I know there's no reason or logic to that whatsoever. I know Segred's recovery had nothing to do with that and everything to do with imubots and antibiotics. That game didn't help my son. It helped *me.*' He gestured supportively with his thoracic legs. 'So. What are you looking forward to, with Tupo?'

Ouloo cradled the cup in her paws. 'I'm very excited for xyr to tell me what gender xe is,' she said. 'I've been planning the party in my head forever. Crushcake with groob jam if xe's a girl, ten-berry fancy if xe's a boy, citrus cloudcups if xe's neither or somewhere in between. I have the recipes saved on my scrib. I know it might not happen for years – there's no way of predicting when kids land on it, xe could be all the way grown by then – but I love imagining the party. It gets a little more elaborate every time. There will be lights and pixel clouds and I'll hire a band if I've got the money for it.'

'Sounds spectacular,' Roveg said. 'Do you have any guesses, as to—'

Ouloo waved one of her paws at him. 'Oh, no, no, no,' she said. 'I won't do that with xyr. Some people – not everybody, but some – think it's cute to make bets on it, but I think it's a stupid thing to do. When I was not much older than Tupo, I overheard my – it's odd for me to say *relatives*, because we don't use those terms among ourselves, but that's the word *you* would use. Anyway, they were talking about me in that way, and most of them thought I'd tell them I was a boy. Had me confused for standards. No, I absolutely won't do that with Tupo. Xe's the only one who knows what xe is.'

'Noted, and admirable,' Roveg said. 'And I have always thought the party sounds like a lovely custom.'

'Quelin don't have anything similar, right?'

'No, not at all. If your parents got it wrong, you let them know, you update your records, and everybody gets on with their lives. It's a casual matter. Nobody hires a band. Which is our loss, really.'

'Well, no matter which recipe I make for—' Ouloo took a shaky breath.

Roveg bent his legs in an empathetic gesture. He'd felt that hesitation before. 'It's all right,' he said. 'Will it.'

Ouloo's eyes narrowed and her jaw tensed. 'No matter which recipe I make for Tupo,' she said with fierce intention, 'all three of you are invited.'

'I wouldn't miss it,' Roveg said. As soon as the words left his mouth, they circled back and slapped him. Oh, he wouldn't miss the party of the child he'd known for four days. Stars, no, he wouldn't miss *that*.

Ouloo watched him as he sat brooding. She picked up one of the eel crackers and offered it to him on her upturned paw.

'They're for you,' he said.

She pushed her paw forward, insisting. 'It's not a cure,' she said. 'It's encouragement.'

It took little time for the two of them to eat the tray clean.

PEI

The kid didn't move, beyond breathing. The colours on the scanner screen didn't vary. The only thing that changed was the rotation of who was watching – Pei, Speaker, Pei, Speaker – every half an hour. The mood in the shuttle was miserable and stagnant, and Pei didn't know whether she wanted things to hurry up so that she could deal with whichever scenario presented itself, or if she wanted everything to hold still for as long as it took for them to come up with a better solution than this.

As neither option was possible, she sat by the med bed, and continued to observe the screen doing nothing.

Speaker came back to the room before it was her turn to take over. 'I need to go to my shuttle, just for a short while,' she said. 'My air supply needs a refill, and I need some food.'

'Oh, right,' Pei said. Ever-present as Speaker's suit was, Pei hadn't thought about the logistics of being stuck in one all day. 'Yeah, of course.' The Akarak began to leave, but something that had been stuck in Pei's craw for hours finally worked itself free. 'Hey, I want to apologise for what happened in the garden. I'm . . . sorry we fought. I was drunk.'

Speaker stopped the suit, and turned to face her. 'You don't strike me as the sort to change her opinions just because she's drunk.'

This assertion wasn't wrong, but Pei bristled at her tone. 'I said I'm sorry we *fought*. I'm not apologising for my opinions.'

'I'm not, either,' Speaker said.

'Stars, can I—' Pei could feel her cheeks going purple, but she reined it in and took a breath. 'I'm apologising for pushing you on topics you didn't want to get into. You didn't want to go there, and I . . . didn't have the wherewithal to recognise that. And I *should* have, even though I don't – I mean, obviously we don't see eye to eye.'

Speaker met Pei's gaze with unflinching directness. 'I don't think you're a bad person, Captain Tem. There are few people who are truly *bad* through and through. I still don't know you. I know you *better*, from what I've seen in here. I think you mean well. I think you want to help people, even though we have very different ideas of what that means. But I won't pretend that I'm comfortable with what you do and what you're a part of. I can't look at you and say, "Oh, I like her as a person, so I'll ignore the life she lives." That's exactly the sort of thinking that allows problems to persist. So, if you want me to apologise in return, if you want me to take back what I said in the garden, I won't. I told the truth. Nothing about tonight changes that.'

'Pei.'

Speaker blinked. 'Sorry?'

'You can call me Pei,' she said. 'That's my name. That's what friends call me.'

'I . . . don't understand. We—'

Pei shook her palm at whatever Speaker was about to say. 'We're *not* friends. I'm not sure that we could be. I don't have any shame about my work, and I don't agree with your take on it. I'd be a liar if I said it didn't piss me off. But I do respect you, and your honesty. I respect somebody with the strength to say things you *know* will piss somebody off, because you believe what you believe. And given that, plus all that's happened tonight, it would be weird for you to keep addressing me like a stranger.'

'What are we, if not strangers and not friends?'

'I have no idea.'

The Akarak thought about that. 'All right,' she said. 'Pei.' She cocked her head. 'Do *you* need to rest, once I get back? I don't know what your sleep cycle is like, but especially since . . .' She gestured broadly at Pei's shimmering scales.

Now it was Pei's turn to be confused. 'What about it?'

'I – sorry, I have no idea what your reproductive cycle feels like,' Speaker said. 'I know that for my species, it's common to feel tired while growing a clutch.'

'It's not like that for us. If anything, I'm restless.'

'I see,' Speaker said. 'Are you looking forward to going to the creche? To coupling, or however it works?'

Pei had meant what she said about respecting honesty, but stars, Speaker wasn't shy. 'That's a blunt question, seeing as how we're not friends.'

'Since you don't know what we are, then how do you know what sorts of questions are too blunt?'

An annoying retort, but Pei couldn't argue it, and was too tired to keep her thoughts to herself any longer. 'I'm feeling . . . complicated about it.'

'Because of your Human partner?'

'No, stars – dammit, see, that's exactly – that's exactly my problem.' Pei exhaled. 'I can explain, but do you actually care?'

Speaker shrugged. 'I'm curious, at least.'

Pei laughed shortly, her cheeks pale green. 'I guess that's good enough.' She crossed her arms over her chest and gathered her thoughts. 'How much do you know about the whole *thing* my species has about relationships like that?'

'Nothing, really, other than it's a common taboo.'

'Okay. The rationale goes that the more time you spend around other species, the more their cultures start to influence you. This is generally seen as a good thing. Most of us would encourage this. But if you extend that influence to a *romantic* relationship, the thinking goes that there's a danger of you abandoning the Aeluon way of doing things in that regard, which—'

'Which means if you start to shimmer, you might not act on it.'

'That's the gist, yes.'

'And . . . sorry, but what's the problem with not acting on it?'

'We don't reproduce easily, and we only get a chance or two, at most. Not acting on your shimmer is a wasted opportunity. No, it's worse than that. You're letting everybody down, kind of.' Pei struggled to articulate her point. She'd never had to explain this in words before, and she wasn't getting the nuance right. 'You've failed, if you let your shimmer go. You've failed the species.'

Speaker thought about this. 'Is this because of the bottleneck? Your near extinction?'

'I honestly don't know. Probably, now that I'm thinking about it. It's just baked in, at this point. We take it for granted.'

'Well, if that *is* the rationale, why would concerns over population growth apply anymore? You're one of the most well-established species in the GC. You're *everywhere*.'

'Yeah, but that's not the point. The point is, this idea's been around for a long, long time, and it's . . . it's calcified. Doesn't matter that there are billions of us on dozens of different worlds. Interspecies relationships are just *not done*. At least, not by most.'

'I was going to say, I met two Aeluons once in Reskit who were part of a feather family. You're definitely not alone in this.'

'No, but those people are on the fringes, and I . . . am not. It would not go well for me, if the people I work with found out.'

Speaker squinted at her. 'But you said your feelings about your shimmer have nothing to do with . . . sorry, what's his name?'

'Ashby. And see, that's exactly the thing I don't fucking understand, because he's not the problem at all. Humans tend to get all their wires crossed in this arena, but he and I talked about shimmering when it first became obvious this was an arrangement we wanted to continue. He understands the difference between social sex and reproductive sex – he really does. His pilot's Aandrisk, and they're close, so he already had an introduction to the concept. It's not the same, of course, but—'

'He has an open mind. And a willingness to accommodate cultural norms beyond his own.'

'Yes.'

'So this *isn't* about you not wanting to couple with someone other than him.'

'No. Not at all. And that's what's so infuriating, because I know it's only a matter of time before people – my people, I mean – find out about him and me. I know it. It's gone on for too long, and I don't want to lose him, so being open about it is the only other option. So if I *don't* go to a creche but I *do* go to my Human partner, then . . . well, then it doesn't matter why I let my shimmer go – I've become exactly the cautionary tale all of this bullshit is based around, even though Ashby wouldn't be my reason for it at all.'

'Then what *is* your reason?'

'*I don't know.*' Pei rubbed her face in frustration. 'There *is* no reason why I don't want to do this. I'm healthy. I'm clearly capable. Everybody I know who's ever gone to a creche comes back saying it's a fantastic time. I'd have tendays to just lie around and have sex and be catered to. I like kids. I like being around kids. I imagine visiting my own would be nice. I have a partner who understands, and friends who would be thrilled, and . . . there's no reason not to.'

Speaker looked at her for a moment. 'Of course there is,' she said. '*You don't want to.*'

'That's not a reason. That's a feeling. Feelings have to have reason.'

'Since when?'

'All feelings stem from something. Even if you can't see it right away, there's always something way down there at the root causing it to happen. Like fish. I'm terrified of the fish we get back on Sohep Frie. Just seeing vids of them makes me twitch. I've been that way my whole life, and I never thought there was any reason for it, until one time, a few standards ago, I was visiting my fathers, and somehow me being scared of fish came up. And my father Gilen, he thinks this is . . . oh, there's not a word for this colour arrangement in Klip. Sad-funny, I guess. Sorry, it's hard thinking back on a colour conversation and having to translate it into sound.'

'I imagine it would be.'

'Anyway, he says that one of my older siblings once told me that the schools of shiver fish we'd see on beach trips would eat me. It apparently took my fathers forever to get me to go swimming again after that. I have no memory of this, at all, but I guess it stuck. It's the same principle with this. Somewhere in me, there is a reason why I don't want to do this. I just haven't figured it out yet.'

Speaker pondered. 'Are you aware that my legs aren't typical for my species?'

'I . . . wasn't, actually. Sorry.'

'Don't be. That's why I asked. It's a genetic condition. I have limited use of them, compared to Akaraks who are built other-wise.'

'Oh. I'm sorry.'

'Again: don't be. I'm not.' Speaker shifted her weight and clicked her beak. 'Two standards ago, Tracker and I were at a market stop. She was having a rough stretch with her lungs, so we found a doctor. The doctor in question was Laru, and I'm sure you're aware of their species' proclivity for genetic medical therapy.'

'I've heard that, yeah.'

'Right. So, this doctor helps Tracker with her trouble, and even though we weren't there for me, she gave me a check-up as well, because why not. Three days later, she contacted us, and she says, you know, I've been running simulations since you were here, and I'm confident I could give you new legs.'

'What, in a genetweak box or something?'

'Yes. Basically, she'd put me in stasis and I'd spend the next four tendays in a genetic manipulation module – a genetweak box, as you say – and when I awoke, I'd have new legs. I'd have to relearn how to use them, but it wouldn't hurt. I wouldn't be aware of anything that happened while I was out. She talked me through the whole procedure, and said Tracker could be there with me the whole time. Given the good care she'd provided Tracker, I trusted her. I liked her. I don't always say that about doctors. But everything she proposed seemed safe and above board.'

'But you didn't do it.'

'No, I didn't.'

'Why not?'

'Because I didn't want to,' Speaker said simply.

'But why?'

'Because I *didn't want to*. And when it comes to a person's body, that is all the reason there ever needs to be. Doesn't matter if it's a decision about a new pair of legs or how you like to trim your claws or—' she gave Pei a piercing look '—what to do about an egg. I didn't want to. You don't want to. That's it.'

'But—' Pei started.

Speaker leaned forward. 'That. Is all. It ever needs to be.'

Pei frowned, her colours swirling uneasily. Inside, she balked at what Speaker was getting at, and took it as proof that Speaker didn't understand, that you could explain cultural differences all day long, but in the end, there were some gaps you just couldn't fill. But a sliver within her gravitated hard toward the Akarak's sentiment, begging the rest of her to come along. Pei was unnerved by this, and her cheeks tinted red. 'Why are you even having this conversation with me?'

'Because it's interesting,' Speaker said. 'And because I think you needed to have it.' She stretched her neck, rocking her head from side to side. 'And speaking of needs, I have to go tend to myself. I'll try to not be more than half an hour.'

Speaker clanked away, leaving Pei with the monitor, the unconscious Laru, and a few too many thoughts that needed sifting through. Tupo exhaled loudly, as xe did from time to time. The sound meant nothing, but Pei's implant interpreted it as sad and impatient, the non-verbal complaint of someone who was ready to move the fuck on.

Yeah, kid, she flashed. *I know the feeling.*

SPEAKER

She needed to take care of herself, but she had to be quick about it. Everything aboard Capt— aboard Pei's shuttle had stayed the same for hours, which was what made Speaker wary about leaving. She wasn't superstitious in the slightest, but her stepping out seemed like exactly the time in which something *might* happen. The last thing she wanted was to be absent for that.

She climbed out of her cockpit, muscles stretching with relief. The suit was as comfortable as she could make it, but stars, it always felt good to get out of it.

The good feeling vanished as she noticed the ruined cake lying on the floor, its formerly fluffy frosting now collapsed. She hated the sight of it, but cleaning would have to wait. She locked a wrist-hook around the nearest pole and swung forward with clear intention. Bathroom. Food. Air. That was her mission here.

After completing the first item on her list, she made her way to the kitchen – if it could even be called that. It was a nook, really, containing storage hammocks and a stick-out shelf with a hot pot and a water tank. It wasn't much to look at, but she liked it much better than whatever the hell was going on in that Aeluon ship. At least here she could see where the doors were.

She reached for one of the dehydrated meal packs she'd been living off of for the past four days – hook bean hash, which she'd discovered to be completely fine. Not as good as the hook bean hash her mother had made, by a long shot, but it was tasty and filling and reminiscent of home. She began to open the package, but hesitated. She'd have to cook it, obviously, which would take ten minutes, and then she'd have to wait for it to cool – and it wasn't the sort of dish you could scarf down in three bites and be on your way. She considered instead grabbing an armload of protein bars, eating one right then, and taking the rest with her. But Speaker was ravenous. Aside from having been out of her ship for hours, she'd been putting the suit through tasks she'd never done before. Lifting things and using tools? Fine. But lifting *people* and using *medical tools* had never been on her to-do list, and it had taken no small amount of concentration to not be clumsy about it. She tore open the meal pack and emptied its shrivelled contents into the hot pot, along with some water. Yes, cooking would take time, but she needed to eat. She'd be of no help to anyone if she continued along with an unfuelled brain.

She hung by her wrists as the meal cooked, soothing her stiff body with the pull of gravity. She closed her eyes and thought of nothing.

Ten minutes later, the timer chimed. She began the careful process of transferring the scalding meal into a bowl, and was successfully not making a mess when the comms panel played an alert. There was an incoming call.

'Stars,' she muttered as a glob of sauce splattered on the floor. Of course. Of course this was when something went wrong. She should've just grabbed the protein bars and gone straight back. She gestured at a wall vox, accepting the call. 'I'll be right there,' she said loudly, pouring the hash back into the pot. She could reheat it later. 'Is everything—'

'Speaker? *Irek ie?*'

Speaker froze, and it felt like Gora stopped spinning right along with her. It wasn't Roveg or Ouloo calling.

It was Tracker.

Speaker was in the shuttle cockpit so fast she barely registered swinging her way there. But oh, oh, there she was – there was Tracker, on screen and breathing and beautiful. Speaker didn't sit in the hammock. She climbed right up on the control panel, pressing her hands against the edges of the screen, feeling as though half her weight had been cut clean away. 'Are you all right?' she cried in Ihreet. She was too loud. She didn't care.

'I – yes, yes, of course, I'm—' Tracker sputtered. 'Are *you* all right?'

'Yes, I'm fine,' Speaker said hurriedly, 'but are you well? Have you taken your medicine?'

'My – *what*?' Tracker said. She was shouting, incredulous. 'Who cares about *that*?'

'I – *I* care, you were having such a bad day when I left, and—'

'Speaker, you've been stuck on a planet *alone*. Alone! For days! And you want to ask me about my fucking medicine?'

Both sisters stared, realising in real-time that neither had considered the possibility of the other worrying about *them*. Baffled and exhausted, they did the only thing that made sense:

They laughed.

'So did you?' Speaker said, holding her forehead in one hand. '*Did* you take your medicine?'

'Yes, sweetheart. I did. I'm fine. I'd forgotten all about having a bad day. That feels like standards ago. Are you—'

'I'm fine. Perfectly fine.'

'Have you had enough to eat? I couldn't remember when the last time was that we stocked the shuttle.'

'Yes, I'm well fed, don't worry.'

'And it's friendly there?'

'Yes, very friendly. There's been no trouble.'

'Shit.' Tracker rubbed the sides of her face with her palms, as if trying to rid herself of a headache. 'I kept picturing you and some – I don't know, some gang of alien bastards fucking with the shuttle, or hurting you, or – I know how stupid this sounds, but stars, I was scared.'

'It's not stupid,' Speaker said. She placed her fingers over Tracker's face, pretending she could hold her close the way she wanted to. 'I pictured—' She shut her eyes. 'I don't want to say.'

Tracker clicked her beak reassuringly, the way she did when

Speaker awoke from a nightmare or had an upsetting day. 'We're okay.'

'Yes,' Speaker said. She pressed her hand against the screen, hard. 'We're okay.' She paused, remembering the context of what she'd been doing in the shuttle in the first place. 'But somebody here isn't. I—' Stars, where to begin with summarising the who and what and how? 'I don't have time to explain. There's a kid in trouble. Medical trouble. I need to get back there, I just needed food.'

'Holy shit. Okay. What—'

Speaker's eyes widened, and she cut Tracker off. 'You have comms. Tracker, *you have comms.*'

'Well, yeah, I – Oh. Of course, you don't know. Comms up here are fine, we just haven't been able to contact anybody planetside. Signal traffic has been a clusterfuck since the temporary satellites were deployed, but I made some tweaks and was able to punch through.'

Never in Speaker's life had she wanted to hug her brilliant sister's head so hard. 'You can contact the TA orbiter?'

'Uh, yeah, absolutely, I—'

'I need to you to flag emergency services. We haven't been able to get a signal through.'

Tracker immediately got to work, punching commands into her control panel. 'Stars, you're gonna make me speak Klip. What are the details?'

'Laru child. Age seventeen. Went into *olotohen* after asphyxiating—'

'Went into what?'

'It's like a coma.'

'Do you seriously think I know how to say *coma*? Or fucking *asphyxiating*?'

'Just tell them there's a Laru child who needs a doctor, and give them the coordinates. Can you say that?'

'Uh – yeah. Yeah, I think so. I can say *Laru* and *need doctor*, at least. What's *child*?'

'*Breggan.*'

'*Breggan,*' Tracker repeated in her thick accent. 'Ugh. Okay, you go help, I'll call.'

'Tracker?'

'Yeah?'

Speaker looked seriously at her sister. 'I miss you so much.'

'I miss you, too. And this is a shitty thing to say, but I'm so glad you're not the one I'm making this call about.' She made a shooing motion. 'Go, go. I'm on it.'

The screen switched off, and Speaker raced back toward the airlock. She grabbed an armload of protein bars on the way.

PEI

The doctor took an hour to arrive, but it was obvious she'd made the best time she could. Her skiff came tearing across the empty desert, and had barely come to a stop before its lone Human occupant jumped out and headed into the airlock. She hustled up to where Pei waited for her outside of the shuttle, wearing an exosuit and carrying a medical bag. She pulled off her helmet, and Pei found herself facing a petite young woman with black hair shaved short around the sides and cascades of piercings encrusting her ears. Her expression was friendly, but her eyes hinted that she was not in the habit of screwing around.

'I'm Dr Miriyam,' the Human said. 'Where's the patient?'

The words hit Pei's implant, and she warmed immediately to the crisp, clipped consonants of an Exodan accent. Ashby's accent. 'Come on,' Pei said, leading her inside.

Dr Miriyam followed. 'Are you the kid's guardian?' she asked.

'No, I'm just – a friend.' She hurried through the hallway to where the others were waiting in an anxious huddle.

'*Ah*,' the doctor said as she saw Ouloo. 'You must be—'

'I'm Ouloo,' she said, her fur fluffing. 'I'm Tupo's mother.'

'Tupo, got it. I'm Dr Miriyam.' She reached into her belt pouch and pulled out a bundle of printed cards. 'I've got my medical licences here if you'd like to take a look.'

Ouloo was confused. 'Oh – I don't need to see any of that. I trust you.'

Dr Miriyam paused. 'Oh.' She looked at the cards for a

moment, then put them back in her pouch with an expression of quiet surprise. 'Usually people ask.'

'I get that,' Speaker said.

'Hmm,' Dr Miriyam said, throwing her a knowing look. 'I bet you do. All right, where's—' She looked to her left, saw the med room door, and headed straight in. 'Oh, boy. Hey, Tupo. Let's sort you out.' She wasted no time in examining her patient. Ouloo joined her in the room; everybody else crowded around the door. 'How long has xe been in *olotohen*?' the doctor asked.

'Six hours, maybe,' Pei said. 'We're not entirely sure when this happened, but it couldn't have been much longer than that.'

'Okay. And what was the trigger?'

'Xe boarded my ship without a suit,' Speaker said.

Dr Miriyam apparently knew exactly what that meant, because she turned her head toward the Akarak with a dumbfounded expression. 'Without a suit? *Why?*'

'I think, um . . . xe was trying to bring me some cake.'

The doctor blinked twice, then shook her head. 'Kids, kids, kids,' she sighed. 'So! We're dealing with severe oxygen deprivation, which—' She noticed the air mask, buried into fur matted with sealant. 'What is going on with this?'

'I had to glue it,' Speaker said. 'The air wouldn't flow without a proper seal. I know it looks a mess, but—'

Dr Miriyam studied Speaker's handiwork. 'No, that's fabulous,' she said. 'Honestly. Kids like xyr can get by without breathing for the first few hours, but getting xyr nose open and some oxygen in xyr blood probably bought more time. That's great.'

Ouloo stood on two legs at the end of the med bed, holding Tupo's back paws in her forepaws. 'Is xe going to be all right?'

'If we're talking six hours, probably, yes, but I need to look at a few things before I can say for sure.' She looked around at the furniture. 'Is this . . . a chair?'

'That's a chair,' Pei said.

'If you say so.' The doctor unsnapped her exosuit, stepped out of it, tossed it into a corner, and sat down, looking mildly perturbed as the chair shaped itself around her. 'Well, that's weird,' she said in a flat voice as she pulled the bot scanner her way. She stared at the colour screen swirling back at her. 'Right. I'm gonna use mine.' She opened her medical bag and began pulling out various tools. 'Anything on xyr scans raise any flags in the last few hours?'

'Not that we noticed,' Speaker said. 'But we don't really know.'

'Neither of our fields of expertise,' Pei said.

'Well, you did the right thing by keeping an eye.' Dr Miriyam pressed her own scanner against Tupo's wristpatch, entered a flurry of commands, and studied the results closely. Ouloo began to rub her toepads against Tupo's fur nervously, her breath tight and halting.

Roveg tapped Pei on the shoulder with one of his legs. 'Captain, if I may?' he said, indicating that he wished to enter the room. Pei let him past, and Roveg walked up behind Ouloo. He wrapped his thoracic legs around her shoulders and torso gently, holding her steady, letting her know he was there. 'It's going to be all right,' he said in a soft voice. 'The doctor's here.'

Ouloo took a deep breath, bobbing her neck in acknowledgement. She reached a paw toward her shoulder and patted Roveg's toes.

Dr Miriyam nodded her head up and down as she read from her own scanner, and Pei knew this to be a promising gesture. 'Okay,' the doctor said. She looked up at Ouloo, her eyes serious but kind. 'I'm going to need to conduct a full tip-to-toe exam once xe's awake, but so far, this is looking good.'

'Oh,' Ouloo gasped. 'Oh, that's – oh, good.'

'We're not out of the woods yet,' Dr Miriyam cautioned. 'But the procedure I need to do won't take long. I'll be using xyr imubots to kick xyr brain back into gear. From what I'm seeing, there's low risk of complications here. But . . . you may not want to be in the room for this.'

'Why not?' Ouloo asked.

Dr Miriyam pressed her lips together. 'Xe'll likely twitch while I'm doing this. Might thrash around, make some involuntary sounds.'

'Will it hurt?'

'Mmm, that's hard to say. It probably *does* hurt, but xe either won't be conscious enough to register it, or xe won't remember it afterward. But it does look . . . upsetting. So, if you want to step out—'

'Like hell,' Ouloo huffed. She glanced back at Roveg. 'Will you stay, too?'

'Yes, of course,' he said, squeezing her shoulders.

'We'll all stay,' Speaker said.

'Thank you,' Ouloo said timidly.

Dr Miriyam looked around, still processing her surroundings. 'Do you have a bucket? A large bowl? Anything like that?'

Pei was not keen on where this question was going. 'I think so, why?'

The doctor made an apologetic face. 'Our friend here will probably, ah, purge xyr stomach contents once xe wakes up.'

'I saw a bucket in the storage closet,' Speaker said. 'I'll go get it.' She walked her suit down the hall.

'And actually, on that note,' Dr Miriyam said, 'we should get that mask off before we start. Don't want it hurting xyr if xe wakes up hard.' She dug around in her bag and pulled out a pair of oddly shaped scissors. She looked around the remaining group, and pointed at Pei's hands. 'Do you think you can hold these?'

'Maybe,' Pei said. She took the scissors, which were made for five fingers, not four, but she found she could manage (a bit uncomfortably, but whatever).

'Can you work on the mask while I get this procedure lined up?'

'Yeah, sure.' Pei scootched past and leaned over Tupo's limp, lifeless head. 'Sorry about this, kid,' she said as she began to cut hunks of fur away, exposing the dark skin beneath.

'So you've done this before?' Ouloo said.

Dr Miriyam paused in typing out her imubot commands. 'I've done this in sims,' she said frankly. 'But this will be my first time with a live patient. I can't say I've ever had a call for *olotohen* before.'

The bit of calm that Ouloo had managed to scrape back visibly evaporated. She didn't make a sound, but her whole body tensed.

Roveg's eyes shifted in their hard sockets. 'Doctor, just out of curiosity, what sims did you train on?'

'You mean the title?'

'Yes.'

'The Sapient Scholar Medical Training Suite. Version eight, I think.'

'Ah!' Roveg said. He patted Ouloo's shoulders and leaned his head closer to hers. 'I know the head of the studio who makes those. Delightful Aandrisk woman. Her team has a *very* good reputation in our industry. I hear their medical sims are practically indistinguishable from the real thing.'

The fur around Ouloo's ears lowered just a touch. 'I'm sorry, Doctor, I'm just—'

'It's okay,' the Human said. 'I know it's been a stressful night. But we're gonna fix that soon.' She entered in one more command and sat back. 'All right, that needs a minute to compile, and then we'll be ready to go. How are we doing with that mask?' She got up and took a look. 'Nice, good stuff. Want me to take over?'

'If you don't mind,' Pei said, relinquishing the scissors and shaking out her cramping hand.

Dr Miriyam pushed up her sleeve and got to it. As she did so, Pei noticed an ornate tattoo on her inner forearm, white ink leaping off of brown skin. The image was in the shape of an

Exodan homestead ship, with a sentence in Ensk woven around it. Most of it meant nothing to her, but Pei picked out the words for *fly* and . . . and *death*? Not death – there was something else added to the word that she couldn't parse. Stars, she needed to learn more Ensk.

'Which homesteader are you from?' Pei asked.

'Hmm? Oh,' Dr Miriyam said with a glance at her arm. 'You know what this is.'

'I do.'

The doctor smiled as she worked. 'I'm from the *Ratri*.'

Pei smiled blue. She knew the name. 'I have a friend from the *Asteria*.'

The Exodan gave her a quick look and a wry smile. 'Our waterball team is better.'

The blue in Pei's cheeks freckled with green. 'He'd fight you on that.'

'Yeah, well, he'd lose, just like his team does under pressure.' She gave one final snip and pulled the mask free. 'Sorry about your new look, Tupo, but it'll grow back.' Pei agreed with the doctor's assessment; the kid now had a wide, patchy border of bare skin circling xyr nose. It looked like xe'd stuck xyr face into a hedge trimmer.

Speaker returned to the room, carrying a maintenance bucket in the suit's hands. 'Will this do?'

Dr Miriyam took the bucket with a nod. 'It'll do,' she said. She set the bucket on the floor next to the bed, then turned her attention to the bot scanner. 'Okay. We're ready to go.' She looked at Ouloo. 'Are *you* ready?'

Ouloo waggled her neck vigorously. Roveg stayed with her, his many legs holding tight.

'All right,' Dr Miriyam said, exhaling. 'Starting neural stimulation in three . . . two . . . one.'

The doctor had been right: Tupo started twitching, and the sight was indeed upsetting. The kid looked like a glitching bot, or something out of a horror vid. There was no life in the movements, no intention or purpose. Pei had so rarely seen Tupo holding still, but this wasn't the youngster who couldn't keep xyr paws on the ground for ten seconds. This wasn't a goofy kid who'd had too much sugar. This was a monster, a puppet, a science experiment gone wrong.

'Oh, I can't,' Ouloo gasped. She remained standing where she was, but whipped her neck around so she could bury her face against Roveg's shell. 'I thought I could, but I can't.'

'It's all right,' Dr Miriyam said, her eyes moving back and forth between patient and scanner screen. 'I know it's hard, but Tupo's doing great. Just a few more minutes.'

Roveg angled his head up toward the ceiling so he didn't have to look, either. Pei found herself glancing aside as well. She'd seen some real shit, but there was something about this that got right under her scales. But as she turned her gaze from the med bed, she noticed Speaker. The Akarak looked uncomfortable, but she hadn't turned away. She watched the grim procedure with intensity, her beak moving with muttered words too soft for Pei's implant to pick up.

What her implant *did* catch was the sudden, drowning gasp that ripped itself from Tupo's throat. The kid's eyes shot open, and xyr whole body bucked.

Dr Miriyam grabbed Tupo's arms, keeping xyr from falling off the table. 'Get xyr head,' Dr Miriyam ordered Pei.

Pei did as she was told, taking Tupo's head firmly between her hands. This, she'd done before – not with a head this fuzzy or a neck this long, but still.

Tupo stopped thrashing almost as soon as xe'd started, and xyr eyes darted wildly around the unfamiliar space. 'What—' xe croaked. The question was left unfinished. Alien as xyr face was, the panicked, urgent expression that flooded it could be understood by anyone who possessed a stomach.

Under the circumstances, Pei wouldn't have minded cleaning the floor, but all the same, she was glad they had a bucket.

Tupo flopped back against the med bed once xe'd finished,

panting shakily. The rest of the room held their breath. Finally, the kid quieted, licked the edges of xyr mouth, and with effort, craned xyr head up.

'Mom?' xe called in a trembling voice.

Ouloo let out a long, cooing wail. Roveg let go of her, and in a split second, she was up on the bed with Tupo, wrapping all her long limbs around her child and babbling in Piloom.

'That's—' Dr Miriyam started to object to the ferocious hug, but she paused, looked at her scanner, and leaned back. 'Yeah, that's fine.' She smiled to herself with a nod.

Pei put her hand on the doctor's shoulder. 'Pretty good first time,' she said.

Dr Miriyam gave a soft laugh. 'Yeah,' she said. 'Pretty good.'

'Thank you,' Speaker said. She nodded her head with respect, Human style.

Roveg exhaled noisily through his spiracles. 'Stars and fire,' he said. 'Oh, fuck, that was a lot, wasn't it? If you all don't mind, I'm going to get some air.' He exited the room, making relieved, weary sounds.

On the bed, Ouloo nuzzled Tupo as though the universe would end if she didn't. Tupo looked drained and confused, but as the seconds went on, a look of concern filled xyr face, as though crucial pieces of what was happening were falling into place. 'Mom?' xe said slowly.

'Yes, Tupo?' Ouloo asked, switching into Klip.

Tupo chewed on xyr lips. 'Don't be mad, but I think . . . I think I did something really stupid.'

Ouloo exploded in laughter. 'Oh, you did, baby,' she cackled. 'You certainly did.' She rubbed her forehead against Tupo's. 'But I'm not mad. I'm not mad at all.'

Day 240, GC Standard 307

. . . .

ALL CLEAR

Received message
Encryption: 0
From: GC Transit Authority – Gora System (path: 487-45411-479-4)
To: Ooli Oht Ouloo (path: 5787-598-66)
Subject: URGENT UPDATE

This is an urgent message from the Emergency Response Team aboard the GC Transit Authority Regional Management Orbiter (Gora System). Though the temporary communications satellite fleet is currently in operation, standard ansible and Linking channels are still unavailable. We will continue to communicate via the emergency beacon network until all communications are restored. Please continue to leave your scribs locked to this channel.

PLEASE READ THIS MESSAGE IN FULL.

We are pleased to inform you that we have restored safe launch and landing conditions above Gora's settled regions. While the clean-up efforts will continue for several days, the airspace above all Neighbourhoods (North and South) now meets our requirements for normal space traffic.

We will be contacting each ship owner to assign you a new launch time and slot in the tunnel queue based on your current travel plans. As all vessels on Gora's surface cannot launch at once, we will be rolling out launch times in stages. Provided that all ship owners follow these temporary procedures accordingly, we are confident that we can have everyone back in transit by the end of the day (240/307).

Thank you for your patience and cooperation.

EVERYONE

Roveg didn't know how it was possible for his ship to have fallen into such disarray in only five days, but he'd certainly managed it. He bustled about his projection room, picking up empty cups and pillows and sim gear with each of his thoracic legs. He usually kept his belongings organised, but he lacked the mind for it in that moment. Everything he collected was shoved unceremoniously into a cupboard and strapped securely for take-off, with no regard for what was being stored with what. He could sort it all out once he was on his way. It would give him something to do, other than fret.

The wall vox switched on. 'You have an incoming call from the ground host,' Friend said.

'Thank you, Friend,' Roveg said. 'Please put it through in here.'

There was a pause as the connection was made. 'Hi Roveg,' said a raspy voice. 'It's me, Tupo.'

'Tupo, my friend!' Roveg said. '*Very* good to hear you up and about. How are you feeling?'

'Fine,' Tupo mumbled, sounding as though xe was embarrassed about the question and wanted to move past it as quickly as possible. 'Hey, um, what time are you leaving?'

'I'm scheduled for a late night hop, so I'll be launching in about three hours.'

'Okay, um, just so you know, you're invited to a goodbye party. My mom's not doing it. I mean, she's helping, but it's my party. It's so I can say thank you for, um, helping me.'

Roveg could practically hear the little Laru's paws shuffling. 'Tupo, I would be delighted,' he said. 'When should I be there?'

'Oh, just, um, whenever you want. I guess not yet, because it's not ready.'

Ouloo's voice appeared in the background, calling from somewhere in the house. 'Stars, Tupo. Tell him 16:00.'

'It's at 16:00,' Tupo said.

'In the garden,' Ouloo called.

'In the garden,' Tupo said.

'Splendid,' Roveg said. 'I'll see you then.'

The child had stopped talking, but xe hadn't ended the call. Roveg could hear Tupo still breathing through the vox. 'Can I ask you a question?' Tupo asked in a hush.

'Of course,' Roveg said.

Another pause. 'How did you bring breakfast to Speaker? Because I know you did, and I want her to have party food, but, um . . . obviously I kind of don't want to do that again.'

Roveg replied with gentle patience. 'I used a drone, Tupo. I didn't go inside her ship.'

'*Oh*,' Tupo said. Xe was quiet a moment more. 'That makes way more sense.'

Pei wasn't going to miss the garden, exactly. She was glad to know that she'd be in the air in a little over an hour, leaving Gora far behind. But with a tenday and a half of transit in front of her, one last touch of grass before she left was welcome.

Everybody else was already on the lawn, seated in a circle. The same decorations as the previous gatherings flocked the bushes, but they were more haphazard than before, and didn't reach as high up. A similar state of almost-but-not-quite applied to the tray of mellow-mallow puddings that lay on the grass in between everyone. The fluff on the top was shaped inexpertly, and the colourful sugary swirls that dusted them were heaped in some spots and nonexistent in others. There could be no mistake whose party this was.

The evening's host sat on xyr back haunches, leaned up against xyr mother, who was seated in the same manner. Ouloo cuddled Tupo close, and Tupo rested against her heavily. Whether xe was doing so out of physical weariness or emotional fragility was immaterial. The kid needed xyr mom. That much was obvious.

'Hi, Captain Tem,' Tupo said with a smile. The patchy fur around xyr nose somehow looked even worse than it had when the glue had first been cut, but that was neither here nor there.

'Hey, Tupo,' she said. 'You know, you can call me Pei, if you want. I'd say we're buds now, right?'

'Oh,' Tupo said. Xyr smile widened. 'Okay.' Xe reached forward, picked up a pudding bowl, and offered it to her. 'They're not as good as my mom's, but . . .'

'I think they're *very* good,' Roveg said, balancing a bowl between two legs and wielding a spoon with a third. 'You certainly didn't skimp on the sugar.'

'Wouldn't be dessert without sugar, would it?' Speaker said. She was eating a helping of the fluffy stuff within her cockpit, using her beak and nothing but. Her pudding, however, wasn't the same as the others. Rather than a plex bowl, Speaker's portion had been served in a measuring cup. The most Akarak-sized receptacle Tupo could find in xyr mother's kitchen, presumably.

Pei kicked off her boots, hugged the grass with her toes for a second, then sat down cross-legged and accepted the pudding.

'Whoa,' Tupo said, slinking xyr neck down toward Pei's feet. 'That's so cool.'

'Don't stare,' Ouloo scolded.

'It's okay,' Pei said. She knew what the kid was looking at. Her shimmer was unmissable, and the golden light of an ending day brought the swimming flecks of blue, pink, and green out brightly. She thought it looked kind of cool, too.

'Can I touch it?' Tupo asked.

'*Tupo*,' Ouloo said.

'I'd rather you didn't,' Pei said. 'I'm pretty ticklish.'

Roveg lowered his spoon. 'Can you explain being ticklish to me?' he asked. 'I have never understood the concept.'

'Yeah, it's—' Pei started to answer authoritatively, but got no further than that. How *did* you explain being ticklish?

Speaker stared at the top of her cockpit, eyes narrow with thought. 'I . . . have no idea how to describe what it feels like.'

'It's like . . .' Ouloo frowned. 'Hmm.'

'Is it painful?' Roveg asked.

'No,' Speaker said slowly. 'It's not.'

'But you don't like it?' Roveg said.

'I don't like it,' Pei said.

'I mean,' Ouloo said, 'I don't mind it.'

'It's not my favourite, but it's not the worst,' Speaker said.

Roveg looked around the group with his hard-shelled face. 'Thank you, this has been incredibly illuminating,' he said.

The sun dipped lower, and the globulbs in the garden brightened in response. 'It's kind of nice,' Ouloo said, 'seeing the sky without any ships.'

'They'll be back before you know it,' Roveg said.

'I know,' Ouloo said. 'And I'll be glad to see them, but . . . it is nice.'

Pei tipped her head back and gazed upward. The wreckage drones had cleaned up their patch of sky, and the view above the Five-Hop was now free of debris. There was no junk, no traffic, no blinking satellites. Nothing but the transparent seams of the dome and what little air lay above. She tried to remember the last time she'd seen a sky that way, and came back empty.

Roveg set his bowl back down on the tray decisively. 'Right,' he said. He tucked in his thoracic legs, planted his abdominal legs firmly against the grass, and with one quick heave, flipped himself onto his back. 'Ahhh. That's better.'

Tupo burst out laughing.

'What?' Roveg said. 'What's so funny?'

'You are,' Tupo said, giggling heartily. 'That looked *hilarious*.'

'Tu*po*,' Ouloo moaned.

'What's hilarious?' Roveg said with good humour, craning his head back toward Tupo as far as his shell would allow. He was well aware that full-bodied dexterity was not his species' strong suit. 'Show me what's so funny.'

'You were like . . .' The little Laru dramatically threw xyrself over, limbs flopping noodle-like into the grass.

'You're the one with crazy legs, not me,' Roveg said. He shifted his eyes toward Ouloo. 'But not you, of course,' he added with conciliatory charm.

Ouloo made a teasing face at him. 'I'm sure,' she said. She rolled over with far more grace than her offspring, and the two snuggled together into one shaggy pile, facing up toward the sky.

Pei followed suit, breathing deeply as she hit the grass. It was peculiar, Roveg thought, hearing sound come from her mouth rather than the implant in her throat, even if the only thing audible was the sway of air. 'That's nice,' Pei said through her talkbox. The words were layered atop the asynchronous sound of her breathing, making the distinction between organic noise and synthetic speech all the more striking. 'City fields are nice and all, but they're not quite *this*, are they?'

Roveg clicked his mouthparts in agreement. 'When was the last time you lay down under a real sky?'

The Aeluon let out another heavy breath. 'Sohep Frie, probably. When I was a girl.' She rolled her head toward him, her cheeks a delicate blue. 'A long time.'

'I've an idea,' he said, 'but only if it's not a bother. Ouloo, is it possible to turn off the garden lights?'

'Oh, that's no bother at all,' she said. As though it were the most casual action in the world, she reached into her belly pouch and pulled out her scrib.

Roveg's frills twitched involuntarily. 'Do you . . . keep . . . *belongings* in there?' he asked.

'Why not?' she said. 'It's been a long time since it was occupied, and I don't plan on it being so again. Might as well use it for something.'

Roveg decided to not pursue that line of questioning any further. He recalled using her scrib in Pei's shuttle the day before. He decided to not think further about that, either.

Ouloo made a couple of gestures at the scrib, and all the lights at the Five-Hop dimmed and deactivated. Roveg's eyes adjusted quickly to the twilight. Stars, but it was lovely out.

Roveg shifted his gaze, and noticed Speaker sitting in her suit, which was likewise in a sitting position. She seemed unsure of what to do. 'Can you lie down in that thing?' Roveg asked.

'I . . . yes?' Speaker said. 'There's no mechanical reason I couldn't. I've just never done it.'

'You've never laid down and looked at the stars?' he asked.

Speaker did not appear to understand the point. 'I live in space,' she said. 'I see stars all the time.'

'We *all* live in space,' Pei said, 'but it's . . . it's different, from the ground.'

'Come,' Roveg said. 'You must give it a try. And if your suit gets stuck, we'll get you back up.'

Speaker was right about the suit's mechanical capabilities, but it was strange to be lying down that way. She didn't spend much time lying on her back to begin with, and doing so in her cockpit was downright odd. But once she'd adjusted to the weirdness – and figured out how to angle the cup of suckingly sweet pudding so that it wouldn't spill everywhere – she took in the view with thoughtful silence. She *did* see stars all the time. The windows of her ship were full of stars far more often than not.

But Pei was right. This *was* different.

'They're so . . . soft,' Speaker said with surprise. 'They're not as sharp. Is that because of the dome?'

'No,' Roveg said. 'It's the atmosphere. It mutes them. And see how they—'

'They move,' Speaker said. She laughed. 'I've read books in Klip that made mention of the stars twinkling, but I thought . . . I thought they were just being poetic. Like they were comparing them to jewellery, or glass. I didn't think . . .'

'That they did that?' Roveg asked.

'Right,' Speaker said.

'Why do they twinkle?' Tupo asked.

'Air currents,' Pei said. 'You know how when you make tea and you look in the mug when it's really hot, you can see the liquid swirling around itself?'

'I don't like tea,' Tupo said.

'You like soup,' Ouloo said.

'Yeah,' Tupo said.

'And have you seen that swirl?' Ouloo asked.

'Yeah,' Tupo said.

'Air does the same thing,' Pei said. 'And it makes the light shining through it wiggle.'

'Which one's Uoa?' Tupo asked. The Laru species' home system.

Ouloo let out the sigh of a parent who'd been asked a good question for which she had no answer. 'I have no idea,' she said.

'Well, let's find out.' Roveg wriggled a few legs behind himself awkwardly, trying to get at the satchel tied around his abdomen, currently smooshed between his back and the ground. 'Tupo, can you reach the big pocket on the side of my bag? I'm trying to get my scrib.' He knew Ouloo's scrib was more handy, but . . . no. Never again. Thankfully, Tupo obliged, and placed Roveg's own scrib into his waiting toes. 'Thank you very much,' he said. He made a few gestures, then held the device up to the sky. The scrib chirped in response, and displayed a map of the stars behind it. 'Let's see,' Roveg said, scanning. 'All right, well, we're not at Uoa yet, but do you see that orangish one?'

'Where?' Tupo asked.

'Yeah, where?' Pei asked.

'Here, follow my leg.' Roveg extended a single thoracic leg and traced it from horizon to heavens. 'Come up from here, go left for a while, and then . . .'

'Oh, I think I see it,' Pei said.

'I don't!' Tupo said.

'Tupo, be patient,' Ouloo said. 'Look where Roveg's pointing.'

'Oh!' Tupo said. 'Yeah, I see it!'

'Do you actually see it?' xyr mother asked. 'Or are you guessing?'

The child scoffed. 'I said I could see it.'

'That's the Aandrisk home system,' said Roveg.

'Huh,' Pei said. Her talkbox carried the word with a laugh, and Roveg shared the sentiment. He'd stood on Hashkath many a time, watching the sun cast haunting shadows across the red rock valleys. That memory came packaged with feelings of warmth and dazzling brightness – nothing he would associate with the pale speck so insignificant alongside the scatter of countless others exactly like it.

'Cool,' Tupo said, and then, a bare second later: 'What about Uoa?'

Roveg did a quick search for it in the star map. 'Ah,' he said regretfully. 'Won't be up tonight. Seems that's a winter star on Gora.'

'What's a winter star?'

'Means you won't be able to see it until the winter.'

Speaker chimed in, after a moment. 'Can you find Iteiree?' she asked.

Roveg didn't recognise the name of the star – and given the tone in Speaker's voice, was a little ashamed that he didn't. He searched; the scrib obliged. 'Let me see, let me see.' He scanned, pointed, traced. 'There,' he said. 'Do you see that row of four large ones that – ah, how to explain – they curve just a bit, like the edge of a bowl.'

Speaker looked; he could hear the frown in her silence. 'Oh,' she said. 'Yes, yes, I see it.'

'Go up from the left-most one about forty-five degrees. Do you see that yellow—'

'Yes.'

'That's it,' he said.

Even Tupo did not break the weighty silence that ensued. 'It doesn't stand out much, does it?' Speaker said, her voice soft but steady.

'None of them do,' Roveg said, 'unless you're looking for one in particular.'

'Do your people have constellations?' Ouloo asked.

'I don't know,' Speaker said. 'I'm familiar with the concept, but I don't know if we did.'

'Do you have them?' Roveg asked, looking in Ouloo's direction.

'I don't know, either,' Ouloo said. 'I don't know much of anything about my species' homeworld.'

'We have them,' Roveg said. 'I used to know some of them. I'm not sure I'd be any good at it now.' He looked to Pei. 'You?'

'They're not a thing for us,' Pei said. 'We only paid attention to the stars that have an obvious colour. Ancient astronomers on Sohep Frie didn't think the others were important.'

Roveg laughed. 'Because they weren't talking to you?'

'Exactly. The coloured stars, though – oh, you could lose tendays reading about Aeluon astrology. Some people still pay attention to it. Blue stars are good luck, yellow stars are bad luck, and so on. It's incredibly stupid.'

'I have *never* heard an Aeluon call superstition stupid before,' Roveg chuckled.

'Yeah, well, this Aeluon's not scared of yellow stars,' Pei said. 'Or prime numbers. Or years where it doesn't snow.'

'Why don't we have constellations on Gora?' Tupo asked.

'Because we don't need them,' Ouloo answered. 'Constellations are so people without tech can find their way around the sky.'

'Yeah, but we couldn't use tech for *days*,' Tupo said. 'Not really. We should have some for emergencies.'

'You should make some,' Roveg said. 'Draw them out and put them in your museum.'

'Oh,' Tupo said. 'I forgot.' The child rolled over, got to xyr feet, and walked off somewhere out of Roveg's line of sight. 'I have presents for you.'

Pei saw Tupo fetch something from a table. Xe returned on two legs, holding three bundles wrapped in scrap fabric with xyr forepaws. 'I wanted to give you all something. You each get a piece from my museum collection.'

Xe handed the first of the bundles to Pei; she unwrapped it without missing a beat. Inside the fabric was an opalescent stone. It was unpolished, but even in the nearly disappeared light, a bit of sparkle winked back at her.

'You get this one 'cause it looks like you,' Tupo said. 'It's pretty but it's also tough.'

Pei laughed delighted green at this. 'I love it,' she said. 'Thanks, kid.'

'Can you help me unwrap this?' Speaker said, cupping her bundle in the suit's palms. 'String is tricky for the suit.'

Tupo picked the bundle back up, unwrapped it with xyr paws, and held up a bright red crystal, nearly the length of Speaker's forearm, embedded in a chunk of grey rock. 'Okay, so maybe this isn't a good present, because it's more for your sister, I think. You said she likes crystals, and I know you really want to see her, so I'm giving you a present to give to her, since we didn't get to meet her. If that makes sense.' Xe placed the crystal back in the suit's hands.

'Tupo, that's perfect,' Speaker said. 'That's a very Akarak sort of way to give someone a present.'

'Yeah?' Tupo said happily.

'Yeah.' She clicked her beak with fondness. 'And tell you what

– next time I come back, I'll drag Tracker along with me. I think she'd like your museum.'

Ouloo beamed. 'We'd love to have you back,' she said.

Roveg could tell what was in the bundle as soon as the child gave it to him, and he was oh-so glad Tupo could not read him. He understood exactly why Tupo was giving him this, and he understood that Tupo did *not* understand how Roveg felt about it, and stars, did he feel complicated.

He unwrapped the bundle and extracted the poem stone.

'I really liked it when you read to me,' Tupo said. 'Your language is really cool.' Xe threw a furtive glance toward xyr mother and lowered xyr voice. 'And also, I thought about what you said about museums stealing stuff, and um, I don't want to be that kind of museum.'

'Thank you very much,' Roveg said, bowing gracefully. 'I humbly accept the repatriation of this fine artefact. I'll give it a place of honour in my gallery at home.' He was being intentionally flowery, but it was also the truth. The cheap knick-knack in his hands now carried with it a sentiment of the present he would cherish, and a reminder of the past he would always loathe. Only the finest art could accomplish both those things at once.

THANK YOU FOR SUPPORTING YOUR LOCAL PLANETARY CO-OP

PEI

She didn't have the colours to express how good it felt to be in space again.

It shouldn't have mattered, in some ways. Her shuttle was the same shuttle. Her chair was the same chair. But there were stars out her window now – not merely above, but all around. Gora grew ever smaller below her, a massive curve shrinking into a modest sphere. The debris field was still patchily present, and seeing it up close was disquieting, but the automated wreckage drones were on the job, scooting this way and that in methodical stripes, passively pulling in junk with their magnetic collection arms. It was surprisingly satisfying to watch.

Orbital traffic was as crowded as expected, but the zippy TA guideships were doing a heroic job of corralling the comers and goers into transit lanes. Beyond the lanes were five clear-cut areas in which all traffic stopped: the safety corridors around the tunnel entrances, through which only one ship could travel at a time. At the end of the corridors, the worm-holes awaited, each held stable by the polyhedral containment cage constructed around it, a net of metal and blinking lights encasing a blacker-than-black sphere that wasn't so much object as absence.

Pei steered her ship into the lane for tunnel number four, and directed her ship to follow the autopilot buoys. She imagined a similar scene would await her on the other side, and that she'd travel to Ethiris' surface in a manner every bit as controlled. She was already looking forward to the point a few tendays ahead in which she was back out in open space, able to fly in whatever direction she liked and as fast as local law allowed. But that kind of freedom was still a ways off. First, she had to get this egg fathered.

No. That wasn't first. First, she had to write to Ashby and tell him she wasn't coming.

She felt childish about the fact that she hadn't written to him the moment comms had been restored. She'd told herself there hadn't been a need to inform him that she'd been delayed. That much would have been obvious when she hadn't sent him a travel update from Gora five days prior, and knowing Ashby, he would've checked the news or done some digging and ascertained what the situation was. But the longer she went without writing him, the more she knew her hesitancy had nothing to do with flight updates, and everything to do with not landing upon the right words to disappoint him with.

With no option but to wait in the queue, she decided it was well past time to suck it up and be an adult about this. She turned to her comms panel, flashed the command for a new message, switched the input format to Klip, and began to write.

I'm so sorry to do this, but I won't be able to

She deleted that, and started over.

I'm so sorry to have to do this. There was a massive delay at Gora, and while I was there, I started shimmering. I found a creche a tenday or so from here, but that means I can't

She deleted that as well, her cheeks spotting yellow.

You know how they say that making plans is the best way to be sure they won't happen? Well,

Delete, delete, delete.

I don't want to be writing this, and I'm having the worst time of knowing what to say. I don't know why this is so hard. I started shimmering on Gora, and I found a creche, but I

Pei exhaled sharply, her cheeks frustrated yellow and wistful orange. She pressed her fingertips hard against the keymap, erasing all of the inadequate words once more.

She tried again.

I don't want

She locked her fingers behind her neck. The shuttle crawled forward, following the autopilot buoys.

She closed the message field, and instead activated the comms camera. With no call in progress, the only thing the screen displayed was herself.

She took a breath, closed her eyes, and dug deep, letting her colours swirl however they pleased.

She thought about the Rin creche, with their cheerful info chip that said all the right things. She imagined taking part in something ancient and beautiful, something every single ancestor before her had succeeded in doing. She thought about how awe-inspiring it would feel to continue that chain and repay all the gifts they'd so selflessly given her. She replayed the conversations she'd had with friends who'd come back from their shimmer and raved about how wonderful it had been. Such a badly needed break, they said. Such a special experience. Good sex and plenty of rest and the lingering sense of a primal purpose fulfilled.

She opened her eyes, and looked at her reflection. There were many colours present in her cheeks, but overwhelmingly, the dominant hues were red, yellow, orange. Fear. Dislike. Discontent.

The sight made her shaky, but there was no surprise in it. Some part of her had known this was exactly what she'd see.

She shut her eyes hard, balled her fists in tight. With clear intention, she shifted her thinking elsewhere.

She thought about Ashby. She thought about his homely, janky ship and the good people who lived on it with him. She imagined meeting them properly this time – no pretence, no half-truths, no holding her colours rigid through every interaction so that her crew wouldn't notice how she felt when he stood close. She thought about what his bed might be like. She'd never been in *his* bed, *his* private space. How would it feel, to exist with him for a while in a context that wasn't secret? She thought, funnily enough, about Dr Miriyam, and how just a few syllables of Klip flavoured by Exodan Ensk had given Pei the irrational sense that this was a person she could trust. She thought about cheese and waterball and hairbrushes and grasshopper burgers and goosebumps and crying and all the other batshit Human ephemera that occupied space in her head now. Every bit was truly fucking weird, but she loved knowing it all the same.

Improbably, she thought of Speaker. She remembered what the Akarak said to her in those long hours on the shuttle, watching over Tupo.

You don't want to, Speaker had said. *That's it. That is all it ever needs to be.*

Pei opened her eyes, and she saw two things.

She saw the bluest blue, dark as the sea, shifting in currents that carried nothing but love.

She saw orange, sharp and sorrowful. This was not incongruous with the other hue. Sorrow was the right thing to feel when there were two doors in front of you and you knew that one of them was going to stay closed.

The decision solidified. It should've felt frightening. It

should've felt wrong. But the longer Pei let it sit, the more she realised that all she could feel was relief. This one choice didn't answer everything for her, not even close. How could it? Life was never a matter of one decision alone. Life was just a bunch of tiny steps, one after another, each a conclusion that lead to a dozen questions more. She still had no idea what she was going to do about her job, or her crew, or anything else. But she knew where she was headed now, and that wasn't nothing.

She brought the message field back up. Once more, she began to write.

Sorry about the delay. There was a huge mess at Gora, and I was stuck there for five days. But I'm fine, and I'm on my way now. I'll tell you the whole story once I'm there.

Can't wait to see you.

She sent the message before she could change her mind. Her blood practically fizzed as she did so.

This was the right thing.

She shook out the last scraps of tension in her hands, and put in a voice call to the TA orbiter.

An Aandrisk man appeared on her screen, his scales green as laughter and his feathers a riotous argument. 'Hey there, I'm Agent Siksish,' he said. 'What's the issue?'

'My name's Captain Tem, I'm ship ID number 9992-3-23434-7A. I'm currently in the queue for tunnel number four, but I need to change my course.'

The TA agent gave her a look. 'Cutting it pretty close there, Captain.'

'I know,' she said.

Agent Siksish punched in rapid commands with his claws. 'You said your ship number is . . . ?'

'9992-3-23434-7A.'

'Okay. And which tunnel do you want to take instead?'

'Tunnel number one.'

He studied his monitors. 'Since you'll be reentering a queue, that's going to tack another hour onto your departure time. Is that going to work for you?'

'Yes,' Pei said. At this point, an hour was nothing.

He entered more commands. 'Okay, there's a guideship coming your way to lead you out of your current queue and over to the next. Just disengage your autopilot and follow when ready.'

'Thanks very much,' Pei said. The call ended. She flashed her commands, and the shuttle pulled out of the lane. She leaned back against the headrest, flicking her inner eyelids.

Holy fuck, she was doing this.

The guideship arrived in minutes; Pei followed steadily along. As her ship swung around, Gora came back into view. The past days there began to mull together in her mind – the people met, the conversations had. An idea began to form. It was a long shot, but . . . hmm. The more it developed, the more she liked it.

She turned once more to her comms monitor and brought up her lengthy list of work contacts. She scrolled through, not entirely sure who she was looking for. She needed someone with the right kind of influence, someone who liked her, someone who – *yes.* She pointed at the monitor as she saw the name *Kalsu Reb Lometton* pop up. Yes, she'd be perfect.

Kalsu, bless her heart, picked up the sib call within minutes. 'My dear Captain Tem!' she said. 'What a pleasant surprise!' The Harmagian woman sat in the ornate office Pei had stood in a few times before, on work trips to the Capital. Pei didn't regularly take contracts that needed Kalsu's stamp, but when she had, the experiences had always been . . . lively.

'How goes it on Hagarem?' Pei asked.

'Oh, you know, weather's fine, beaches are lovely, politics are a hellscape. The usual.' Kalsu glanced at the lower corner of her display. 'Doesn't look like you're in the neighbourhood, so I assume this isn't a social call.'

'You are correct, as always,' Pei said. Kalsu never missed a detail, which was precisely why she was great at the job she never stopped complaining about. 'I was hoping to ask a favour.'

'For you? Anything, anytime.'

'Well, wait until you hear it. I don't know if this is something you've got the pull for.'

Kalsu's tendrils curled with intrigue. 'A challenge! How exciting.' She leaned in and lowered her voice. 'It's nothing improper, is it?'

'Kalsu, come on, it's me,' Pei said. 'Of course not. And actually, that's exactly why I called *you*. This one's no good if we can't do it above board.'

'A *legal* challenge. My favourite. Come, come. I want all the details.'

Pei smiled blue, and continued to nudge her ship in the right direction. Strings could always be pulled.

· · · · · · · · · · · · · · · ·

ROVEG

They'd changed the archway.

When you landed at the Noble Harbour Spaceport, and you exited your ship, the sight that greeted you was that of a decorative stone archway, dripping with vines and crowning the walkway to the customs building. Roveg had seen it dozens of times, on everything from childhood vacations to his state-mandated departure. But this time was different. He couldn't see the archway this time, because they'd removed it and replaced it with some garish light installation instead. Roveg had braced himself for a return to a place he thought he'd never set foot in again; he hadn't been ready to see it move on without him.

The thing that hadn't changed was the smell, an overwhelming perfume that shot straight to his soul. The air was humid – deliciously, ideally, correctly so – and within it danced the scents of sun-warmed ponds, hosed-out fuel lines, the cabal of food vendors he knew to be waiting around the corner, and the pheromones of countless members of his own species, both fresh and fading, telling him stories about people nearby and already departed. He had run into other Quelin from time to time in the past eight standards – exiles like him – but never more than one or two at once. Never in a way where they were the majority within a social space. Roveg hadn't been in an environment populated by Quelin and *only* Quelin since his last time at Noble Harbour. He'd forgotten what it was like to not be the odd one out.

Except that he *was,* of course. He could smell the disgust rising sharply off passersby who saw the ruined branding on his shell. No one else landing at Noble Harbour that day had a pair of Enforcers awaiting them on the other side of the hatch. At least he'd been downgraded to only two Enforcers, Roveg noted with grim humour. There had been four escorting him on his way out.

It was time for this unpleasant business to begin. He spread his thoracic legs, preparing to be searched. 'Enforcers, I humbly submit myself to the will of the Protectorate and to your authority,' he said. Every word felt rotten as he formed them in both mouth and throat. Their taste lingered even as the sounds left him. 'I am Roveg, and I have an approved appointment with the law office.'

One of the Enforcers marched up and scanned his ID patch while the other wasted no time in opening the satchels strapped around his abdomen and on the front of his thorax. The first Enforcer looked at her scrib as the patch scan completed. 'Your appointment was scheduled for 14:00,' she said.

'Yes,' Roveg said.

She looked him in the eye. 'You are late.'

'Yes,' he said. 'I apologise, there was a—' He stumbled. Oh stars, oh fuck, he couldn't remember the word. It had been so long since he'd had a formal conversation in Tellerain that he couldn't remember the fucking word. '—a disaster along my route and I was delayed. I have arrived as quickly as legally possible.'

Roveg spoke the words with grovelling inflection, but the Enforcer made a note on her scrib, undoubtedly marking both his tardiness and his rusty Tellerain. Roveg's heart sank. He'd been here barely a minute, and already he had the heavy sense that this trip would be for nothing.

Dammit, he had to try.

The Enforcers escorted him to the law office, one on either side, neither touching nor speaking. Roveg could feel the stares of the crowd as he made his way. He was accustomed to being stared at by other sapient species, and no longer paid them any mind. These stares, though – issued forth from eyes just like his own – these chipped away at his shell, carving out tiny pieces of himself and leaving them to bleach in the sun.

He was here for Boreth, he told himself. He was here for Segred, and Hron, and Varit. He repeated their names in his mind, over and over, a chant of courage to carry himself forward.

The law office was stark and far too bright, like all institutional facilities were. It was incredible how a nearly empty room could feel so much like a threat. The only thing present was a circular workstation in the dead centre, staffed by a lone legal officer. Roveg replaced the chant of beloved names with a nervous review of all he'd prepared for.

They'll ask you about your work, he thought, *and you have nothing to fear about that. Be clear that you only make vacation sims. They'll ask you where you live, and whether you live with other species. You live alone, and they can hardly fault you for living in a mixed city – where the hell else would you live, if you can't live here? They'll do a hemolymph scan. They'll probably check your bots. They'll go through your scrib, and that's fine, there's nothing untoward on there. You triple-checked. If they press you on being late, press back about why you're here. You're for tradition. They love that. Play it up. You remember how. Boreth. Segred. Hron. Varit. You can do this.*

You have *to do this.*

The officer looked briefly up from his workstation, smelling as though he'd never laughed at a joke in his life. 'You must be my 14:00,' he said, gesturing commands at a terminal.

'Yes, I'm Roveg,' he said. 'And I apologise. There was an accident—' he'd had time to remember the word '—and it resulted in an unavoidable delay.' He opened a satchel (the Enforcers watched intently as he did so) and pulled out a carefully wrapped bundle of pixel prints and info chips. Evidence of his home, his work, his finances, his medical history, his travel route, his entire life. He'd spent tendays putting it together, and even though he'd gone through it over and over to ensure that every single box had been checked off, his spiracles flared at the thought that he'd forgotten something. The Enforcer who had scanned his patch looked at him, and Roveg didn't have to guess why. He knew he stank of worry.

Roveg presented the bundle to the officer courteously, holding it with four sets of toes. The agent looked up at this. 'That won't be necessary,' he said.

Roveg felt as though every one of his knees was about to buckle inward. No. No, they had to give him a chance. They couldn't turn him away without even giving him a *chance*. 'But – please, I—'

Something popped out of a machine at the workstation – a label, of some sort. The officer picked it up, burned six different stamps into it, and handed it to Roveg. 'Affix this to your torso, as close to your face as is practical. The glue on the back will break down after a tenday.'

Roveg picked up the label. It was made of stiff plex, and the text on it was bold and ugly.

TEMPORARY TRAVEL PERMIT
EXPIRES: 277/307
WEARER IS A KNOWN CULTURAL DEVIANT
AND MUST BE ACCOMPANIED BY A LAW
ENFORCEMENT ESCORT AT ALL TIMES.

Roveg stood silent, staring at the most precious object in the galaxy, now resting in his toes. To say that he was confused was an understatement. Surely there had been some mistake, but he wasn't about to stand there and tell them that perhaps they *shouldn't let him in*. 'Do I . . . not need to give an interview?' he asked with caution.

The officer flexed his legs *no*. 'According to our sapient immigration agreements with the GC, the fact that you are currently contracted by a parliamentary employer, were convicted of a non-violent crime, and have served the first eight standards of your life sentence means that you are exempt from the interview requirement for a temporary travel permit.' The officer's scent burned with disapproval, but his inflection indicated he had no choice but to comply. The law, after all, was the law.

Roveg did rapid calculus. There had unquestionably been a mistake. He had no idea what contract or employer they were referring to. But should he voice that? Would it be worse to ruin his chances here and now, or for them to find out after the fact that he'd taken the permit under false pretences?

Boreth, he thought.

He peeled the backing off the label and stuck it firmly to his torso, straight below his head. The glue smelled atrocious. He did not care. 'Thank you,' he said, putting every ounce of energy he possessed into sounding and smelling calm. 'You have my assurance that my behaviour will be exemplary.'

'That'll be for your escort to gauge, not me,' the agent said. He pointed across the room. 'You may stand in the waiting area over there until she arrives.' He picked an info chip up from his workstation and handed it to Roveg. 'Your employer's letter of sponsorship made a request for us to provide you with this upon arrival. The contents, of course, have been reviewed.'

Roveg took the chip, no less confused but very ready to end the conversation before further questions were asked. 'Thank you very much,' he said. He headed toward the waiting area, and the Enforcers departed, their disapproval more potent than the agent's.

Once all eyes were off him, he took his scrib from his satchel and plugged in the info chip, trying his best to look nonchalant even though he was desperate to know what the hell was going on. The chip contained two documents, one of which indicated that it was to be read first.

Dear Roveg,

How delighted I am that you have accepted our contract to create environmental sims for the Galactic Commons' cultural education archives! There are woefully few materials of this sort featuring Quelin locations, and I am delighted we have found a talented native citizen such as yourself to help us fill this gap. After all, the Quelin are an enormously valued member of the GC, and we are eager to properly celebrate your species' rich culture and complex history.

We can discuss the particulars of payment and deadline once you have returned to Central space. On this chip, you will find a list of the public sights we hope you will scan and map for your eventual sim, provided that access to these areas is allowed under the rules of your permit. Given your delicate legal situation, I am including this information with your sponsorship letter rather than messaging it to you directly, in the interest of complete transparency. I also request that you capture imagery from your sons' First Brand ceremony, which I understand is serendipitously happening during this assignment. It would benefit our citizens greatly to better understand this fascinating tradition.

As a personal aside: our mutual friend Gapei Tem Seri sends you her warm regards. She and I both wish you the best of luck with this project. I can't wait to see the end result.

May you enjoy the safest of travels,
Kalsu Reb Lometton
Second Deputy Director of the Export Oversight Office,
GC Department of Border Regulation

Confused was no longer the appropriate word for what Roveg was feeling. He was totally, thoroughly stunned.

He remained that way even as his escort arrived – a sturdy-shelled woman who he would've found attractive had she not smelled as though she were looking for any excuse to throw him in a prison pit. 'My name is Officer Greshech,' she said, her inflection as icy as her scent. 'I will be your escort during your temporary stay on Vemereng. You are not permitted to go anywhere without me. You are not permitted to enter any building without my approval. You are not permitted to engage in any conversation topics that have not been expressly approved by me. You will provide me with a detailed proposal for your activities by 06:00 each day. Failure to comply with these requirements will result in reversal of your permit, as well as . . .'

Roveg fixed his eyes on her as though he were listening with all the focus in the world, and let her bureaucratic droning wash over him. He took his mind happily elsewhere, and began entertaining the first glimmers of something he was going to make. It would need an immense amount of work, but he could already picture the colours, the shapes, the way he wanted it to feel. He was sure it would be beautiful, but he tucked that imagining away for a later time. First, he would meet his sons. He would see their faces, learn their adulthood scents, maybe even touch them if allowed. He had never seen them with hardened shells, and had spent tendays steeling himself for the possibility that he might not recognise them. As he stood there with a garish legal document glued to his thorax, this idea no longer troubled him. They were his boys, and however they looked, they, too, would be beautiful.

. . . .

SPEAKER

'Speaker?' Tracker called down the hall.

Speaker was awake, but hadn't left her bed. She had no plans to do so anytime soon. It was very, very morning. 'What?' she called, lying flat on her belly, not bothering to lift her head.

'Are you expecting a mail drone?'

Speaker thought. She hadn't ordered anything recently. 'Might be that hull paint you bought?'

'That's what I figured, but . . .'

'But what?'

'Well, its delivery address is for the *shuttle*, not the ship.'

Speaker raised her head. 'That's weird. Who's it from?'

'I have no idea who—' Tracker paused. 'Is this that Quelin you met?'

Speaker got up. 'Let it dock.'

The crate the drone delivered was small, and not particularly heavy. Within the crate was an unmarked box, and tied to the top of this with a bit of ribbon was an info chip. Speaker picked up the chip, plugged it into her scrib, and read the message that appeared on screen.

Hello Speaker,

I hope me sending you something unannounced isn't an intrusion. I thought about contacting you ahead of time, but you know I can't resist a surprise.

I'm taking a risk here, in sending you a gift that I have not been able to test. I admit, I'm not sure if it will work. You see, I did some digging after we left Gora, and it turns out that the GC Medical Institute has brain maps of every known sapient species. I've never worked with a map that wasn't part of a pre-built sim design template, so building off of such raw material was quite a challenge. If this doesn't work as I hope it will, I'd appreciate hearing exactly what went wrong, so that I might try again with improved results.

But, in the optimistic scenario that it does *work: I fervently hope this is a positive experience for you (and for your sister, and whomever else you wish to share it with).*

If you ever find yourself near Chalice, please do come say hello. I'd love to throw you that party I promised.
Kindly,
Roveg

PS If you are wondering, my sons are doing very well.

'What is it?' Tracker asked.

Speaker had an inkling – a bewildered, sceptical inkling, but an exciting one all the same. She opened the box, and her suspicion was confirmed.

Roveg had sent her a sim hub, a box of one-use slap patches, and a download drive hand-printed in Klip. *Wushengat*, the label read.

Flower Lake, she remembered.

On the back of the drive were instructions in tiny print:

1. *Lie down or sit somewhere comfortable.*
2. *Place a slap patch on the back of your neck, right over your brain stem, with the red stripe facing upward.*
3. *Turn on the sim hub. You'll hear a ping when it connects to your patch.*
4. *Plug in the drive.*
5. *Close your eyes and wait until the count of ten for the sim to load.*

Tracker moved into Speaker's periphery. 'You're not seriously going to plug that thing into your head, are you?'

'Oh, yes, I am,' Speaker said. She put everything back in the box, gathered it beneath her less dominant arm, and headed back toward the bedroom.

'Speaker.' Tracker swung after her. 'Speaker, hang on. We can't use—'

'We *don't* use them. That's not the same as *can't.*' Speaker handed the box to her sister. 'Can you take this?' She nodded toward their bed, which she couldn't climb to one-handed.

Tracker took the box with her feet, frowning. 'You could hurt yourself,' she said. 'That's some modder shit. That's some hackjob—'

'It's not hackjob,' Speaker said. 'Roveg's a professional. He knows what he's doing.'

'Yeah, for *other types of brains.* Do you not want to think about this?'

'I thought about it.'

'For *two seconds.*'

Speaker sat down on her bed and pulled a cushion behind herself, letting it support her weight. She looked her sister in the eye. 'I trust him.'

Tracker continued to frown. With slow reluctance, she handed the box over.

'Thank you,' Speaker said. 'And if it'll make you feel better, you can sit with me while I do it.'

'Oh, ho, I absolutely will,' Tracker said. She swung herself into bed and sat directly across from Speaker.

'Okay,' Speaker said, setting the hub down. 'Sit somewhere comfortable, check. Put a patch on my neck . . .' She opened the box and took one of the patches out. It was thin, no thicker than a bandage, and somehow soft despite the wires running through it. She applied it to the back of her neck, right below the base of her skull.

'Does it hurt?' Tracker said.

'No. It feels like . . . nothing,' Speaker replied. She switched the hub on. A mild warmth spread through the patch. The hub beeped as a connection was made. 'All right,' she said, holding up the drive. 'Here goes.'

'If you so much as *twitch*, I'm ripping that thing off,' Tracker said.

Speaker crinkled her eyes, reached out, and put her sister's palm over her own heart. 'Here,' she said. 'If I start to feel worrisome, you can shut down the hub.'

She inserted the drive, closed her eyes, and began to count.

One. Two. Three. Four. Five. S—

Everything hit all at once.

There was light. She had stood on dozens of planets, and on moons, too, in marketplaces and transit stations and parks and spaceports, all basking beneath alien suns. But in each of those situations, her view was confined to the window of her mech suit, a metal-framed border that stood between her and every vista the galaxy had to offer. The only places she'd ever been without her suit were ships and shuttles, and these, too, were made of metal, of walls, of end points. Here, in this illusion Roveg had built, there was no separation between *herself* and *the world*, nothing cutting her field of vision in half. Everything was impossibly, unimaginably, overwhelmingly bright.

There was the openness. Again, this was an experience she

thought she knew from standing planetside and seeing the ground stretch flat in all directions. But without her suit propping her up, without it protecting her from her surroundings, the sheer size of this place made her feel so, so small.

There was the sensation that swept across her skin, which immediately registered in her mind as danger. There was an air leak somewhere, she thought. There was a busted valve, a damaged seal, a hatch or bulkhead about to pop. It took her several moments to reassess the feeling, slowly, like an explorer. Like a scientist. The pressure hadn't changed. She could breathe just fine. The air wasn't leaking. It was simply *moving*. With a small, trembling cry, she realised what that meant.

She was feeling the wind.

'Speaker?' Tracker said. Hearing this was uncomfortably dissonant, because Speaker knew her sister was seated right in front of her, but they were no longer in the same place. Her voice came from nowhere.

Speaker found her words, with effort. 'I'm fine,' she said, her voice quavering. 'I'm okay.' *I'm okay*, she repeated to herself, though she wasn't entirely sure of that – not because the sim was hurting her, but because it was just *so much*.

Roveg had built a world for her, and she'd entered it on the shore of a lake. She was kneeling directly on the sand – creamy white and sugar-soft. The water had an amethyst tint, and lapped tenderly against time-polished stones. A forest ringed the lake, its trees heavy with flowers. A paddle boat just her size was tethered to a post, and bobbed in the purplish ripples. Some kind of tiny golden arthropod meandered just ahead of the waves, darting here and there with comic quickness. And all around her, all through the sand and up to the trees, stood practical posts made of smooth white wood, each carved with notches an Akarak could swing from.

She did not climb the posts. She did not go toward the boat. She remained kneeling, and dug her hands into the sand. She clenched her fingers, then stretched them out, then pushed them in deeper. She tried to think of something to compare the feeling to. A bowl of cooking starch. A bag of hydroponic soil. The ash you cleaned out of an engine filter every few weeks. No, none of those things came close to what the sand felt like. All of them were small, contained, packaged. Everything she thought she understood about *touch*, about the sensations of the worlds she visited, about what a world *was* . . . all of it was wrong. Completely wrong.

She'd never been anywhere before.

Speaker reached up and tore the slap patch from her neck. Reality returned with a jolt, and she shivered from head to toe, even though her ship was warm and dry. Her ship. Her bed. Her sister. All existing within the compact scale she'd always known. It was terrible to look at now, and yet, it was all she wanted. It was familiar. It was safe.

'Hey, hey,' Tracker said. She held Speaker's wrists gently in her hands. 'Hey, whoa, what's—'

Without a word, Speaker fell against her sister and began to keen like an injured child. The cries ripped themselves from her throat, reflexive and untethered, each a warbling wail. Tracker did what any twin would do in response: she held the other half of her soul tight, saying nothing, holding fast, giving the pain space to pour itself out. Speaker didn't know why she was acting like this, but she couldn't stop it, either. She keened and keened until her throat felt raw.

'I've never,' she gasped at last, 'I've never – we've – we don't – we don't understand—' She clutched at Tracker as though she were falling. 'We don't understand *what it would be like.*'

Tracker nuzzled her, stroked her head, rubbed beak against beak. 'Oh, my heart, my heart, my heart,' she said, speaking the words like a lullaby. 'What happened?'

Speaker pulled back a bit, tried to breathe, tried to think. After a moment, she reached over, picked up the slap patches, and offered the box to Tracker. 'You need to see it,' she said.

Tracker stared at her, but did not protest as she had when

Roveg's crate had first been opened. They were in a different space now, the two of them – that place of wordless understanding only siblings shared, a place brought into being when one cracked herself fully open. Speaker needed Tracker to see what she'd seen, and so, Tracker would go look. She put on a patch. She closed her eyes. She breathed normally . . . until she didn't anymore. Her breathing stopped, then sped up, then caught, then shook – not in the way that made Speaker wake her up in the night, but in the same way that Speaker's had before she'd cried out.

Speaker held Tracker's hands tightly, feeling her sister's pulse race against her palms.

'Oh,' Tracker gasped. 'Oh – oh, fuck.' She laughed, sort of. The look on her face went from joy to grief, and Speaker felt it echo in her bones. Tracker shook their clasped hands urgently. 'Come back in with me,' she said. 'I don't want to be here alone.'

'Do you want to stay in it?' Speaker asked.

'*Yes*,' Tracker said. 'Stars, yes.'

Speaker replaced the patch she'd torn off, and went back to the lake.

Tracker looked strange. Speaker had never known a life without Tracker in it, and she knew her sister's body as well as her own . . . but she'd never seen Tracker off a ship without a suit. She'd never seen her in full sunlight.

Tracker evidently felt the same, from the way she gaped. 'Do I look as small as you?' she asked.

Speaker knew what Tracker meant. She didn't know what to make of her sister – who had always been larger than herself, who had always been tall and strong – looking so fragile and delicate on a breezy shore. Speaker began to crawl toward Tracker, intending to reassure her, but an unexpected sensation made her pause. She cocked her head, moved forward a hands-width or so, and laughed. 'You have to try this,' she said.

'Try . . . what?' Tracker said.

'Crawl,' Speaker said. 'And make sure your belly is touching the sand.'

Tracker gave her a quizzical look, but got down on her fore-limbs and crawled forward. 'Ha!' she cried. She rocked her torso back and forth, granules of sand spilling out below her. 'Oh, that feels so *weird*.' She looked at Speaker, her gaze burning bright. 'What else can we try?'

They learned the feeling of sand together. They learned the feeling of water on their legs, and of floating in a boat, and of laughing after the boat flipped. They climbed a tree and hung from the branches. They lay on the ground and looked at the sky. They spent hours in Roveg's favourite place, forgetting every chore and fix-it list that awaited them in the ship they could no longer see. The lake wasn't real. It wasn't real, but it didn't matter. They would never feel a real world this way, Speaker knew. None of her people would, not in her lifetime. But maybe . . .

. . . maybe one day, one of them would.

The sim wasn't real, but their bodies were, and there reached a point where even a purple sky and sugar sand couldn't distract them from their growling stomachs.

'We can come back after we eat,' Speaker said. 'Or any time.'

'Yeah,' Tracker said. 'Ready?'

Together, they peeled their patches off. They blinked at their home as though they'd never seen it before. They reached out without speaking, and held each other's hands.

'What do we do with this?' Tracker asked, nodding at the hub. 'We can't keep it just for us.'

Speaker popped the drive out and held it in her hands, running a finger over the label Roveg had written for her. 'We make copies,' she said, 'and we show everyone. We give it to anyone who wants to know what a world feels like.'

'And what will that do?' Tracker said.

'I don't know,' Speaker said. 'I just want them to see what we saw. Feel what we felt.' She turned the download drive over and over in her hands, savouring the memory of the imaginary. 'I don't know if it'll do anything. I don't know if anyone else will care. But I think that's what we have to do.'

Day 119, GC Standard 308

· · · · · · · · · · · · · · · · ·

OULOO

Ouloo awoke not out of habit or rhythm, but thanks to a smell. She pulled her head from beneath her hind leg and drew in one deep breath. That was all it took to get her up and running.

Something was on fire.

The direction of whatever calamity had arisen in her home was easy to place, as there were lights on in the kitchen, and a great deal of bustling and clanking from said-same. She stumbled through the door, paws tripping over each other in haste, untended fur puffed in alarm.

'It's fine!' Tupo yelled in the aggravated tone of someone who had hoped to remedy a problem without being noticed. 'It's totally fine!' Xe stood at the pot filler, blasting water into a smouldering cooking pan. Steam and smoke mingled together over the carbonic remains of whatever it was xe was trying to scrape out.

'Tupo, what—' The burst of adrenaline that had awoken her was still waging war with her sleep-addled perception, and it took her a moment to fully digest the surrounding scene. The kitchen, which she'd left pristine at bedtime, now looked as though the contents of her cupboards had violently expelled themselves onto every conceivable workspace. Raw batter dripped from a tilted bowl stacked atop several others. Used spoons and cups lay scattered about. Beneath the smoke, there was the powerful smell of cooking oil, which was explained by the soggy stack of rags set atop a spilled puddle in an apparent attempt to mop it up.

The baffled reprimand preparing to launch from Ouloo's tongue dissolved as Tupo turned xyr face toward her. 'I wanted to make you breakfast,' xe said mournfully.

Ouloo closed her eyes, took a breath, and approached the sink. 'What were you trying to make?'

'Sunrise dumplings,' Tupo sighed.

Ouloo peered into the blackened pan, now parsing the molten shapes of what could conceivably have been sunrise dumplings, or an attempt at them. They were one of her favourites, when not reduced to slag, but why a child who rarely could be found at the stove would attempt a dish this intricate was beyond her. 'What gave you that idea?' she asked, taking both pan and spatula. She began to pry the ruined bundles out.

Tupo's paws shuffled. Xe was as tall as xyr mother now – a development that had happened in a blink, and one Ouloo was coming to terms with – but still so soft and clumsy in how xe moved. An adultish body housed with childish spirit. That was what adolescence was, she supposed, but stars, Ouloo wished she could've kept her little Tupo just a short while longer.

'Well,' Tupo said, 'we don't have any guests docking today, and we've got lots coming tomorrow, so I thought . . .' The shuffling intensified. 'I thought maybe I could give you a break.'

Ouloo wrestled in a most parental way between melting over her child doing something kind for her, and the fact that she *did* have a full guest list the next day and really could have used an uninterrupted sleep and a kitchen that didn't need to be cleaned again. 'You silly sweetie,' Ouloo said, melt winning out.

She nuzzled Tupo's head with the side of her neck, then blinked. 'Did you trim your fur?'

'Yeah.'

The trim was extraordinarily uneven, but never in a million years would Ouloo voice that. She hadn't asked Tupo to trim xyr fur, and she would not add an asterisk to this victory. 'It looks good,' she lied, then added, honestly: 'It's nice to see your eyes.'

Tupo mumbled something unintelligible, looking pleased.

'Well,' Ouloo said, surveying the kitchen. 'How about we clear some space, and then I can take over the dumpling production.'

'No,' Tupo said. Xyr neck raised up assertively. 'I. Am making. Breakfast.' Xe lowered xyr head and shoved it against Ouloo's side, nudging her toward the door. 'Go back to bed. Or do something else.'

'But—' Ouloo began to fret over the mess, the wasted oil, the probably ruined pan. Her child glared back at her, frowning mightily. 'All right, all right,' Ouloo said. She ran her tongue over her incisors as she thought. 'But maybe . . . maybe sunrise dumplings are something we could make *together*, another time. I can teach you how. What if right now, you made melon porridge?'

Tupo's neck drooped. 'That's not as fun.'

'You're good at it, though. That last batch you made was pretty tasty.' This was also true, even though the presentation had left much to be desired.

Tupo looked simultaneously reluctant to admit defeat, and relieved to be given an out. 'Well . . . okay.' The glare returned. 'But you can't help.' Xe took the pan and spatula back, and gave her another shove. 'Go away.'

Ouloo laughed and surrendered her territory. 'Okay,' she said, backing out of the kitchen. 'Okay. You're the boss.'

Going back to bed was out of the question, so Ouloo headed for her grooming cabinet, and thought through the day as the robotic hands washed and curled. Much as she preferred to see her dome filled with visitors, business had been good and steady, and a day with no guests was a rare opportunity to knock out projects in a leisurely manner. She could touch up the paint on her shuttle, she thought, but it wasn't urgent, and wasn't the sort of work she was in the mood for. The scale scrub stock in the bathhouse was getting a bit low, but she wasn't about to make a new batch of that with the kitchen as it was. Oh, but the garden – she'd almost forgotten, with how busy she'd been. She'd received some new plants for the garden nearly a tenday ago, which were still waiting in their drone crates. She'd been so excited to receive them, but *everything else* had gotten in the way, as so often happened. Yes, that was the perfect thing to do on an empty day. She bounded out of the cupboard once the grooming program was complete, properly coiffed and full of energy.

'I'm going to the garden,' she called as she headed for the door. 'Please don't burn the house down.'

Tupo presumably heard her, but the only reply she received was the sound of something non-breakable clattering to the ground, followed by muffled swearing.

Ouloo walked through the door without another word. She didn't need to know.

She ducked over to the office to grab a slice of her neighbour's jenjen cake to tide her over, then loaded up a pushcart with the drone crates, plus garden tools and paw covers. Ships and shuttles criss-crossed overhead as she ferried her cargo down the path – some landing, some ascending, some orbiting high above. Just another day. There had been a time shortly after she'd bought the patch of planet beneath her feet when the closeness of the sky-borne vehicles made her crane her neck all the way back every time one of them passed. She remembered Tupo – so fluffy and heart-achingly small then – crowing the categories of ships in view. *That's a cruiser! That's a cargo hauler! That's a . . . uh . . . a ship!* The charm of that habit had quickly worn thin, but Ouloo couldn't deny that she'd shared in the sense of amazement fuelling it. She had thought, then, that she'd never grow tired of looking at those incredible constructs, that they'd always be a bit magic to her. And they were, when she actually took the time to stop and think about it. But she didn't need to look at every single one anymore. They would always be remarkable to her, but in the present moment, the thing that grabbed her attention most was the ground she now stood on. The ships above were strangers, machines carrying other lives and other plans. The world inside Ouloo's dome was small, sure – but was there any world that wasn't, when you stacked it up beside everything else? The dome was *her* world, that was the key thing. She had started with a blank slate and had built something upon it. She could put a sign here, slap some paint there, change whatever didn't suit her fancy. That was a powerful thing, to Ouloo, more powerful than the biggest ship with the biggest guns. A ship like that was good for only one kind of job. The Five-Hop, on the other hand, could be whatever she wanted it to be. That was more compelling to her.

The path wound its way into the garden, its paved edges now softened by bowing branches and playful vines. The summer ferns were exploding with new leaves, each still spiralled tightly inward around itself, waiting for the right moment to unfurl. The eevberry bush was in full bloom, and the pollinator bots diligently wove their way from flower to flower, ensuring there'd later be fruit to fold into pastry dough.

She parked her cart by a bed filled with mistdrops, though not for much longer. These, she would replace with the newcomers. She opened the smaller of the two crates, revealing thirty egg-like capsules, waiting in tidy rows cushioned with protective foam. The capsules were transparent, and within each stood a small plant anchored in ghostly blue grow-gel. She'd been told all of the plants' names ahead of time, as well as how to care for them, but every variety in this box was a mystery to her, a species she'd yet to meet. She selected one capsule at random and cupped it in her forepaw, turning it this way and that in admiration. It was a curious thing, with corkscrewed branches and circular leaves accented with delicate blue stripes. The plant was small but verdant, the roots white and healthy. A shadow fell over both Ouloo and the plant as some vessel hummed by overhead; she paid it no mind.

Ouloo replaced the capsule among its friends, put on her paw covers, picked up her shovel, and got to work – not with the new plants, but with the pretty white-blossomed mistdrops that were about to meet their end. She felt guilty tearing up plants that had nothing wrong with them. They were healthy. People liked them, she was fairly sure. But she didn't want them anymore, and that was that. It felt slightly foolish, to have put so much time and effort and water into something destined for the composter, but what had been lovely then was just background now, and she was ready for colours and shapes she hadn't played with before. It didn't make her feel any less bad about ripping up the fat roots, but it did keep her from hesitating. She assuaged her guilt by telling herself that plants got eaten and trampled in their natural environs all the time. That was the way life worked, and she was allowed to have a hand in it.

A clot of dirt landed in Ouloo's fur, just above the seam of her glove. She frowned and flicked it out of her fresh curls. Truth be told, she didn't enjoy the actual work of gardening very much. It was fine, as tasks went. She'd much rather do this than muck out the water filters or scrub a gummy engine. But the thing she enjoyed about gardening was *having a garden*. She liked imagining it, and she liked sitting in it when it was done. The middle bit of digging and pruning and getting sap on her paws and dirt in her fur and a crick in her back – that, she would happily do without. But you didn't get a garden if you didn't do the middle bit, unless you hired somebody else to do it, and then it wasn't really *yours*. It would never match the garden in her head, if she did it that way.

Not that the garden around her *did* match the one in her head. It had the sort of feeling she'd hoped for, and it served the purpose she'd intended, but the shape and the look were little like what she'd imagined at the start. She hadn't planned on putting a *seshthin* tree in the middle, or that the eevberry bush would take over its entire bed, or that she'd ever rip out the mistdrops she'd been so in love with five standards ago. And no matter how hard she worked on it, there was always something missing. She'd step back and look, and she'd think, *yes, that's fine,* or *hmm, well, I'll try again in a few weeks,* but it never felt *done.*

On some level, though, that didn't matter, because the garden wasn't *for her.* If she'd wanted flowers all to herself, she could've just planted them around her house and left it at that. No, this garden was for her guests, and that's why she'd chosen the *seshthin,* which Aandrisks loved the smell of, and why she'd chosen the blue eevberries instead of the purple ones she'd preferred, for the sake of her Aeluon guests, and why she was prepping this bed for the crate beside her now. The new plants were all vegetable starters, and they'd been sent by Speaker – not *by* her, exactly, but *through* her. She'd procured them from one of her countless contacts, after an ongoing message exchange about Akarak recipes had led Ouloo to the question of whether Akaraks still cultivated any plants from their homeworld. They did, Speaker had written, but she didn't know of any grown for purposes other than food.

Ouloo had thought about that, and decided it was a wonderful idea. If Akaraks couldn't enjoy cake in her garden, then she'd grow food for them to bring home. What each species took away from her wasn't important. The only thing that mattered was that they felt welcome. And if they didn't, well, then she'd figure out why not, and give it another go.

The mistdrops came up easier than she'd expected. She raked the bed smooth, put down a layer of compost, and got ready for the tricky part. The thing about the Akarak vegetables was that they needed the right kind of atmosphere, and this was the reason for the second crate, which contained all the components for a large, air-locked terrarium, complete with its own pint-sized life support system. Ouloo was eager to see it assembled, but first, she needed to put the plants in the ground, and she couldn't do that inside a tank filled with methane. Speaker's last letter had relayed the advice of a contact named Arikeep – *Farmer* – who assured her the plants would be all right in oxygen-rich air for a short time as they were coming out of stasis, but not for more than an hour.

Ouloo was not worried. She knew how to work fast, when need be.

She dug a small hole with her trowel, retrieved one of the capsules, and unsealed the lid. Nothing about the plant changed, of course, but she knew that with the seal broken, the tiny stasis gadget inside had shut down. The cells within the plant were now waking from their interstellar slumber, remembering how to ferry water and carbon, how to make sugar from sunlight.

As gently as she could, she pulled the gel-cased roots from their container, and placed the delicate plant in the waiting ground. She brushed dirt around it with her paws, tucking the roots in, making sure the stem had the purchase needed to stand on its own. The gel would dissolve, in time; the roots would spread far, forever seeking. She cleaned some dirt off a leaf with the tip of her toepad, and nodded with satisfaction. This might not be her favourite part about having a garden, but she couldn't deny that lush little plants in a fresh bed looked awfully nice. Nothing felt quite so clean and pleasing as the start of something new.

She picked up her trowel, and dug another hole.

ACKNOWLEDGEMENTS

Ending a series is bittersweet, especially given how seismically this one shifted my life. Like all big things, I could never have done this alone.

On the professional side, the biggest of thanks to Molly Powell, Oliver Johnson, and Seth Fishman for their constant support and good advice. Hugs all around to the amazing teams at both Hodder & Stoughton and Harper Voyager US, as well as to my publishers worldwide.

On the personal side, thanks to Susana, who helped me reverse engineer some tricky bits, and who usually knows what I'm trying to say better than I do. Thanks to Greg, the best Girl Friday and my friend forever. Thanks to the Hammers for charging my creative batteries when nothing else would. Thanks to my friends and family for putting up with my nonsense, yet again. Thanks to my wife, Berglaug, who brings me more joy than all the words in the dictionary and stars in the sky. (Is that too sappy? Probably. I don't care. If only one scrap of my writing outlives me, I want it to be the one that says that I loved her, and so I will write it wherever I can.)

I've said this many a time before, but here's one more for the road: neither me nor these books would be anywhere if it weren't for legions of people who I don't know at all. To my backers and fans, to the lovely people I've met the world over, to everybody who wrote me letters and hugged me at cons and told me their own stories and cracked me up and made me cry – I will never, ever be able to tell you how grateful I am. Thank you for this amazing ride. I can't wait to show you what's next.

WANT MORE?

If you enjoyed this and would like to find out about similar books we publish, we'd love you to join our online Sci-Fi, Fantasy and Horror community, Hodderscape.

Visit hodderscape.co.uk for exclusive content form our authors, news, competitions and general musings, and feel free to comment, contribute or just keep an eye on what we are up to.

See you there!

HODDERSCAPE
NEVER AFRAID TO BE OUT OF THIS WORLD